The Last of Ancients

by

Terri Nixon

Best wishes, and enjoy!
Terri

Published by Lynher Mill Publishing
Plymouth. UK.

Paperback Edition 29 September 2013
ISBN 978-0-9926956-0-6

The Dust of Ancients

by

Terri Nixon

Lynher Mill Publishing

For Rob and Dom. My boys. With all my love.

Illustration by Ian Brown. fyredance.wix.com/ianbrown

Prologue

Worlds within worlds; feared, denied, yet irrevocably enmeshed. It was not always so.

The day had begun to fade before the villagers gathered at the circle, and dusk crept rapidly over the high ground and softened the harsh features of the moor, but nothing could disguise the malevolence of those beautiful, deadly stones. Talk was scarce and conducted in low voices, from mouth to ear with barely a sound carrying in the damp air, but most remained silent and stared, grim-faced and pale, at the flat granite slab in the centre of this place that had always been a haven of reverence and worship.

They came, at last, into the cold from a nearby round hut: a babe in arms and his trembling, ashen-faced mother. Faces that instinctively twisted to see them just as quickly looked away, and the last of the murmurs fell silent while two pairs of furious eyes, watching from the darkest hollows of the heath, turned to one another in horrified recognition of the truth.

Loen felt his brother's hand on his arm and shrugged it off. 'I know! The fault is mine, I do not deny it.'

Borsa sighed. 'What you have done –'

'Cannot be undone.'

'These idiot mortals already believe we are responsible for every killing frost, every crop-scorching sky. To lie with one of them, Loen! Worse, to create a _child_ –'

'Enough! I am still your king!' It came out as a harsh

1

whisper, but Loen could have shouted it and gone unheard by these people who, as Borsa said, walked in awe and superstitious terror of the moorland elementals. Yet he had subdued one of them with nothing more other-worldly than his own beauty, and the barest hint of wordless suggestion. The irony tasted bitter now; there had been a certain dark humour at the ease with which he had deceived this woman, whose people so vehemently despised his own, but it had been swept aside by disbelief at this terrible judgement.

'Hear this, Borsa, and remember,' he managed, his jaw tight and aching. 'What I have done is wrong, but it is nothing when held up against the deed that foul mortal intends. If he …' the words choked off in his throat, and he took a deep breath. 'If he harms my son, I swear by all the elements I will be the death of his line. My own hand will end it.'

Borsa's nodded, but his voice was flat. 'I will stand beside you, as your brother and your subject.' His voice turned pleading. 'But you must know you have done a terrible thing! You have endangered your own people as well as these innocents.'

Loen tore his gaze from the awful scene before him, and his own words both surprised and dismayed him. 'Nevertheless I cannot wholly regret it, even now.'

Magara had captivated him from the moment he'd first seen her; the sister of the village chief, powerful in her own right and a strikingly beautiful creature. He had watched outside her hut night after night, unseen by the villagers: the elementals were fully human in size but, when the need arose, could appear no more substantial than a passing breath of wind. Wrapped in the darkness, Loen attracted no attention as he waited for her.

She had emerged, that perfect, crisp winter's night,

framed briefly in the doorway, the faint glow from the moon glancing off golden hair braided tightly to her head. Even in this half-light she had the bearing of royalty – a worthy partner. She hurried around to the pit area at the back of the group of huts and still he waited, heart beating fast until she reappeared, her attention on re-adjusting her shift.

Loen glanced around, and released the shadows that had cloaked him before stepping up to her, silencing her startled cry with a firm hand on her mouth. Frightened blue eyes stared at him, and he felt her tense to strike, but he smiled and she relaxed under his touch: there was nothing to fear, he was just a traveller, a passing moment of passion and promise … his mind eased hers without a word passing between them.

Their union was purely sexual. They made no sound beyond the low, breathy murmurs of mutual pleasure, and as they parted in silence he had seen a glow forming around her: the beginnings of his child in a glistening aura that fell about her like a cloak, formed of some exquisite fabric only he could see.

He never made himself known to her again, but over the months he watched her belly swell and took deep satisfaction in the knowledge that the woman would bear a child who would carry his enchanted, but ultimately weak blood, mingled with the strength of that of the humans. A child he already loved, and who would one day become ruler over all the moor.

***

The night of the birth was unseasonably balmy. Magara watched with sleepy appreciation as women hurried to her with cool water and herbal preparations, and she expected

3

fear to take hold but felt only the tingle of pleasant anticipation; soon she would see the face she had dreamed of seeing for so long, feel the heartbeat that had been her own, hold the solid warmth against her skin. Her child.

Her pregnancy had confirmed her suspicions about the stranger she had lain with: there had been no sickness when she woke each morning, she had suffered no aches or stiffness as her back bent to support the weight of the growing child, and now the time had come her pains were mild despite the obvious advancement of her labour.

The stranger's sudden appearance out of the shadows had set her heart racing in shock, but an easy calm had fallen over her as she'd looked into his eyes; such a clear, vivid green. When she had discovered she was to bear his child her first instinct was not fear, but a deep and fierce surge of joy — any child born of such a man would reflect the beauty to which she had so willingly surrendered. Every day she had looked out over the moor, and once or twice she thought she saw movement in the grass, but she never saw the stranger again.

Late summer lightning bloomed soundlessly on the horizon as the boy took his first gulping breaths; Magara could see the flare through the half-open door covering, and sent a silent message out into the night: *you have a son, my beautiful bringer of storms. Please ... know him.*

The new-born's cries were the only disturbance in the still air, and the villagers attending the birth looked at one another in shared pleasure at the arrival of another healthy life, but their delight quickly soured. The elderly woman who had delivered Magara of her son took a closer look at the black-haired boy and backed out of the hut, mumbling. Unwrapped and unwashed, the baby squalled

4

while Magara cast about for something in which to swaddle him, puzzled but too relieved and exhausted to give it much thought.

The door-covering was swept aside again and the hut emptied of all but mother, child and the new arrival, a tall, broad-shouldered man, bearded and fierce-looking. Magara held her son to her breast and smiled proudly up at her chieftain brother, but the smile faltered as she saw his face.

She found the formal words at last. 'I greet you, Ulfed. I offer you and our people the gift of this baby boy –'

'Who fathered this child, Magara?'

Magara looked away from his accusing stare. 'I do not know.' Many of the village men had been happy to claim the honour of starting the child with the chief's kinswoman, but there had never been a moment's doubt in her mind.

Ulfed's voice was softer now and it was as if he was reading her mind. 'It was no-one here, was it?'

In response to his tone Magara opened her mouth to tell him a carefully selected portion of the truth, but before she could speak the old woman burst back into the hut, raising shouts of alarm from outside. Two women came in after her, protective of the new mother.

The midwife raised an arm to point a shaking finger at the child. 'You must cast it out, let the evil ones take back their fiend before it destroys us!'

Magara drew an outraged breath and pulled the baby closer, her eyes going from the woman to Ulfed. 'She is mad! What can she know of my child?'

The woman's terrified eyes locked onto Magara's. 'I see much that is hidden,' she whispered, almost in tears. 'The child is fair to look upon, but its soul is stained.'

Ulfed gestured to the two women hovering by the

doorway in nervous excitement. 'Take her out.' He sounded bleak now, and the pain of the decision he must make was clear on his face. Magara went cold at the sight of it.

The women removed the distraught midwife with difficulty, leaving Magara and Ulfed to face each other in the sudden, frightening silence. She held the warm, squirming bundle closer still as her son took his nourishment, feeling a pleasurable ache at her left breast, and the sympathetic leaking at her right. Tears burned her throat but would not fall.

Ulfed remained silent, but Magara had no need of explanation and the dread took root, winding its way through her veins and stealing her ability to speak, even to plead for mercy. The midwife was held in high regard, her pronouncement would not be questioned, and therefore Ulfed's choice was simple; let the child starve or end its life swiftly. It was no choice at all.

***

Now, one full day after the birth, Loen stared in disbelief as the villagers brought mother and child to the circle. Surely the chief must be willing to risk the judgement of his goddess, whom he always judged so merciful? He himself had not even looked fully upon his son, but love for the child burned in him nevertheless, and, if the elements that sustained him had forced a choice, that love would prove the worthy victor. Did these mortals not revere their children in the same way?

The woman barely had the strength to walk by herself, and was supported on both sides as they crossed to the stones, her chest hitching violently as tears of terror carved bright rivers into her cheeks. Ulfed stepped forward and took the child from her grief-weakened grip, and Loen could see the chief's hands were trembling as he cried to the darkening skies.

'We beg your forgiveness for this woman, who has turned her back on you, and on her own people, and coupled with a creature of enchantment. We ask you to restore your favour upon us.' He raised the baby above his head and his voice started to shake. 'We offer this tainted child to you, as –'

'No!' Magara's barely maintained composure dissolved. Ulfed's pleading words dried up, and he wept openly as he laid the child on the stone slab in the centre of the circle, while Magara's supporters became her jailers. She sank to the ground in stunned, throat-locked silence as Ulfed stepped back from the stone.

Loen stared in horror. Had he really believed this man might find the strength to defy his precious goddess? He started forward and felt Borsa's grip on his arm.

'Where are you going?'

'I can take the child, they will not see me –'

'No, but think! They will see the babe vanish before their eyes! And then the mother will be put to the knife instead. You would wish her blood on your hands? Her who you chose in selfish greed, and whose life you have destroyed because of it?'

'But my child –'

'You must not! You have done enough.'

Borsa was right, Loen knew it, but unspeakable grief ripped through him at the sight of the knife poised above his son and, unable to look any longer he lurched away. Dragging a breath that seemed to come from the depths of the rock-strewn earth beneath his feet, he clenched his fists and felt a stirring around him, pressure building until the air itself seemed to push at him with hard, insistent fingers. He raised his face to the sky and his voice rolled out across the moor; ancient words of untested power, commanding obedience from the elements, fury and bitterness fuelling his demands.

The rains came first: sudden, freezing, heavy. A weighty curtain falling across the gathering by the stones, all but drowning out the bewildered cries from the villagers as they ran for shelter. Then the winds swept across the moor, a hollow boom rising to a shriek that split the evening air.

Loen felt his brother pulling at his arm, trying to drag him away, but shook him off once more. Ulfed raised the knife higher above his head, his head twisting wildly around in superstitious dread, clearly wondering if this act had further angered his goddess instead of pacifying her.

The only person unmoved by the storm was Magara. She remained, stupefied, on her knees at the foot of the stone, where the baby boy lay unprotected from the storm, his tiny legs kicking, fists beating at the air in futile anger. Loen silently exhorted her to rise up, to save her child, but her mind was unreachable.

The storm's ferocity grew, and Loen's heart tightened in sudden fear; he had merely exchanged one mortal danger for another. Once more he cried out his demands, this time for calm, but this storm had been born from the wildness of his rage and was equally beyond his control. Thunder set the earth trembling, and lightning stabbed the hills, now close, now on the distant horizon. Always deadly.

Confusion and indecision twisted the chief's expression and Loen knew he had only one chance and it was already slipping away. He moved swiftly, and was almost at the stones when he felt his hair lift from his scalp and a hideous blue-white light engulfed him. He crashed to the ground, tasting wet earth and hot, burned air, and for an excruciating moment his senses were heightened to an unbearable degree; the thunder seemed to crack his skull wide open, and each blade of grass beneath his cheek was a separate laceration in his skin.

He tried to rise but numbness crept over him, stealing his strength until he couldn't even raise his head. He struggled for every too-short breath, his heart hammering in terrifyingly erratic bursts, and acknowledged, with dull finality, that the lightning had no loyalty to its creator. He lay, helpless, feeling his life ebbing away into the churned mud and he was aware of Borsa somewhere above him, weeping, crying promises of revenge, but they made little sense.

His ancient flesh was withering now, drawing in on his bones as it paid the price for longevity, but there was no more pain. He was past that. He heard the outraged screaming of the child and twisted his gaze once more to the tableau at the stone circle, hope flowering in the darkest corner of his heart. But as his vision faded he saw Ulfed come at last to a decision and the chief's hoarse, sorrowing cry echoed among the stones.

The knife swept down.

Chapter One

Bodmin Moor, Cornwall. 1990

The old engine house rose from the rough hillside, glassless windows glaring down, the crumbling chimney standing stark and black against a blameless blue sky. Laura stared as if it was the first time she'd ever seen it; why did it suddenly seem so frightening? She wasn't a kid anymore, she was a teenager now, and it was just a lump of stone after all. She'd even sketched it several times, this one and the others that dotted the moors by her village, and they were among her favourite drawings. But today it looked different, almost menacing, and she made one last attempt to dissuade her younger brother from his determined march towards it.

'If someone catches us it'll be me who gets into trouble, I'm supposed to be in charge.'

Tom snorted. 'Who's going to catch us?'

Without waiting for a reply, even if she'd had one ready, he parted the safety wire and scrambled down the short, grassy slope to the overgrown tunnel. Laura glanced back wistfully at the disappearing daylight and sighed, then she crawled under the flaking warning sign. The ground was hard under her knees in the tunnel, and the memory of warmth and home, just ten minutes behind her, seemed impossibly distant.

Her unease grew as they descended and she shivered, picturing piles of bones lying forgotten and crumbling in the hollow hills. What if there were actual ghosts drifting in these tunnels? She thought she felt a whisper of movement against her skin, and her mind wanted to shrink in on itself; she could feel it closing in, and the tunnel seemed to be doing the same until all she could think about was how the roof would soon be brushing the top of her head. Even the roots of her hair seemed alert to the imminent touch of cool, living stone.

Laura's breathing quickened. 'Turn the torch on, Tom.'

'I'm saving it for later.'

'Turn it on *now*!'

He did, but instead of comforting light, it created strange shapes and shadows that came to life as he moved the narrow beam around the inside of the tunnel. Laura determinedly swallowed an exclamation of fear and tried, instead, to focus on something. A single stone, caught in the light for only a second but captured by her artist's eye. She concentrated on its colour, its roughness, the way it lay, snug and ordinary against its neighbour. Her constricted mind opened a little, and she felt her breathing ease. It was just a tunnel after all, incapable of moving, no narrower than it had been when she had first entered.

It went dark for a moment, then her heart froze as a face loomed, inches from her own, with glowing red distended cheeks and staring eyes. She screamed and Tom took the torch from his mouth, laughing. Laura slapped him hard on the shoulder and he did it again, adding a low growling noise before removing the torch and shining it in her face. This time she just gave him a withering look, and he wiped the torch on his jeans before turning back down the tunnel.

'You should never have taken this dare on,' Laura said to his grubby backside as she tried to keep close.

'Me?' Tom protested. 'Soon as Mike said about this place you were keen as mustard to show him how brave you are!'

Michael was the same age as Laura, and for each of them he held a different allure: ten year old Tom was in awe of his popularity and daredevil reputation, Laura was just starting to notice his laughing blue eyes.

Uncomfortable with her brother's observation, she returned to the attack. 'You're already in trouble anyway, getting kicked out of youth club. What if someone saw us?'

'They didn't.'

'Well what if something happens then?'

'Like what?'

'Anything! It'd be easy to have an accident somewhere like this.'

'Yeah, easy for a *girl.*'

Laura ignored him. 'Anyway, I reckon Michael was just winding us up, there's no cave.'

'No?' Tom's voice held a grin now and Laura saw the shadows change, elongating. Her brother stood up and swept the feeble beam around the massive cavern in an attempt to see all their surroundings at once.

Laura joined him, her heart lightening with relief. Thinking about how impressed Michael would be, she put her annoyance to the back of her mind and cupped her hands around her mouth to let out an experimental hoot. The sound bounced back and, encouraged, they jumped up and down and whooped and howled, each trying to outdo the other in volume and variation.

After a while Tom began walking around the edges of the cavern, stopping now and again to peer into holes in the wall, and shining his torch above his head to look for the ceiling. Following the thin line of light Laura saw it arc above them, lumpy and surprisingly high; they had clearly come farther under the moor than she'd realised. She waited by the entrance to the tunnel as Tom went deeper into the chamber, suddenly feeling horribly alone. The thought of them becoming lost, wandering down here forever, crept into her mind, along with the realisation that no-one knew where they were. Abruptly the fun was snatched from the day.

She called out, embarrassed by her own wavering voice, 'All right, let's go now!' There was no answer. Tom's torchlight vanished and Laura struggled against swiftly increasing alarm. 'Tom!' she shouted again. 'Don't muck about, I want to go. Come *on*!' She waited in the darkness, mentally cursing her brother but at the same time wanting nothing more than to see his annoying face again.

The torch bobbed back into view and she heard an excited cry: 'Come and look at this!'

Laura glanced back at the relative safety of the tunnel, then, finding a thread of courage she picked her way, hands outstretched, across to where Tom had disappeared again behind a stony outcropping at the far side. When she found him he was shining his torch on a large wooden box, pushed back several feet onto a wide shelf.

He played the light over it from end to end. 'What do you think's in there?'

'How should I know?' Laura snapped, anxious to leave despite the find.

Tom handed her the torch and boosted himself onto the ledge. 'Keep the light on the box.'

She was tempted to tell him to get lost, and to take the torch and get as far away as possible, but instead she sighed and directed the beam just ahead of him. The ceiling was still high enough for him to stand, even in this tiny chamber, and he scrambled in until he was right beside the box. His body blocked out some of the light, but Laura heard a scraping sound and realised he was prising off the lid – something in her baulked at the notion and she turned uneasily away.

That was when she saw the first one.

On the periphery of the circle of torchlight stood a figure half the height of her brother, but no child had ever looked like this; the huge head perched on slender, almost delicate shoulders tilted towards her, and all she saw of its face was a bulbous forehead and a wide slash of mouth, before the torch fell from her numbed fingers and clattered to the ground. It went out, plunging them into a chilly blackness she could almost feel on her skin.

'Hey!' Tom's voice held a trace of fear along with irritation. A scream locked in her throat, Laura had to get the light back just so she could breathe, but she couldn't move until, in the silence following Tom's protest she heard a scratching, scurrying noise in the huge cavern behind her. Galvanised by the sound, she groped swiftly by her feet but her outstretched fingers instead found the stone floor with bruising impact.

Tears of pain sprang to her eyes, but still she could make no sound through her tightly pressed lips. What if the batteries had come out and were rolling around in the dark by her feet? With a surge of relief she found the torch and snatched it up, switching it on in the same movement and flashing it wildly around. There was nothing there except an annoyed-looking Tom, and the wooden box with the lid now standing open.

'Who rattled your cage?' he demanded. 'Shine that thing back in here a minute, I've found something brill. Look!'

The beam shook wildly as Laura brought it reluctantly back towards the box, keeping her head screwed back over her shoulder, her eyes aching with the strain of trying to penetrate the seemingly solid blackness. How could she have imagined something like that? But she would rather believe she was going mad than bring it to irrefutable life

14

by speaking of it aloud.

'Keep still!' Tom grabbed her hand and directed the torch beam to the object he was trying to show her.

A jar. That's all it was, a crummy little jar with a decorated lid, while out *there* were … what? Goblins? Gnomes? Did those things even exist outside Enid Blyton books? She tuned out Tom's excited voice, trying to detect any more rustling sounds, but there was nothing. Slowly her heart began to return to its normal rhythm; she must have imagined it, built something solid from the shadows –

'Ow!' Tom's shout cut through her concentration. 'Something stung me!'

Laura swung the torch so the light illuminated the corner of the ledge. Finally the scream came out, short and terrified and, unable to speak, she slapped Tom's arm and pointed.

There, standing on wizened legs, shrivelled looking yet oddly menacing, was the creature she had seen before. His head now swivelled to stare at Tom, and his hand reached out to take the jar. With his other hand he jabbed a small, long-tined pitchfork at the boy's leg, eliciting another shout of pain, this time laced with bewildered horror.

Tom scrambled back, still holding tightly to his prize, and began to drop his leg back off the ledge in preparation for running away. But as Laura reached out to steady him she felt a sharp stabbing pain in her own thigh and screamed again, instinctively kicking out. Tom slipped, and the jar crashed to the floor. The sound of it shattering was deafening in the tiny space, echoing off the stone walls, and each piece of pottery seemed to make its own audible clatter as it landed.

Tom immediately began coughing, dragging in harsh breaths, and Laura saw his face was covered in blue-grey dust that coated his lips. Each breath dragged more of the stuff into his mouth, and his eyes were wide with dismay and revulsion. She was about to try and bang him on the back when she was halted by a howl of rage from the creature on the ledge.

Her head swam as she heard a noise behind her and turned to see two more of them, one brandishing a short, sturdy piece of wood, while the other had taken off his belt and was swishing it angrily in front of him. It was an almost comical act that struck a darkly amused note in Laura's mind despite her terror: this was proof it was only a dream … she pinched the skin on the back of her hand hard enough bring fresh tears to her eyes, but nothing changed.

The goblin-things were almost upon them now, and Tom was right behind her, still coughing, shoving her forwards in his attempt to escape. She couldn't move of course, but he didn't know that until he pushed her aside, and then she heard him moan quietly. The tiny sound spurred her; she was the big sister, she had to take charge. She swept the torch from side to side, searching for some way past the creatures but suddenly that belt-weapon didn't look so funny after all, it had a large buckle on the end and was cutting the air with a heavy whooshing sound.

The goblin-thing behind them had dropped off the ledge and was moving towards them, huffing in angry little coughs. To Laura's bemusement he actually sounded as if he were crying, and she swung the torch around to shine full on him. Sure enough, tears were running down his wrinkled face, leaving tracks in the dust and plopping off his chin onto the dark green jacket he wore. Laura was so astonished she could do nothing but stare, as he crouched beside the broken jar and began to scoop the pieces into his pockets.

Tom tugged at her arm to bring the light around once more on the two newcomers, but she was paralysed by a strange kind of sympathy for the ugly little man. He lifted his face to hers, as if drawn by her fixed stare, and her compassion dropped away, replaced by crushed ice that crept through her bones and froze her breath.

The creature opened the hideously outsized mouth to shriek his fury through great, gulping sobs. 'Cursed! Oh, *cursed* you are! Wicked children, you should never have come here!'

Behind Laura, Tom stopped coughing and burst into shocked, rasping tears. She wanted to comfort him, but her eyes were fixed on the little man as he carried on scooping up dust and broken pieces of clay, and her fascinated attention was only torn away when she realised the cavern behind them was now as empty as it had appeared when they arrived. The creature climbed back onto the ledge and melted into darkness, and the sounds of his furious distress faded.

Tom's sobs subsided into hiccups. 'What was it?'

'I don't know,' Laura muttered, 'but we're getting out of here *now*.'

Together they made their way across the huge cavern, making slower progress than Laura would have liked as they kept looking over their shoulders; she swept the torch across and behind them as they went, but they remained alone. When they were halfway across they both had the same, unassailable urge to be out in sunlight again, and simultaneously broke into a run, fighting each other to be first into the tunnel. Tom won, and took the torch from Laura.

Crawling behind him, Laura could imagine the creatures closing in on her from behind, could almost hear them - they were small enough to run, hunched but still on their feet, and so vivid was the picture that, when the goblin-thing in her mind reached out to grasp her ankle she jerked away and screamed. Tom cried out too, and half-turned, shining the torch in her eyes.

She pushed at him in panic. 'Just go!'

At last she saw sunlight above Tom's head, reaching weak fingers along the roof of the tunnel as if to draw them out. Each impact of her knees on the stone floor made her wince, but she didn't slow. Tom disappeared from sight as he reached the entrance, and Laura pulled herself out after him and stumbled up the slope and under the wire. Her strength spent, she sank to the ground, relishing the feel of the grass under her hands and the breeze on her burning face, and then, with no warning at all she was crying. There was no embarrassment, no awkward sniffling and turning her head away, she let out the shock and relief in a wash of sobs that hurt her chest and made her head ache.

Tom reached out and touched her arm. She saw her own terror reflected in his eyes, but neither spoke. Eventually she got to her feet, and this time it was he who followed her.

'Lau?'

She looked back at him and gasped; she was staring at someone she didn't know. Tom appeared much older, his features more finely cut, even his eyes seemed longer, more oval, had a greenish tint ... then she blinked, and he was just Tom again.

'There was nothing there really, was there?' he said. 'Just shadows.'

Laura hesitated, and saw his guarded determination fade as a frightening blankness took its place; acknowledging the truth could tumble him into some dark place from which he may never return.

She swallowed hard and shook her head. 'No. Just shadows.' And when she got home and peeled down her jeans to look at her bruised knees, the red mark on her thigh that welled blood when she squeezed it might have been caused by anything; a loose stone in the grass, a bit of rusted warning sign, even an insect bite. There was nothing to say it had been made by a tiny pitchfork. Nothing at all.

***

Deep below the surface of the moor a tall regal woman beheld the sorry sight of a misshapen little man hunched before her, sobbing out the story of a broken jar, a lost treasure and the wickedness of human children. Deera felt coldness worming through her and leaned on her plain wooden staff, praying for the strength to remain on her feet, as she contemplated the full horror of what had happened.

Loen's dust, frantically gathered by his grieving brother, now lost to the human world. He would be able to claim the revenge promised him by his brother so long ago, but at what cost to her own family? Dread clutched at her heart and she raised the staff in two shaking hands, poised to deliver punishment.

But the fatal words never came. Instead the creature lifted his head and whispered through his tears: 'Jacky Greencoat knows a secret, yer majesty, a big, old secret. Spare Jacky, and Jacky will tell.'

A short while later the heavy curtain was pushed back and a slender boy stepped into the chamber. He was almost a man now, the future king, and Queen Deera swallowed tears of mingled pride and fear.

She took a deep breath and went to him, taking his hands in hers. There was no other way but to speak it plain. 'Maer, you have always known your life would be in danger should Loen find the means to return.' He nodded, light blue eyes fixed on hers, evidently sensing the worry behind her deliberately measured tones. She sighed. 'The jar is broken. The king's spirit was freed and has taken hold within a new form, a child of the new village.'

'But surely that is good?' Maer said with a relieved smile. 'If he has found a living form already he will have no need of mine.'

'I would give my life for that to be true, but the child is fully human.' Deera struggled to remain calm. 'Loen can only use it for a short while, to grow, to become strong enough to take over a more suitable body. But not yours!' her voice rose as she saw fear start into his eyes. 'I will not allow it.'

'Then who do you mean him to have, mother?'

He was just a boy again now, and Deera longed to take him to her breast as she had done in times past to soothe him. But she could not.

Instead she took a couple of steps away, drawing her cloak tighter around herself. Her fingers brushed the symbol of royalty emblazoned on the cloth over her heart, the blade crossed through with lightning, and she took strength from it. 'I have recently learned of another child; half mortal, half elemental,' she said. 'He lives far away, out of our reach and must be protected, kept safe from all dangers, and only brought here when the king is ready.'

'Brought here? By whom?'

'By you, Maer.'

His eyes widened briefly in excitement, then he

frowned. 'I do not shy away from such a duty, but why must it be me?'

'It was I who allowed the jar to be destroyed, and in accordance with Borsa's promise I owe the king a body. If it is not to be yours, it must be this half-mortal child. His situation is perfect: he has no parents, his guardians are elderly in mortal years, and he is wise and fair. He will appeal to the king's vanity as well as his needs.'

'How do I find this boy?' Maer asked, and she could hear his eagerness now, at the prospect of travelling.

'You will use the Doorway to go directly to him – it is simply a matter of readying yourself.'

'Now?'

'Yes, my love, you must leave now. You must return at least once in every full cycle of seasons or you will become weak and ill, and age too quickly. My brother Gilan will tend to the boy at those times and you will take over his duties here, watching over the village boy.'

As she moved forward to embrace him she saw the light of adventure brightening his expression, and her heart eased a little. She would miss him, but he would have the chance to learn something of a world she could scarcely imagine. Most importantly, he would live.

Chapter Two

The boy who showed up at the park that morning was like no-one Richard had ever met before. He just stood there, hovering on the fringe of the argument the gang always had before the first pitch of the day. Steve had seen him first, and nudged Richard. They both stared and the boy stared back, unfazed and almost arrogant-looking, only the tiny hint of nervousness saving him from serious ridicule. He looked to be about fifteen, the same age as most of the kids in the game, but he was way too pretty for a guy.

A couple of the team yelled out, 'Hey, beautiful!' and, 'Where's your purse?'

The boy's nerves visibly melted away under the open taunts, becoming a wry smile, and he called back, 'It goes better with my other dress!'

The masculine tone blew that angel-boy look right out of the water, and Richard grinned. 'You throw?' The boy nodded. 'Okay, guys, argument over. Meet our new pitcher.' Richard tossed the ball, and the blond boy caught it easily and moved closer to the group.

Afterwards, he caught up with Richard as he started across the park. 'Thanks for bringing me into the game.'

'Hey, don't thank me, you pretty much won it for us. Best knuckleball I ever saw.'

'Thanks. You're Richard, right?'

'Yeah, Richard Lucas.'

'Dean Mayer,' the boy offered. 'Just got here a couple days ago. My parents thought I should come live with my uncle, figure I'll get more chances in the city.'

'Cool, good choice.'

'Yeah, they're okay. What are your parents like?'

Richard kept his gaze fixed ahead and swallowed hard. 'Don't have any. Not since I was eight.'

'That's rough. How'd they die?'

'Car wreck.' After seven years the grief still struck Richard breathless and he deliberately brightened his expression to shake the feeling. He gestured to a kiosk at the edge of the park. 'You wanna get a drink?'

'Sure, that'd be cool.'

They discussed the game, and Dean's surprising skill as a pitcher, considering his unfamiliarity with the game itself, then as they sat drinking coke in the autumn sunshine, talk turned to school.

'I guess you'll be going to Highland Park High,' Richard said. 'I go there, it's not so bad.' He narrowed his eyes. 'But if you ever tell anyone I said that I'll have to track you down and kill you.'

'Message received and understood,' Dean said solemnly. 'So, what are the girls like?'

Richard whistled and shook his head. 'Now you're asking. Bet you had your pick at your old place, huh?'

Dean shrugged. 'About as much as you do here.'

'Yeah, right.' Richard took a drink to hide his flush. He knew girls generally liked him, although he'd never been able to figure out why, not that he'd tried too hard; it was embarrassing to think about it at all. Girls were a mystery, and some of them were downright terrifying with their spray-on skinny jeans and artfully tousled hair.

He communicated none of this to Dean though, as two teen princesses swayed by, giving both boys a long, inviting look as they went.

'Wow, they're really up front out here!' Dean whispered, and Richard laughed, causing the girls to turn back for another look. One of them gave a coy little wave, curling her fingers one by one over her palm, before swinging around to give maximum flounce to her hair. 'I don't know about you, but they scare the hell out of me.'

Richard grinned. 'You and me both,' he admitted with some relief.

Dean raised his coke bottle in a salute. A tiny smile touched his lips 'Well then, here's to discovering a little courage.'

***

Maer – no, he must think of himself as Dean now – watched Richard surreptitiously as they made their way back across the park a little later. The boy was very self-assured for fifteen years old, and already undeniably handsome, bold-featured with thick black hair falling untidily over arresting, clear green eyes. No wonder girls were drawn to him. He walked with a long, easy stride that belied an average height, and as Dean walked beside him he felt the associated kudos of being with a boy people genuinely liked. This would be no chore, but a whole new life. A human life! He still felt unsettled and a little sick from his journey through the Doorway, but he couldn't deny the thrill of anticipation, nor the sense of achievement in picking up the new speech patterns so quickly. He'd listened to all the boys throughout the game, noting the subtle differences and strong similarities, and adopted the ones that were closest to his own. It was starting to feel natural already.

'Shit.' Richard stopped, looking towards the perimeter fence.

Dean followed his gaze. 'What's up?'

'See those guys over there?'

'Yeah. What about them?'

'One of them owes me something.'

'Oh. Okay, you want to go get it?'

Richard cast him a crooked smile. 'Are you kidding? I think it may involve broken bones.'

Dean gaped at him, but only for a moment, then he shut his mouth and set his shoulders firm. This was what he was here for: to protect this boy. He felt a little vibration of fear – he had never lifted a hand in anger in his life – but he was a prince, he had a duty to perform, and now was the time to prove he could do it.

Four of the boys by the edge of the lot had broken away from the fence and stood closer together now, watching them. Dean stole a glance at Richard and was astonished, and somewhat dismayed, to see the smile hadn't left his face.

Richard's eyes stayed on the boys. 'How fast can you run, Dean?' he asked mildly.

'Run? Um, pretty fast I guess.'

'Good. I suggest you start now.'

'Suggest again.'

Richard glanced at him and the smile was still hovering around his mouth, but he had a serious look in his eyes. 'Look, this isn't your fight, okay? You seem like a nice guy and these assholes have no quarrel with you, but if you stick around you're liable to get all caught up in something you don't need.'

'There are four of them and one of you!'

'I'm not going to pretend I can take them all, but you don't have to get involved.'

'So what, you're going to stand here and wait for those guys to come over here and kick you into the middle of next week?'

'No, I'm going to run too, when it's time. Go on and

get out of here, Dean, I'll catch up with you later.'

'Screw that.' Dean felt the thrill separate into strands of excitement and fear, and he saw Richard's chin come up and his hands curl into loose fists. He mirrored the action, feeling a fluttering deep in his belly. It was really going to happen; newly arrived in this incredible land and already he was facing his first fight.

'Hey, Lucas!'

'How's it goin', Tanner?' Richard sounded older than his years as he returned the hostile greeting with a friendly one of his own. He had barely raised his voice, but it carried clearly across the park. The biggest of the boys, who looked a couple of years older than Richard, was already walking towards them.

'You little bastard, you're going to wish you'd stayed home with gran'ma and granddad today.'

Richard glanced at the sky. 'Why, is it gonna rain?' He still sounded calm, but Dean could see his knuckles whiten and his breathing change as he readied himself. His own heartbeat speeded up as he drew himself taller, and Tanner threw him a curious but unimpressed look. The other three trailed by a few yards, this was clearly between Lucas and Tanner.

'You know, if you hadn't been such an asswipe over that whole thing with Steve Shelby, you would never have gotten arrested,' Richard said. This was no way to defuse an incendiary situation, but that didn't appear to be his goal. He stood rock steady as Tanner came within striking range, and Tanner scowled.

'Who the hell do you think you are, Lucas, making me look a total jerk?'

'Did that all by yourself, my friend,' Richard said. Dean saw the tightness of his jaw and realised extreme anger had been there all along, hidden behind the insolence.

But Tanner was too wound up to notice. 'So who's your pretty little friend?' he said, looking at Dean properly for the first time and raising an eyebrow. 'You two going to slide off for a little boy-fun after I kick your ass?'

'This has nothing to do with him,' Richard said. 'Or them,' he added, gesturing at Tanner's friends. 'Come on, Tanner. What do you say we finish this once and for all?'

'Just you and me?'

'Just you and me.'

'Sure. Back off, guys,' Tanner said, turning to his cronies, and from where he was standing Dean saw something Richard clearly hadn't: Tanner winked.

Before he could open his mouth to warn Richard, Tanner had turned back and thrown a punch all in one swift movement. His fist connected with nothing more solid than the air where Richard's head had been a split second before. His balance was thrown off, and Richard planted a sneaker square in the seat of the older boy's pants, and pushed.

Tanner went sprawling and Dean groaned: humiliation was hardly going to bring about the end Richard wanted, and he started to say so but a sudden stinging blow beside his left eye sent him staggering backwards. He turned to see one of Tanner's friends sucking his knuckles and grinning, although tears of pain stood out in his eyes.

'Enjoy that, pretty boy?'

'More than you did by the looks of things — are you crying?' Dean returned, and felt a twinge of pride as he heard Richard laugh.

After that everything became a blur of adrenalin and swinging fists as Tanner and his friends weighed in. Dean ducked under a flailing arm and delivered his first ever punch, to his assailant's jaw. He heard Richard grunt, and looked up to see him taking a series of body blows from

Tanner, but before he could get to him Tanner had gone down beneath a swift karate chop to the back of his neck. Richard straightened and flashed Dean a brief grin, rubbing the edge of his hand. He jerked his head towards the fence, where their fight had attracted the attention of the rest of Tanner's cronies.

'I think it's time,' he said, and Dean nodded.

They ran.

Through the park towards the wooded area beyond ... something familiar at last, amidst all the noise, and the heavy bellowing of traffic. Dean felt relief surging in his blood. The road, when he had first seen it, had struck a note of such terror in his soul he'd felt momentarily faint. Of course there were new roads in the village near his home, but he'd never imagined such monstrous byways as these. The two boys hurtled, side by side, into the blessed greenness of the trees, hearing the thunder of boots on the grass behind them.

Once there was a healthy distance between them and their pursuers, they ducked in behind a large elm tree and stopped. Something about the sound of Richard's breathing struck a suspicious note, and a glance sideways confirmed it: he was laughing. Dean wondered if he realised he was hardly out of breath. He'd checked his own speed at first, not wanting to alert Richard to any strangeness, nor to leave him behind, but he'd quickly realised it wasn't necessary, he had extra speed here but nothing even close to the way he was at home.

The thought of home, and what it meant to be here instead, clenched his gut for a moment, but Richard's words banished the feeling. 'You're quite something, Dean.'

'Something what?'

'Something else!' Richard said, and clapped him on the

shoulder.

For one born to royalty and adoration, the simple gesture of acceptance and approval from this half-mortal boy gave Dean a surprisingly warm rush of pleasure and pride.

'Where's whatshisname?' he said, turning to hide the flush he could feel on his face and neck.

'He's coming.'

'Then why are we hanging around here?'

Richard's smile fell away. 'Because this isn't over yet, and it's damned well going to be before today is out.'

Even as he spoke they heard the sound of crashing footsteps in the undergrowth, and Richard stepped out from behind the tree, directly into Tanner's path.

'There you are, you fucking coward!' Tanner spat, dragging in deep breaths.

Richard glanced beyond him. 'Where are your buddies?'

'Coming.'

'Tell them to back off, no tricks this time.'

Tanner looked at him, amazed, then barked laughter. 'Or you'll what?'

Richard shrugged. 'We'll just out-run you again, you know we can.' He folded his arms and leaned against the tree. 'And then I'll make sure everyone knows you need help to fight a kid three years younger than you.'

Tanner stared at Richard, and Dean wasn't entirely surprised to see a new expression there: Richard had already won, although neither he nor Tanner knew it yet.

'You little —'

'Just you and me, Tanner,' Richard said once again. Eventually Tanner nodded, and Richard levered himself off the tree. He walked up to Tanner and held out his hand. Bemused, Tanner shook it, then glanced over his shoulder to make sure his friends hadn't seen. They arrived in the clearing just in time to see him step away from Richard, and looked at each other with evident satisfaction.

'Stay out of it,' Tanner said.

'Sure,' one of them, the one who'd hit Dean, grinned.

'I mean it this time. I don't need no help with this little shit.'

A chorus of murmuring as his friends fell over themselves to agree, and Dean caught Richard's eye and nodded his understanding: the rule went for him too.

'You know, you keep telling me how 'little' I am,' Richard said to Tanner. 'Let's see how well you deal with little shall we?'

Tanner swung and, once again, Richard's quick movement avoided contact. He let fly a short, controlled punch that smacked Tanner on the cheekbone, then turned easily to avoid Tanner's furious retaliation.

He continued to step out of reach for several minutes but eventually Tanner's superior size and weight carried him forward, knocking them both to the ground, and Dean winced as he saw a large fist swing into his new friend's ribs. Richard gripped Tanner's shirt front and dragged him around until he was able to roll on top and straddle him.

They fought hard for control, and Tanner's hands flashed upward and gripped Richard's throat. Dean almost stepped in then: Richard's eyes had closed briefly in pain, but he brought his own hands up and out between Tanner's outstretched arms, breaking the stranglehold, then shot his own fist out and clipped it hard under Tanner's chin, snapping his head back. He adjusted his position, pinning Tanner's wrists to the ground above his head.

He leaned in close. 'Stay away from me and my friends, you're done here.'

Tanner started to struggle, but Dean saw realisation in his half-hearted movements and it wasn't simply because Richard was astride him; one powerful shove might have unbalanced the younger boy enough for Tanner to turn the situation around. But there was a fierce light blazing in Richard's eyes, an absolute conviction in the rightness of his own actions, and it was obvious Tanner saw it too and was just as jolted by it.

Dean would see that look time and time again in years to come, and his belief in the boy, and the man he would become, would be strengthened by it. For now though, there was just the insane urge to laugh with relief that it was over, and that he had upheld his vow of protection, at least as far as he was needed. Tanner's friends were less easily cowed, but then they hadn't been subjected to that intense gaze. They moved together and readied themselves for Tanner's order to step in, but Tanner shook his head.

'Not now. Later. When you're not expecting it.' He spat this last at Richard, who nodded. Tanner was merely saving face, but this was no time to bait him with it.

'Look forward to it,' he said, and rose in a single, fluid movement, allowing Tanner to clamber to his feet. 'Later, guys.'

His grin, and the little wave he gave, nearly kicked the whole thing off again and Dean sighed with relief as Tanner called his gang away: it was pretty clear that, charisma and charm aside, Richard Lucas was going to be one hell of a full time job.

Chapter Three

Cornwall 1991

The first hesitant signs of spring appeared. Tom didn't question why he no longer felt the urge to play on the moors with his friends, and whenever someone else did he gave the same answer: he was too old for playing, and besides, there was money to be made. Working people wanted their dogs walked, and were willing to pay good money to someone with the time. And if he confined his walks to the upper slopes of the village by the old mill rather than the flat, lower ground by the mines, well what of it?

Today Laura had scooped up a chunky stick from the path in their garden, and persuaded him to phone the curate and offer their services with his little collie. The curate was busy enough to be grateful, but it still rankled that Tom would have to split the takings when he was used to doing this alone. He'd been so annoyed he'd barely noticed when she'd crossed the road outside their house and headed towards the stone circle, instead of turning right and going up the hill, but he followed anyway, and let Kelpie off the lead as soon as they were safely away from the road.

As they went farther onto the moor the ground beneath their feet became uneven, wet and a struggle to cross, but once they'd passed the first of the black chimneys that scratched the sky Tom began to feel a new kind of excitement, and it seemed to lift his heart higher until it felt almost as if he had to float to keep it in the right place inside him. His mouth stretched in a smile he had no real reason for, and his stride became easier, longer, more confident. Why had he stayed away from here for so long?

Laura didn't seem to share his pleasure. 'This ground's so boggy, it's hard to find somewhere solid to walk.'

'It's okay here. Besides, you chose this way.' His own feet were finding their way unerringly from one solid piece of ground to the next and he enjoyed the feeling. Then Laura gave a yelp, and her arms pinwheeled as she fought to remain on her tussock, and Tom was only a little ashamed to feel a spiteful flash of humour before he grabbed her hand. The whole incident had taken a split second but the satisfaction of his unexpected effortlessness on the unsteady ground abruptly deserted him, along with the ease itself. He and Laura supported one another, and together they crossed to higher, dryer ground, relieved to leave the bogs behind.

Kelpie raced ahead, then back to them, yelping with impatience until Laura hefted the stick she'd picked up and hurled it across the grass. 'You are going to give me half the money for this, aren't you?'

'Yeah, s'pose.'

Kelpie bounded back to them, laughing around the stick in her mouth, and dropped it at Laura's feet.

She threw it again. 'You'd better! If it wasn't for me you'd have just taken Mrs Bowden's annoying little terrier down Langstone Lane and back for fifty pence. This is getting us a couple of quid easy.'

Tom wandered away for a bit, trying to ignore Laura's stupid baby talk as she called encouragement to the dog. Why should he give her half the money anyway? She didn't have to come, he never asked her to. She probably wanted to save up for some make-up to impress Michael

33

Hart; she thought he didn't know she fancied Michael, but everyone knew really. It was embarrassing.

'Pull your weight then!' she shouted at him, tossing him the stick. It hit the side of his hand and he felt a wash of anger as he sucked at the scratch. The sun disappeared behind a cloud and he shivered in the sudden gust of wind, and for a second he recalled, with absolute clarity, a dream he'd had last summer, the night after the trip down the mine.

He'd been in a large, single-roomed building, surrounded by fire and searching for a jar, desperate to protect it. At last he'd found and seized it with a cry of relief, but the contact had seared his skin, jerking him into wakefulness to find his hand still hurt. When he put the bedside light on and looked there had been a very faint mark there, and the pain lit the shape of a circle beneath his skin. Within five minutes it had faded, leaving him wondering if he'd imagined the whole thing. Outside, thunder had rumbled and Tom heard the muted sounds of his parents hunting around for candles in case the lights went, but something told him the storm would soon fade.

The next day he'd learned the youth club hall in St Tourney, from which he'd been banned for fighting, had burned to the ground following a lightning strike. He'd told Laura about his hand but at her look of horror he'd backpedalled and played it down; he'd needed her to assure him it was nothing, but the way her face had gone white had scared him more than the dream.

Now, sucking at the coppery taste of blood on the side of his hand, Tom tried to push the memory to the back of his mind where it belonged. He threw the stick hard, and felt his mood lighten as Laura whistled in admiration.

'Whoa, nice one!' she laughed, as Kelpie shot after it. Tom felt a prickle of pleasure at his sister's praise and, as if to celebrate, the sun came out again and he felt the urge to run.

'Beat you to the top!' he yelled, and without waiting to see if she followed, not caring if she didn't, he took off up the hill.

By the time Laura arrived he was sitting on top of Lynher Mill Barrow. The granite lintel was cold through his jeans but he felt more like his old self: the confused mixture of feelings had gone and he was happy to be out of doors and earning a bit of money at the same time. The winter had been too long, too much time to think.

Laura bent over, hands on knees, panting almost as much as the dog loping up behind her. 'Well, you didn't hang around.'

Tom laughed. 'It was a race!' He took hold of the stick again but Laura stayed his hand.

'Wait a bit. She's pretty old now, don't forget.'

Tom ignored her and threw the stick. Kelpie looked at him for a moment, then back to where the stick had gone, and trotted off down the hill once more. 'See? She wouldn't go if she didn't want to.'

Laura sighed. 'Just be careful.'

For a while they sat in silence, looking out towards the village where they'd grown up.

'Where will you live?' Laura said suddenly.

'Huh? When?'

'You know, when you grow up. When you leave … what's the matter?'

But Tom couldn't answer. What was she thinking? He'd never leave! And she mustn't either. He became aware that she was looking at him, puzzled. She didn't even realise what a terrible thing she'd said.

His voice came out very small. 'You're going to move away?'

'Yeah, 'course I am, eventually. I'm going to live in London, or America, or maybe Australia. I'm going to be an artist. And a teacher, a really nice one that everyone likes.' Misreading his dismay she reached out and squeezed his arm. 'It's okay, you can come too, I won't leave you on your own here in this dump!'

She gazed away into the distance again. 'We can be the best brother and sister team ever, travelling the world wherever the kids need us. Bit like Mary Poppins, but with less singing!' She giggled, but Tom didn't share the joke, he was filled with a horror he couldn't explain, even to himself. He felt at the granite he was sitting on: without using his hands he couldn't tell where flesh ended and rock began.

He knew, absolutely and without doubt, that if he were transported somewhere else, no matter how exciting it was, he wouldn't be able to breathe. He stared at Laura as she gazed away, she was obviously seeing something different from the rolling hills and dotted rock formations, and the distance on her face made her look like someone he had never known.

'No,' he whispered, 'we can't –'

'Yeah, we can. I know it seems like a long way off, but one day you'll be able to go wherever you want. Anywhere in the whole world,' Laura told him, and he supposed she was trying to be comforting but it was the most horrible thing he'd ever heard.

She carried on talking of far off places, the biggest, most exciting cities, and as she spoke his hands clenched tighter and tighter and his eyes squeezed shut to block out the pictures she painted. He had an awful, ashy taste in his mouth, and his throat was dry. He coughed and it hurt a little, but the scratchiness did not go away.

A cold wind gusted across the side of the hill, cutting

around the back of the nearest chimney stack and making his eyes snap open again at the sudden, eerie whistle it made. He realised Laura had stopped talking, and was staring at the darkening sky with an awe that was rapidly turning into fear. She turned to him, mouth open in an unspoken question, but he ignored her and stood up, calling to Kelpie.

When the dog did not appear, Laura's expression changed to one of accusation. 'I *told* you not to –'

At that moment the air around them pulsed with blue light, and sharply cracking thunder ripped across the moor. Laura screamed, and Tom gasped as the light left dazzling prints in the air when he blinked. How beautiful. Rain began to fall, the heavy droplets pattering onto the rock where he had been sitting, and falling, freezing, down the back of his neck. He smiled.

The next flash came almost immediately, and was even brighter against the dark charcoal skies. Tom started down the hill at a run, and when Laura yelled at him to wait he ran faster. The thoughts that twisted and tumbled in his head were clear, although he couldn't have put them into words:

Serve her right! If she doesn't want to stay here, then let her feel the moor now. Let her live it, breathe it, learn to respect it. How could she even think of leaving?

The rain slid off his face and into his hair as he ran, faster still, pretending not to hear his sister's shouts. Eventually he stopped to look around, breathing hard, but with fierce exultation making his blood sing. 'Kelpie!' he yelled, and the word whipped was away by the wind even as it left his mouth.

Another flash, each step of the stroke producing a sharp crack so it sounded like a short machine gun burst. The air smelled hot, felt heavy despite the wind and the rain, and the sky was swollen and dark, purple-grey. Tom's heart beat fast and hard and it was not entirely due to the exertion of running. He remembered how easy it had been finding his way across the boggy ground, and how then, as now, his heart had seemed to float free in his body, as if he didn't need it at all. He had never felt this alive before, although he knew the storm posed a real danger. Maybe even because of that.

'Tom!' Laura screamed, and at the same time he heard a yelping sound from below him, where the ground evened out.

The euphoria melted away and he started to feel cold and uncertain; the area would be boggier than ever after even a short spell of such heavy rain. Laura must have been thinking the same, and she pushed past him in her desperation to get to the dog. Frightened now, Tom followed. He was still aware of the occasional flash, and crack of thunder, and a stinging sensation in his palm, but as he plunged into the black ooze behind his sister he no longer delighted in the power of the storm. Kelpie was just ahead of them, her legs fully immersed now, frantically leaning forward towards the firmer ground just beyond her.

Laura was calf deep in mud. 'She won't go under, it's not deep enough just here, but she's terrified. Let's just be calm for a minute, okay?'

Tom stopped. 'Hey, girl,' he said to the frantically thrashing dog. 'What are you doing, eh? Hold still now. Hold still, there's a good girl.'

Laura uttered similar, mindlessly soothing words as they both stepped carefully through the marshy ground, trying not to panic Kelpie further. She drew close enough to reach out and grasp the dog's collar, and with Tom's help she ran her hands down the trembling dog's legs, breaking the suction, talking quietly to her, stroking the filthy black and white coat as the softly whining dog licked them both in turn.

Tom carried Kelpie back onto the worn path. 'Storm's eased off.'

Laura fixed the lead back onto the dog's collar, and scowled. 'Just as bloody well. Why did you run off and leave me?'

'You're older than me! How come you're such a wimp?' Tom snapped back.

Conversation died as the clouds began to disperse, and they walked miserably along the pathway back home. Tom shivered as his body warmed and made him more aware of his cold, wet clothing. He could see Laura doing the same, and wondered how he could have enjoyed the storm so much: it had been really uncomfortable as well as scary. His hand burned and stung and he pressed it against his sodden jeans, grateful for the cooling sensation, but reluctant to look at it in case he saw that circle again.

He was about to apologise for running off when Kelpie gave a sudden lurch and toppled over onto the wet ground, her sides heaving. Tom dropped to his knees, barely noticing the pain of scraped skin as he lifted her head and saw her large brown eyes glaze over.

'Kelpie!' Frantically he ran his thumbs over the patch between her eyes where she loved to be rubbed, trying to bring her back, but it was no use. Her brief struggle had ended, and her head, cradled in Tom's lap, took on the impossible weight of all his anguished guilt.

Chapter Four

Chicago, Illinois. 1993

Richard slammed the trunk down and slipped into the driver's seat. 'How long 'til your flight?'

Dean shrugged. 'Three hours, a little more.'

'Traffic's light, we should make O'Hare in around a half hour.'

'Okay, great.'

Richard glanced at him as he drove, reluctant to push the conversation: he knew Dean wasn't happy to be going home. During the past three years they had learned a lot about one another, and gauging one another's moods had been one of the most valuable.

One of the most surprising, however, had been the day Richard had discovered Dean wasn't American at all. The accent had fooled him for several weeks, and it was only when his new friend had fallen asleep on the couch and begun muttering that Richard had realised. He had waited a day or two, listening carefully, and spotting the occasional slip only in retrospect. The kid was good.

And the kid was British.

Holding off had been fun, but Richard's curiosity had finally won out. 'So, where'd you grow up?' he'd asked one afternoon as they left school, he on his skateboard, Dean walking alongside as usual.

'Little place, middle of nowhere. You wouldn't know it.'

'Maybe I would, you never know.'

Dean shot him an exasperated look, but there was

nothing to indicate he had anything to hide. Richard was impressed.

He jumped off the board and scooped it up. 'Come on. You know pretty much everything there is to know about me, but I don't know anything at all about you. We never go to your place, and I've never met your uncle. So - where did you live before? You just said 'the country', could be anywhere.'

'Okay! If it means that much to you, I lived in a place called Lynher Mill.'

'Liner like a ship?'

'No.' Dean spelled it out for him. 'Lynher's the river that runs through it.'

'You're right, never heard of it.'

'Toldja.'

'Yeah, but we both know *why* I never heard of it.'

Dean was indignant 'I didn't make it up, you know.'

'Nope, I guess it exists alright.'

'Sure it does.'

'In England.'

Dean looked trapped and Richard grinned, enjoying the moment. 'Don't worry, I only figured it out when you crashed out after the game and talked in your sleep.' This time the look Dean gave him was actually dismayed and Richard felt uncomfortable; the guy looked ready to run. 'Hey, it's okay, you didn't say anything embarrassing.'

He'd tried for light, but Dean clearly wasn't matching his mood. 'What *did* I say?'

'You can drop the accent now,' Richard reminded him. 'You just said something about some meeting or other, and a jar.' He couldn't remember the details: the accent had taken his attention away from the words.

When Dean spoke again it was obviously a relief to be able to use his natural tones freely at last. 'Alright, yeah.

I'm English, I was born in Cornwall. The reason I took on an American accent was because ... well, you saw the reaction when I arrived, right?'

'Yes, Ma'am!'

Dean shot him a rueful grin. 'Precisely. Can you imagine how much worse it'd have been if I'd showed up looking like a girl *and* talking like Prince Charles? I'd have been toast.'

Richard conceded this was probably true. 'So what now? You going to keep the pretence going in school?'

'Nah. Why bother? People are getting used to me. Might as well stop talking like an idiot.'

'Hey!' Richard aimed a lightning-quick blow at Dean's upper arm and apparently deadened it quite satisfyingly. 'Don't forget you're outnumbered here, Brit.'

Dean rubbed at his arm. 'Yeah, but I can move pretty fast, for a girl.' He grabbed Richard's board and slid it ahead of him before leaping on. Richard had watched him into the distance, reluctantly admitting that Dean rode the board with far more grace and ease than he ever would.

Now, driving to the airport three years later he noticed that, despite acquiring a natural American undertone, Dean always slipped more noticeably back into his English accent the closer he came to returning to his home country. He had also grown quieter and more easily rattled than usual, and Richard's curiosity was threatening to get the better of him again.

Instead of giving in to it he changed the subject. 'You want me to come in to the terminal with you this time?'

'No point. You may as well get back and get ready for the party. Amy'll be waiting.' Dean smiled, but it looked forced.

They parted company, as usual, at the entrance to

terminal five, and Richard watched Dean disappear into the crowds. Something clearly bothered him about going home, so why wouldn't he say what it was? The question continued to eat away at Richard's thoughts, distracting him as he walked back to the car. He didn't see the man leaning on the driver's door until he had almost walked into him.

'Can I help you?' he said, irritated.

The handsome, garishly dressed stranger merely stared at him, making no attempt to move aside. He seemed to be waiting for Richard to speak again but Richard waited him out. Irritation had dissolved into mild uneasiness, but he kept it hidden as he waited for the man to get out of the way.

At last the man levered himself off the car and walked around to stand behind Richard, who remained still but calmly altered his grip on the car key. He was ready to turn the moment he felt the slightest movement behind him.

The man spoke at last. 'You're pretty stupid really, aren't you?'

Whatever Richard had been expecting, it was not that, and when he turned it was in surprise rather than the defence he had been poised for. '*What* did you say?'

'Do you usually keep your back to strangers in parking lots?'

'What's it to you?'

'Like I said – stupid.'

'Not as stupid as leaning on my car, asshole,' Richard snapped, privately acknowledging it wasn't the wittiest thing to have said. Nor was it the wisest: the stranger's narrow face tightened, and he moved his face closer until Richard could smell the gum on his breath.

'I've been watching you. You've got a sloppy way of

staying alive, you know that? You need looking after.'

Richard almost laughed out loud. His unease had dissipated but fascination kept his attention on this strange guy: why did he talk like a cheap copy of The Godfather, yet look more like Willy Wonka? And who the hell was he anyway?

'I wouldn't worry yourself too much. I'm still here.' He turned dismissively back to his car and opened the door. The man's demeanour changed abruptly, and he moved to Richard's side and held out his hand.

'My name's Gary Sharpe.'

Surprised into an automatic response, Richard shook it. 'Richard Lucas. But you'd know that, right?'

'Right.'

'Okay, since you're still playing stupid games I guess I'll be heading off now.'

Richard waited for a second to see if the strange man would respond, and when he didn't he slid behind the wheel and pulled the door shut. He hesitated as he reached to switch the engine on, and instead lowered the window.

He studied Sharpe for a moment. 'You know, if you're running some kind of protection crap, you've got the wrong guy. I'm eighteen years old and I'm nobody. Look at this car. I don't have any kind of money, and I don't move in the kind of circles where people end up owing it. If you'd really been watching, you'd know that too.'

'Oh, I do know it, Richard, I do. Goodbye now.' Sharpe gave him a disarming smile and Richard's unease crept back: even for Chicago this guy was totally weirding him out. He twisted the ignition key and, without looking back he took off out of the parking lot just a little too fast for cool.

Later that night he was feeling very cool indeed. He lay stretched out on the sand beside Amy Griffin and felt just as cool as can be. Amy's hands were travelling over his body with deliciously light, feathery strokes, and her breath brushed his neck as, ignoring the hoots and yells of their friends partying just across the way, she lifted one long leg over his and lay full length on top of him. He enjoyed the softness of her sun-warmed skin on his, and wrapped his arms around her while the party went on around them, loud and lively in the summer evening.

When Amy's touch became too sweet to endure he led her away into the cover of the trees and took her there, revelling in her breathless gasps and the way she urged him on with her lithe body. Her hands moved all over him, gripping his waist, then moving across his back like tiny, soft animals with minds and libidos of their own, sliding into his hair, then back down to his hips to pull him even harder inside her.

Afterwards she lay tucked against his side, her fingers tracing small circles on his chest. 'I guess you've had a lot of girls,' she said, noticeably shy for the first time since he'd met her.

'Nope, just you and … okay, two others.'

'Really? Wow!'

Richard shrugged. Many of the guys he hung out with were happy to hit on anyone that looked at them twice, but he'd always needed some sort of connection to take it a step further. Amy had a quick and clever brain inside her admittedly gorgeous head, a fact that tended to go sadly unnoticed, and he wanted her to know he was different.

'I don't fool around, that's all.'

'No, hey, it was a good kind of wow,' Amy assured him, lifting her head to peer at him closely. 'I mean, I know what most of these guys are like, and let's face it, you're kind of a catch –'

'Get outta here!' Richard abandoned defensive, and instead felt a coil of pleased embarrassment snake through him.

'And that's why!' Amy laughed. 'You seriously have no idea, do you?'

'I know *you* like me, and since you're kind of cute yourself, I'll take that as a compliment,' Richard said, and smiled, anxious to drop the subject. 'So, why don't we head back and show everyone the 'hot couple' know how to party?'

It was past midnight when Richard saw the face that sucked all the enjoyment out of the night as easily as it sucked the air from his lungs. He had slipped off to ease the burden of too many Buds, smiling at the tipsy singing that followed him, and humming along under his breath. He found an area away from the others and, after what seemed like an age he finished and zipped his jeans. When he turned to leave, the tune froze in his throat. He stared at the man who stood, spot-lit by moonlight, on the path just fifteen feet away.

The freak from O'Hare.

Richard opened his mouth to shout but no words came out, and he felt sick and vulnerable out here alone, bare chested and shoeless. His head, previously pleasantly woozy, now sharpened with the crystal clear vision of his own body, face down in the lake.

As he struggled for breath he was startled to see Sharpe raise a hand and waggle his fingers in a greeting.

'You take care now, Richard!' The voice drifted across the short distance between them and although it was hardly more than a whisper it ripped into Richard's head like a scream.

He finally managed to speak. 'Who the hell *are* you?'

But his words hung in empty air; Sharpe had disappeared into the shadows beyond the little pool of moonlight. It would have been impossible to follow, barefoot as he was, and in any case his leg muscles felt as though they had been replaced by sponges. Making his way back to the group he tried to rationalise how it could be that he had seen the same weirdo, so many miles apart, twice in one day. A guy, moreover, who seemed to know him, and exactly where to find him. He couldn't. Coincidences happen, sure, but this? No way. No way at all.

'Hey, music man, play us a song!' Steve yelled, as he moved back into the firelight. Richard shook his head, but the guitar was already sailing towards him and he caught it purely by reflex. Hands trembling, he slipped the strap around his neck and strummed a few chords before taking it off and handing it back.

'Can't, sorry,' he mumbled.

Amy came over and slid her arms around him. She had been swimming, and her wet costume should have felt cold against him but he was numb. 'Too much to drink?'

Richard had never felt more sober. He took a deep breath, not sure whether he could say what was on his mind without sounding paranoid. In the end it was easier just to nod, and accept the good natured jeers of his friends. He was rewarded by a brilliant, if slightly lopsided smile from a tipsy Amy as she pulled him down to lie next to her by the fire.

'Play for us tomorrow, okay?' she murmured, already half asleep. 'I love it when you play.'

'Sure.' He manoeuvred his arm under her back so her

head fit in the hollow of his shoulder, her hair tumbling across his chest in a heavy, damp curtain he still couldn't feel properly. Soon the gentle sound of snoring accompanied the songs that were dying out, along with the fire, but Richard's eyes stayed wide open. He kept looking around as the darkness crept into the clearing on their little beach by the forest, and he wondered if he'd ever sleep again.

Almost a week later he had dropped Amy home after a date, and as he was walking back to his car he glanced across the road – directly into the face that had plagued his dreams and waking moments alike for the past six days. Fury washed over him and, as Sharpe stepped back into the clump of trees marking the edge of the park, Richard took off after him. He swiped at the branches that flicked into his face, bemused and frustrated by the speed with which the man had vanished.

The attack happened so quickly he barely had time to gasp. An arm fastened across his neck, dragging him backwards and cutting off his air. His hands went to his throat, and he briefly felt the frightening strength in the wiry arm that was choking him, before he was slammed back against a tree.

The arm disappeared and Richard sucked in a breath, only to hold it in his lungs as he felt a sudden, painless pressure against his chest. He looked down to see a narrow blade pressed against his leather jacket, directly over his heart, and he closed his eyes to block the sight. Then he opened them again quickly; he needed to stay alert to his attacker's intentions. The man was clearly, and puzzlingly, furious.

He leaned close, his eyes fixed on Richard's, his mouth

a thin, tight line. When he spoke it was more like a hiss. 'Oh, but this would be *so* easy!'

Richard let his breath out slowly, trying not to focus on how exactly how easy: the blade had already sliced the thin outer layer of the leather. Still, and to his relief, his uppermost emotion was anger. 'Are you going to tell me who you are and why the hell you're following me?'

The knife remained pushed against his jacket – although the inner leather was tough the blade was sharp enough to do some real damage in the right hands, and, remembering the strength of the arm that had clamped about his throat, Richard judged bleakly that these were undoubtedly the right hands.

'You have come close so many times, you stupid kid,' Sharpe breathed, and, more bewildered than ever, Richard saw there was real rage in his eyes. 'This has just been to show you *how* close, see?' the man went on. 'Don't tempt me, boy, just don't. I don't want this situation any more than you do, so … don't push it.'

Stepping back, he removed the weapon and, with a stare of such malevolence Richard felt it right down to his boots, he walked away. He must have known Richard was once again too shaken to follow him, because he didn't look back and Richard remained by the tree, replaying the incident in a bemused, angry loop. He had no idea what to do. Go to the police? With what? He whirled and slammed his fist against the tree, relishing the thin pain of scraped knuckles that overshadowed the deeper confusion and the fear he hated to acknowledge.

'Dammit!' he yelled, and hit the tree again, letting the more familiar fury take him past this moment of uncertainty and into the next step; he would have to talk to someone else. Dean was still in England and Richard felt his absence more keenly than ever, but maybe some of his other friends had seen this freakazoid around too.

The subject came up at the gym. Richard had just finished bench presses, and lay getting his breath back while Steve Shelby returned the weights to their position behind him.

Steve frowned as he looked down at him. 'What happened to your neck, man?'

Richard sat up and grabbed a towel to wipe the sweat off his face. He wasn't sure whether to say anything anymore, the urgency had faded, replaced with a sense of unreality more easily dismissed. 'It's just a bruise,' he said at last.

'Not what I asked. You get attacked or what?'

'Kind of, yeah.'

'What the hell's that mean?' Steve persisted, 'You did or you didn't. What happened?'

Richard sighed, looking for an accurate description that didn't sound too bizarre. 'This guy, I've seen him before. He threw me against a tree, told me it'd be real easy to kill me and then let me go.'

'What?' Steve stared at him, a half smile on his face. 'Don't tell me you, of all people, just stood there and took that?'

'It was pretty hard to argue, he was holding a knife on me at the time.'

The smile vanished. 'Shit, that's different. You should go to the police.'

'And tell them what?' Richard shot back. 'Some guy told me to take better care of myself? Christ, Steve, what are they going to do about something like that in this city?'

'You said you'd seen him before,' Steve prompted as he followed Richard to the showers, clearly conceding his point about the police.

'Yeah. At the beach, and once at the airport. Said the

same thing both times, but this was the first time I saw him so … angry.'

'At you?'

As closely as he could, Richard related the main points of the three incidents, and when he was done Steve reverted emphatically to his original assertion. 'You've got to tell someone. I can't believe he gave you his name, how dumb is that?'

'It's probably not his real one,' Richard pointed out, too embarrassed to admit he'd given his own in return although he sensed it had not been necessary.

'Whatever. You may not think the police'll do anything, but you should at least tell them. File a complaint, take out a restraining order. Guy had a knife, Rich, what exactly are you waiting for? If Dean was here he'd tell you the same thing, so do it. Okay?'

Richard rubbed his chest, feeling the phantom pressure of the blade, recalling how little effort it would have taken to slip that wicked-looking piece of steel through his heart. Did he really want to anger him further? He knew his own take-shit-from-no-one reputation preceded him, so maybe the guy was testing that?

But Steve wasn't finished yet, although when he spoke it was in unusually quiet, worried tones. 'Think about something else before you decide to sit on this: two out of those three times you saw this guy, Amy was just a few feet away.'

His words would reverberate in Richard's mind long past the moment he realised that nothing he did, or said, would have made a difference.

Chapter Five

Laura ran, her mind blank, all concentration focused on the slapping of her trainers on the road, and a moment after passing through her front gate she was across the road and onto the heath. Now there was just the steady, solid thump as she pumped across the dry grass, and the wordless moan that blessedly prevented coherent thought from settling in.

Finally, breathless, she reached the first of the old engine houses and collapsed at the foot of the chimney. The empty heathland stretched away ahead of her and, with nothing new or unexpected on which to focus, unwanted thoughts invaded her mind once more.

Six months ago, the love that had been unquestionably hers for sixteen years had been cruelly and abruptly ripped away, leaving her as bitterly empty as her mother's seat at the kitchen table. A misplaced footfall on the stairs, one single moment on an ordinary day, and lives were savagely torn apart, twisting the shape of a family until it could never be right again. The baby her mother had been carrying had also died.

Laura, Tom and their father had drifted around each other like ghosts, too numb to offer comfort, each fighting the shock in their own way. But little by little, pictures previously turned to the wall in stark denial had been faced into the rooms again, as anger and grief had melted into the need to see her. To speak to her, even if no answer was ever forthcoming.

Laura had drawn endless pictures, frightened she would forget her mother's face if she wasn't constantly re-creating it in her sketch books. The pictures were good, better than good really; they captured the gentleness, and faint wistfulness she'd sensed in Vivien sometimes, and although they were just line drawings with a little shading, they had life in them that even some of the photos of her could not portray. Laura couldn't make her smile though, the mouth had been lovingly and expertly drawn, but it never seemed to turn up the way it had in life.

They had gone just a week ago, their diminished family, to visit the grave with those two names carved into the grey marble:

Vivien Riley 1952-1993.

Benjamin Riley 1993 -1993.

Standing there in the incongruously bright sunshine Laura had reached out and touched her mother's name, and sobbed unashamedly. Her father had let her go until she was spent, then gathered her and Tom to him and held them close. The healing had begun.

But now this new splash of poison had hit her life.

On her way out after lunch, her thoughts had, for once, not been on her mother, but on her artwork, specifically the picture she had drawn three years ago. The day of what she had come to think of simply as "the mine thing." After she'd been sent to bed that night she had taken up her pencil with shaking hands and opened her sketch book, and moments later there he was, staring back at her once again, and the tears she'd drawn on his ugly face almost seemed to drip as she looked at them.

For the first time Laura had felt something other than pride in her talent; she hated it. She tore the sheet from the book and was about to rip it up, but something made her look more closely. She saw fear in the set of the creature's brow, fear she couldn't remember putting there, he had been angry not frightened, so why should she have drawn him that way? She stayed her hand, hating the perfection of the picture but unable to destroy it. Eventually she slid the paper into an empty folder and sat looking at it for a long time. Whatever superstitious fear was stopping her from tearing it up would fade soon enough, and in the meantime Tom must never see it.

She didn't pick up her sketch book again for three years. The pictures of Vivien had been the first ones she had drawn since that day, the little stack growing and growing until Laura began to see the futility of it, and made herself stop. It was time to move deeper into her own life, a life that had, through tragedy, put her at the heart of the family, and she owed it to her father and brother to fulfil that role as best she could. She shuffled all the pictures of her mother together and opened the box under her bed that she'd stuffed with drawings on all sizes of paper over the years, going back to her first scribbles as an infant.

There was one tiny, framed picture among the scraps, a drawing on which her mother had written "Laura," and the date: 1983. Laura had been six. She had come home from an afternoon on the moors with Vivien and Tom, and had sat down to draw as usual, half her attention on Fraggle Rock, the other half idly plucking pictures from her head and transferring them to paper. The shape that had emerged from her sweeping pencil that evening was of a woman dressed in odd clothes; a tight-fitting tunic over leggings criss-crossed to the knee as if to keep the material from flapping. She had long hair tied back, and the merest hint of very fine features, and the tilt of her head seemed to convey deep curiosity. Stunned by the detail in a drawing by such a small child, Vivien had asked who she was but Laura had shrugged. 'No-one,' she said. 'Just a lady.'

Vivien had placed the picture with pride on the mantelpiece, even though it was a torn scrap of paper and not properly finished. Her father had given Vivien the smallest frame he had in his workshop, and she had kept the picture in full view for nearly ten years. Now it lay here, in this plastic box, and it had no-one to love it anymore. Laura's eyes stung, and as she looked away her glance fell on the blue folder containing the drawing of the creature in the mine. But although her hand hovered over it she couldn't make herself open it. Instead she dropped the drawings of Vivien on top, making sure not even the tiniest bit of blue showed through, but it didn't make any difference; the picture was as vivid in her mind as if she held it in her hand. She shoved the box back under her bed, and tried very hard to lock the sadness away with it. A walk would help.

As she passed the living room on her way out she had heard a raised voice: Aunt Sylvia. Always sensitive to anything that may upset her father, Laura had stopped to listen and, if necessary, intervene. Instantly all dim and dusty thoughts of old drawings and their subjects were swept from her mind.

'… say that, Martin, but Laura is sixteen, she has a right to know. Vivien would –'

'Don't talk about her …' It came out cracked and whispery, and for a second Laura hated him for sounding so defeated.

'I'm just saying it can't upset her now,' Sylvia persisted.

'What about me? You think it won't upset me? For God's sake, I lost my wife and my baby –'

'And I lost my step-sister, don't forget that!'

Martin continued as if she hadn't spoken. 'And now you want to take Laura from me too?'

Laura's heart stuttered.

'Not take her away,' Sylvia said, 'just tell her the truth.' It sounded like something she'd said many times and was tired of repeating. 'She'll thank you for it in the long run, you know she will, and she's a level-headed girl, Martin. But she's *my* level-headed girl, not yours.'

Head spinning, Laura backed away from the living room doorway, and as she came up against the banister she heard the clarification she didn't need, and the words burned as she pulled open the front door and stepped blindly out into the chilly afternoon.

'Sylv, please! You *gave* her to us – '

She'd started to run.

Sitting hunched over on the dry, scratchy grass by the chimney she thought about how Martin had always called her 'my precious girl' when she was no such thing. Tom was his precious boy, she knew that much: she had seen photographs of her mother pregnant, and of Tom right after he had been born. There were pictures of her too, only now she realised her parents' expressions of triumph and devotion had been nothing but lies.

Laura thumped the ground beside her, desperate to give voice to the tightness and anger that wound her insides into tangled springs. She wanted to scream out loud, to smash something, to exhaust herself all over again, it was easier when she was too intent on catching her breath to think. But now the questions kept coming: if Sylvia was her mother, who was her father? Was he even alive? Why had they given her away? And did everyone know except her?

'Liars! I hate you!' she screamed, the words suddenly past her lips and out in the air like a swarm of wasps. She began ripping out handfuls of stubbly grass, but it was unsatisfyingly short and fell through her fingers before she could throw it. A second later she felt a hand touch her shoulder, and screamed again, this time in shock. She scrambled to her feet, staring wildly at the boy. Where the hell had he come from?

'Don't scream again,' he begged, a tentative smile just about warming the edges of his otherwise cool expression.

She took a deep breath, embarrassment momentarily overtaking her anger. 'I won't, ' she said. Then raised an eyebrow. 'Unless you're an axe-murderer, then I'll just do it louder.'

'Good thing I'm not then, 'cause that actually hurt!' he confessed, and inserted a finger in his ear and waggled it. She couldn't help but smile back, her sixteen year old body reacting independently of her mind to his nearness, and to the way he stared straight into her eyes.

Exotic both to listen to and to look at, he was a leftover from the New Romantic age; lean-featured, with dark eyelashes and brows at odds with long, floppy blond hair. His faint American accent lifted him further out of the mundane.

He stood like a film star, with one hand in the back pocket of his jeans, the other sweeping his hair back from light blue eyes, all catlike moves and easy charm. The leather straps on his wrists emphasized their slenderness, and his low slung belt did the same for his waist.

She realised she was staring and coughed, tossing back her own long, dark hair. 'You must be cold.' She gestured at his shirt, oversized but thin, and he shook his head.

'I live in Chicago most of the year, this is nothing.'

'Oh, right,' Laura shook off the twinge of disappointment. What had she hoped, that he'd just moved to the village to take away all the pain she had just been dealt? Actually, she acknowledged with a stab of guilt, he seemed to have done a pretty good job so far and they'd only been talking for a moment.

Something must have shown on her face, because he reached out and touched her arm. 'Sometimes it's better to talk to someone you don't know,' he ventured.

'Talking won't help,' she told him, inwardly wincing at her own sharpness of tone, but he didn't appear bothered.

'Okay, but if you change your mind the offer's still there.'

'It's just all so, so ... *deceitful*,' Laura said, realising that, helpful or not, she did want to talk after all. Had to, in fact. As they stood there face to face, she told him, first of all about the loss of her mother, her struggle to cope with it and to be a steady, calming influence on her father and brother, and finally what had had driven her out onto the heath in a fury of betrayal.

When she had finished there was a silence broken only by the summer wind, snapping at the boy's shirt and whistling as it caught the side of the abandoned engine house.

When the boy eventually spoke he sounded much older than the seventeen or so he appeared to be, and his expression was hard to read. 'Okay, just so I've got this right: this woman told you she loved you, but that was a lie, yes?'

There was edge to his words, and she lowered her gaze to the grass. 'No, I'm sure she did love me, but –'

'Still, it must make it easier to let go of her now you know she wasn't your real mother. I mean, you don't miss her anymore, right?'

'Of course I do! Who the hell do you think –'

'Laura, think about it,' the boy said, interrupting her with a grip on her hand. 'The way she was with you your whole life hasn't changed. And in the same way, your father is still your father, who else could he be?'

58

'But why didn't they tell me?' Laura began to cry again, but the anger had gone out of it. Now she felt as if a tiny piece of her soul had been removed, leaving a space she didn't know how to fill. Before she knew what had happened the boy's arms were around her and he was rubbing her back with firm, soothing strokes.

Later she remembered the deep feeling of peace that came over her, but without being able to pinpoint the moment. There were no words she could remember, just gentle murmurs and the constant, steady movement of his hands on her back.

At last she pulled away, rubbing at her eyes like a child. 'What's your name, anyway?' She remembered he'd used hers although she couldn't recall telling him what it was.

'For what it matters, I'm Dean.'

'You don't sound very American.'

'I'm not.'

She frowned. 'You said you live in Chicago.'

'I do, but I was born here. I moved out there a couple of years ago, that's all. The accent sticks pretty quickly though.'

Laura looked more closely at the boy. She had lived here all her life, surely she'd have remembered growing up close to someone so – *go on, admit it, he's gorgeous.*

He seemed to read the question in her face, and shook his head. 'I didn't go to your school, I lived nearer to Liskeard. I may have seen you around though, you've got a brother haven't you?'

'Yeah, Tom.' Her stomach twisted as bitter memory resurfaced. 'Except he's not really my brother, is he?'

'Of course he –'

'I should have realised before,' Laura said. 'Tom's tall, like them, but look at me! Little Miss Dumpy.' She sighed, hating her own shrill tone. 'I should have realised,' she repeated, more quietly.

'He's your brother,' Dean insisted. 'You've grown up together, spent your time sharing things, watching TV –'

'Fighting,' Laura supplied, a smile edging its way past the misery. 'You talk far too much sense for a teenager, d'you know that?'

Dean smiled too. 'I've been told I come off kind of preachy at times.'

'Who told you that?'

'Friend of mine back ho ... uh, back in Chicago.'

'Some friend,' Laura said archly.

'Nah, he's okay. It's thanks to him I wasn't kicked into the middle Lake Michigan when I first showed up. I don't think I made a great impression to start off with.'

'I wish I could just take off and make a fresh start somewhere,' Laura said enviously, looking out over the moor towards Plymouth.

'I'd never have left if I didn't have to,' Dean said, and Laura could sense the ache in him as he reached out to brush his fingers across the ivy-clad stone of the chimney.

'Well why don't you move back? You're old enough to make up your own mind, surely?'

'I will, but not just yet, I have stuff do first. Until then I'll have to make do with coming back whenever I can.'

'How long will that take?' Laura heard the eagerness and blushed, turning to look behind her to hide it, and letting the movement carry her away from Dean in case he thought she might leap on him at any moment.

'I don't know. How's Tom?' The sudden change in conversation made Laura blink, but she answered anyway, anything to keep him talking.

'He's fine. A typical adolescent pain in the ass, but he's okay.'

'He'll be fine, we all make it,' Dean assured her, then it

was his turn to blush. 'I'm doing it again, aren't I? Sorry.' He sat down and patted the grass beside him. 'Wanna sit for a bit?'

Laura pretended to consider, but only for a moment. 'Why not?'

They talked for a while, about Dean's move to Chicago, his life there and his best friend Richard, who sounded a bit of a handful and a decidedly dodgy influence. Before long she felt herself becoming pleasantly drowsy. She tried to keep her eyes open, and once she saw Dean turn to stare directly at her with the strangest expression on his face, but her eyelids grew heavier and heavier. It was bliss to close them just for a second, even though she was sitting upright.

She drifted.

***

Deep underground, the low hum of voices grew into a buzz as the gathering numbers swelled. There was a call for silence at the far end of the cavern, and reluctantly the moorland dwellers ceased their excited speculation.

Casta, Prince Consort, spoke again. 'Your queen,' he said, glancing at his lady. Deera stepped forward, the royal staff clasped in her left hand, the direct link to the heart. The last of the whispered conversations ceased abruptly and all eyes turned to her. Casta watched with a familiar surge of pride as Deera began to speak, holding every being before her suspended on the invisible thread of her gaze.

'The time has nearly come,' she told her people, and against the sudden shifting and muttering, she continued in a calm, even tone, telling the story they knew as legend, reinforcing it as fact. They listened, rapt, as if they were children and she were telling them a tale to send them to bed with wonderful dreams.

'At the moment of Loen's death,' she concluded, 'his brother Borsa, my ancestor, swore to help him return. Now the task falls to me, as the last remaining ruler of that royal line. You have made a life's work, all of you, of protecting Loen's spirit, contained within the dust of such of his body as Borsa saved. But now he is almost ready to take his rightful place as your king, and as *your* protector in return.'

As Deera waited for the cheers to taper off, Casta, in turn, waited for the gathering to realise what they had been celebrating; some of those with quicker thought processes grasped that this would mean the end of Deera's reign, and gave embarrassed coughs, looking down at the ground. Deera glanced back at Casta and he was amused to see a smile fighting her stern expression and only just being bested. He called for silence again, and when they had it Deera spoke.

'The jar was broken three cycles ago, as you know ...' more mutterings, and a plaintive voice denied culpability, but in tired tones, as if the owner had repeated his plea so many times he no longer fully believed it himself.

'Jacky Greencoat is not to blame!' Casta bellowed, making Deera flinch. He touched her shoulder. 'Sorry.'

Deera nodded. 'No, he is not to blame,' she agreed as the noise subsided again. 'Greencoat was performing his duty, as have his predecessors every day since the king's death. The child who broke the jar is now acknowledged to be the last descendant of Chief Ulfed, so how can Greencoat be blamed for destiny finding a way to fulfil itself?' She paused to allow her words to sink in, and Casta saw passionate relief on the face of the little spriggan at the back of the room.

'A curious boy,' Deera continued, 'nothing more, yet that mortal child now holds our future within him. He breathed the king's dust, enough to capture the treasured and lost spirit, and now Loen works within him to become stronger every day, strong enough to rise again and return to us.'

More cheers, and Casta and Deera let them run their course before Deera spoke again. 'There is something else.' It was time to unveil the next part of the story; the secret, protected for thousands of years, now to be brought out and given like a gift. The faces of their people held many forms of curiosity; some were simply and openly fascinated, some tempered with wariness, some downright suspicious. Casta understood: secrets were not tolerated easily, unless they were secrets shared by all against their common enemies.

Deera continued, 'Many of you have been asking us where Prince Maer has been travelling, and what he has discovered.' Nods and murmurs. 'Now we can tell you: shortly after the jar was broken we learned of another boy, whose body will be far more fitting for King Loen than the pitiful human he now inhabits. Maer has been this boy's companion these few cycles, and his guardian, and will bring him to us. Very soon now.' Excited murmurings swelled the cavern as Maer himself entered, and Casta raised a hand in greeting. But Deera was queen now, and not mother; she ignored him and went on, 'A protective watch will also be kept upon the mortal boy Riley during the time it takes him to become fully grown. Every effort must be made to preserve Riley's health while he nurtures your king. He must remain on the moor, under no circumstances can he be permitted to move away lest the king's power diminish. Loen will soon have his time, the time denied him when his child and rightful heir was offered in sacrifice to their goddess. Now go. Be vigilant. The boy Riley and his kin are under our protection from this day until Loen decrees otherwise.

***

The wind blew hard against Laura's back and she drew her knees up tight against her chest. Something scratched at her cheek and she twitched, feeling roughness on her skin as it pressed against the ground …

The ground?

She sat upright, her skin stinging as her cheek peeled away from the dry grass. Surely she hadn't been sleeping out here? She hadn't done that since she was a little girl, exhausted from playing chase with Vivien and Tom.

The memory tested her feelings, and she found some of the sense of betrayal had eased. An image flashed into her head: the mysterious boy, called … something short. He had held her, soothed her, told her … told her what? He hadn't seemed the type to leave her alone out here on the heath, yet if she couldn't even remember his name how could he have been real?

The moor was as deserted as it had been when she had run, shocked, from her home. No more sign of anyone now, than there had been when she arrived at the mine. The more Laura thought about it, the more it made sense that the encounter had happened in her mind: how likely was it there would have been a boy like that living here all this time and she hadn't seen him, or even known of him? This wasn't a city, it was a tiny village, barely more than a dozen houses and not even a village hall of its own.

'Jane bloody Farmer would have known all about him,' she muttered; her friend had a way of attaching herself to any good looking boy who came within snaring distance, look how she had moved in on Michael Hart. No way someone like that would escape those predatory clutches. No, he had been beautiful, and she wouldn't mind dreaming about him again sometime, but a dream was all he was.

Even those dreams that impact hugely on waking soon fade as reality takes over, and after a few more minutes spent wondering about the boy, Laura put him out of her mind and turned in the direction of her home and her family. Today it would be enough just to accept the love they offered, to blot out the questions, and to know that someday those questions would be asked, and answered. But not today.

Chapter Six

The crowd was bigger than expected for a first gig. Richard picked up his guitar and glanced at Steve, his eyebrow raised and a weird mixture of satisfaction and nervousness battling it out in his stomach. Steve gave him a thumbs up. 'We have an awesome sound, plus we're hot as hell. What's not to love?'

Richard lifted the strap over his head and let the guitar settle at his hip, the familiar weight relaxing him. 'Yeah, you're right. We'll blow 'em away.'

'Bummer Dean couldn't be here for this,' Steve said, picking up his sticks and sliding onto his seat behind the drum kit. 'When's he due back?'

'Couple days yet, I pick him up Tuesday.'

'And Amy? Rather go to a swim party than support her guy's big break? Or did she just want to party alone? Can't say I blame her, you'd just cramp her style.'

Richard smiled and flipped him the finger before plugging in his amp. 'It's not just a swim party, Linda's her best friend, she's gonna miss her. She'll get to see the next show. *If* she wants. It's not even her kind of music.'

'Crap. It's everyone's kind. She'll love it, and she'll be totally impressed and showing off how she knows us.'

'Well she likes vocals and guitar, says it takes talent. But drums? Everyone knows how easy it is to just hit stuff with sticks.'

Steve returned his one-fingered gesture, and Richard grinned and began tuning his guitar.

***

Twelve miles up the lake, Amy changed into her swimsuit, listened to her friends talking and laughing and, all the while she was telling herself how lucky she was to be right here, right now, she was wishing she was back in Highland Park. She'd miss Linda soon enough, but right now all she wanted to do was hide in a dark corner of the club and lose herself in Richard and his music. After almost a year together she still shivered whenever she heard him sing – his voice was raw, strong and pitch perfect. Unique. And he had been one of the few people, male or female, who didn't let her bouncy blonde hair and infectious giggle blind them to the rest of her. But then Richard was different in a lot of ways.

She remembered the day they'd met, just after Linda had started seeing his friend Dean, his clear green eyes had fixed on hers and he'd seemed to see right into her. It had been disconcerting at first, then his mouth had lifted in that unexpectedly sweet, shy smile and she'd felt her insides twist with the need to make him do it again. Linda and Dean had barely lasted a week but she and Richard were stronger than ever, and just the thought of his low, soft voice in her ear, and those strong hands exploring her body was enough to …

'Hey, Amy! You ready?' Linda's impatience cut through her thoughts and Amy guiltily shook off a wave of irritation; when Linda was gone Canada would seem like a world away. This was her night.

She fastened her bikini top and kicked her clothes into a pile. 'I'm ready.'

'Dreaming of Mr. Lucas?' Linda said with a wink.

Amy laughed. 'Wouldn't you be?'

'Hell yeah!'

'Well he's all mine!' Amy poked out her tongue, then

turned to beat them down to the lake.

As soon as her feet touched the water she stopped, hardly noticing her friends splashing past her. She looked out over the calm, sparkling water at the yachts heading for Winthrop Harbor further along the lake, and a chill washed through her. She felt a prickling sensation in the small of her back, and turned to stare back up the beach, empty but for a family packing the last of their belongings away.

There was no-one else there, but the feeling remained, and she suddenly found herself remembering the strange guy Richard had told her about. He had finally gone to the police to make his report but Sharpe hadn't been found. Yet.

'Hey, *Amy*! If you're gonna daydream all night, we'll just have to duck you under to wake you up!' Linda laughed, splashing back to her. Then she frowned. 'Hey, you okay? You know I'm just kidding, right?'

Amy relaxed as the prickling vanished: talk about paranoid. 'Sure, of course. Just felt a little weird for a second, I'm okay now. Race you to the raft?'

She plunged into the water, the chill blasting away the uncertainties of a moment ago, and set her mind towards making the most of her last evening with her best friend.

***

The show was going better than Richard had dared hope for. The mix of music was hitting the right spot, it seemed: a hybrid sound born of his first love, rock, blended with traditional blues. He and Steve had worked hard on the set list and it showed in the constant flow of new faces, both male and female, coming to the front of the room to get a better look. His voice was definitely rougher now than when he had first started out, but it seemed to work. He thought of Amy out by the lake with her friends – with some of these looks stripping the clothes off him he felt even more naked than she would be by now.

He wondered if she had spared him a thought all evening, and then remembered the look she had given him just before she'd left. Her small hand on his chest, wide eyes raised to stare into his, the mischievous tilt to her luscious mouth.

His sudden grin as he launched into the next song brought a wave of cheers from the floor.

***

Amy fished in her pocket and sighed. Damn. 'Linny, I left my keys,' she called out.' They must have fallen out of my pocket.'

Linda looked back down the beach. 'Want me to come back with you?'

'No, you can wait here, I'll just be a minute.'

'Actually I think I'm going back with Jenny and Kate,' Linda said, 'save you driving out around my place again.' She came over and hugged Amy. 'So cool of you to come, I know you're missing Richard's big show.'

'Hey, he'll do more shows, but you only have one leaving party.'

'Well thanks anyway. I'll see you Monday, okay? Call me when you get home so I know you didn't break down or anything.'

'Okay, see you later.' Still with her swim bag slung over her shoulder, Amy waved and ran back down the small path to the top of the beach.

The last car drove away. She listened to the engine and the stereo fading together and, as silence fell, she felt suddenly small and alone. It wasn't dark yet, but the edge of the sky was blurring into the lake and the half-moon cast a pale glow over everything. She looked around nervously as the shadows swayed with the gently lifting water, but couldn't see her keys anywhere. Double damn! She was about to head up the path again when she saw a movement out on the water.

Squinting, she focused on the raft, on the lean, square-shouldered figure outlined in faint moonlight, Richard! He must have finished the set early. She waved, and something in his hand glinted as he waved back. Amy laughed out loud as she realised he must be holding her keys. Sneaky sonofabitch, how the hell had he managed that?

She dropped her swim bag and pulled out her wet swimsuit, for once not minding the cold, clammy feel of the wet scraps on dry skin. Her eyes remained fixed on the raft as, smiling with anticipation, she ran into the water and began to swim.

***

The club was emptying fast, the band had finished to gratifying applause and two encores, and Richard was still on a high as he packed away the equipment.

'Told you they'd love us!' Steve twirled his sticks above his head and played a brief tattoo on Richard's back when he leaned over to unplug the amp. 'We going back to your place for a drink?'

Richard wrapped a coil of wire around his fist and tucked it away. 'Yeah, Amy should be headed back anytime now. She's driving Linda home first though. Let's finish up here and go celebrate.'

The guys were still congratulating themselves and each other when, a little past midnight, the door to Richard's cabin burst open. Linda stumbled in, took one look at Richard and opened her mouth to speak, but burst into tears instead.

He scrambled to his feet, ice cold from head to toe, his heart slamming against his rib cage hard enough to hurt. Somehow he managed to take hold of her, but she was shaking so violently he could hardly understand her.

'She, she went back … she, oh god she forgot something, her … her keys or something. We left her. Christ, Richard, we *left* her!' Linda's eyes were wild, looking anywhere but at him. 'I went with Jenny, I thought Heather was still there, but I swear, soon as we realised she was alone, we turned right around –'

'What happened?' he demanded. When she didn't answer he gave in to the heat of fury, and shook her until her teeth snapped shut and blood began to flow over her lip. 'Linda, *what happened?*'

She raised her face to him, her eyes blank now, her voice flat. 'Amy's dead.'

Chapter Seven.

Cornwall, 1999

L aura looked around at the cottage she and Michael
Hart had shared for three years. Although it looked
no different, and was still chock full of her stuff, it
felt oddly empty now he'd gone. She wondered how long
it would be before it began to feel unreal that he'd ever
lived there at all. Certainly she'd never imagined it could
happen; she'd been convinced her hopes for him would
come to nothing once he'd clapped eyes on Jane Farmer,
particularly after that awful school Christmas disco when
they'd got together. She'd been utterly heart-broken,
forced to smile, congratulate them and then watch them
go through the rest of the school year glued to one
another's side. The life and soul of their year group.

But Jane had, predictably enough, been unable to hold
onto Michael. Long before she had left Cornwall he had
realised her party-loving persona was nothing more than a
brittle shell, hiding an insecurity that manifested itself as
bitchy humour. She had a knack for prompting guilty
laughter, but seldom joined in herself. Laura still felt the
undercurrent of their shared younger childhood as a sweet
remembrance, and was sure it must have remained deep
down in Jane's heart, but it had been getting harder and
harder to bring back to the surface.

When Michael had first asked her on a date after he
and Jane had broken up she had, to her immediate regret,
said no, and then waited with bated breath to see if he
would repeat his request; loyalty could only stretch so far,
and, after all Jane had shown none to her. He had asked

her again only a day later and this time she had almost snatched his hand off. They had been happy together for a long time, his urge to explore was something she had always understood and admired, and she told him she would go anywhere with him. She'd meant it, too, and they had begun their life as a couple with every intention of remaining one. Until now.

He hadn't been the cause of their break up, it was all down to her. All her childhood fantasies of travelling had remained just that; leaving Lynher Mill just wasn't an option. At least for Laura it wasn't physical, but Tom couldn't leave the moor, it was that simple. Any time he was away for more than a few hours at a time he would get panicky and short of breath, and a prolonged trip further than ten miles from his home made him physically ill.

Every now and again Laura would catch him looking at her with a raw, scared expression but he never spoke of it aloud, and a few years ago Laura had tentatively broached the subject of hypnosis.

The strength of his reaction had startled her. 'No!' Then he'd sighed. 'I don't want to know, Lau. Right now it was just a dream, see? I can tell myself that and get to sleep at night. Someone tells me I truly believe, deep down, that I saw some fucked up little pixie, and where's the dream theory then? They'll throw away the key.'

Her mind flew to the picture in her drawing box, relieved she had not shown it to him, as she'd often wanted to if only to confirm she had it right. 'Well what about me? I was there too, so how come I'm not scared to leave this place?'

'You are.'

'No, I'm not. What scares me is leaving you and Dad. If I could make you come with me I'd move, even if it was just to Plymouth.'

'Well maybe you're just tougher than me. Look, I can't help it if I can't get my head round it yet. It'll get better.'

But it hadn't, if anything it had got worse.

So here she was. Still. Michael had gone, with a single, huge backpack, his passport, and an expression freer and happier than she had seen him in far too long. For a moment she found herself wishing she could have been the one to make him smile like that, but the man she was already missing was the man who would always be a companion, a warm friend, an enthusiastic lover – but no soul mate. There had been regret on his face as he left, but the sudden uncertainty on his face had melted into relief as, somehow, she'd found a smile of her own to send him away with.

So that was that. And this was a turning point in a life in which turning points had been few and far between. A chance to take stock, re-evaluate everything and maybe take some of Michael's wanderlust and … just borrow it for a while, see how it fit?

Her heart beat a tiny bit faster, and it made her aware of her breathing, and the lightest sensation of her own touch on the back of the armchair as she brushed by it; she was alive, and letting that life pass her by. But she *could* do it, couldn't she? Not like Michael, and not so far away as to be out of reach should Tom or her father need her, but teaching in Plymouth couldn't be that different from teaching in the village. She'd managed teacher training every day at college, and they'd been fine without her then. If nothing came of it, fine – at least she'd have tried. It was mad: the mere thought of moving thirty miles and suddenly the possibilities seemed infinite.

Laura smiled at the notion. She stood still, her eyes fixed on the piles of books and CDs Michael had been sorting through, but instead saw a bright classroom with chattering children, and beyond the window, more buildings; cars; people; noise. Life.

'Hello, the house!' she called ten minutes later, pushing open the front door. She went down the hall, brushing the walls with her fingertips as she went, a throwback to childhood she had never quite shaken off, just as their family greeting remained built into their lives, even now.

'Enter and declare yourself!'

Taking over their father's business had done Tom good, given him a valid and palatable reason to stay here in Lynher Mill, and he'd been like a new person since he'd taken on the lion's share of the work. He sounded pleased to hear her call, and Laura smiled as she went into the kitchen. 'How's business?'

'Not too bad. People buy vile prints on their holidays 'cos they're cheap as chips, then want 'em framed so they look like the real thing to take home. Mad bastards.'

'That's emmits for you. Where's Dad?'

'Mercy mission, we ran out of coffee. So you'll have to wait 'til he gets back, unless you want something a bit stronger? Sun's over the yardarm and all that.'

'What does that actually mean, anyway?'

'Means you're allowed to get pissed without the neighbours gassing about you.'

'Oh, let them.' Laura took a can of cider from the fridge. 'Here's to suns. And yardarms, whatever they are.'

Tom grinned. 'And here's you living in a seafaring county. The yardarm's what a square sail hangs from. Sun

75

rises over it around noon in the North Atlantic, therefore,' he checked his watch, 'go for it.'

She pulled the ring back and took a long swallow, then let out a small, polite belch. 'Pardon me. God, I needed that.'

'So he's gone then?' Tom said, his tone cautious now.

'Yep, he's gone. Chasing ... I dunno, rainbows? Dreams? Whatever people chase when they go away.'

'Well I wouldn't know that, would I?' Tom turned the conversation back onto Michael before she could work out if there was any bitterness in the retort. 'You okay about it?'

Laura shrugged. 'I think so. Feels so empty there though, I just needed to get out for a bit. Even you're better company than the pile of ironing I've got at home.'

Tom grinned. 'We can go down the Miller's Arms later, you might find some local talent to take your mind off Mike.'

'He *is* the local talent, you berk. I'll probably see his mum and dad in the pub, toasting their boy's success in getting away from me!'

'Now you're being a berk,' Tom said. 'He was mad to let you go.'

'We let each other go.' Her throat clenched suddenly, and she swallowed hard. 'Let's not talk about it anymore, okay? How's Dad doing?'

'Not too bad, he's ... ah, you can ask him yourself.'

'Hello, the house!' Martin called out. 'Get the kettle on, the cavalry's arrived!' He came in, limping slightly from the rheumatoid arthritis that had persuaded him into partial retirement, and stopped when he saw Laura. He peered closely at her, eyes narrowed, and then put down his carrier bag and walked straight towards her with his arms open.

Laura hugged him close, breathing in the familiar woody scent of his work jacket, and the tears came from nowhere. She held on to him, vaguely aware of Tom quietly leaving the room, feeling her father's arms around her, his large hand patting her back as he murmured soothing nonsense. For the first time since she'd been sixteen she truly understood how it felt for Tom to know this was his home.

***

Chicago. 1999.

'You lot surplus to requirements tonight then?' Dean gestured to the raised platform where Richard was settling himself on a stool with his guitar. There was no band behind him, and he caught Dean's eye and pulled a face, implying nerves. Dean snorted. *As if.*

'They just wanted acoustic background music,' Steve said. 'Apparently the full band's too noisy for a book launch party, so we get to drink ourselves stupid for once, like you.'

'Lucky break,' Dean said, and lifted his own beer, making sure Richard could see it quite clearly. He was rewarded with a grimace that made him smile into his glass: the only thing Richard really disliked about performing was knowing everyone else could relax with a drink, while the one person who needed it most had to stay clear-headed.

As the evening progressed it was clear Steve was taking advantage of the situation, flirting with every girl in the place, including the author of the book the party was celebrating. He was also becoming amusingly maudlin as he came over to stand by Dean just before the end of the first set.

'He's totally got it,' he said, waving his bottle at the stage. Dean nodded. 'I mean, he's got it all. Which should be seriously fucking annoying,' Steve went on, 'but it's okay, you know, because he like … doesn't realise it.'

'Right.'

'I mean it. The guy can't even figure out why girls like him. I mean *genuinely* can't figure it out.'

'He knows they do.'

'Yeah, he *knows*, but he doesn't *understand*. Thass what I'm sayin', you know?'

'Yeah, I know,' Dean assured him, trying not to laugh. 'But it's okay, right? Got it.'

'It's more than okay, it's … it's right. *He's* right. I ever tell you what he did for me back when we were kids?'

'Once or twice. Besides, I was there, remember?'

'He took on the biggest motherfucker in Highland Park for me –'

'I know! Stop leaning on me, ya pisshead!'

'I love him, man,' Steve said, and grinned lopsidedly. 'I'm not, y'know, queer or anything, but I fuckin' love him, that's all. If that asshole had done anything to him –'

'What? What asshole?'

'Weird guy with the knife. Bad dresser. He didn't tell you, huh? Figures. I need to pee.'

A *knife?* 'Wait! Steve!'

But Steve had wobbled off to find the rest room, leaving Dean staring after him, a dark suspicion forming; "weird," and a "bad dresser"? who else could it be? Gilan's methods and his own were poles apart, but the thought of his uncle threatening Richard just to prove a point … He shook the image off, swallowed the surge of helpless anger, and took refuge at the buffet table behind which a flustered-looking girl was creating artistic open sandwiches. She was by no means the prettiest girl in the room but her happiness seemed to draw people to her, and her sweet nature kept them there.

It was hard to get close, but Dean squeezed in behind the table, returning her smile. 'He's sounding good.'

She looked up at the stage. 'Doesn't he always?'

'Blimey what's this tonight, the Lucas love-in?'

The girl laughed and popped a piece of cheese into his mouth. 'I'm allowed, Dean.'

The room swelled with applause as the set ended, and after a few minutes Richard joined them. 'Thank God, I'm starved,' he said, grabbing one of the girl's beautifully crafted and garnished sandwiches, and ripping into it.

'Dammit, Richard!' She shoved a plate at him.

'Sorry, babe. These are awesome.'

'I'm surprised you had time to taste it, the way you scarfed it down.' She reached out and brushed a crumb off the front of his shirt, and he placed his own hand over hers, imprisoning it against his chest. Dean watched the look that passed between them and wondered if he should walk away. They'd been seeing each other for well over a year now and he knew Richard was absolutely gone – in fact he'd seen the ring box go into Richard's jeans pocket just a couple of hours ago.

Caitlin Warner was one of those girls that just creeps quietly into your life and sits waiting to see if she's noticed, not minding too much if she isn't. But Richard had noticed. They'd been at a party down in Winnetka where she was catering, and Richard had spoken to her out of politeness and admiration for the food, and because he hadn't been able to resist making the obvious joke about her name and her chosen profession. If anyone else had said it, Dean was pretty sure Cait would have shoved a whole cheesecake in their face.

An hour later Richard had pulled Dean aside. 'Dean,

she's amazing. Can you get a lift back with Steve? We're going out by the lake.'

And that had been it. Dean had watched as the pain of losing Amy gradually faded, and love filled the place where it had been. Tonight, Richard was going to ask Cait to marry him and it didn't take a genius to work out what her answer would be; she kept sneaking sidelong glances at him and her eyes were so filled with pride and affection it was hard not to smile.

He shouldn't have allowed this: Richard should have had nothing to tie him to this land. But his happiness was infectious, and he was so alive with it Dean couldn't bring himself to deny him. If it came right down to it then Cait would have to come back to England too, and if Loen saw them together maybe he would show some of the mercy he'd once been famous for – maybe he'd allow Richard to live.

'Okay, I'd better get back,' Richard said, breaking into Dean's thoughts. He leaned in to kiss Cait, before making her growl by sneaking a bread roll from the pile. 'Can we find someplace quiet later?' he added, looking genuinely nervous now.

She nodded. 'Sure, what's wrong?'

'Nothing's wrong, just need to talk okay?'

'Okay.' But as he walked away Dean saw her expression turn troubled. He knew exactly what she was thinking as she cast suddenly miserable eyes around the room. It was filled with beautiful, impeccably made up girls wearing necklines that plunged front and back, with jewels glistening at slender, tanned necks and wrists. And as Richard took the stage again these beauties surged forward, eager to get themselves noticed.

Cait had never understood how he could remain unmoved in the face of such temptation, but Dean had told her so many times not to worry. He wanted to tell her again now, that Richard wasn't going to throw her over, but in the end it was unnecessary: throughout the set Richard kept his eyes on her, and Dean saw a gradual lightening of her expression and felt her relief.

He jumped as a hand landed on his shoulder and he was pulled into a bear hug.

'Deano! My man! Stop eating all this amazing food, leave some for us.'

'Wow, Steve, you're still standing?'

'Just barely, my friend, just barely. Hey, Cait, how's it going?'

'Okay, I think,' she said, her knife a blur as she cut thin slices of cucumber to twist and garnish the last few sandwiches. She cocked an eyebrow ironically. 'You drunk yet?'

'Working on it, honey.' He grinned at her and crossed his eyes, and she laughed.

'Doing a good job on it by the looks of things.'

'May I say you're looking gorgeous tonight?' Steve said, dropping a kiss on her forehead.

She pushed him away, still laughing. 'You may, but then I'd say you were *definitely* drunk!'

'Aw come on, I know you only have eyes for the guy with the voice, but I thought all the chicks loved the drummer?'

'Oh, I do love you, Steve. How could I not?' Cait said, and looked up at him through her lashes and affected a tragic voice. 'But Richard is a cruel master, and if he finds out I have a shrine to you hidden behind my shoe cupboard he'll beat me black and blue, and lock me in the basement. Again.'

'Yeah, he's a real sonofabitch,' Steve agreed ruefully. 'Well, when you manage to escape his evil clutches, you come to me, okay?'

'Okay. Now move out of the way will you? People want to eat.'

Steve threw his arm around Dean's shoulders. 'Come and have another drink with me, we never talk anymore.'

'You're not talking now, you're slurring,' Dean pointed out, and waved to Cait as he helped Steve out to the bar. Better not to bring up the "weird guy with the knife" again now, but he'd keep a closer eye on things, for sure.

Later he saw Richard take Cait's hand and lead her out through the double doors to the garden beyond, and when they eventually returned, arms linked around each other's waists and both smiling, their closeness pulled a powerful image into Dean's mind; a lovely but troubled teenage girl, running from a terrible truth into the arms of stranger on the moors, and into his heart for good.

He looked at Cait, her left hand proudly displaying its new, tiny solitaire diamond, and he noted the way she leaned into her new fiancé as if she couldn't bear not to be touching him. His gaze went to Richard, alight with pride, and, even as he took pleasure in their evident happiness, he ached with a fresh envy, born of the knowledge that he would never know that joy for himself.

Chapter Eight

D eera viewed the man before her with thinly veiled mistrust. His departure meant her beloved Maer would soon return, two reasons to be content, but still her misgivings persisted; quite aside from Gilan's shadowy dealings with the coastal elementals – of which he believed she knew nothing – he was unpredictable, and he carried with him a deep-seated anger he sometimes had trouble controlling. And he was her brother, which made it hard to distance herself, no matter how she felt about him and how much the other Moorlanders reinforced those feelings.

Deera sighed. Sometimes she wondered if she had chosen the right path after all, acting on Greencoat's story, until she remembered the danger her son was in. Such a mixed blessing to be young and strong, with a physical beauty that would appeal to a vain being who had been much lusted after himself. Indeed, she acknowledged wryly, if he hadn't been, none of this would have happened.

She heard Casta clearing his throat behind her, and it brought her thoughts back to the matter in hand. 'You know the descendant is now married,' she told Gilan. 'He travels home today with his new bride.'

'Maer has been foolish to allow such a chain to bind Lucas to his homeland. Still, he is lucky to have found a wife, some of us are destined to be alone.'

Deera ignored his sulky expression and persisted. 'So you are ready to leave?'

'Yes, exalted Highness.'

'You know you don't have to call me that.' Deera was conscious of the staff she held, but uncomfortable at the tone with which Gilan had addressed her. Respectful enough words, but delivered with the bitterness he had never bothered to conceal. Of course, had he been born first he would be ruler now, and unlikely to be searching for any means to relinquish the title. But then he would also be most unlikely to have a son to protect in the first place.

She realised her thoughts were wandering once again, while Gilan was staring at her with chilly impatience. 'Very well, I wish you speed and good fortune,' she said, but with no feeling behind the formal blessing. There was no need: the boy – no, he was man now – would remain protected, without need of niceties.

Deera laid down her staff and moved into her husband's comforting embrace, remembering how excited Maer had been to discover, not only that something could be done to save his life, but that it would involve such adventure on his part. He returned regularly, each time bringing news of the one who would unwittingly save them. Now grown into manhood, a musician and an educator, Richard Lucas was apparently already showing signs of a strength and authority Loen would use well when he took that body, and the spirit of the man, for himself. Her mind welcomed the knowledge Maer brought, but Deera was uneasy in her heart, particularly when her son took up his uncle's duties with Riley.

'I do long to see him again, Casta,' she said, 'but what if Loen should sense his presence and try to take over?'

'He knows to keep his distance,' Casta said. Sometimes his absolute faith in his son was exasperating, did he never worry about him at all? 'Would you rather he stayed with

Lucas?'

'Of course not, but passing through the Doorway is so harrowing for him,' Deera fretted.

'And staying there would age him too quickly and he would become ill. Who could cure him in the human world?'

'I know you're right, but still I –'

The air grew abruptly heavy, and the light created by Casta's and Deera's combined energies dimmed. They stood still, holding on to one another's forearms and breathing slowly and steadily. The pressure built and tightened around them, and just when Deera felt she might collapse, order gradually began to restore itself. The Doorway was closed again. For the moment.

'So, Gilan is gone,' Deera said. 'I would be so much more content if only someone other than Maer could be trusted to watch over Riley.'

Casta squeezed her hand. 'Try not to worry. Enjoy him. I must go: the Foresters are holding their meeting early for my convenience, I shouldn't keep them waiting.' He draped his cloak about his shoulders, the lightning and blade symbol falling neatly over his heart, then frowned. 'There was something else, wasn't there? It slips my mind for the moment, the opening of the Doorway has addled my brain.'

Not so Deera's; matters concerning her subjects were always easily to hand. 'You agreed to speak to Gerai, if you can find him.'

'Ah, yes, of course. The man must stop vanishing when there's work to be done, it's becoming difficult.'

'Do not go easy on him, Casta.'

'I will speak to him on my return from the forest.' He promised, and bent to kiss her. 'Be at ease, my love, Maer will soon be here.' She watched him leave, knowing that, no matter how reassuring his words, he would never understand how terrified she was. The next time the air thickened and her breath grew short, she welcomed the sensation: Maer was home.

Upon her son's arrival a short while later, she drew him to her and held him tightly. He looked tired and a little ill, but hugged her back warmly, then outlined what she already knew; Lucas had married a girl named Caitlin, and was even now driving back across the country towards their home and their new life together.

'She's really good for him,' he finished, the remnants of human speech patterns still colouring his words.

But Deera was less impressed. 'Remember why you are there,' she reminded him. 'I do not know why you have allowed yourself to become so close to this man, Gilan has always watched quite effectively from a distance.'

Maer's eyes narrowed, but he did not question her pronouncement. 'It was different for me, I was just a child,' he said instead. 'I had no-one else, and besides it was the best way to remain at his side. But we've grown up together and to be truthful I know him better than I know ...' He broke off, blushing, and Deera could guess what he had been going to say: *than I know you.*

She brushed away the apology that hung in the air between them. 'You will betray this man, and bring him here to his death,' she said softly. 'Is this the basis of your friendship?'

Maer looked stricken at her words. 'Maybe Loen will realise he doesn't need to kill anyone,' he said. 'What if he isn't the beast you make him out to be? He was a well-loved king once, there must be something of that left. He might yet spare Richard –'

'There is something I haven't told you,' Deera interrupted in growing desperation. Maer's gaze remained questioning but silent, and she took a deep breath. 'You have heard of Loen's intended revenge upon the descendants of the Chief Ulfed, who destroyed the babe?'

'That he will wipe them out by his own hand? Of course, everyone knows –'

'There is more. This part no-one else knows, not even your father. No-one except Borsa's bloodline, which is now only Gilan and myself, and you of course. Loen swore that if he fails to be restored and carry out his revenge, there will come chaos and terrible storms, and a darkness which will destroy our race forever.'

She saw a flicker of real fear at last, but the light of hope still dominated his expression, and her lips tightened. 'This is our last chance for survival, Maer. Borsa made a vow to his king even as he became king himself. We owe Loen a body, but that body is not yours, it is this man's. Do not fail me, and do not fail your people.'

Deera's tone had turned cold and, seeing her son pale at the sound of it she pressed her advantage, taking up her staff and planting it firmly upon the stone floor between them.

'Do not confuse your loyalties, *Prince* Maer,' she said. 'You will bring this man back as soon as you are ordered to do so. From the moment Loen takes him you will obey every word that comes from his mouth, because that mouth belongs to your king, not to your friend. Do you understand?'

'Yes, Highness.' He did not shrink back, and his tone was even, but she saw his heart was closed to her as he turned and left the chamber.

***

'Are you coming in?' Caitlin Lucas looked across at her new husband as she unlocked her safety belt.

He gave a jaw-cracking yawn and shook his head. 'Huh uh. I trust you, you know what I like. I'm gonna grab a few more Zs before it's my turn to drive.'

'Okay.' She leaned over and brushed her lips across his temple, and although his eyes remained closed she saw the smile touch his lips. She topped up the fuel and stepped into the small shop, trying not to think about how fast the time was passing – the honeymoon was almost over, but Chicago was another day away, which meant another stop somewhere down the road, another chance to pretend they were the only two people in the world until real life got hold of them again.

She was picking out some of Richard's favourite savoury snacks when she noticed a man standing very still, neither buying nor browsing. Her curiosity was caught by his clothes, which bordered on flamboyant, but as he looked around and caught her eye she was struck by a disquieting sense of … *wrong*. Something about his expression was at odds with the way he was dressed: the closed, tight expression on his narrow face belied the gaudiness of his shirt and pants, and gave him the faintly sinister look of a bitter-hearted clown. She finished her shopping in a hurry, and crossed to the cash desk.

Afterwards, everything rushed together into one brief, terrifying moment. She saw Richard getting out of the car, his face barely visible through the flyer-pasted window but his movements urgent; the door banged open, the bell jangling, and the two men who appeared in their midst covered the six people in the shop, all too effectively, with small handguns. They appeared to be looking for someone specific, but that couldn't be right, because they were turning towards her.

Richard, running. One gun was coming around to bear on her, the other trained on the horrified cashier; the door crashed open again; a blur of movement; two guns spitting. Such a surprisingly sharp, light sound.

Cait stared, bemused, as the basket of shopping dropped from her hand. Someone had shoved her in the chest, but there was no-one near her: she had stood alone from the moment the gun had swung in her direction. Richard had burst through the doorway and now stumbled backwards, his dark t- shirt suddenly glistening. Cait saw his body hit the door jamb and then he fell, half in and half out of the shop.

She felt light-headed, weak, and there was a dull pain starting somewhere behind her breastbone, warmth coursing down her ribs, but all she could see was Richard, so still … she had to get to him. She tried to take a step forward, his name on her lips, but no sound came beyond a high, thin whistling.

Then blackness rushed in and she could no longer stand against its insistent beckoning. The last thing she saw was the man in the bright clothes leaning over her husband's still body, hands outstretched, and she wanted to scream a warning but it was too late …

Chapter Nine

Cornwall, July 1999

Maer stood by the edge of the village green, leaning on the garden wall that ran the length of Martin Riley's house. Laura had gone in ten minutes ago, he had looked on with a sad hunger, and a strange kind of pride; she was still recognisable as the teenager he had met six years ago, her anger had been dark then but it had not eclipsed the freshness of her face, and the shifting colours in her silver-grey eyes. Every time he had returned he had sought her out, feeling a new kind of pain as he watched her start her life with her childhood friend Michael, but taking some pleasure, at least, in her contentment.

And she was drawing again. He saw her often, out with her paper and pencils, and whenever he could he had sat behind her unheeded, surprised to see, not the landscape in which she sat reflected on the page, but bustling, busy streets; people; traffic; markets bursting with their strange mixtures of clothes and toys, and foods he could almost smell even as they appeared beneath her pencil; parties filled with smiling people, hands brushing each other, eyes finding one another, always something else to see the more you looked. Her talent was uncanny and fascinating, and made all the more so by the fact that she did not have regular, first-hand experience of the kind of life she drew almost obsessively.

Now, cloaked in daylight, Maer waited by the gate of the house in which she had grown up. She had only been there a few minutes when he heard footsteps on the road, and watched as Martin limped up the path, a jar of coffee in his hand. A moment after he had gone in, shouting the usual Riley family greeting, his son came out and closed the door gently behind him. Maer bit his lip, hoping Tom wouldn't go too far from the house; the urge to remain here, to try and catch another glimpse of Laura, was almost painful. Her name tasted rich and sweet on Maer's lips as he whispered it aloud, and the memory of holding her as she wept still haunted him. Since that day she had barely been out of his thoughts. He hadn't told anyone about her, not even Richard; no words could do justice to her and so he didn't try.

To his guilty relief, Tom went into the workshop. He looked fine, natural, in control for the time being. Maer allowed himself a wry smile: knowing how the majority of mortals viewed supernatural beings, he couldn't help but consider how they'd react if they knew what was happening right under their noses.

In the common vernacular: they'd freak.

He drew fresh sunlight around his form to reflect a minor shift in the light, and sat down to think about his mother and the way she had spoken to him. She really *had* been his mother one minute – warm, strong and gentle, eloquent in her gladness at his return – yet a moment later he had been whisked back to the first time he had seen her in her role as Queen Deera. She had held the council in thrall then, barely raising her voice and yet in total, unquestionable command, and no-one had dared speak against her.

This had always been taken as a sign of respect, and so it was, but now Maer realised such a respect must necessarily be liberally lined with fear. She was a queen through and through, and today she had spoken to him as such. He let his head fall into his hands as he contemplated the thought of bringing Richard back here, to his spiritual death. And afterwards to have to watch that familiar, beloved form being manipulated by the ancient, power-hungry King Loen.

'I can't do it,' he whispered aloud. 'Not to Richard, it's all –' Realisation struck, sending his thoughts whirling and slamming back to the simple truth: he could leave, right now. Go back to America and find someone else! His mother had no idea what Richard looked like, the only other person who knew was Gilan, and he wouldn't care who was chosen as long as his sister was deposed as queen.

He stood up, his heart fizzing with relief, and turned as he heard laughter coming from the Rileys' cottage garden. Laura and Tom had pulled open the double garage doors as wide as they would go, and were beginning to pull boxes and paint pots out onto the grass.

'I'll do the surfaces, you do the floor,' Laura called, snapping on a bright yellow pair of Marigolds and brandishing a scouring cloth.

'Okey doke.' Tom switched the radio on and began larking about with a long-handled mop, dancing with it.

Maer watched for a while, enjoying the sound of Laura's laughter, then he turned to go; there was nothing to report here.

He made his way back across the moor, trying to work out how best to find a likely stranger and gain their trust. That would be the tricky part: manipulation of mortals was limited to a mild form of hypnosis, more an acute talent for persuasion than anything else. And it lessened with distance from the moor. Up here it had allowed him to convince the sleepy, emotionally drained Laura he'd probably never existed, but it would not be enough to make someone follow him back to England. Still, there had to be a way …

'No, Maer.'

He stopped, startled, and turned to look behind him. Casta was sitting on a nearby boulder, his arms folded across his broad chest. 'Do not waste your time.'

'What do you mean?'

'I know how hard this must be for you,' Casta said, moving aside to make room. 'But to begin with, your mother knows all she needs to know about Lucas: Gilan does his job well, and you yourself paint an extraordinary picture whenever you return. You cannot help it; your love for this man loosens your tongue, your desire to share his achievements, your pride in him ... you share more than your words.'

'But how did you know what I was thinking?'

'I know you, and I could see there was new purpose in your step, a new light in your eyes.' Casta's voice was gentle, but his expression did not invite argument. 'I know how close you and Lucas have grown, but you have to accept that he was a task you were given, nothing more.'

'He's a good man,' Maer said stubbornly. 'And he has family again now, he has Cait. He doesn't deserve to die just because he has the right manner and appearance.'

'And the man you would have chosen in his stead, would he have deserved to die? Would he not be just as random a choice as Lucas? Maer, you are thinking like a mortal.'

'It is hard not to.'

'Hard, but not impossible. Maybe you need to stay here for a little longer. Gilan will do a good – '

'No!' The dark work of this so-called guardian went no way at all towards making Maer feel better about coming home. Even Amy's death, accidental as it had seemed, raised an ugly question mark since Steve's throwaway comment about the knife.

'Maer, you must do this. It's for the good of your people,' Casta insisted. 'Do you not think Lucas would willingly give his life to save yours?'

'It's not the same thing. You're talking about *killing* him!'

Casta looked at him, clearly struggling for more persuasive words, then lowered his head. 'You have lived long among humans, and taken their ways as your own.' He sighed and it was deep and heavy, as if the sound came up from the rock beneath him. 'Very well.'

'What do you mean, "very well"?'

'I see you will not be moved despite my words. Listen well then: Lucas's life may *possibly* be spared. This will anger Loen and we may pay a heavy price –'

'Spared?' Maer stared at his father, heart thudding.

'It will be hard, and it will be dangerous, but with care we may succeed. Loen will take Lucas's body as planned … wait!' he held up a hand as Maer started to speak again. 'Tom Riley is lost, or soon will be. When Loen is strong enough to leave him, there will be nothing left of him except that body. A mortal body, but strong enough to be saved if it is taken quickly.'

'Saved for Richard?'

'If we are swift,' Casta reaffirmed.

Maer fought down the fierce joy he felt, cut through as it was with guilt at the realisation of what Casta was saying. This was Laura's brother.' We cannot save Tom at all? Are you saying he must surrender himself totally to Loen?'

'It is already near to being accomplished, we know this.' Casta was firm, allowing no room for false hope. 'Riley grows confused easily, and tired. And the more tired he becomes the easier it is for Loen to come forward, to take control. It is regrettable, as is the loss of any life, and at best your friend may lose his memories of his former life. Or he may retain them all and be sent mad – he may not recover from such madness.'

'But he would live?' Maer persisted.

'Yes, he would live. But I have said it is dangerous and so it is – we rely completely on Loen's mercy. That he will have Lucas's body but not his spirit will displease him greatly.'

'Father, I swear –'

'Enough now.' Casta's tone gentled. 'Will you come down with me and sweep away the harshness that has passed between you and your mother?'

Maer shook his head, his mind still spinning. 'I should remain here until Gilan returns, but I will see her before I pass through the Doorway again.'

'I will tell her you will continue in your task. With a lighter heart, no doubt?'

'Yes!'

'And you make your vow to me here, now: you will bring him?'

'I will bring him. My word on it. And, Father?' Casta turned back, and Maer touched his arm. 'Thank you.'

***

Tom watched his sister carefully as they carried the trays out into the garden. Sometimes he felt older than everyone, wiser and more sensitive to the world around him – he didn't understand it, but he welcomed it. In darker, more uncertain moments he had an idea the moor was repaying him for his loyalty, and the thought would strike a deep discord in him. Those were the nights he found himself jolted awake, shivering, and all too often with tears sliding into his pillow.

Today though, he concentrated on Laura, He had caught the odd flash of quiet reflection throughout the afternoon as she helped him clean out the workshop, but he had to admit she appeared surprisingly together despite the break up with Michael. He watched closely for any signs of unhappiness, but she kept up a lively chatter and didn't seem to be hiding anything. And it wasn't like she'd never find anyone else. Even he had to admit she had turned out quite pretty, although her long dark hair was permanently pulled back in a scrunchie and a bit of a mess on the whole. Her eyes were unusual, rarely looked the same shade of grey two days running, and she had a sweet smile. If only she'd dress a bit better he was sure it wouldn't be long before someone else asked her out.

He and Laura arranged the plates and cups on the wooden lawn table, and while Laura went back into the house to bring out their meal, Tom went in search of his father.

Martin was in the workshop, admiring the freshly scrubbed surfaces and neatly squared away tools. 'She's got you organised at last then.'

'Seems so. D'you think she's okay?'

'I think she is now, yeah. She was kind of brittle before, but when she smiles now you can see she's feeling it.'

Following Martin back out into the garden, Tom was touched as he realised how much their father actually noticed. He was a quiet man, but he watched, he took note and he understood. On impulse Tom reached out and squeezed his shoulder.

Martin patted his hand and for a second the evening was perfect. Time seemed to freeze, and Tom was acutely aware of everything around him: the grasshoppers buzzing, a distant car; the warmth of the evening sun on his forearms and face; the feeling of deep peace stealing through him.

He opened his mouth to say something, and abruptly the good feelings dropped away. He felt his heart race at the fleeting sense that someone he loved was in terrible danger - the feeling lasted for no more than a second and was replaced by an urgency that actually propelled him forwards a couple of steps.

He vaguely heard Martin's voice, muffled, unreal, calling out to him, and then there was a sudden, burning pain, deep in his chest cutting off his breath ... oh, Christ! Heart attack? He stumbled to his knees, dimly aware of his father leaning over him although he looked thinner and all wrong. Tom saw the mouth moving, but he couldn't hear the words. He collapsed onto his side, gasping. And then the pain was gone, as suddenly as it had hit. Nothing, not even the residue of the burning sensation, remained. His hand went to his chest and found the place, high on his left side, but there was no wound, nothing to explain it.

He blinked and struggled to a sitting position against his father's restraining hand. 'I'm alright,' he insisted, pushing the hand away. 'It was just a stitch or something.' He climbed to his feet, avoiding Martin's incredulous stare.

'Bloody hell, Tom, some stitch!'

Tom saw worry furrowing his father's brow, irritating as hell; it was pretty obvious everything was alright now. 'Leave it, okay? Let's just go and eat, before Delia Smith blows a fuse,' he said, gesturing to Laura who was coming out of the front door with a laden tray.

'Wait!' Martin caught at his arm as he started to walk away. 'What the hell's the matter with you?'

'Nothing. Let me go.'

'Nothing? One minute you're all sweetness and light, the next you're behaving like some spoiled adolescent.'

Tom struggled with rising anger, but took a deep breath and forced a conciliatory tone. 'Sorry. You were right, it was a hell of a stitch, but it's totally gone now.'

Martin let go of his arm but his eyes, still hurt and angry, fixed on Tom's. 'Alright, that's all I wanted to know.'

But as he walked away across the garden Tom felt the anger coming back harder, stronger, as overwhelming as the pain had been, and he was just as powerless to control it.

***

Maer looked on with growing horror as the scene unfolded. He had arrived back in the village, light enough to float, relief peeling away the layers of guilt and misery that had lain across his heart for so long. Arriving outside the Riley home, he had been in time to see Martin go in to check the progress on the cleaning of the workshop, and to feel his own breath cut off in shock as Tom had staggered and fallen barely a heartbeat later.

Before he'd had time to take another breath it had been over, but as Tom shoved his father's helping hand away the sudden animosity between the two men was palpable. There could be only one explanation: Loen was pushing forward, fighting Tom for control, and it seemed he was winning. How strong was he now? Strong enough? Maer felt a chill creep through his veins.

Laura had appeared from the house and immediately latched on to the disharmony between her father and brother. She spoke briefly to each of them, and when neither took their gaze off each other long enough to explain the problem, she slammed her cup onto the table and left the garden, her face bewildered and angry. She brushed unknowingly past Maer at the gate, and, seeing the tears in her eyes he had to fight the urge to throw off the sunlight and go after her.

Instead he turned his attention back to the two men at the table. Martin's hand was clenched beside his plate, and Tom was lounging against the bench's backrest, his eyes burning across the table at his father. Maer's heart began to pound, it was uncanny to think such an ancient being was looking out through those cool blue eyes, and he couldn't help wondering what Martin was seeing. Their voices had risen, making it all too easy now, for Maer to hear what he had been struggling to hear before.

'What on earth has got into you, are you mad?' Martin was saying. 'Because every now and again I find myself believing you actually are. Not just a bit strung out, but clinically bloody insane!'

'Shut it, I'm not interested.'

'You go from doting son to toddler with a tantrum in the blink of an eye. No-one knows where they stand with you!'

'Oh don't give me that, you can't wait to shut me out when *she's* here,' Tom snapped.

Martin recoiled as if he'd been spat on. He rose, furious. 'Stop trying to push it onto your sister, you pathetic little shit. You've always been the same; you have a problem you can't deal with so you shove it all onto someone else. Well it won't work. You may be a great hulking tough guy to look at, my son, but you're weak.'

'Oh?' Tom also stood, and he towered over his father. 'How weak do you have to be to kill someone?'

Martin stared at him. Maer's breath locked in his throat, and the skin on his forehead tightened. He gripped

99

the top of the gate.

'What?' Martin was hoarse from shouting, his shaking hands gripping the table in an attempt to steady himself.

'Thought that might shut you up.'

'Killed? You had an accident? What, in the van?'

'I was thirteen. Too young to drive, but yeah, they did reckon it was an accident now you mention it.'

'Too young to ... thirteen?' Martin was now sheet-white. 'Tom, *what did you do?*'

'I was in the right place at the right time, and one little push was all it needed.' Maer moaned aloud as Tom went on, 'The baby had no place here. No more children could be born in this line.' There was sick realisation on Martin's face now, but Tom continued, his gaze fixed somewhere above his father's head. 'It was supposed be just the baby, but she died too.' Tom faltered and his voice faded until it was barely audible. 'That was wrong,' he whispered, then let out a choking sob. 'Th, that was ... oh god ...'

Tom's eyes rolled back in his head, and Maer realised Loen was retreating, leaving the stunned young man pinned at the thigh between bench and table. Martin sucked a sudden harsh breath, his mouth dropped open and his eyes flew impossibly wide as he reached for his son, clawing at the air. Maer could see greasy sweat breaking out on his face, saw his chest hitch as he dragged at the air, then the hand reaching for Tom fell limply to his side.

Tom swayed in shock as he watched his father slump forwards, smacking into the table with his forehead and sliding sideways on the bench; Maer could tell he had no recollection of what had passed between them. He watched, helpless, as Tom stumbled around the table to pull at Martin, tugging frantically until he came free. Then Tom lifted a tear streaked face to scream for help and, although he already knew it was too late, Maer moved forwards.

The moment he had arrived at O'Hare, and seen Steve Shelby there instead of Richard, Maer realised something was wrong, but Steve's first words sliced him away from his senses.

'Richard's been shot.'

Dazed with shock he barely took in the details as Steve drove them out to the hospital, and the fact of Cait's death elicited a small moan of horror and grief, but he couldn't speak. There was a flash of fury that Gilan had not prevented this – after all that was why he was there – and then the only thought in his mind was how close he had come to losing his closest friend. How then, would he feel when he had to hand him over to Loen?

And then it hit him. He found his voice and it shook badly. 'What day did it happen?'

'Saturday. Last day of their honeymoon.'

'What time?'

Steve looked blank for a moment, then shook his head. 'Jesus, what does it matter? Around lunchtime? Just after maybe. I got the call, drove out to where it happened. Some dipshit little place north of the city, but they saved him. They brought him back yesterday. Hey, don't worry,' he added, more gently, 'he's going to be okay, they said so.'

Maer nodded but couldn't answer, his thoughts had veered to Tom, collapsing in his garden at teatime on Saturday, and he had no words.

The hospital corridors were full of people, all of them

hurrying somewhere, some chattering with relief, some tight-lipped with worry or pain, all too many red-eyed with quiet misery. Maer knew his face was expressionless, it had to be, because he was numb from head to toe.

Richard was asleep, his skin as white as the sheets folded neatly at his waist, the hospital gown bulky across his chest where the bandages lay beneath the thin material. Maer felt sick; if Loen was already sufficiently aware of his intended host that he could pick up his pain and transmit it to his current one, how would they be able to prevent him from taking him over, mind and body?

'They took him off the machines this morning.' Steve spoke quietly but Richard opened his eyes at the sound. For a second he stared right through Maer, then he blinked and focused properly. 'She's gone, Dean,' he whispered. He licked his lips and tried again. 'She went without me.' He closed his eyes again and said nothing more, holding his breath as if denying himself the air that gave him a life he didn't deserve, or need, now Cait's had been taken.

Maer leaned over him, worried. 'Rich, hey – you need someone? Something for the pain?'

Richard shook his head briefly and breathed again, but didn't open his eyes. Maer reached out and touched Richard's shoulder, trying to convey all of what he wanted to say in that one touch. A tiny nod told him Richard understood, and Maer stepped out of the room, tight with fury, wondering where Gilan had been while Richard lay dying in a gas station doorway.

Chapter Ten

May 16. 1643. Stratton Hill, Bude, Cornwall.

The darkness was lifting, although it was not yet five o'clock: pre-dawn. He could see men donning their helmets, checking armour – he glared at his own misshapen, useless breastplate where it lay in the mud beside him, and tightened the thongs on his tunic, looking enviously upon those lucky men with sufficient armour for the task ahead.

The task. Ah, but it was hopeless! Stamford was dug in with his Parliamentarian army around the fort on the top of the hill, and they outnumbered the Cornish Royalists by at least two men to every one. Orders to march here by night had been wisely conceived, but the men were so tired now it was hard to think of victory, to believe it might yet be theirs.

The order came: they were to march in four columns, Sir Bevil Grenville's column would approach from the west, word was carried on whispers to preserve their advantage over the Parliamentarians.

A few feet away, John Bartholomew sent him a hungry grin, his eyes gleaming in the first grey light.' Ready, Stephen?'

The soldier hesitated; Stephen? Yes, of course he was Stephen, why had his mind momentarily told him otherwise?

'We'll send them back to Hell,' he confirmed. His heart thumped so hard now he could feel it under his hand, even through the leather tunic that had once promised to afford some small protection, but that now seemed as useless as the thin shirt he wore beneath it.

John jerked his head at the discarded breastplate. 'Sourton Down?'

Stephen nodded, frowning at the memory. He'd been part of the secondary attack on Dartmoor, when the Parliamentarians had panicked the initial wave of dragoons into retreating, colliding with the men who had come behind them. Brought down beneath the stampede, Stephen remembered the rage with which he'd watched the chaos that had ensued, and the sudden, unexpected thunderstorm that had sent the king's army spinning back into safety - the moor was no place to be in a storm, particularly carrying a sixteen foot iron pike.

'That storm has much to answer for,' Bartholomew observed. 'Had it not been for the lightning we should be tucked in our beds now.

'Aye, well, storm it did, and the retreat led us here.'

Bartholomew snorted. 'The retreat was good sense – leaving Hopton's portmanteau for them to find was not. The king's *orders* were in there!'

'Well Stamford is determined to ensure those orders will come to nothing, and so here we are. He has chosen a good place to make his stand though: this hill is nigh on unbreachable.'

Bartholomew looked towards the distant encampment. 'Word has it some of those whoresons used the mill at Lynher to sharpen their weapons.'

'And what of the miller?'

'Dead. Along with his brothers.'

'They will be avenged a hundredfold,' Stephen said, his voice rich with bitterness, and they waited in silence, contemplating the atrocities committed on the innocents at the mill.

Then it was time. They looked at each other for a long moment, then Bartholomew clapped him on the shoulder and the column turned to begin their march.

To their left walked Anthony Payne, a giant of a man at over seven feet tall, right hand man of Grenville himself.

'Penhaligon?'

As Stephen turned in enquiry, Payne frowned and gestured to his own armour, then at Stephen's leather tunic. 'May God go with you, man,' he said, troubled.

Stephen was about to reply when the shout went up: 'They have heard us!'

The element of surprise was lost – what chance now? Fear and courage linked hands within the king's army, and the men readied their weapons and didn't look back. They pushed up the hill, cutting down Parliamentarians with a ferocity and determination made all the stronger by their being hopelessly outnumbered.

To Stephen's right, a man fell, a musket ball in his throat, and ahead two more fell to Stamford's soldiers. The smell all around was rich and hot; sweat, blood, smoke from flintlocks hanging in the air, making the men's eyes water. Still they fought on, for King Charles, for their country and, right here and now, for their next breath.

They gained some ground on the hill, forcing the enemy back, but ammunition was short and victory was, without doubt, a distant hope. As Grenville's men were readying themselves for a last concerted effort to push through, Major-General James Chudleigh appeared on the hill before them, his pike men behind him. At his signal they charged down the western slope, felling Grenville's men, smashing deep into his column.

The conflict raged on, but it grew harder to see friend from foe amid the universally muddied coats and bristling pikes. Stephen felt the heat of a blade slashing at his thigh, and glancing down saw his red breeches stained darker with blood. The wound was shallow, and he knocked aside a further attempt by the same soldier, bringing the blunt end of his pike around to smash into the man's face, shattering his cheek and jaw. The man went down, Stephen fought on.

A scream from somewhere on his left, just one scream among the hundreds, yet this one struck at Stephen's heart – he saw John Bartholomew on his knees, his hands over his face, blood dripping from behind hooked fingers.

Stephen shouted loud enough to strain the muscles in his throat. 'John!'

John's hands dropped away and he raised his shattered face, unseeing, but tilting his head towards the sound of his friend's voice. 'Stephen? I cannot see you!'

'I will come back for you!' Stephen cried and, in a fresh burst of fury he levelled his sawn off pike and charged forward.

A pulse of light bloomed away to the east, over Bodmin Moor; another storm – but victory could not be stolen from them again. Stephen's charge carried him deep into the oncoming ranks, spearing one of Stamford's men through the heart. He felt only a dark, savage elation when he saw the man's eyes bulge as he fell, dead instantly.

As Stephen struggled to tear his weapon free from the body, a blow from behind knocked him forwards and he stumbled in the mud. Breathing hard, knowing he was already dead, Stephen twisted onto his back to face his killer. Squinting against the sky he saw, for a second, not the filthy, blood encrusted tip of a pike, but a gleaming blade wielded by a man whose countenance held an unexpected expression of extreme sorrow.

The image shifted, and his true enemy stood above him: just a stranger's bloodied mask after all, as exhausted and numbed as his own. He could not find hatred for this man, even now. The pike swept down, found its place. Pain and blade roared together through Stephen's chest – yet he knew it had missed his heart because he was still living, still had his eyes open, he could feel the steel tip of the pike between his ribs, glancing off bone and slicing deeper. Agony twisted and burned inside him and he prayed for the Roundhead to tear the blade free and pierce him again, to end it.

Somewhere far away he could hear screams, and it seemed they were for him, yet crying a different name. At last the Roundhead jerked his weapon back and Stephen knew then he did not need a second blow after all; blood was bubbling out of the wound and he couldn't draw a good breath, the remaining circle of light was diminishing fast. He remembered his promise to John and tried to call to him, but the pain was circling his ribs and he was unable to suck in even the tiniest gasp of air.

He was weightless. Rising like a leaf in the wind above the battle ground, where men of both armies lay in terrible numbers, blood soaking into the grass and mud. And there, his own body, unprotected by armour that might have saved his life, his left side soaked in blood. There was a darker patch where the wound still bled – for a moment. He saw his own eyes, bright green and horrified, staring back at him, then they closed as his head slipped to the side and the last breath left his body. Just one of so many shattered corpses on the hillside.

Nearby was his dearest friend John Bartholomew, still on his knees, his blind eyes raised to the sky as if he could see Stephen and could somehow reach out and join him. Stephen tried to tell him he was sorry, but he had no substance; no mouth with which to call, no ears to hear the horrific sounds of the battle that still raged. Not even eyes to see, and yet he did see it, and he remained there: this weightless, formless being, until he saw someone pull John to safety, back through the ranks.

I am dead! the terrifying knowledge beat against his mind like a solid blow as he felt himself spinning away. *Lord, have mercy, I am dead ...*

No! Not this time ...

Richard's eyes snapped open. His heart was pounding hard and heavy, he wasn't even sure if he'd shouted out loud. As his room filtered into view the lingering vision faded. The unknown man he'd thought of with great affection as John, the battle on a hill somewhere he'd never been, accents he'd never heard. And the pain.

That was the only thing that had been real, and what had, no doubt, triggered the vividly detailed dream. Sweating despite the chill in the room, he shoved the covers down to his hips and the words drifted in his hazy consciousness, coated in mystery. *Not this time?*

'What the hell does that mean?' he whispered. He reached out shakily for the bottle on his bedside cabinet: to hell with his stupid notion of coming off medication, if dreams like that were the result then bring on morphine addiction. Jesus ...

As the intensity of the dream inevitably faded, Richard found his mind taking the treacherous path back to the gas station, and then to the funeral. The grief was still as sharp, and sometimes he wished the pain was too, at least it made him feel as if he were paying, in some miniscule way, for letting Cait go to her death. But what would happen when he was healed: how would he justify being alive then?

His grandparents had collected him from the hospital to attend the funeral, and he'd felt the strong hand of his grandfather around his back, supporting him. He'd looked across at Cait's parents; who was there to support them? Only each other, and it couldn't be enough.

In the semi-darkness of his room Richard forced himself to swallow the pills, and his throat was so tight he had to chase them with mouthful after mouthful of water. He felt tears leaking from his tightly closed eyes and, since he was alone, he let them come.

It seemed this was part of his penance – it hadn't felt enough like a dream to allow him to forget the feeling. The details, yes. Specifics, faces, even names would all fade in time, but the feelings of helplessness and horror would be with him every day of his life.

He welcomed them.

Chapter Eleven

Chicago, August 2010.

'So, what do you think?' Dean sat forward, hands clasped between his knees, trying not to let his anxiety show.

Richard shuffled the papers in his hand and shook his head. 'You went ahead and arranged all this?'

'This is a real opportunity for you.'

'Dean, you did this without even *consulting* me?'

Dean sat straighter; there was something in his friend's expression that was profoundly unsettling. Something diamond-hard. It reminded him of his mother, and he found himself responding with an almost unconscious deference. 'Okay, I'm sorry. I should have asked first. But it's not set in stone, you can always call them and say you've changed your mind.'

'*I've* changed *my* mind?' Richard flung the papers down on the coffee table.' I can't believe you did this, what the hell were you hoping to achieve?'

'I don't know,' Dean returned, allowing a little ice to enter his own voice. 'How about fun? How about learning? How about re-discovering what you're best at?' He waved his hand to take in the guitars leaning against the walls, the half-finished music scribbled in pencil and full of crossings out, the piano, unplayable beneath the stacks of books. 'You've lost yourself, mate,' he went on, sounding sad. 'You and the guys had something really good, and you've just let it slip away. Not their fault. Yours. You need this break.'

Richard picked up a hand-painted acoustic guitar, then shook his head and replaced it. He'd been doing that too much lately, things were even worse now than they had been in the months immediately following Cait's death; dark hatred and the need to physically rebuild his strength had driven him on, and then, for a while, he had even seemed back to his old self. His teaching job kept him focused on the positive, passing on his love of music to eager young minds, and the band had kept on playing to enthusiastic crowds. For a while.

But Dean hadn't been able to ignore the gradual slipping of the façade his friend had presented, and no matter how hard he tried he couldn't stop it. The easy laughter that had never been more than a sideways glance away, the creative talent and simple joy it brought him, even the roguish taste for conflict that was as deep a part of him as everything else, all were fading under Dean's helpless watch, leaving someone he barely recognised.

Eleven years after Cait's death Richard moved through his days visibly exhausted, and whereas his gaze had often pinned people with an unnerving intensity, now it just slid off their faces as if they didn't exist. Nothing seemed to light him up anymore. He slumped back against the couch now; something was clearly bothering him, other than the idea Dean had sprung on him today. He seemed uncertain whether to speak, and when he did it was oddly stilted.

'Had another weird dream last night.'

Dean's gut clenched and he hoped his reaction didn't show, but Richard's gaze was focused elsewhere, remembering. 'It kind of reminded me of the one I had right after Cait died, the battle dream, remember?'

Dean nodded; it had been a long time ago but the way Richard had told it he didn't think he'd ever forget – nor was the location of the dream something to ignore.

'There was this guy,' Richard went on. 'Name was Jack. I don't think he was American either, but I believe it happened here in the States this time. He was on a hunting party, never been hunting before, I could feel his excitement. I mean really *feel* it. His friend got excited too.' Richard frowned and rubbed his chest. 'Shot him by accident.'

'Killed him?' Dean was cold now, but the chill wasn't on his skin, it never was. This chill had pierced his bones and he could do nothing to warm it.

'Yeah. And although I felt the shot I know it wasn't me, because I can remember seeing him standing over ... over the body, begging to be forgiven but it was too late. He was destroyed by what he'd done, they were really close friends. Christ, imagine doing that to your best friend.'

Dean flinched, he couldn't help it. 'It was just a dream, Rich.'

'I guess.' Richard sat up again, to Dean's relief he was obviously looking for a change of subject. He gestured at the chaos in his front room. 'What the hell is wrong with me? I can't seem to even write my own stuff anymore. It's been too long to feel this way, I need ... something.'

'You need a fresh start, somewhere completely different. And believe me, Cornwall is the perfect place.'

Richard picked up the paperwork again. 'And this is the way to do it? Quit my job and just take off?' But he was sounding less determined to dismiss it now, and Dean felt his heart quicken: it might still work.

'What better way?' he said. 'Off-season, no tourists, doing something you love and sharing it with people who'll really appreciate it. And you don't have to quit, just take a sabbatical.'

'And how old are these kids?'

'It's a primary school, they're aged five to eleven. You'll be working with the older ones on this project.

112

Look, Richard,' he allowed an impish grin to cross his face, confident now that he'd breached the Lucas defence, 'are you going to say yes now, or are you determined to torture me for the rest of the day?'

Richard sighed. 'I guess I'm saying yes. Although torturing you has an attraction to it.'

'Yes!'

'When do we leave?'

'Three weeks' time. I've got a flight two days before yours, so I'll have chance to get a B&B sorted before you arrive. Listen, Rich – you've made the right choice, you'll thank me for it.'

Richard finally smiled. 'Yeah, right. Now get out, looks like I've got an important call to make. My boss is gonna love me.'

***

Lynher Mill, September 2010

Laura clipped the lead onto the puppy's collar and called down the hall, 'Tom! We're just off out for a bit. You okay?'

'Fine, don't worry!'

Standard question, standard answer. Satisfied, Laura gave the lead a shake and set off up the lane. As always by this time of year the volume of traffic had slowed right down, and most of the holiday makers had left, although there were lights on at the bed and breakfast across the village.

Halfway up the hill, she stepped off the road and onto the moor and let Captain off the lead, wishing she had a decent share of his energy as he bounded off up the track towards the ruined windmill. There was an odd feeling in the air tonight; a sort of melancholy mingled with a cautious kind of awakening; the two emotions battled briefly and she wondered at that prickle of sadness until she remembered the date. Her father's birthday.

Eleven years on, the question remained: what had caused the heart attack? Tom had been devastated and unable to offer any explanation, even much later. He'd remembered being angry with Martin, that they'd argued, but not what it had been about, and the next thing he'd remembered had been dragging his father away from the table to lay him on the grass.

His grief, and the fear of what that inability to remember might mean, had not lessened over the years, in fact it distressed him more as the time went on and Laura's brief dream of moving away had fizzled and died. She had almost been able to see it in the mirror each day; her bright optimism, her lively interest in everything, fading into this ghost of a woman who moved through life with quiet efficiency but little else. If her mother's death had set her on this grey path, and Tom's panicky dependence had kept her gaze fixed firmly ahead, then the death of Martin Riley on the same day Michael had left, had taken the last glimmer of light in her life and quietly, completely, snuffed it out.

Her only concern since then had been Tom, and for a long time that had been enough to give her some kind of purpose, but tonight life seemed once more to be trying to take hold in the cold places inside her. The weather was unremarkable, the landscape exactly as she had always known it, but something about the evening was brushing her with a tingle of hope, and of possibility. For a moment she pushed back against it, remembering how shock and tragedy had followed the last time she had felt real excitement, but as her mind cleared she recognised the strength of her own need and stopped fighting.

Captain's innocent excitement and curiosity was infectious: she watched him explore, sniff, examine – and found she too was looking around with newly opened eyes. Hers was a bigger world but, like the black lab's, it could be explored one piece at a time; no need to move on until she was ready. And now maybe she was. As she walked she let her thoughts run free, and felt a new kind of energy in the air that helped them grow, fleshing them out until they ceased to be 'what if,' and became 'when.'

It felt like the perfect night for testing the strength of her new resolve. Rather than take Captain back to Tom's house then slink back to her own, she made the decision to call in at the pub. Not something she'd have contemplated doing alone, not before tonight, but there would never be a better time, it would be full of people she knew anyway: colleagues, people she'd grown up with, no-one would stare at her, and it would be nice to sit and chat with them, and drink a nice cold glass of cider.

She sang as she walked, a deliberately silly Monty Python tune that made her smile as the sun slid over the horizon and night crept across the moor. As she rounded the corner at the foot of the hill she stopped dead, the song dying on her lips. Standing absolutely still by the edge of the road, staring out over the darkening moor toward the mines, was a man in a long black coat, his hands clenched against the chill from the wind blowing off the heath.

There was something intense about his stance, as if he were poised on the edge of flight and, fascinated by the taut energy she perceived, Laura too remained motionless, watching.

He actually seemed familiar in some vague way;

memory clawed at her, trying to scratch away the layers, but it was no good. She looked more closely, wondering if he was simply someone she had known from school, or a parents of one of her pupils.

As if he felt the weight of her gaze he turned towards her, but she still couldn't see his face and was none the wiser.

'Sorry to stare,' she called out, her voice cutting across the quiet road, sounding brassy, even to herself, in the quiet evening air. 'I just wondered if I knew you, that's all.'

The man shook his head, his face an unreadable map of shadows and faint splashes of light from nearby houses. 'Pretty sure you don't.'

Laura noted his accent, and that memory scratched harder but it was no good, she didn't know any Americans. 'Sorry,' she said again. 'Didn't mean to intrude.'

'Not a problem. Really.' He went back to this thoughts, and Laura hesitated. Now they had exchanged greetings, would it be rude of her to simply walk away?

She chewed her lip thoughtfully for a moment. 'Well, 'night then.'

'Huh? Oh, yeah. 'Night.'

Laura whistled Captain to her and fixed the lead onto his collar, a little self-satisfied grin on her lips; she had just voluntarily called out to a complete stranger, without a second thought. And he hadn't chased her away, hadn't ridiculed her, had done nothing but answer her civilly, if a little distantly. She relaxed into the discovery of her own tiny core of courage, but that odd familiarity was going to bug her.

When she walked into the Miller's Arms two minutes later the memory clicked into place. The reason was standing at the bar: tall, slender, white-blond hair flopping over his brow in exactly the same way as it had seventeen years ago. In her dream. The man outside had definitely been a stranger, but this was ... Dean! The name flashed into her mind, the name she hadn't been able to remember, even immediately on waking, but she was sure that was it.

'Dream, my arse,' she said aloud, and he jumped. His eyes widened as he saw her, but just a little. Not terribly surprised, she thought, but then, *I'm* not the one who's supposed to be the figment of someone's imagination.

'Laura. Hi. You're all grown up.'

'Dean. Hi. So are you.' She carefully matched her cool tone to his as she secured the puppy's lead to the leg of a barstool, before straightening and looking at Dean properly.

The extraordinary light blue of his eyes hadn't changed of course, the beauty of the bone structure hadn't faded, and the easy elegance with which he had stood out there on the moor all those years ago was mirrored in the way he lounged against the bar now. That's what had sparked the memory outside, even before the stranger had spoken he had reminded her on some deep level of the boy on the moors.

'What was that about a dream?' Dean asked, finishing his drink and signalling the landlord.

'I woke up, you'd gone. I thought I'd dreamed you. You have to admit it was something of a surreal experience,' Laura pointed out. The incident still held no substance for her; even now, with Dean here in the flesh she couldn't attribute any sense of reality to it. So how could he just turn up out of the blue, and just start talking to her as if they were old friends?

'Yeah. Look, I'm sorry about that,' Dean told her. 'I actually stayed with you for a while, but I had to go. I was late, my flight –'

'It's okay, you weren't obliged to stay with me.'

'I felt bad though,' he admitted. 'Can I buy you a drink to make up for being such a prat?'

'No argument from me. Pint of Strongbow, please.'

She waited until the drink was in front of her, then traced shapes in the condensation on the glass. 'Do you have any brothers?'

'Nope. Why, got a friend?'

His presumption, and the grin that accompanied it, surprised her into a laugh. 'Very good. No, I saw someone outside. Only from a distance, but he sort of reminded me of you. Definitely American though, not like your half-assed Dick Van Dyke accent.'

He snorted. 'Thanks. That'll be Richard. Hardly think we look alike though.'

'I couldn't see him properly, but anyway that's not what I meant. He had the same kind of, I don't know, tension? Like he was about to take off across the moors. You have that. As if you think someone's standing behind you about to go: 'boo!' Dean's glass wobbled and sloshed beer onto his wrist, and his eyebrows came back down from where they'd shot into his hairline.

Laura grinned. 'Sorry,' she said, sounding anything but. She passed him a bar towel and watched him mop at his sleeve, enjoying her own ability to tease in spite of her general nervousness at seeing him. In fact she was disappointed to find she wasn't remotely drawn to him anymore. In the back of her mind, for all these years, there had lurked this mysterious dream-boy: wise beyond his years, not to mention beautiful, and now here he was and while he hardly looked different at all, whatever had been there when she was sixteen had gone. Probably just a case of her hormones settling down.

'So, have you moved back now?' she asked, just to make conversation. The new sense of freedom was still bubbling just below the surface, it was a rare and precious feeling and she didn't want to lose it.

Dean shook his head. 'Not yet, but I'm thinking about it. I just brought Richard here to get his act together a bit.'

'This the same bloke you talked about before, the one who calls you names?'

'Good memory. Yeah, that's the one. He's a bit – directionless at the moment. Anyway, I'm on good terms with the head teacher here, and found out the local primary school was looking for a special project leader for Christmas. I think it'll do him … okay, what have I said now?'

'That's my school,' Laura said, not bothering to hide her annoyance. 'I know a couple of others who applied to lead that project, so how come they're taking on someone who doesn't even live here?'

Dean shrugged. 'Maybe they wanted some fresh ideas from a different culture? Chicago is certainly different to this place. Who knows? Look never mind Richard, let's talk about you. You teach now?'

She opened her mouth to reply but was distracted as the door opened and Captain began tugging at the leg of the bar stool, yelping happily.

Tom gave Laura an odd look, surprised to see her here, then stooped and pulled at the puppy's ears. 'Alright, you old bugger?'

'Yes, I'm fine thank you.' Laura dodged as Tom straightened with a grin, and moved to clip her around the ear. 'Dean, this is my brother, Tom. Tom, this is Dean, um …'

'Mayer. We've met.' Dean held out his hand and Tom took it, his eyes widening slightly, and the grin faded. The

119

handshake was brief, almost to the point of rudeness.

'Yeah, back along,' Tom said. 'Alright then?'

'Can I get you a drink?'

'No, let me get you one. Least I can do.' Tom's tone indicated otherwise, but he waved a ten pound note at the landlord, who immediately picked up Dean's glass to refresh it.

'You remember Dean from when we were kids?' Laura asked.

'Hardly kids, Lau. Don't you remember? Dean helped me when Dad, uh, when Dad had his heart attack.'

Laura blinked in surprise; surely she'd have remembered seeing him again? Her emotions had been all over the place back then, certainly, but to forget him completely? Again?

'I think I'd gone by the time you came back,' Dean muttered into his drink. 'I'm so sorry to hear he didn't make it. But I couldn't stay.'

'Again.' Her tone was dry.

'Look, what could I do?'

'Anyway, cheers, mate.' Tom raised his own glass to Dean but didn't look at him, and Laura was aware of the reappearance of his old brooding frown. All the good feelings were starting to slip away and she was desperate to regain them.

She tried to lighten the atmosphere again. 'This is such a tiny place, you must be bloody good at hiding,' she said to Dean,

'You'd be amazed.'

'Or maybe you've been avoiding me,' she teased.

'Just busy.'

A taut silence fell over the little group, and as it stretched, Laura noticed that, despite her brother's surface gratitude towards Dean, he couldn't disguise his keenness to keep his distance.

It was embarrassing, but conversely it made her more determined to stay and talk. 'So, Dean. Are you and your friend staying with your family?'

Dean gazed at the door, as if he would like to escape through it. 'Uh no. They live in Liskeard now, we're kipping down at Lynher Rise B&B.'

'Oh, right. Never been inside there. Nice place?'

'Seems alright.'

'Good. Mrs Trethowan runs it, doesn't she? Nice landlady?'

'Nice enough.'

Heavy silence.

Laura tapped Tom's arm, bringing him back from somewhere in the middle distance. 'Dean's friend got the job I was telling you about. The Christmas music project?'

'Oh, yeah.'

'Starts tomorrow, should be interesting.'

'Right.'

More silence.

'God, this is painful!' Laura exploded. 'Dean, thank you very much for everything you've done for me and my family. Nice to see you again, hope your friend doesn't get too bored at his new job. Tom? I'm going home. I'll drop your laundry down in the morning on my way to work, okay? 'Night, both of you.'

***

The door swung shut behind his sister and Tom turned back to his drink, wishing he'd been a bit more forthcoming. Bad feelings had begun to creep back lately, very bad ones, and Laura had been the only thing keeping the shadows at bay. Now she had left he felt alone in a growing pool of darkness.

He stole a glance sideways at Dean Mayer, who had taken a good sized step back as soon as they had completed the formality of the handshake. It was strange: there had been some kind of nervy reaction there, and their palms almost felt fused together for a split second. Hopefully Laura hadn't noticed how he'd almost wrenched his hand away.

He moved a bit closer, curious. Mayer stepped back again and put his glass down too heavily on the bar. 'I'll make sure she's okay, it's dark out there now.'

The moment he had gone Tom felt that pull vanish, as if someone had cut a thread that had been constantly twisting, pulling Mayer and himself closer with each turn. The pub returned to life around him, noises making sense again now; the fruit machine, the click of cue against ball on the pool table, laughter from the far end of the bar. He checked over his shoulder but no-one had noticed anything out of the ordinary. When he finished his drink and untied Captain's lead, a few locals raised a hand in casual and wordless farewell. Situation normal.

He'd intended to go home, but once outside he crossed over the road onto the grass verge at the edge of the heath. He saw the shadow of a man, standing as if turned to stone, and briefly recalled how deeply visceral that pulling sensation had felt with Mayer. He felt the phantom of it again, but it was gone just as suddenly once he moved on.

The sky was dark out here, no reflected street lights, no tower blocks with lights swarming over the sides like glowing insects. Just a perfect canvas on which the stars lay, impossibly distant, yet more real than any city skyline he could imagine.

He walked on into the blackness, past the stone circle

that always gave him a nameless, crawling sensation in the pit of his stomach, and when he reached the closest of the mines he sank down at the foot of the chimney and rested his head against the cool stone. Peace stole over him and he closed his eyes, letting the insistent shadows take over the last pinpoint of clarity in his mind.

Chapter Twelve

'You did well to bring Lucas back, the king will soon be ready. But it may yet take a while longer.' Deera faced her son in consternation. 'How will you make sure Lucas remains close by?'

Maer stared steadily back at her, the tension between them not forgotten, but set aside for now: as her son, as well as her subject, he must obey her. It was in his blood. 'He will stay, Mothe ... *Majesty,*' he corrected deliberately, but felt a twinge of guilt as she flinched. 'His job will give him the satisfaction and the enjoyment he has been missing, and he will spend his last mortal days imparting something of lasting value.'

Despite his even tone, the pain of those words cut deep and for a second it hurt to breathe. He sat down quickly, noticing Casta standing in the shadows, and clung to his father's promise.

Best not even think of what would happen if the switch failed, if Loen took the body and Richard became nothing more than a wasted spirit, formless, useless and confused. He wouldn't be alone if so; the moors were full of restless souls. Sometimes they tried to take the bodies of mortals who strayed too close, and occasionally they succeeded, but only the strongest, most desperate of spirits, who had died in their right minds. Richard would not, in all likelihood, be so fortunate.

'As soon as Loen declares himself ready I will deliver Richard to you,' Maer said, then turned to his father. 'Your promise stands?' He saw the flicker on Casta's face a split second before he realised his parents had not discussed this.

'Promise?' Deera turned to Casta. 'What have you said?'

Maer's heart faltered; if the matter had not been brought before the queen, how could it even be considered? He swallowed a groan of dismay. Too human by far, his feelings.

'I told him Lucas might not have to die,' Casta said. Deera's silence commanded more information, and he reluctantly gave it. 'Whatever else Loen may be, he is royalty, and such a noble nature demands he cannot deny his saviour a chance. Lucas will have a mortal life still, as miserably short as those lives are.'

'But –'

'You can see how important it is to our son, Deera! He needed my reassurance that Lucas need not be harmed if it can be avoided.'

'Maer, your compassion for this man worries me.' As gentle as her words should have been, Deera's voice was edged with steel. 'You know what will happen if Lucas is not delivered.'

'No, I know what will happen if *no-one* is delivered!' Maer said. 'We could give him anyone. Who's to say there's no-one better out there? Some vagrant with no family. I could go back –'

'There is no time!' Deera snapped, and Maer struggled for an argument but she was right. There was no turning back now.

Deera continued, her tone frighteningly formal now. 'Listen well, Prince Maer. You have been charged with the deliverance of the mortal Lucas to save your king, and to prevent the curse from destroying your people. Do you understand?' Maer remained silent, hating her in that moment. 'I said, do you *understand?*'

'I understand Richard is my friend –'

'You cannot speak of true friendship with a mortal. He will grow old and die before your eyes, as will his grandchildren.'

'But he would still have had his life!'

'And so he will,' Casta put in, gentler than Deera and cooling Maer's anger with hope once more. 'He will be devastated at the loss of his familiar shell, and he will likely hate you for causing it, but you will be able to watch him, in Riley's form, as he lives out the promise of life he was granted as a child.' He touched Maer's arm. 'We will continue to protect him as best we can, for he is worthy of our deepest gratitude.'

'Casta,' Deera said, with none of her usual affection. 'I trust you do not forget the consequences of failure?'

'I do not forget, My Queen,' Casta bowed with his body only, his own eyes not breaking contact with hers. 'I would merely remind you that Loen must realise his one true descendant deserves —'

'Wait!' Maer's gaze snapped between his parents. 'How can he be descended from Loen? The one get of Loen's seed was sacrificed —'

'No, he was not.' Deera turned her gaze on him, and from the corner of his eye Maer sensed the relaxation in his father's stance, as if he had been physically unpinned. 'There was confusion. A storm. Ulfed panicked, he struck a severe blow but not a fatal one, and the child was snatched away by his mother before the ceremony could be completed.'

She allowed Maer a moment to absorb this news, then continued, 'Mother and child fled into the hills and were taken in by the spriggans, who healed the child's wound. We have learned this from the spriggans themselves, who have held this secret all these many cycles. The boy was raised there until he was old enough to make his own way.'

'But all the way to America? How could any moorland spirit leave the land for so long?'

'You forget, Maer, the child was only half faery. The mortal heart is a wandering one, and he would have been born with a human's strength. Loen himself was bold, impetuous, any child of his would have been the same, yet also felt the pull of his human side. Like to like. He had royal blood and human wanderlust – a combination destined draw people to him, yet drive him from his homeland to seek the wider world.'

Casta put a comforting hand on his Maer's shoulder. 'Go now. Lucas will return from his walk soon and you must be as you always are. Be his friend if that is what you wish, the Elements know he has need of one.'

Maer walked back towards Lynher Mill, feeling the September wind pressing his shirt against him but not feeling the chill of it. So often he'd had to pretend to feel the biting Chicago winters, sometimes he forgot and only realised his mistake when Richard reacted with amazement to shirtsleeves in below freezing temperatures. He longed to be the same as his mortal friends, even while he smiled at their discomfort, but he never could be.

In the twin room at the B&B he lay on his bed, flicking through the pages of Richard's motorcycle magazine, not looking at the pictures or reading the text, but seeing past them, back into the life he'd made in America. From the outset it had been an education, and a pleasure, far more than a duty. Although … despite everything, Maer couldn't help smiling as he remembered the times he'd had to step in and prevent a fight from breaking out over something stupid; Richard had an absolute authority about his presence, but those who felt the need to challenge that steel often found themselves on the wrong end of what it pleased Steve to call a Lucas-knuckle sandwich.

In the light of what his mother had revealed, Maer now recognised those flashes of authority for what they were: the undeniable, bone-deep assurance of one born to be king whether he knew it or not. But although Maer was already grieving for his human friendship he must remember he was royalty himself, and the lives of his people were at risk. He threw the magazine aside and groaned. He had learned of Loen's curse too late, if only his own body could be substituted he would gladly have given it but the physical connection with Richard was already there.

The connection. How could that possibly have happened over such a distance? And yet Loen had felt the pain of the gunshot, and that had, in turn, manifested itself within his host, only to vanish as Richard lost consciousness. The link must be stronger than anyone suspected; Maer wondered if Tom had baffled doctors with constant chest complaints, with no perceivable cause, as Richard fought his way back to full recovery. Or maybe it was just that one, horrifically traumatic moment that had sealed everything, and then nothing more since? He could ask Gilan if only he could bear to speak with him.

At last though, he could cease to worry about his uncle. Twice every cycle he had surrendered care of Richard into those dangerous and greedy hands, then walked the moors each sleepless night in a constant state of anxiety – with good reason it had turned out. Now he himself would be able to ensure that no harm would befall Richard Lucas. Not yet. And, armed with his father's word, he could make sure that when the time came Richard's spirit would not be cast out into nothing. It had to be enough.

Chapter Thirteen

Six forty-five a.m. If ever there were words to make you pull the duvet up around your ears, those were only beaten by 'first day of term.' Laura's mind began to let go of the usual fragments of inexplicable and bizarrely disconnected dreams, and instead wandered to the day ahead. Year one: faces she'd come to know last year in reception class, gradually losing their shiny, new-person gloss and gaining confidence – often this meant becoming more troublesome, but they were always an interesting challenge. Once she got herself out of bed that was, which was even more of one.

She wandered, bleary-eyed, to the shower, and closed her eyes while the water needled her into life. Dean's friend would be arriving today, ready to set the ten and eleven year olds alight with something apparently only he was qualified to give. It was hardly fair; year four teacher Simon Finn would have been just as good and wouldn't have cost the school a penny extra, unlike this bloke who they'd probably paid to fly in from Chicago, putting their budget back months. Which would they sacrifice first, art materials or the planned new playground equipment?

Working herself into a sour mood at these thoughts, Laura pulled on her teaching attire: long skirt and baggy jumper, and raked a comb through her long hair before tying it, still wet, at the nape of her neck. It hung heavy and uncomfortable down her back but it would dry eventually. She wished she could wear jeans and boots, but Mrs Edwards would have a fit.

At the thought of the school's head and her husband, Laura suppressed a heavy sigh and reminded herself she must be more charitable: Gail and Graham Edwards were simply looking out for her. They had "taken her under their wing," – she could almost see the air quotes when she thought about it – after Martin's death, which was very kind, but she wished they'd take less of an interest in her love life, or lack of it, and stop nagging her about her scruffy clothes.

She applied a touch of mascara, ruffled her fringe, then pulled a face at herself in the mirror. 'Job's a good 'un,' she said, and gave a wry smile; Tom would have something to say about that; he was forever on at her to make more of herself. Maybe she would, next summer, but just at the moment the weather was turning chillier and that meant boots and sweaters, and he'd just have to nag.

She called on him with his washing as promised, but he was already in the workshop so she left it inside his front door and yelled out to him rather than disturb his early start. That meant no chatting over a coffee today and so, with plenty of time to spare Laura took the path around the back of his cottage, and started across the field on the more roundabout route to the little village school.

As she rounded the hedge she was surprised to see Dean walking towards her, focused on the ground and on course for a collision.

'Morning,' she said. He looked up, and for a second her vision wobbled; he seemed indistinct, a vague shadow. Then she blinked and he was there again. 'Early morning constitutional?'

'Kind of. Just showed Richard up to the school, thought I'd take the scenic route back.' He still seemed distant, with an urgency about him at odds with someone out for a stroll.

'Well, better make the most of the walking weather before it turns nasty I suppose,' she said. 'Although as I seem to recall you don't feel the cold like us mere mortals.'

Dean's head jerked as if it were on a string, his eyes suddenly huge in an otherwise expressionless face. 'What?'

God, what had she said now? 'You glamorous Chicago-types. Remember I once asked if you weren't cold on the moor with only a thin shirt?'

He smiled, a little distractedly. Laura felt his impatience to move on, and grew embarrassed for both of them. 'Um, I'm going to be late if I don't get going,' she said. 'Nice to see you, enjoy your walk.'

'Yeah. Yeah, thanks. Have a good first day. And be nice to Richard, okay? He's pretty nervous.'

She had begun to walk away but turned, walking backwards now. She raised her eyes skywards and shook her head. 'He's a grown man, Dean, I'm sure he'll be fine.'

***

Maer watched her cross the field, and let out a shaky breath, returning to his thoughts. Seeing her elicited, as always, a confusing mixture of pleasure and sadness. Like every other mortal, she moved through her life with no knowledge of what lay just ahead of her and it was a blessing, this gift of ignorance, since her loss was not something he had the power to prevent no matter how deeply he wished otherwise.

Tom's fate was already sealed but if Casta's plan worked his body would live on. Of course it couldn't be allowed to remain here, not with a stranger inside it; Richard would have to go back to America, and, if his mind miraculously survived the trauma intact, he would not take a great deal of persuading. Laura must be led to believe her brother to be dead, and her grief would be crippling but at least her own sanity might be spared. It was small comfort, but Maer had to take what little he could from a terrible situation.

He had not accompanied Richard to the school, that was another lie. Since Gilan was nowhere to be found he had spent some time this morning watching Riley himself and it had not made for happy viewing: the man was close to the edge. His mind in turmoil as he unconsciously battled his intruder, he would stop in his tasks and stare fixedly into the distance, but it was impossible to tell what he saw.

He had stood in his workshop earlier, the door wide open, his hands hanging limp at his sides. Then, guided by Loen's curiosity, he had reached out and brushed his fingers across the teeth of a small, extremely sharp saw hanging on the wall. He showed no sign of pain, or even awareness of what he'd done, but Maer saw the blood drip to the floor and his own fingers closed tight, and he'd uttered a sympathetic hiss.

At that tiny sound Tom's head swivelled until he was staring, seemingly straight at Maer. Maer did not move. His heart pounded as he saw Tom's blue eyes narrow, then turn back to the shadows of the workshop just as Maer heard footsteps on the lane outside: Laura.

He stared at Tom, frantically willing him to wake. Laura's booted footfalls came closer and Maer heard her at the gate. She wouldn't see him of course, but Tom seemed more aware than any mortal could be of his presence, and if he challenged him he'd have to make himself known.

Then Laura shouted, and Tom jumped. He raised his left hand, staring at his fingers in confusion, and Maer let out a sigh of relief. This time Tom did not hear him although the sound was louder. How aware was he that something was wrong with him?

'Tom! Did you hear me?' *Oh, Laura, don't come in here, don't ...*

'Yep. Thanks,' Tom called back, obviously just as eager to avoid her. He grabbed a cloth and wrapped his fingers in it, and now Maer could see from his expression it was starting to sting.

He needed to report the way it had been Laura's voice that had brought Tom back, reaching a part of him untouched even by the pain of his self-inflicted cuts. This might be significant, or it might simply be the closeness they shared after losing their parents, it was up to Deera to decide but she had best be told quickly, things were moving at a frightening speed now. Maer stepped swiftly around the back of the building and took the little path towards the edge of the moor, so deep in thought he hadn't realised Laura had taken the same path. Caught unawares he had almost cloaked himself before realising it was too late, and everything she said had made him twitchy; by the end of their brief conversation he was convinced she thought him at best simple, at worst rude, but hopefully not in any way sinister.

He watched her pass through the gate and out onto the main road, and finally, reluctantly, turned away himself. But as his gaze slid away, he started in shock at the sight of a familiar shape at the bend in the path, watching Laura where his own eyes could not follow.

Gilan.

Laura had walked right past without seeing him, but to each other they were as visible as the rocks themselves and he began to appreciate just how unsettled Richard had been to see Gilan, in his guise as Gary Sharpe, appear out of nowhere back in Chicago. He was now certain his uncle had arranged the shooting that had killed Caitlin, which meant he had caused Richard's injuries too: the one sent to protect him had instead almost killed him.

Rage began a slow, deep burn as Gilan smiled with bright good humour, then waved and walked away, following Laura's path.

'Don't you dare ...' Maer breathed, his hands curling at his sides: Laura was under the protection of the Moorlanders for now, but if Gilan found out she was adopted he would no longer be under any obligation to stay his vicious tendencies.

Maer was suddenly very frightened indeed.

***

For a small school, Lynher Mill Primary certainly managed to make its fair share of nerve-shredding noise. Laura knew it would only be a matter of half an hour or so before she tuned it out and was able to think straight again, but for now, as she crossed the playground, she winced at the shrill screams of a group of year three girls, dodging around her as if she were nothing more than an inconvenient tree growing in their path.

The new ones were easy to spot: four and five year-olds in smart winter coats, clutching at their parents' hands. Some of them were already eyeing each other as potential playmates, peeking at each other around grown up legs; others were being picked up and cuddled, tears wiped, promises of teatime treats whispered into small, chilled-pink ears.

As she rounded the building she saw him. He had his back to her and was deep in conversation with the headmistress, but that taut, poised-for-flight stance she had noticed last night was unmistakeable. As dark as Dean was blond, shoulders square under a long black wool coat, he wore the forbidden jeans and black engineer boots but Laura was ready to bet no-one would chastise him for it. His hands were speaking in the air, their movements relaxed and graceful in contrast to that tightly controlled energy - no doubt he was explaining his wonderful plans to Mrs Edwards with a nauseating assortment of buzzwords.

She tucked her head down and hurried towards the main entrance, but she wasn't quick enough: Mrs Edwards beckoned her over. 'This is Richard Lucas,' she beamed, clearly smitten. 'Mr Lucas, this is Miss Riley, our year one teacher.'

'We almost met yesterday, briefly.' Laura took the hand he proffered, and raised her face with a guarded smile. Her first impression was of untidy black hair and very little else, but as he brushed it back from his forehead she was assaulted by the greenest eyes she had ever seen – thick lashed and clear. She barely took in the rest of his features, but was vaguely aware of a pleasant voice uttering random words to which she nodded politely. With an apologetic glance at Mrs Edwards she excused herself to prepare her class. Hell, hell, hell! That was all she needed.

He was a banana skin incident waiting to happen.

Twenty minutes later, on autopilot as the children filed in, Laura instructed them to find a place on the carpet for circle time. While the noise rose and fell behind her and the teaching assistant handed out name stickers, she found herself staring out of the window at the spiked chimney stacks in the distance, her fingers itching to hold her sketchbook and pencil again. She had often felt intimidated by the moor, its vastness, the way it surrounded the little village and her home and seemed to press in on it, but today, *now* in fact, she was fighting the urge to just walk out there, to feel the fresh air on her face, to walk to those mines and touch her fingers to the stone, then to sit down and draw again. Not the city and its bustling life and busy people, but this place, the mossy towers, the crumbling ruins …

'Laura!'

She jumped; her teaching assistant was looking at her a little impatiently. She shrugged her apology. 'Just realised I've wasted the whole summer holidays,' she admitted.

The TA pulled a face. 'Haven't we all? Takes getting locked in the classroom with a bunch of five year olds to realise we really just want to behave like them. Right, first off, Callum has forgotten his dinner money …'

By lunchtime the day had melted back into its usual lump of ordinariness. The morning had passed quickly in the usual blur of mixed up PE kits, games, and squabbles, but the noise made no more impact on Laura now than the bellow of constant traffic would to a lifelong city dweller, and no more thoughts of walking on the moors stole her attention.

She sat at one of the children's tables in her classroom with her lunch, checking through home-school contact books and writing a short welcome note in each. Still looking at the book in front of her she reached for a small wrapped cheese, and her fingers knocked it instead, sending it rolling to the floor.

'Bollocks!'

'Gesundheit,' said a low, amused voice in the doorway.

Eyes fixed on the floor, Laura would have known who it was even without the accent. The banana skin moment; life really was that cruel.

'Typical,' she said on a sigh, and looked up to see

Richard Lucas leaning on the door jamb, a smile touching features that were undeniably, and annoyingly, beautiful. Without the shapeless black coat she could also appreciate the neat physique, all but disguised beneath a casual, loose-fitting denim shirt – she tried again to disapprove of his attire but it was difficult.

'Mr Lucas. What can I do for you?' She picked up the cheese but did not unwrap it, reluctant to eat in front of him. He levered himself off the doorway and came over to sit on one of the small chairs opposite her. Determined not to stare at his face, she fixed her eyes instead on the wide, plain leather band around his wrist, and the long fingers laced on the table in front of him. It didn't help much.

'Miss Riley, isn't it?'

'It is. Are you enjoying your first day, Mr Lucas?'

'It's great!' His enthusiasm leapt to the fore, then adjusted to match her politely distant tone.' I'm sorry to disturb your lunch, but I was wondering if any of your kids would be interested in helping out with the project?'

'Helping out?'

'Yeah. I'm asking all the classes from first grade ... uh, year one, upward. Not a major drain on their time, but we do have certain roles I think they'd enjoy.' He paused, evidently noting her growing disapproval, then shrugged. 'I won't ask you to release them for a couple weeks yet, but maybe you could quietly sound out those who may like to help?'

'I see. How many are you looking at?'

'I guess maybe three or four? I have to ask the other year groups too.'

Five minutes in the door and already he was muscling his way through the school. Laura fixed him with a cool look. 'If it's alright with you I'll let them settle in, *then* maybe get a feel for those who may be most useful to you.'

He sat back, looking disappointed. 'Miss Riley, I think you misunderstood me. I don't want those who're most useful to me, I was asking if you think any of your class would enjoy helping.'

'What happens if no-one wants to get involved?'

'Then no-one gets involved. Likewise if you feel their time is better spent elsewhere. I swear I'm not here to take over.'

She blushed, caught out. 'I never thought –'

'Sure you did.' His extraordinary eyes fixed on hers, and beyond the thick dark lashes that drifted slowly down as he blinked, she saw an absolute refusal to accept the lie, even for form's sake.

His tone remained friendly though. 'I don't blame you, Miss Riley, I really don't. Some outsider – worse, an American – comes into your domain and starts fishing for your co-operation? I'd flat out refuse, but you didn't, so thank you.'

Laura frowned. 'These roles you're looking to fill, are they noisy ones?'

'Very.'

'Then I'm sure you'll be beating them off with a stick.' She liked it when he smiled, his expression softened and he looked infinitely more approachable. She relented. 'We do musical activities on Tuesday afternoons – maybe you could pop in sometime, introduce yourself and what you're doing, and see for yourself if any of them seem keen to pitch in.'

He studied her for a moment. She recognised that look already, it felt as if he were seeing through any veneer of politeness to the raw self beneath. It was unnerving but not altogether unpleasant, and when he smiled again she felt the force of it, of him, settling in her bones and knew she was in trouble.

'That would be great, thank you. I'll stop by in a week or so, after we're all settled and they've had chance to see me around the school a little.'

He rose with the kind of ease that should never have been possible for a grown man from such an uncomfortably low chair. Laura found herself wanting to watch him constantly out of pure fascination, so to distract herself she reached for her drink carton and, as with the cheese, she knocked it flying instead.

Richard's hand shot out and caught it. 'Should've let it fall, if only to hear you curse again.' He grinned as he handed it to her, and Laura relaxed and smiled back.

'Oh, don't worry, I'm sure you'll have plenty of opportunities, I'm good at making a total arse of myself.'

When he'd gone she found herself staring at the seat he'd occupied – was spinsterhood throwing fantasies at her at last? Not one, but two beautiful men had appeared in her life, right at the very moment she'd known she was finally ready to live it. Dean was all languid hands and boneless, catlike elegance, and Richard possessed the same poise, but he had a taut, dangerous edge – the panther to Dean's Siamese.

It was both strange and exciting and, after the eleven passionless years since Michael, something of a relief to know she could still feel this way. She stood up and went to the window. The moor was exerting its pull on her again, and this time she connected Richard's closeness with the feeling, and the thought of it sent a chill through her. It had seemed that, as soon as he was gone from her presence, both this morning and now, she had sought to fill the empty space. And the only thing that seemed to satisfy her need was to drink her fill of the heath. Those bleak, rolling, grey-green hills, undermined by tunnels and caverns that held deeper secrets than most people could ever dream of.

She stared past the playground without seeing it, out into the distance where the engine-house ruins rose against the grey sky. Perhaps life was giving her one last chance; after all these years giving of herself maybe it was time to seize what had been laid in her path – this man.

She remembered the way his voice had hardened when he detected he was being lied to, and how his eyes had glinted. She shivered, and in her mind the moors and Richard Lucas became one entity: wild, beautiful, and potentially very, very dangerous.

***

Richard walked away from the school gates that afternoon with a sense of deep and unexpected well-being. Despite the noise and boundless energy of these kids, much younger than he was used to teaching back home, he felt peaceful, and with that peace came the urge to create. It crept over him like drawing on an old, favourite sweater, almost-forgotten but still shaped to his form, and his pace quickened. In the room at Lynher Rise, fingers plucking tunes from his head and transferring them to his guitar, he was deep in re-discovery and it was a long moment before he realised Dean had come in.

'Hey,' he said, deadening the vibrating strings with the flat of his hand. 'What do you see?' He gestured to the papers strewn in front of him, pencil marks telling the tale of at least an hour's solid work.

'I see someone who really should be thanking me,' Dean said, smiling.

'Thank you. I mean it, seriously.'

Dean flopped across his bed. 'Welcome. You can buy me a drink tonight.'

'Ah come on, you know the bar isn't really my thing. Why don't I get some beers and we can go out on the moor –'

'No!' Dean's voice was sharp, but he went on quickly. 'Most of the school staff will be at the pub tonight anyway, celebrating making it through the first day back. You could do worse than network a bit.'

'*Network*? Are you kidding me?'

'Alright, but you know the kind of thing; get to know them on a personal basis and they'll be more happy to help out. Don't tell me there's no resentment that they gave the job to an 'outsider'?'

'I'm sensing some,' Richard admitted. It'd been tougher going than he'd expected, particularly with the fourth grade teacher who'd been commonly accepted as a certainty for the job. 'You know a guy named Finn?'

'Know of him, but that's all. I gather he was considered for the project.'

'So how come I got it? I never realised I was taking anyone's job when I agreed to this.'

Dean shook his head. 'It was never "anyone's job." Look, you may as well know: the whole project was my idea, okay? Last time I was over I got talking to Mrs Edwards, put the idea in her head, and later she called me up and said she'd got the go-ahead from the board of governors. She had to advertise it within the school, but the truth is, without you there would *be* no music project.'

Richard's pleasure faded; he'd been manipulated and it didn't sit well. Seemed his instinctive balking at the idea hadn't been over-reacting after all, and he'd let Dean talk him round so what kind of an idiot did that make him?

'You went too far, Dean,' he said at last. 'I don't want

to be accused of using an incredible place like this for my own ends, and now I feel like I should quit.'

'What happened to "thank you"?' Dean protested. 'Anyway, you think I did this just for you? I happen to think you'd be good for this school, and for the kids. But yeah, go on, let your pride get in the way of using your talent for something good why don't you?'

Richard's own anger flared. 'What the hell has gotten into you? You go ahead and arrange all this, convince me it's a great idea, haul my ass all the way over here then make me feel like I'm the one dumping everyone else.' He stood up, his guitar held loosely in his hand – it felt so natural there that to put it down would have left him feeling ... unarmed somehow. *Unarmed? Against Dean?*

'I'm sorry you feel like that,' Dean said quietly.

His conciliatory tone cut through Richard's taut resentment and he shook his head. The thought of leaving had given him a painful twist inside in any case. 'Look, it's been kind of a strange day,' he said. 'Good, but strange. So I'll play your game; we'll go to the bar later and I'll try and build a few bridges.'

'This mean you're going to stay?'

'I didn't say I was *going* to quit, just that I felt like I should. Still do. But I can't argue with this,' Richard gestured again at the proof of his renewed faith in his own work, then a reluctant grin found its way onto his face. 'Besides, if I don't stay I'll never see the adorable Miss Riley again.'

Dean blinked.' Laura?'

'You know her?'

'Sort of. We met when I was nineteen, I was over here when ...' He tailed off and Richard saw the connection slip into place on his face even as his own heart contracted.

'When Amy died. Damn, Rich, I'm –'

'It's okay. Go on.'

'Well, I'm sorry.' He glanced at Richard again, then went on, 'Anyway, the day before I flew back to Chicago I met Laura on the moors, she was going through kind of a crisis, That was it until last night. She was in the bar with her brother Tom.'

'Crisis?' He wanted to know everything Dean did about Laura, and felt a mild sting of jealousy as his friend shrugged.

'Not really sure she'd want me telling you. Anyway, we only spoke for a few minutes.'

'And she remembered you?'

'Why wouldn't she?' Dean put on a wounded expression, and Richard was charmed into a laugh.

'So, you guys talk at all?'

'A bit, she didn't stay long. I'd seen her a couple of times since, on trips back, but never to talk to.' He seemed distant, regretful. 'She's lost a lot of what made her, well – sparky. She had some spirit back then.'

Richard thought back to the classroom and the escaped cheese, and his lips twitched. 'Oh, I think you may find it's still there.' He ignored Dean's curious look, satisfied to contribute something himself to the Laura puzzle. He stretched, feeling the bones pop in his back. 'Okay, I'm gonna hit the shower. Then let's go early and eat in the bar; I don't know if it's the same everywhere but if this place is anything to go by, British school meals deserve their reputation.'

As he stepped under the shower Richard found himself thinking back to how things had been at the age of nineteen; the summer the band had clicked and found their sound; the summer of loving and losing Amy.

The summer he'd met that freak show at O'Hare.

Abruptly another memory forced its way through, and

Richard stood still, breathing deeply as the hot water streamed over him. His eyes closed, all he could see was Cait; the blood; the dazzling lights in the ceiling ... there had been nothing more to his recollection: the next thing he knew he'd woken in the hospital and learned he'd failed her. Natural enough the thought of Amy should trigger those memories, but instead it had been the memory that crazy son of a bitch. Why?

For years he'd barely spared a thought for the man, yet now, here, the memory of his name brought Richard out in goose bumps, despite the warmth of the water. 'Sharpe.' The words were swallowed by the splattering of the shower, but as the name breathed across Richard's lips he felt his skin tighten and the hairs along his arms prickled. Even the name seemed to have some unsettling power over him, and suddenly this place didn't feel so peaceful after all.

Chapter Fourteen

Striding the heath in the gathering darkness, Gilan clenched his fists tight enough to hurt as the thoughts twisted and writhed in his pounding head. He had put aside plans – lucrative, if of questionable morality – to attend to the problem with his own people, and who knew when he would be able to take up those plans again? All this would be more palatable had things not suddenly started working in Deera's favour; that she should succeed was unthinkable.

His sister would get all the glory, the decrepit King Loen would rule again, and Lucas would even be granted a new life. Even the queen's precious son would come out of it well: the hero, deliverer of his people, and what would be left for the queen's brother? Nothing! It could not be allowed to happen.

Loen was lying low inside his host for now, conserving his strength in order to take control of his new form. By the time he was released from Riley there would be nowhere to go but into Maer, Gilan would see to it, and then where would the wonderful Deera be with her promises?

As for Lucas … oh, how he wished he'd sliced the throat of that insolent boy when he'd had the chance, or let him bleed to death eleven years ago. That had all been Maer's fault: allowing Lucas to marry, not putting an end to things before they had gone that far. It was common sense, for Thunder's sake! There should have been *no* anchor for the boy in America – once again it had been left to him to sort out the mess, just as he'd had to the last time Lucas had surrendered his heart.

Getting rid of Amy had been easy enough. He'd played

145

the light and shadows just right, and although up close it could never have worked, she had been thinking of the boy, and in the semi-darkness the calling of her name had been all it had taken: she had swum and swum until, exhausted and frightened, it had only taken a brief revelation of his true self and she had panicked and gone under. He hadn't even had to lay a finger on the stupid girl.

The wife though, that was something else again. Caitlin Warner, not as attractive as some of the girls who had thrown themselves at Lucas it was true, but she had possessed a certain charm and the young man had clearly fallen in love with her. Maer had allowed it, even encouraged it, and time in which to undo the mistake was short, but it posed no great challenge to Gilan's determination.

It was so simple even Maer could have done it, and would have, if he had possessed the wit and the fire. Two men, fighting in the back lot of the gas station had been subjected to Gilan's own brand of mild hypnosis: a single glance at the ridiculous amount of money he was prepared to part with had placed them firmly in his thrall. Click, click. Just like that. He had even provided the weapons. So, there she was, paying for gas and food while her new husband dozed selfishly in the car. Perfect.

Except Lucas had somehow sensed something was wrong, and as a result Gilan had had to move equally fast. Too late to stop one of the fools from panicking and shooting Lucas, he had thanked the stars that at least the wife had been hit too, and instinct had initially pressed him to simply walk away. But back then his obedience to his queen had been unquestionable so instead, the concerned bystander, he had knelt and lain his hand on Lucas's chest, leaning on the wound hard to staunch the flow of blood. He had felt the tingle in his fingers as his limited power drew pieces of shattered bone back towards the surface and closed the wound a little. The bleeding eased.

A brief exploration revealed no exit wound, and Gilan rose, enjoying the way the previously arrogant young man stared up at him, recognition and grief battling the pain in his eyes. Pain won and the eyes closed, a groan escaping on his surrendering breath as he slipped under.

Now, as he stalked the moorland, Gilan acknowledged that, personal feelings aside, he'd done the right thing. If he had been the one to allow Lucas to die he would never be permitted to return, and would certainly never be deemed a suitable ruler when Deera was discredited. No, he must appear blameless, set apart from any disaster that threatened the rule of King Loen.

And so he would continue to support his queen in public, and privately he would set about making sure Lucas was unable to come to the moor when Loen was ready. Loen would have the meddling prince Maer's body, and he himself would have the restored King's gratitude – for as long as it was useful.

***

Richard and Dean ducked into the low-ceilinged pub together on the wave of a joke, their laughter bringing curious glances, then smiles, from those nearest.

'Help you?' the barman asked. Dean, more familiar with the place, ordered two pints of lager while Richard looked around, wishing he'd come in here before – it was a beautiful place.

The woodwork was dark and glossy, the back of the bar and a good deal of the ceiling hung with an odd assortment of items: old hunting horns; dark and stained leather tack; tankards; horse brasses; even a heavy, antique-looking farm implement of some kind at the end of the bar near the restaurant area. Along the back of the bar were rows and rows of pewter tankards, photos and newspaper cuttings of local interest.

There was so much to look at he almost missed her.

In fact he saw the man first. Tall, looked to be in his early thirties, maybe a couple of years younger than himself. He stared at the newcomers through a shaggy fringe, his expression set and unreadable.

'That's Laura Riley's brother Tom,' Dean murmured, and then Richard saw Laura herself, standing beside the table with a pool cue in her hand. She met his gaze and held it.

Her hair was tied at the nape of her neck as before, but the exertions of the day had taken their toll and the escaping curls bounced as she blew them away from those lovely, silver-grey eyes.

A flush crept up her neck at the frankness of his stare but she didn't look away, and he couldn't have even if he'd wanted to: he was seeing her curvy figure hunched to fit into the child's classroom chair, her fingers playing with the wrapping of her runaway cheese, her annoyance a tangible thing.

She had seemed stern, almost severe in reaction to her embarrassment, but an undeniably lively spirit had flashed at him from behind the set, polite expression and whatever she was thinking he wanted to know it. All of it. He wanted to sit with her and let her talk until he'd uncovered the reason for the drab clothes and lowered eyes, and he wanted her make her laugh until she was helpless with it, until that sombre reserve was nothing but a wisp of memory.

He felt a cold beer pressed into his hand, and raised it in her direction with a smile. As she smiled back, an expression of blatant, yet sweet invitation, he realised the reticence was already receding, and felt a sudden lifting of the spirit he hadn't experienced since …

Abruptly the feeling vanished and he was left cold and shaken. He turned back to the bar, his jaw tight, his chest tighter.

'What? What's the problem?' Dean hissed.

'I don't know, it's just, I feel …' Richard shook his head.' I'm gonna grab some air, okay?'

'Rich! Finish your drink at –'

'I'll see you in a bit.'

Outside in the windy twilight, Richard pulled the collar of his coat up and walked away from the lights of the village, out towards the standing stones; a few scattered, sloping lumps of granite set in a rough approximation of a circle. As he approached them a chill crept through him that had nothing to do with the weather, but he shoved his hands deeper into his pockets and kept walking.

Roughly at the centre of the circle there was a larger, flatter rock standing at about hip-height, and seeing it he felt surge of revulsion roll in his gut. He was suddenly certain he was going to be sick; a light sweat broke out on his forehead, and he swallowed hard and unbuttoned his coat, breathing deeply until, gradually, the feeling passed. He waited for a moment and when it didn't return he approached the rock and reached out to brush his fingers across it.

Nothing. Weird. He sank down onto the slab, trying to think in a straight line, but each thought took a U-turn back to the same place: Laura.

Okay, so stop fighting it. What was it about her? She was pretty, not beautiful in the way some of the girls back home were but there was something about her, a freshness and honesty that pulled at him somewhere right down inside where there were no words, just feelings. It had been the same way with Cait. His friends had been surprised when they had got together, those who didn't know him as well as Dean and Steve had all said the same thing: you could have anyone you want, why her? But Cait *was* the one he had wanted, with her wide, happy smile, her snub nose and the uptilted blue eyes that had fascinated him with their directness. He had told her he loved her after just a couple of weeks and when he could see she didn't believe him, he vowed to prove it to her every day of the rest of their lives together. And he had.

Except it had all ended just two years later. Richard saw over and over again those eyes fixed on him, wide and confused, a split second before the second bullet had smashed into him and that was the last he had seen of her until the day they buried her. She'd looked so peaceful then, and beautiful, maybe for the first time in her life, but she hadn't looked like his Cait; it was the life in her that had tied their hearts together, and now that was gone. He'd barely been able to do more than glance at her before he'd turned away, the bright agony of grief sending him stumbling from the room.

Richard lay back on the stone, feeling the coldness of the granite through his coat and the wind tugging at his hair and shirt. He closed his eyes and took a deep breath, then let it out slowly, feeling some of the tension drain away, absorbed by the land that surrounded him and the cool night that enfolded him. Vaguely aware of distant sounds; a single car on the road, a couple of cats arguing in the village, the low hum of a distant aircraft, he felt himself drowsing. *Bad idea, Richard, you could sleep the whole night away out here …*

He opened his eyes and looked up through the scudding clouds, and abruptly his heart stuttered in shock. A face: larger than life and bearded, both fierce and fearful, the bushy eyebrows drawn down in painful regret. Without warning, an intense stitch sank deep into Richard's chest at the site of his old wound, and he gasped and half-rose, his hand pressed to his side, trying to breathe slowly – for a second he equated the sensation, not with burning bullet, but with ice-cold blade.

Although half-curled over the pain, his gaze was fused to the vision above him and he saw the face dissolve quickly into another: this one thin, coldly smiling. Richard heard again the almost toy-like crack of guns and recognised the new, narrow cloud-face staring down at him.

Fury obliterated the last of the pain and brought him to his feet. the unsettling feeling he'd had in the shower resolved: now he knew without any doubt that Gary Sharpe had been in the store when Cait had died, bending over Richard with hate in his eyes but healing in his hands, like some bizarre, dark angel of deliverance.

I don't want this situation any more than you do ...

This was too screwed up for words: Sharpe didn't want to help him, yet was compelled to? What was he, some kind of bodyguard? Employed by whom? The questions twisted around themselves in Richard's head, but the fact remained: Sharpe had first arrived shortly before Amy's death, and the last time he had seen him had been in that store, that black August day in 1999. He had to have been responsible for both Amy's and Cait's deaths, and the only connection between them was Richard.

'Christ!' He felt a whole new kind of agony now, one that rose and crashed inside him like high tide, full of guilt and horror. 'WHO ARE YOU?'

Lightning pierced the gloom, striking the moor some distance away and Richard's breath caught at the violence of it. Nauseous again, he bent over, hands on his knees, heart pounding. He was slowly drawing himself to a standing position when he heard someone calling.

'Richard! Hey, Rich, where are you?'

Richard raised a hand and saw he was trembling. He was used to the sensation of helpless fury, but now at last he had a focus; he would find Sharpe, one way or another. 'I'm here,' he said, and was relieved to hear his voice sounding clear and strong as it cut through the deepening dusk.

'Wow, did you see that lightning?' Dean said, coming into the circle.

He seemed strange, faintly ethereal and Richard stared at him, beginning to feel distanced and light-headed again. 'Yeah,' he managed. 'Freaky huh?'

Dean gripped his arm. 'You okay, mate?'

Richard started to nod, then shook his head. 'I feel kinda weird,' he admitted. 'I'll sit for a minute.' He made for the stone slab but Dean pulled him away again.

'Oh no you don't, you're coming away from here and back into the pub. You've just broken that poor girl's heart and you've got some fixing to do. You've been up here long enough.'

'What?'

'You've been dozing up here, idiot. Won't do you any good in this weather.'

Richard held firm for a moment, frowning. Asleep? Maybe. He remembered lying down, but nothing else. He shook off Dean's hand. 'Okay, you don't have to drag me around like some kid.'

'Sorry,' Dean said, and he sounded it.

Richard's anger subsided and he started back to the

village feeling something important may have just passed between them, but his thoughts were still too fuzzy to work it through. 'How strong is English beer?'

'Depends on the drink. Yours was only lager and you barely had a sip anyway. Why?'

'I can't even remember what happened back there.' Richard gestured at the stones receding behind them.

'You're still tired, maybe jet-lagged.' Dean said. 'You were lying on the rock when I first saw you, but by the time I shouted you'd already woken up.'

Richard recalled he'd had a particularly violent and vivid dream after Cait had died, but the details eluded him and he felt only the residue of an unsettling sense of misgiving.

Dean was ripping into him again and his concentration was broken. 'I mean, she gives you a really friendly, even, dare I say it, "come hither" look, and you just walk out? Bloody hell, Rich, you should've seen her, poor girl.'

'Oh, crap.' Richard remembered Laura's stricken face and his stomach twisted in remorse. 'I didn't mean ... it was just that I was ... shit.'

'Well I wouldn't go that far, but you weren't nice.'

'Don't try to be funny, Dean. What the hell do I say to her now?'

'What do you want to say?'

Good question; what did he want to say to Laura Riley? Plenty, he knew that much, but there was something in the back of his mind urging him to keep his distance.

And not just for his own sake.

Laura had watched him go, mortified for the second time that day. First time in years she'd sent a man an openly inviting smile and what had he done? Turned around and run like his ass was on fire. She sat down, her heart hammering, her face hot and pulsing with embarrassment. Tom's eyes narrowed but he didn't say anything, and as soon as a respectable time had passed so it wouldn't look like she was running away, Laura left.

At home the first thing she did was pull the plastic box out from where it now lived, behind the sofa. On top of the pile were the drawings of her mother and, after a moment of aching sadness Laura took out the sketch book that had lain there, untouched, ever since. She flipped open the cover and found a blank page, and with her eyes on the pure white sheet she reached into the box again, fingers going unerringly to the corner where her pencils always rolled, and grasped a stub of HB pencil.

She settled on the sofa and closed her eyes. Her hand hovered over the page, and then his face rose before her, the strong lines of cheek and jaw transmitting from memory to fingers. The pencil moved over the paper with quick, confident strokes and she opened her eyes again, but did not see what she was drawing, only what she wanted to appear. The thick black hair was only suggested, the darkness of brow more apparent, the eyes looking out at her in black and white but their colour vividly painted in by her own mind.

A quick line or two hinted at a faintly smiling mouth, and the open collar of a shirt revealed the wide sweep of collar bone and the smoothly muscled throat. She ran out of paper just below his chest, and her fingers twitched with the feeling she should be adding something, but she didn't know what.

She made herself stop, looked at the picture again, then

groaned and threw the sketch pad aside. What on earth possessed her to bring the image of that raw, masculine beauty into her house? How was that going to help get him out of her mind? And how she was going to face him at work … the thought went hand-in-hand with the need for wine and, after a quick shower, she changed into her night clothes, poured herself a large glass and drank half of it straight down before topping it up again.

Back on the sofa she turned on the TV and made herself sit through Coronation Street before looking at the picture again. When she finally allowed herself to glance down she remembered the feeling of those extraordinary eyes on hers, and her hand shook, spilling wine down her favourite dressing gown. She crossly brushed herself down with a tissue, then picked up the pad again and frowned.

She had always been able to pluck that indefinable *something* out of the person she was drawing, the thing that made them real, and use it to bring her drawings to life. The pictures of Vivien, of the complete strangers she had secretly sketched on the bus to college, even of the imaginary woman in the strange clothes, all had that uncanny touch of vitality. Not so this likeness of Richard Lucas. Thank god. No, it really was a good thing.

She tore the picture from the pad, prepared to scrunch it up, and then hesitated; it had been a mistake to draw it, and it wasn't even as good as her other work, yet despite not wanting to look at it again she couldn't quite make herself throw it away. The thought of it gave her a momentary, superstitious shiver, and abruptly her memory presented her with another image that had made her feel the same way, a drawing made in the aftermath of another encounter.

The two pictures belonged together. With shaking

fingers Laura reached into the box and found the blue folder, and, keeping her eyes averted in case she accidentally saw the other drawing, she slipped the picture of Richard on top of it, shoved the box back out of sight and curled up on the sofa again.

Gradually, as the level in the wine bottle lowered, she allowed herself to think about what had actually happened that night. Not much: he'd smiled, she'd smiled back - and hadn't *that* taken some guts – did she seem too keen then, predatory even? Did she have broccoli in her teeth? Should she have maintained the cool exterior she'd been trying so hard for when she'd seen him at school?

Maybe. But why? She'd seen something reciprocal when he'd fixed her with those wide-set green eyes, and although he unsettled her to some degree, in the end he was just a man. As Stephen King would say: he pulled his pants on one leg at a time. No doubt he scratched his arse too, just like any other man. Just like Michael. So what was it that made her want to disregard the long-familiar voice of caution and reticence, and accept that there was an attraction between them? Then again, when the project was over he would leave, as Michael had left, and she'd be alone again. Maybe she was better off fighting it after all.

Maybe, maybe, maybe.

'I don't care,' she said aloud, 'at least before he goes he can bring me back to life again.'

And that was it. When Richard Lucas looked at her it wasn't like a brother looking at a sister, a pupil at a teacher, a colleague at a colleague. It wasn't even like Michael looking at her in the early days. Under Richard's steady gaze Laura had felt herself coming alive, and more than anything she treasured that feeling, needed to experience it again. Hadn't she felt a long-forgotten sense of adventure unfolding tentative green shoots inside her, just last night when she was out walking Captain? And moments later who had she seen?

Fate: sometimes you had to let it do its thing.

Chapter Fifteen

ichard stopped outside the door of Mill Lane Cottage. Twice he raised and lowered his hand, then finally he took a deep breath and knocked – probably too soft to be heard, which was just as well, he still didn't know what he was going to say.

Partly relieved, partly disappointed, he turned to leave a moment later but stopped as he heard the sound of a bolt being scratched back, then the door jerked open. Laura stood there, sucking at the sleeve of her dressing gown, her grey eyes wide and crossing slightly. She didn't look at all surprised to see him.

'I did it again, you made me do it again,' she said.

'Do what again?'

'I spilled my wine.' She waved her arm at him and the movement seemed to throw her off balance. She grabbed at the door and stared at him. 'Why are you here?'

'I have no idea.'

'Oh.'

Her expression told him he'd screwed up again. When was he going to stop being such a jerk?

'I mean,' he went on, 'I wanted to talk to you, but I have no idea what to say.' *Or whether you'll be too hung-over to remember in the morning*, was on the tip of his tongue, but he bit that part back. In fact he wanted to laugh, and then to gather her weaving, curvaceous form in its ridiculous fluffy dressing gown, lay her on her bed and watch her fall into her dreams with that same smile on her face she'd sent him earlier.

'Why don't you start by telling me why you did a bunk from the pub?' Laura immediately looked horrified to hear herself saying it, and clamped her sodden wrist to her mouth again.

'That'd be a good start,' he agreed, 'and I'd like to try. But it may be easier for both of us if you let me come in?'

'Oh.' This time it was accompanied by a wide, if slightly skewed smile, and she stood back to allow him in.

The room was small, dimly lit, a complete mess, and as close to paradise as Richard had ever encountered. The sofa had remote controls strewn across it, the TV magazine open at today's page, and a collection of enormous cushions that barely left room for sitting. A sketch pad and a tiny stump of pencil lay on the coffee table; mis-matched bookcases, with books piled in every direction sharing space with DVDs, pictures, of wildly varying size and quality, and ornaments from the exclusive hand-made-by-children range: bumpy clay figures with Piccasso-esque features.

A selection of candles burned on the mantelpiece, giving off a warm, vanilla scent and throwing shadows at the walls and ceiling. Richard stood still, drinking it all in, and a feeling of peace and warmth stole through bones he didn't even realise had been cold until now.

'Want a drink?' Laura said. She picked up the empty wine bottle, then gave him a sheepish look. 'Sorry. Coffee?'

'Coffee would be great. But I think I have to say this right now or I'll just say it wrong.'

'You don't have to.'

'No, I do. Back there in the bar, when you smiled –'

'You did it first.'

'Yeah.' He stopped. She wasn't making it easy, just watching him with those huge eyes that changed shade every time he saw them. She was sitting on the sofa now, but he couldn't bring himself to do the same: if he allowed himself to relax in this heavenly room he'd never be able to leave, and Laura being so close was only making it worse. 'I just want to say, I'm sorry for running out on you.'

'So why did you?' She spoke softly, and no longer sounded the slightest bit drunk.

He searched for the words, but it was a struggle. 'You made me feel something I didn't think I should be feeling,' he said at last, but Laura was still bewildered.

'I don't understand. Are you married?' Her face was alternately shadowed and haloed by candlelight, lovely in its earnestness, and he finally pushed aside one of the huge cushions and sat next to her.

'I was,' he told her. 'I can't believe I'm going to tell you all this, but if you're ready to hear it I'd like you to know it all.'

She sat in silence while he told her about Cait. When he got to the final day he felt the horror of it all creeping through him again. 'I knew something was wrong, but I couldn't get there in time. Safety belt was stuck, or maybe I was jerking at it too hard, I don't know. By the time I got there it was too late, they shot her. She died right there, in the middle of the store.'

'Oh, god ...'

'I couldn't get to her, she was standing all alone, with ... with blood pouring down her. If I'd gone in with her like she asked, if only I'd –'

'Richard, don't.' Laura reached out and took his hand.

He shook his head: it felt wrong to be taking comfort from this woman, but her touch delivered a sense of release and he sighed, relaxing at last.' When you smiled at me, I felt something I hadn't felt since Cait,' he said quietly. 'You started something inside me working again. Some ... I don't know, some rusty old mechanism I've left alone all these years.'

'Is that a bad thing?'

'I felt like I was betraying her memory.' A long pause, they were both starting to tense again.

'And do you still feel like that?' she asked at last.

'No.' The word left his mouth on a sigh, and then she was in his arms. Warm and solid, her lips brushing his jaw, her hands slipping around the back of his neck, she was no longer the ghost of a lost love but a living, vibrant new flare of hope. He kissed the edge of her mouth, felt her face turn towards him and her teeth close gently on his lower lip, and as she moved into him the kiss grew deeper, until he was lifting her, turning her so she lay under him.

She found the bottom of his shirt, and then he felt her warm fingers on his skin, slipping around his waist. He sat back, keeping his eyes on hers and shucked off his coat and shirt. She drew him back down to her, and was sweetly hesitant as she cupped his jaw to kiss him, but soon grew bolder and let her hands drift down to his chest.

Then she stopped. 'What's that?' Her fingers rested at the puckered scar midway up his ribcage.

He hesitated, then said quietly, 'I was luckier than Cait.'

Laura drew a sharp breath. 'That's why you couldn't go to her.'

Looking down, Richard could see a new brightness in her eyes, reflecting the flickering candlelight. He needed her to understand. 'Nothing else could have stopped me.'

'No. I don't imagine it could.' She reached up and brought his face back down to hers, kissing first his lips and then his neck, and he felt her burying her face against his shoulder, felt a dampness there as her tears slicked his skin. He didn't want her sorrow, didn't want her to feel his pain, only wanted to obliterate it, and he lifted her chin, rubbing gently beneath her eyes with his thumb. She rewarded him with a trembling smile and slid lower to kiss the scar, sending a powerful current racing through him.

One pull of her dressing gown cord and all thoughts of watching her sleep were torn from his mind; he ran a finger down from her jaw, following the long, smooth contours down across her stomach. Without her shapeless, baggy clothes she was surprisingly slender, yet sweetly rounded at breasts and hips. He rested his hand at her waist and she shivered, and he felt her own hands first on his hips, then creeping towards the button on his jeans.

He helped her, with breathless urgency, then lay beside her and began to explore further. She was more than ready, and with a small sigh of pleasure he rolled on top of her. As his hips moved down and forward, she arched again, crying out wordlessly against his neck. They rocked together, his movements slow and deep until she gave a tiny gasp and tensed; the sudden clench of her muscles around him sent him spinning towards his own release and the room went black around him.

Somehow he held onto her, her name was trembling on his lips but he couldn't speak and he felt her hands tighten on his waist as if she too could feel his weightlessness and was frightened he might float away. When the last tremors had faded he lowered himself to lie next to her, breathing hard, feeling her heart pounding against his chest as she turned into his embrace.

Her hair smelled like the vanilla from the candles and the heavy softness of it brushed his chest as she moved even closer, as reluctant as he was to lessen the intensity, to break away and become separate people once again. His arms tightened around her and he kissed the top of her head, waiting for his heart to slow enough so that could speak, although he didn't know what words might come tumbling past his lips. In the end he said nothing, and neither did she, and after a while he felt her grow heavier in his arms as she drifted into sleep.

Gratitude for having found her swelled in his chest and his heart tightened as, in the flickering glow of the tea lights, he watched her face relax, felt her hand slide off his back so her fingers brushed the back of the couch, and felt her breath against his skin. The sense of perfect rightness at being here, with her, pushed away any hint of guilt at the speed with which they had fallen into each other; there would be no awkward, mumbled apologies in the morning. He closed his own eyes, felt the smile on his lips and let himself slip into his first perfectly peaceful sleep in eleven years.

***

Laura woke sometime in the early hours, aware of the discomfort of a cushion zip digging into her back. The candles had long since burned out but she felt Richard lying beside her, his breathing deep and contented, and the memory of the night wrapped her in quiet joy. She lay very still, not wanting to wake him, but he was evidently a light sleeper. He took his hand from where it lay across her and stroked her jaw with a kind of absent-minded affection, and dropped a kiss on her temple, and she snuggled closer, loving the sleepy hoarseness in his voice as he asked her if she were comfortable.

'Absolutely.' The zips of a thousand cushions digging into her skin couldn't have persuade her to move. She felt him laugh gently, and a moment later the cushion was lifted away. 'Okay. Now I'm comfortable,' she conceded. On impulse she kissed his chest, tasting the light, salty tang of clean sweat and feeling the heavy, slow thump of his heart beneath her lips.

The next time he spoke his voice was low, but urgent. 'Honey, I can't possibly go back to sleep now.'

She smiled, although she wasn't sure she had the energy to even move, let alone make love again. 'Why not?' she whispered back.

'Because I'm damned freezing, that's why.'

She erupted into giggles, smothering them against his shoulder, and he wrapped both arms around her and pulled her on top of him. She looked down, seeing the outline of his features and nothing else. 'I think you're a bit of a turd on the quiet, Mr Lucas,' she said, and he laughed. Feeling his body, lean and strong beneath her own, the smoothly flexing muscles as he moved, she decided maybe she wasn't so tired after all. His hands locked into the small of her back and as she bent to kiss him she felt him stir against her thigh, and his lips curved in a smile that matched hers.

'Let's warm you up then,' she breathed, and pressed her lips to his throat, feeling his deep groan go all the way through her.

Energy was not a problem.

Later she led him to her room where they slid under the blissfully warm duvet, and Richard fell asleep again immediately. She lay awake for a few minutes, trying to pick out the details of his face in the dark, but all she could see through the shadows was the curve of his shoulder and the deeper black of his head. Smiling, she too slept.

Morning threw its grey September light through the thin curtains, she could see it just beyond her closed eyelids. She remained motionless, trying to work out if Richard was still with her, if he ever had been. What a cruel dream it would have been otherwise. But she couldn't hear him breathing ... Her eyes flew open and there he was, watching her.

'*This* is what I wanted,' he said. His voice, husky with his first words of the day, stroked Laura through with a rush of heat.

'What is?' she managed.

'Last night when you let me in and you were almost falling down drunk –'

'I was not!'

'Sure you were. I just wanted to carry you up here and watch you sleep.'

'That was all?' Laura said indignantly.

'At the time, yeah. But the sex stuff wasn't too bad.'

'I suppose it was okay,' Laura conceded. 'Considering I was "falling down drunk".'

He smiled then, and reached out to touched a finger to her cheek, and she turned her head to kiss his palm. She felt his chest rise and fall in a contended sigh as she moved against him. His arm curved around her, holding her close against his side, and she felt she could stay there all day, learning him with her fingers, letting her toes run the length of those strong, beautifully muscled legs ...

'Hell!' She jerked upright and stared at the clock. The intention was there but it took a while to remember how to tell the time, and then she groaned. 'Second day of term and I'll be lucky if I make registration.'

Suddenly she was nervous about letting him see her naked. Last night she *had* been a little drunk – on him as well as on wine – and there had been candles. Candles were kind, and extremely flattering. Now though, there was only the harsh, unforgiving daylight, and her fingers wrapped around the top of the duvet, keeping it close to her chest as she eased to the edge of the bed. She shrieked as Richard whipped it away.

'There. Now I've seen you.' He demonstrated his approval by pulling her back and kissing her, thoroughly and with undeniable enthusiasm, then sat back against the pillows with a sweet but faintly wicked smile. 'Now, you can either lie there with your eyes shut, pretending that if you can't see me, I can't see you, or you can get that timid little ass of yours in the shower.'

'Turd,' Laura re-affirmed, and climbed out of bed. For revenge, she dragged the duvet with her as she went, but Richard lunged after her and pulled it off again, leaving her naked on the landing and helpless with laughter.

***

Maer waited at the mouth of the mine and looked around, not sure what he expected to see but reluctant to descend before he saw it. He didn't want to be out here today, leaving Richard vulnerable, but there was no doubt where his friend had spent the night and that was something that must be reported as a significant development.

For the most part it was good: with Laura here for him Richard would be less likely to leave his job and go back to America, and of all people, Laura was probably the only one who could drive the shadow of loss from his soul. And Cait would have approved of her.

But just the thought of them together caused him physical pain. For Laura he would have given up his longevity and grown old with her as a mortal. He would have left the moor and let his true nature wither and die to be with her – and he would do the same to protect Richard if he could.

But he could neither be with Laura, nor could he save his friend's life. He loved them both, and he loved them equally, and he was going to destroy them. He felt like screaming his impotent anger at the skies as legend said Loen had done, and that despairing part of him would have welcomed the same deadly result.

To encourage Richard had been one thing, letting him know how he had hurt Laura last night just by the act of his leaving, but as Richard had faced the little cottage on the hill Maer had found himself torn: half of him wanted Laura to turn him away, to spare them all this twisted tragedy. But when Richard did not emerge from the cottage Maer had returned alone to the bed and breakfast, telling himself that, of all people, Richard deserved this short burst of happiness before the chance of it was wrested from him forever.

This morning Maer stood against the chimney stack, preparing to pass on this news, and still something kept him above the ground. It wasn't until he glanced behind one last time that he understood his own instincts: the thin, nimble-footed figure that appeared on the horizon was as unmistakeable as it was unwelcome.

Gilan had never been one to walk for simple enjoyment of his environment, there was no doubt he was up to something but Maer had no idea what, or how to find out. It was a worrying thought. He stood still, trying to blend into the stone itself as Gilan passed in the distance. The temptation to track him was strong but it would achieve nothing if Gilan knew he was being followed: he would almost certainly divert to some innocent activity. Better to hope it was something on his own crooked agenda and nothing to do with Loen and Richard, although the hope was a hollow one.

More importantly, with Gilan out here no-one was watching Tom. Maer left the mine and moved quickly back towards the village: the man must not be left alone, not now the time was so close.

***

Gilan found who he was looking for after a satisfyingly short search. He hadn't lost his touch then, no matter what his sister thought of him. It was part of what made his illicit dealings with the coastal elementals, the trigoryan an arvor, so successful and it galled him that, yet again, he wasted time trying to clean up Deera's mess. But it would work to his advantage in the end.

He sat down by the entrance to what the locals now called Lynher Mill Barrow, an ancient burial mound set high on the moor, and waited. After a short while he heard movement behind him and turned: Jacky Greencoat hesitated beside the entrance to his hiding place and looked at Gilan with a mixture of fear and defiance, but he dropped his burden of plants through the gap beneath the stone lintel as if they were suddenly too heavy to hold. Or perhaps he was getting ready to run? But no, even he wouldn't be so stupid.

'I need to talk to you,' Gilan said. Greencoat nodded miserably. He'd obviously been expecting something like this, and Gilan felt a little cheated: being second-guessed by a lowly spriggan wasn't flattering. 'Not out here,' he added, waving his hand to encompass the open space around them. Without checking to see if Greencoat was following, he led the way up over the slope and away from the barrow, wondering if that little fool Maer had stopped playing hide-and-seek yet.

He suppressed a laugh at the thought of his nephew, standing against the side of the chimney as if he could remain hidden – maybe it was worth taking off after Lucas while he was unprotected? But things had gone too far here and he was too visible now, only someone below the sight-line of the Royals could bring about the failure of Deera's plan.

And who better than little Jacky Greencoat? His guilt alone made him the ideal choice: he would do his utmost to redeem himself in the eyes of his queen, and as long as he believed Gilan to be working in her interests he would obey without question. Besides, with any luck Lucas would get himself splattered across the nearest road like his parents and save them all the bother of doing it for him.

'Come with me.'

Maer was nowhere to be seen as Gilan led Jacky into a wide, natural hollow surrounded by yellow dwarf furze. He knew the prince wouldn't waste time following him up here, being the little goody golden shoes he was, he'd probably gone off to watch over Riley instead since Gilan was shirking his duties.

He settled himself into the grassy hollow, taking his time over it and enjoying the fact that Greencoat's nerves were, by now, stretched to breaking point. 'Your actions have caused us great distress,' he said at length.

'Yes, sir,' Greencoat muttered.

'However, there is a way you can redeem yourself.'

'Sir?'

'As you know, your queen is planning a way of giving Loen the body of the mortal Richard Lucas.'

'Yes, sir, I was the one who told her –'

'She must be stopped,' Gilan snapped. Why couldn't the spriggan just shut up and listen? His simpering was starting to rub away at Gilan's thin layer of patience but Gilan's words halted his anxious babble. The eyes were wide in the ugly little face, the effect almost comical, but Gilan had little time and even less tolerance. 'If Queen

Deera succeeds, it will bring about the downfall of our race.'

'But, sir –'

'The plan is dangerous!'

Greencoat shrank back, then sat down abruptly on the ground, pulling his head down into his skinny shoulders. 'That body is too human,' Gilan went on, more quietly now. 'Loen will have no more success with it than he is having with Riley. He means to destroy Riley as the last descendant of Ulfed, but what will he be left with? No. He must not take over Lucas, and yet Deera will not listen to reason. The only way Loen will be able to rule safely is if he were to take over a full-blood faery.'

'Y-you, sir?' Greencoat sat up straight again.

Gilan stared at him for a second, then uttered a short laugh. 'Me? I'm loyal enough, never doubt it. But since there is a perfectly good, strong and above all *young* body available, don't you think that would better suit your king?'

'Are you speakin' of Prince Maer, sir?' whispered Greencoat, his expression twisting in terror.

'That same, yes. And you, Greencoat, will have the chance to make up for *your* terrible failure by ensuring Deera also fails. It is for her own good, and that of our people.'

'But he is her son –'

'And I am her brother! Do not forget to whom you speak. And do not underestimate Loen's faith in me: when he rules I will be his chief advisor, and as such I will have the power to secure his forgiveness. Or otherwise.'

He could see his threat had hit home and Greencoat sat quietly, his hands jammed hard between knobbly knees, the ragged ends of his dusty trousers shaking along with his legs.

Gilan leaned in close. 'Deera must not know of my part in this,' he said in a snake-soft voice, but his eyes were hard as granite as they bored into Greencoat's. 'It must be seen to be a failure of her plan and nothing more, nothing attributable to any one of us. Even you. Lucas must either leave the moor forever, or die. Either way, spriggan, see to it.'

'W-what of the girl, my lord?'

'That is no concern of yours, now go.'

Watching Greencoat's retreating form, Gilan knew he'd done the right thing, and his mind turned to the moment to come, when he presented the king with his first gift to celebrate his new reign. Loen's curse would come to pass after all; Ulfed's line would die at his hands, with Laura Riley.

Chapter Sixteen

Tom flexed his fingers, and winced; one day and night hadn't helped much. The cuts were minor enough, but he used his hands a lot so there had been little chance for them to heal. As for how it had happened … he ran his fingers under the tap, washing the dried blood away, and patted a piece of paper kitchen towel to the cuts. As he applied fresh plasters he tried not to think too hard about the fear that had clawed at him as he'd come to his senses in his workshop, but oh, dear God, he'd been breathless with it. He had swayed, dizzy, and gripped the edge of the workbench. *How had he got there?*

He had no recollection of even dressing himself. He'd been in his own bed, deep in some dream – no, not just some dream, *that* dream: the underground cavern and the man in the dusty green coat who had somehow become his servant – and the next moment he was standing there in his workshop, bleeding and confused.

Now, in his brightly lit kitchen he knew it to have simply been sleepwalking; it'd happened before when he was particularly upset or tired, and something about that Dean bloke in the Miller's Arms had definitely unsettled him, probably because the last time he'd seen him they'd been out there in the garden tending to his dying father. Time had seemed to have got away from him then too.

But even so, if he'd managed to dress himself, descend the stairs, go out to the workshop and open up, all without so much as a stubbed toe, how had he managed to cut three of the fingers on his left hand? Ragged cuts too, more like the skin had torn …

Tom's vision abruptly narrowed and he dropped the first aid tin. He left the kitchen on shaking legs, and the path, so familiar to him, was like a foreign country now as he followed it around to the side of the garden. He dragged open one of the workshop's double doors, snapped on the light and slowly walked to where he'd come back to himself yesterday morning. Then he looked at the wall to his left.

Hanging neatly on matching brackets was a selection of saws of varying sizes. Tom stretched out his left hand, turned it palm up, and the bandaged fingers hovered, trembling, below the teeth of the smallest and sharpest of them. The serrated edges were flecked with dark brown.

Tom moaned, a soft, wounded sound. If something like this could happen, if he could inflict this kind of damage on himself without waking, what was he capable of doing to others? Then a chill swept down his sweating back: he already had, hadn't he?

Images of lightning, of burning circles in his child-palm. A school disco. Laura, distraught, returning home with tales of betrayal: Michael, the boy she liked had chosen Jane Farmer, her best friend. She had told Tom about it, and that night Michael's house had caught fire and been destroyed.

Kelpie. Driven to terror by the storm – her death, his fault. At ten years old the knowledge had sat, troubled yet manageable, in his typically flexible consciousness, and as he'd grown older other, more pressing matters, had thrown casual layers over it, not banishing it but hiding it at least.

Now those layers were starting to slip. Something was tugging at the edges, forcing light to fall on what, even if it must be endured as a child, should have lain in shadow forever after. And Tom Riley stood in his workshop, his eyes closed, breathing deeply through his nose, his mouth firmly shut against what must only be a scream if he were to let it out.

***

'Think we should arrive together?' Richard said as they approached school.

The playground was empty, school had started, but Laura had the feeling neither of them would be reprimanded by Mrs Edwards today . 'I don't see why not. We're both young, free and single.'

Richard grinned. 'I was hoping you'd say that.' He kissed her, cupping her jaw with both hands, and her own face felt small and fragile with those long fingers framing it. She loved the feeling of being cared for instead of being the carer.

Later that morning she heard him singing, allowing himself to be all but drowned by the off-key but enthusiastic bellowing of around twenty ten and eleven year olds She listened, smiling; personal feelings aside and no matter how convenient an appointment Simon Finn would have been, he could never have got the kids so utterly involved on only the second day – those year six children were heart and soul behind Richard Lucas. As was she.

At lunchtime he caught up with her in the playground. She munched her apple and kept a watchful eye on the children, but her thoughts were spinning and they were not good. Not anymore.

'Hey.'

She turned. He kept his distance and was looking as troubled as she felt. Her heart froze, and he seemed to sense her fear and stepped closer, touching her hand, wordlessly telling her he had no regrets. Still, the piece of apple she had just swallowed seemed to stick in her throat, and she felt her eyes watering.

'We have to talk,' he said. 'Maybe today, after –'

'Mr Lucas! Mr Lucas! It's Carly's birthday and I'm going to her house!'

'Yes, can you come to her house for tea?'

'*I'm* going to be ten next month, can you come to mine too?'

Richard kept his eyes on Laura and she nodded, her stomach still knotted despite the tenderness of his touch.

Eventually he had to turn his attention to the group of girls who tugged at his coat. He smiled. 'Carly's birthday, huh? Awesome. Happy birthday, Carly.'

'Can you come?' Eager, breathless little voice, and Laura wished with all her heart she could change places with Carly, to be that young again, with an innocent crush on a handsome teacher, to sigh over pictures and a scribbled signature on a piece of schoolwork.

'It sounds so cool and I'd love to,' he was saying in regretful tones, 'but I have a lot of work to do. I have to write some more songs for you to learn, and besides, you don't want boring grownups at your party, spoiling the fun. Tell you what though, why don't you save me a piece of cake?'

The group scampered away, giggling. Laura had used the break in conversation to take a few deep breaths, and felt more under control. It had only taken a couple of hours of separation to bring reality crashing down around her ears and she could tell he'd been thinking along the same lines: this could never last. He was going to leave at Christmas. What had she been thinking?

'I'll come by your class when school's out,' he said. 'Maybe we can take a walk?' She nodded again, not trusting herself to speak, and felt only relief when the whistle blew for afternoon school.

All afternoon Laura felt mildly nauseous. She tried to fix her thoughts on the way it had been last night, and even more so this morning, when there was only tenderness and laughter between them, but all she could see was the bleakness in Richard's eyes when he'd come to her at lunchtime.

Still, the need to hear his voice again was so strong she had to make an excuse to walk near his room. Perhaps if she hadn't she would have accepted that bleakness, and matched it with a resignation of her own, and in time maybe she would have forgotten how he'd made her feel in the space of one day, and one indescribably sweet night. Perhaps she'd have just found the strength to let it go.

But listening to him, talking to those kids with earnest and honest enthusiasm on the other side of that door, changed everything. His voice was like oxygen to her. Never in her entire life had she been hit this hard, not even by Michael. Richard had come along for a reason, woken her from a long, dull, dreamless sleep she hadn't even been aware she was in. He had touched her, loved her, and brought her to vivid, explosive life again; that wasn't something she was going to throw away so easily. And it flowed both ways between them, she hadn't imagined that.

She went back to her own classroom, holding the sound of him in her head and the memory of his laughter in her unburdened heart. Her mind was made up, and for what may have been the first time in her life she felt absolute certainty in her decision. She was going to fight for this, for him, and she was going to convince him she was worth fighting for, too.

At the end of school, when the children had gone and Laura was tidying books and chairs away, he appeared in the doorway, still looking anxious and unsettled. She put the last of the chairs upside-down on its desk and turned to him. 'Right, now we walk,' she said, hoping she sounded stronger than she felt, 'and you can talk.'

Outside it was breezy, but Laura didn't bow away from it, she needed the wind on her face. She looked straight ahead as they walked, waiting for him to gather his thoughts, to form them into words. She steeled herself against what he was going to say, ready to counter it with her own arguments, but when he did speak it was so sudden, and so blunt, she stopped dead.

'I love you, and I'm not going back to America,' he said.

She stared at him, and didn't even realise her mouth was open until he gently pressed it shut with one finger. Then she noticed that finger was shaking, and so was the hand he quickly took away and shoved into his pocket. His usual poise and confident, fluid movements had temporarily deserted him, he stood in the road like a nervous child, but his eyes were fixed on hers in something suspiciously like defiance. *I've said it, now what are you going to do about it?*

'Um, good,' she said at last, 'that'll save me getting a passport.'

'What?'

'Well, I spent most of today trying to work out if I could bear to say goodbye to you,' she clarified patiently, 'and it turns out I couldn't. So …' She shrugged, and had to fight the urge to laugh as she watched the tension in his face melt into relief: he'd had the same reality check, and they'd each retreated to battle it alone and both come to the same conclusion. So much more satisfying than one trying to persuade the other.

He stepped forward and pressed his lips to her forehead and his hands were steady now, on her

177

shoulders, but his voice shook instead. 'You realise this is completely insane after one day?'

'Little bit, yes. And do *you* realise I don't know anything at all about you?'

'Same here. Must just be lust after all,' he said in regretful tones.

'Damn. Is lust worth moving to England for though?'

He tilted his head, considering. 'How about we try it one more time to make sure?'

'I suppose it's only sensible,' she said. 'After all, if you're going to give everything up for such a shallow reason, you need to be sure you're going to enjoy it.'

His smile lit the afternoon, and he took her hand. They walked out of the village, following the natural, tourist-flattened path towards the mine ruins and Laura noted with pleasure and relief that he seemed completely at home here.

'So what do you do, you know, for fun?' he wanted to know.

She hesitated; no-one else knew of her pictures, not even Tom. The only people who'd cared were dead now but she was ready to let someone else in, and who better than a man who understood the urge to create as he did?

'I used to draw,' she said, 'but I haven't for a while. Until last night. And get this, sometimes what I draw comes to life.' He looked blank, and she told him about the picture she'd drawn of him. 'Then an hour later, who turned up at the door?'

'Wow, awesome. Actually I remember seeing your sketch pad on the table. Maybe you could draw me a nice big pizza. Extra pepperoni.'

'Good idea.'

'Can I see some of your pictures sometime?'

Laura nodded. 'You'll be the first in a very long time.'

He looked as if he was about to throw a casual 'cool, I'm honoured,' kind of comment, but then he caught sight of her face and realised how important it was. 'Thanks,' he said quietly instead, and pulled her closer and they walked in silence for a little while.

'Why did you come back with Dean this time?' she asked eventually. 'You never did that before, did you? I'm sure I'd remember.'

He climbed up onto a grassy mound and pulled her up beside him. 'No. I was having kind of a midlife crisis back home —'

'Midlife crisis! What are you, thirty?'

'Thirty-five,' he said, 'but I think I've been middle-aged since I was in my twenties.'

'How come?' Laura could have kicked herself as she saw his expression falter. Of course: Cait. 'Richard, I'm sorry.'

'Hey, don't be.' He shook at their linked hands and she saw the smile was back, if a little sadder.

'So, why this time?' she asked again.

'I hit some kind of a brick wall with my writing. Teaching is great … well, you know that, but what I was doing wasn't enough. There wasn't the scope for creativity and it didn't seem like I was teaching those kids anything real. Any other teacher could do my job just as well.' He sighed. 'My own writing hadn't really worked since Cait was killed.'

Laura thought of her box of drawings, abandoned since her mother's death. 'I'm not surprised.'

'To be honest, I am. I always wrote best when I was in darker place. But losing Cait that way was different. Dean says it's probably guilt.'

'That's ridiculous: you couldn't do anything for her, he knows that!'

'Yeah. And I do too, in my head, but in my heart? That's something else again.' He paused, then let out a big breath. 'It's not the first time I lost someone. My college girlfriend died at a swim party.'

'Oh my god …'

'I wasn't with her, I was with the band back in Highland Park, we had our first live gig. Amy went for a swim after the others left, and they think she must have gotten a cramp, she was right out by the raft but she didn't make it.'

'That's awful,' Laura breathed. 'I'm so sorry.'

'Thanks. Things sucked for a while, then I met Cait.' He gave her a brief smile and she sensed his need to lighten the mood. 'Anyway, Dean told me he was heading home, maybe even for good, and that he'd fixed up this project. I was pretty mad at first, but I let him talk me into it.' He slipped an arm around her shoulders. 'Damn, I'm glad I did.'

'Damn, so am I!'

He grinned and tugged her hair . 'So, are we gonna talk about me the whole time?'

'Yep, you're far more interesting than me. Tell me about you and Dean then, was it like you see it in all those teen movies; you two hanging out with the coolest gang in the school, fighting off the girls, winding up the teachers, winning all the football games?'

Richard laughed and sat on the grass. She sat beside him, leaning into his warmth.

'Nothing like that,' he said. 'To be honest I hardly ever saw him in school. We never shared a class, didn't hang out together much. And in college we had different schedules and I barely saw him then either. I had the band, he had his interests, track mostly.' He shook his head and smiled. 'He was so fast, it was incredible.'

'But you're best mates?'

'Yeah. He'd spend a lot of time at my place during breaks, holidays, stuff like that. He lived with his uncle, and they didn't really get on so I never went there. But my grandparents loved him, and he loved them.'

'Your grandparents?'

'Yeah, my parents died when I was a kid.' Laura squeezed his arm and he smiled down at her. 'It's okay. At least now it is. Now I can just be grateful I had Gramma and Grandpa for so long. When their time came I was already in my late twenties. They'd helped me deal with losing Cait, and then it was my turn to help Gramma cope with losing Grandpa. But there wasn't long between them and I know she wanted to go to him.'

'God, that's so sad,' Laura said quietly, 'but in a way it must have helped. You think they're together?'

'I'm sure of it. I'm not saying they're in any kind of Heaven, that part of my belief is … well, kind of complicated. Not sure I can explain it even to myself. But I'm sure Gramma found Grandpa, wherever it was she went to look for him. And my Mom and Dad went together too. It's better that way, don't you think?'

'Yes, I suppose so,' Laura said, . 'But what about you and Cait? You might have gone together too, but you didn't.'

'No, we didn't.' Richard looked at her with a warmth that crossed the air between them and settled in her heart. 'Fate had something else up her sleeve for me I guess.'

Laura smiled as she remembered her thoughts of last night, before he'd even turned up. 'Gotta love that Fate.'

'So what about you?' Richard asked. He drew her to her feet and they started away from the mine. 'Pretty sure it's your turn to let me into your life a little. I, uh, I know about your father, Dean told me. I'm sorry.'

Laura sighed. 'Thanks. You of all people understand that no matter how much you want to keep hurting, to feel the grief that keeps them with you, eventually it slips – not away, but further down in your mind.'

'And then the guilt kicks in, for not mourning them every day. Hard to know which is worse.'

'Precisely.'

'So what about your mom?'

'She died in a fall when I was sixteen. She was expecting my baby brother. There's another example of loved ones going together.'

Now it was Richard's turn to look shocked. He stopped walking, but she held up a hand.

'We've both been through it, I don't think we need to keep telling each other how sorry we are. I'll stop if you will, okay?'

'Deal,' Richard agreed, and squeezed her hand.

Laura started walking again, it was easier than looking at him. 'Besides, I'm adopted,' she said. 'Turns out my mother was actually my aunt.' She laughed suddenly, for the first time seeing the funny side. 'How Jeremy Kyle is this? And it gets better: I don't know who my father is. Aunt Sylvia couldn't cope on her own, so she gave me to Mum and Dad after I was born. I'm just glad Mum never knew I found out.'

'So where is she, this aunt?'

'She moved to Liskeard I think.' Laura told him how she'd overheard the news, and how she'd come to understand they'd loved her every bit as much as they'd loved Tom. 'And I'd had them to myself for three whole years,' she added.

'Lucky parents, is all I can say,' Richard observed.

'Flatterer.'

'Yeah. Did it work?'

'Always. Remember that, it's useful to know.' She enjoyed his low, throaty chuckle and the tingle it gave her in the pit of her stomach to hear it.

Their walk was leading them back around towards the village. Laura was staring at the sky trying to spot the first star, and only realised how dark it was getting when she looked back down and found it hard to see what lay ahead. At the same time she sensed a change in Richard: he drew away from her slightly, and she felt the chill against her side where he had been. Their conversation fell off and he seemed to be staring at one point in the distance.

Following the direction of his gaze she made out the crooked shapes of the standing stones. 'They can be quite spooky in this light,' she said. He didn't answer. Instead he stopped and turned back to face the way they had come. 'It's okay,' she went on, 'we can keep going, this way leads us back to the village too. In fact it's – '

'No. We'll go back that way.' He sounded different, harsher.

'This way's quicker,' she tried again, and when he faced her she fell back a step. The lines in his face were drawn deeper, cutting dark furrows around a mouth that was no longer mobile and sensual, but a single hard line. His eyes were in shadow, unreadable.

The unformed fear from yesterday breathed through her again, that sense of danger that lit the edges of him, setting him apart from everyone else. It seemed that, right at this moment, he owned the moor. He stood here for maybe the second or third time in his life and he claimed the land and everything on it, including her. He looked as though he might knock her aside without the slightest hesitation if she stood in his way.

Laura's fear quickened as she looked at him. She saw

183

the hard set of his body beneath the coat and of his jaw above it; she saw his hands, hanging at his sides and clenched tight enough for his knuckles to gleam like naked bone in the dusk ... those long fingers that had touched her so gently, with a strength born of love, not violence.

Not knowing she was going to do it, Laura stepped towards him, rather than away as her terrified brain was screaming at her to do. Instead she let instinct take over and reached for one of those hands, and covered it with her own. He didn't look at her, kept his stranger's face towards the stones but, as Laura stood patiently, she felt his fingers open and curl around hers one by one, as if moved by some deeper part of his consciousness.

Heart hammering, Laura reached out with her free hand and touched his cheek. With gentle insistence she brought his face around until he was looking at her, and he blinked and let out a shuddering breath.

'Oh God, Laura ...' He let go of her hand and grabbed her to pull her close, and she could feel him shaking. The buttons on his coat dug into her forehead and cheek, but she didn't care, all she felt was a rush of inexplicable protectiveness. She held him until she could feel his breathing return to normal, and then she led him back the way they had come, away from the stones.

Chapter Seventeen

ichard sat opposite Laura in her kitchen, watching her carefully. She was studying him too, and he wondered how frightening he'd seemed to her, and if it was half as frightening as he'd seemed to himself. He'd tried to explain as they'd walked back, but now, such a short time later he could barely bring the feeling back to mind. She seemed calmer and more relaxed too, maybe the experience was fading as quickly for her as it had for him.

'I'm sorry,' he said again, 'I honestly don't know what happened.'

'Look, it's been a mad couple of days, you're tired, in a strange place. It's easy to jump at shadows out there.'

He shook his head. 'At the time it seemed like something terrible was happening, and afterwards I know I felt like I deserved a good kick in the ass, but I don't feel any of it now, and I can't re-create that feeling. I can't explain it to myself either.'

'Then don't try. I'm not just saying it, it's really fine.'

He sensed no pretence in her calmness, and relief brought a smile to his face. He cleared his throat and lowered his voice to just above a whisper. 'I can re-create other feelings though.'

Her eyes fixed on his, wide and grey, and utterly innocent. 'Prove it.'

Later she lay tucked against his side, her arm across his waist. He curled a stray piece of her hair around his fingers and listened to her slow, deep breathing. Her response to his declaration that he intended to stay with her still made him smile, still sent a warmth winding through him, still lifted his heart. Of course it wouldn't be that easy; his work permit would run out eventually. Maybe in time she'd change her mind, decide to come back to America with him, but for now he was happy to stay here as long as his visa allowed.

'How much of Cornwall have you seen?' Laura murmured, and she sounded so drowsy and content he felt his own sleep creeping towards him, making his bones blissfully heavy.

'Just Lynher Mill, and the road that got me here.'

'So nothing then. Why don't we go somewhere this weekend?'

She pulled herself up until she was resting her hands on his chest, blowing her messy hair out of her eyes.

He pinched her nose shut, just to watch her reaction. Nothing. She was good. 'You going to show me the sights?' He switched to wrapping her hair across her eyes.

'I may do. Or I may just throw you off Land's End, turd,' she grunted, slapping his hand away.

He laughed. 'How can I refuse such an offer?'

Laura snuggled back down, tracing the line of his ribcage down to his stomach and eliciting a delicious shiver. She *was* good.

'It's Friday tomorrow,' she said, 'we can get some leaflets, go for a drink and decide where we want to go,' she said. Then, a little cautiously; 'Are you staying here tonight?' He hesitated, and she picked up on it. 'It's okay if you don't, honestly. I'm not expecting us to spend every night together.'

'I need to talk some stuff over with Dean –'

'I said it's okay. You take up too much space anyway,' she said and he heard the smile in her voice. 'And you snore like a rhino.'

He bent to kiss her. 'And you grunt like a hog,' he told her. 'Can I stay a little longer?'

Her smile widened.

***

Maer watched Tom go back into his house, the workshop closed for the day, the light fading more quickly now as the year crept towards its end. Another day closer; Loen had lain low but he was also, inevitably, another day stronger, the more so for not testing that strength.

Once Tom's light had come on Maer left the little cottage, and walked across the village and up to Lynher Rise B&B. Rather than go inside he sat on the stone wall in the garden, hoping the fresh air would clarify his thoughts.

Trying to put it to the back of his mind was useless, and potentially dangerous. He'd already realised that if it was discovered Laura was adopted she would no longer be under the Moorlanders' protection, and Gilan's field would lie wide open. It would be hard, but timing was everything: the truth about Laura's past must be protected right up until the switch, then revealed immediately afterward.

He jerked upright as the thought occurred: Did Tom know his sister was adopted? If so, Loen would as well. But he wasn't a danger to her yet, Gilan was, and that one was as unpredictable as the wind in his loyalties – who was to say he'd even spare the girl until she could be given to Loen? Maer clenched his hands on his knees: he had to try to get her off the moor.

His gaze fixed on the westernmost part of the horizon, watching the sun sinking lower until the hills had taken it into themselves, and its light was lost. The air grew cooler,

Maer could feel it on the exposed skin of his face and hands, but of course it was not discomfort, merely acknowledgment of the change.

He still longed for the ability to physically experience the change in the seasons, for his body to respond in the same way as the mortals all around him; to hug their clothing tighter, to blow on their hands as he'd watched Richard and his friends do for years. He'd mimicked their actions through necessity, yet he could not feel the effects. In Chicago it had been cold so often, yet he'd never enjoyed the cosiness of a huge sweater and the warmth from the fire. Richard could wrap himself in his favourite coat, cup icy fingers around a steaming coffee cup, and Maer could see the slow pleasure stealing across his face. Maer could do the same, could make the same expressions but with him it was all fake, all show.

More lies.

'Hey, Deano.'

Maer jumped as the voice, soft though it was, cut through his thoughts. Richard pushed open the gate and came to sit on the wall next to him. Even in the shadows Maer could see he was troubled. He didn't say anything, just waited.

Finally Richard took a deep breath and pushed it out on a sigh. 'Something freaky is going on,' he said.

Maer tensed. 'In what way freaky? You're in love?'

'No. Well, yeah. But it's not that. I feel strange here.'

'Here as in England?'

'No. At least, I don't think so. Here as in … here.' He waved a hand to encompass their darkened surroundings. 'I don't understand it, there's something about this place that, sort of pulls me in, and yet ...'

Maer looked at him closely. 'Yet what?'

'Doesn't matter.'

'Rich, come on, you can tell me.'

'Alright, it terrifies me. It repulses me.' Richard said. 'I feel like I need to get away, right now, but if I did I'd need to come back or die. What kind of sense does that make?'

Maer's heart was hammering. 'But yesterday, your writing, your music, I don't – '

'I know! Look, I don't understand it either. And it's not all the time, just now and again I get this feeling, deep down, that something's not right.'

'Not right how?'

There was a long pause, Maer waited with his nerves tightening with every second that passed, reluctant to speak, but barely able to stand the silence.

'Okay,' Richard said at last. 'Laura and I were walking on the moor. We were fine, talking, learning a lot about each other, and suddenly I got this feeling like if I took another step it'd be the last thing I ever did.' He rubbed at the left side of his chest, Maer doubted he even realised he was doing it.

'So what did you do?'

'I wanted to turn back. Laura said the other way was quicker, and ...' He fell silent, in such confused misery that Maer wanted to tell him everything, to explain those feelings and urge him to get out, get away while he still could. But it was too late now.

'You what, mate?' he asked instead.

'I could have hurt her,' Richard said. 'I was mad, felt like I was standing in my own home and someone was telling me where I could and couldn't go.'

'So what happened?'

'I stood there, just staring at those damn stones, and if Laura had spoken again right then I don't know what I'd have done. But she didn't.'

'What did she do?'

'She took my hand.' Richard's voice shook and Maer reached for his shoulder, feeling the rigidity fall away at his touch. 'She made me look at her, and as soon as I saw her it was over.'

'Just like that?'

'Yeah.' Richard sounded exhausted now. 'And there's something else.'

'What?'

'That guy I told you about, back home. Gary Sharpe, remember him?'

Maer's heart lurched. Surely Gilan hadn't been stupid enough to show himself? 'Of course I remember,' he said, calmly enough.

'He was there when Cait died. Right there in the store.'

'Christ, you never told me that!'

'I hadn't realised until yesterday. I know I blocked a lot of what happened. But when we talked about Amy yesterday I guess it triggered something. I finally saw the guy who saved my life. Sharpe.'

'So your stalker saved your life?' Maer tried to make his tone light but Richard sighed, and it sounded like it hurt.

'There's nothing funny about this. You know what it means?'

'I'm sorry, I didn't mean ... I'm sorry.'

Richard shook his head, staring at his hands. 'If he had something to do with Amy's death *and* Cait's, then they were both my fault.'

'Come on! Neither of them was your fault. Amy got cramp while she was swimming. And I know you feel bad about Cait going into the shop alone, but it would still have happened –'

'No, Dean. He was watching me and Amy before, he knew the place on the lake where we always went to party. Steve warned me and I didn't listen. I'm telling you, this freak, whoever he is, killed both of them to make whatever fucked up point he was trying to make to me.'

'What point? This is mad.' Maer paused, and added, 'And kind of egocentric actually.' He wondered if he should have said it, but the expected angry reaction did not come.

'It looks that way, sure. But you know I'm not one of those people who thinks the world spins just for them. And you didn't see Sharpe. You didn't see the … the *hate* in his eyes.' He stood up and began pacing the garden. 'For some reason he was supposed to be watching out for me, but I could see what he really wanted to do with that knife, and it wasn't to use it as a warning.'

Maer felt sick. Gilan had not only been careless but dangerously provocative. Of course Richard was going to make the connection.

'I've got go back for a while, track him down, find out why he was 'protecting' me,' Richard said, pacing faster now, and Maer caught his arm as he passed.

'You'll never find him,' he said. 'It was eleven years ago. And you think the name he gave you was real? Whatever his plan was back then, whatever his motive, it won't bring Amy and Cait back.'

'You think I don't know that?' Richard rounded on him. 'But how can I just let him stay out there when he's murdered two innocent people?'

'And if you do find him? Digging him out from whatever hole he's in may just make him kill a third!' Dean snapped, desperate now. 'And it probably wouldn't be you. Think about it.' Richard stared for a moment, then the tension left him and he sank back onto the wall. Maer pressed home his point, wracked with guilt at the pain he was causing. 'It wasn't you before was it, Rich? It was someone you loved. Both times.'

'You don't have to spell it out.' Richard's bleak tone told Maer the message had been understood: once more he had managed to persuade Richard not to return to Chicago, Loen would have him after all. Maer felt his own spirit shrink a little more at the knowledge.

***

The next evening Richard met Laura in the Miller's Arms, armed with a pile of leaflets. He was a little pissed to see Tom sitting with her, but he'd have to get to know the man sometime.

He ordered his drink, using the time to compose himself, and then went over and offered his hand to Tom. 'I don't think we met properly,' he said. 'Richard Lucas.'

Tom reached out and, as they shook hands, Richard felt his heartbeat triple-thump but as Tom pulled back, also a little quickly, the sensation passed. It was worse than meeting a girlfriend's parents.

Small talk bounced between Tom and himself in the form of a list of questions: Whereabouts in America do you live? How long have you taught music? What's the name of your band? What kind of car do you drive? And, unspoken but louder than all of it: Exactly what are you doing with my sister?

He tried to convey an honest answer to what had not been uttered, by respectful body language and by his deference to Laura, but he could see Tom's mistrust in every movement, every look. And every now and again he felt a little queasy, and an uncomfortable prickling sensation crept across the exposed skin on his hands, face and neck.

'We're planning on a trip,' he said when the questions had run their course. 'Can you recommend anywhere?'

'Depends what you want.'

'Well, I guess I'd like to see what Cornwall is famous for: beautiful coastlines, history, you know the kind of thing.'

'Land's End.'

Richard grinned, despite the difficulty of the atmosphere. 'We can't go there,' he said, 'she'll probably throw me off.' He reached out, without thinking, and pinched Laura's nose shut. Laura laughed but the next instant Tom had grabbed his wrist and twisted it away from Laura's face.

'Don't you ever lay a hand on her like that again!'

Richard tore his arm away, coming to his feet, and only just stopped himself from hitting the douchebag square in the mouth. 'You ever grab *me* like that again,' he said, his voice iron, 'and I'll knock your damn teeth down your throat.'

The two men stared at each other, Tom breathing hard, Richard barely breathing at all as he slowly sat back down. His eyes were still locked on Tom who was looking at him with a different expression now, maybe he could actually see the anger Richard felt pulsing in his head, maybe it showed in his eyes.

He was aware his looks were deceptive, that his average physique did not speak of enormous power, but over the years he had grown to understand that his strength showed anyway, and that some people just felt compelled to test the quiet, easy-going charm that lay over it, hiding it – until he needed it.

'We can go to Land's End,' Laura said at last, to cut through the taut silence that had descended over their table.

After a pause Richard broke the stalemate, although the challenger in him rebelled: Laura was more important. 'Okay, it's a date.' He stood up again. 'If you'll excuse me,

I think it's my round.'

'Count me out,' Tom said, also rising. 'I've got stuff to do back at the workshop.' Richard could see him drawing himself up, preparing to make a huge effort. 'Sorry I grabbed you.'

Richard nodded. 'Sorry I seem to have gotten off on the wrong foot,' he returned, but they both knew the apologies were empty.

When he had gone, Richard bought two more drinks and brought them back to the table. Laura was looking at him with a strange expression and his heart sank.

'Look, I know I shouldn't have –'

'Yes you bloody should! He was bang out of order.'

'Well you look pretty mad,' he pointed out. Laura took a sip of her drink, avoiding his gaze. She seemed less annoyed now, but still troubled – why hadn't he just taken it with a grain of salt?

'I'm not mad at all,' Laura said at last. 'I just don't understand why he behaved like that with you.' Then she sighed. 'But okay, if I'm honest, the way you just sort of flared up reminded me a bit of last night on the moors. It bothered me.'

Richard nodded, he kept forgetting they'd only just met: it felt like they'd been together half their lives already. 'I don't have anger management issues, I swear.'

'But?'

'But I do have a problem with people treating me like crap.'

'Good,' she said.

He studied her for a long moment, then shook his head. 'You're an enigma, Laura Riley.'

'No, I'm not. I'm your bog standard, average woman whose brother wants a serious kick in the arse. If anyone's going to treat you like crap, it'll be me thanks very much.'

Chapter Eighteen

Early on Saturday morning Laura twisted the key in the ignition with a long-missed sense of freedom. She felt like a child on a school outing as she pulled the car out onto the main road.

Richard sighed. 'Are we there yet?'

She slapped his leg, and out of the corner of her eye she saw him grin, and smiled back.

Last night's strange behaviour was a distant memory, although it was Tom who'd concerned her more. What was his problem, did he think she was going to up sticks and move to America? It was understandable, to a degree, but she'd have to disabuse him of that notion when she got back. For now she was happy to be heading off into the last of the year's dubious warmth with Richard beside her.

He pulled the CD out of the player. 'Laura's driving CD,' he read aloud. 'Rewrite on pain of death. Okay, I'm officially scared now. Who was that little warning for?'

'Michael.'

'Michael?'

'Michael Hart. My first love, childhood sweetheart, all that stuff. He went travelling. End of heart-warming love story.'

'Guy must have been insane to leave you behind. But I'd like to buy him a drink sometime.'

'Oh, you're such a smoothie!' Laura slotted the disc back. They headed down into Cornwall, both singing along with the admittedly ropey music, and Richard didn't seem aware she stopped now and again in order to hear him better; even absently accompanying these old, familiar tunes he sounded incredible, and totally unselfconscious.

She kept stealing glances at him beating time on his thigh and gazing out of the window at everything they passed with deep pleasure. As if he'd come home.

By lunchtime they had explored all they could of Land's End without paying more than the parking fee. Laura dawdled in the little craft workshop, admiring the jewellery and the cat who slept beside the work area, and when she caught up with Richard he was sitting on the cliff, looking out over the sea. Towards his real home, she realised with a twinge of apprehension.

She sat beside him. 'You okay?'

'Very okay,' he said, to her immense relief. He put an arm around her shoulder. 'I was just looking out there, at how wild it is.'

'You like it here?' Laura leaned close, and he opened his coat and wrapped it around them both.

'Hell yeah. This coastline is incredible. I mean, look at that spray.'

Laura followed his gaze along the headland to where the sea crashed against the rocks, sending up a white curtain she could almost feel on her skin. Seeing it through his eyes she began to appreciate all over again what she'd grown so accustomed to over the years, and for a while they sat together in easy silence, listening to the roar from below.

'It's getting cold,' Richard said at last. 'Want to head inland and show me someplace else?'

'You've seen all you want to see here?'

'This is what I wanted to see, the wild part. The old part.'

'Excellent, that'll save us about a million quid. We can afford to go and get lunch somewhere,' Laura said, getting to her feet. She missed the warmth of Richard's coat around her, but getting back into the car was almost as good: she hadn't noticed how cold the wind was out there on the cliff.

She started the engine. 'Where do you want to go?'

'You're the boss, surprise me.'

'That's how bosses behave where you come from, is it?' Laura asked as she drove out of the car park. 'Come to think of it, what was your boss like, back in Chicago? Anything like Mrs Edwards?'

'There were certain ... similarities,' Richard conceded and, glancing at him, Laura was surprised to see a faint blush. Then it clicked.

'Oh God, don't tell me your other boss fancied you as well! Was she a crusty old warhorse too?'

'No, he was a little younger.' Richard grabbed the wheel as she began to laugh. 'Watch where you're going, you'll get us killed!'

'Sorry, but that's priceless!'

'Ha ha,' he said darkly, and tapped the dashboard. 'Eyes on the road, missy.'

They stopped in Penzance for lunch, taking their fish and chips down by the harbour to eat. Laura found herself kicking her feet against the wall they sat on, like a child. But looking sideways at Richard as he gazed out over the water she felt anything but childlike. His eyes caught the rays of the sun and fired them back out to sea, their vivid colour enhanced by the raw daylight, and when he tipped his head back to watch the gulls circling greedily overhead she remembered how good his skin felt against her lips and had to fight the urge to lean over and bury her face in his neck. She contented herself with the promise that tonight she would experience the man again, but today was about the person; about companionship, and about learning one another.

Having experienced the passion that ran deep in those beautifully structured bones, she was now discovering that that passion was not just for physical love but also for life. For fun. They'd spent an hour poking around ruins and rock pools and he'd thrown a lump of seaweed at her yelling, 'Look out, it's alive!' Her instinctive shriek and dance away had doubled him up with laughter, and he didn't even stop when the same piece of seaweed had found itself stuffed down his shirt thirty seconds later.

'Bude,' Laura announced as they arrived in the North Cornwall town. 'Origin of, um, Budey things.'

'I hear they're looking for tour guides around here,' Richard said as he shut the car door. 'Sounds like it could be your kind of job.'

'Smart-arse. I haven't been here since I was about six!'

'Some excuse,' Richard grinned.

He fell silent as they walked through the town and she thought he might be bored, but looking at him she saw only deep fascination with every detail of the place. Inside the small museum by the canal, he showed an even more intense curiosity. Laura watched as he moved between exhibits, reading all the plaques, missing nothing.

'Hey, look here – it says a whole bunch of Cornish miners emigrated to the States in 1770 to work there.'

'Don't blame them,' Laura said, 'although one hole in the ground must be pretty much like another.'

'Says they went to work the copper mines at Lake Superior.' He looked at her, his eyes widening and she could actually see his thoughts arranging themselves. 'That's pretty close to where my family is from. This may sound a little weird, but what if I'm descended from one of those miners?'

'You think that might be why you feel such a strong pull to this place?' Laura came to stand beside him. 'It would make sense, you may have heard stories as a kid that you'd forgotten about but are still in your head. Is there any way of finding out?'

'No-one I can ask directly, but I may be able to track the family back that far on the 'net.' He turned back to the picture board and studied the photos. 'It'd explain why I can't seem to stay away from the mines: something in the blood maybe.' He laughed suddenly, a relieved sound. 'Racial memories! I was never certain they were real, but this makes so much sense now. I thought I was going nuts!'

The puzzle resolved in his head, he talked excitedly most of the way around, taking an even deeper interest in the displays. But when they reached the civil war section he seemed to retreat from her again. He stopped before a stand that allowed visitors to measure themselves against the height of a local civil war hero. Laura watched him as he studied the pictures, frowning.

'I've heard of this guy,' he said.

Laura came over and read the notes. 'Anthony Payne? I haven't, and I'm English. Bad, bad teacher. He's a bit tall isn't he?'

'Says here over seven feet, not something you'd forget. But the name seems familiar too.'

He wandered off, peering closely at the displayed artefacts, running his hand over the protective glass in front of a selection of weapons, and as he reached a display of armour his fingers clenched shut in a fist and his expression tightened. She thought she saw him mouth a word; 'Useless.' Then his hand dropped away and he looked at her, unfocused at first, as if coming out of a daze.

'Sorry, got caught up there for a minute. Look, I could use some air, you ready to head out of here?'

'Good idea,' Laura said, unsettled. 'It's time we started heading back home anyway, traffic'll be getting heavy soon.'

Richard was quiet on the drive back; he replied to Laura's questions and observations but she soon fell silent, sensing his need to think. It obviously pleased him to think his roots were here, and the idea warmed her too; it seemed to anchor him there by her side more firmly somehow, as if it would be harder for him to leave.

Why should he leave anyway?

Because I don't want him to.

You know he doesn't want to either.

Neither did Mike, at first.

Richard is different, he'll –

'... Never leave you.'

The voice followed her thoughts so closely it took a moment to realise he'd spoken aloud. She looked away from the road for a moment, his eyes were fixed on her face, and now they had lost their excited spark they were gentle again.

'Promise?' she said, and it came out as a whisper.

'On my life.'

'Don't –'

'Come on. Looking at your face back there, Laura, you were already saying goodbye. If you've changed your mind, I think you should know I'm a very difficult guy to get rid of.' Relief lifted her mouth in a grin, and she allowed the car's speed to increase again. 'Unless you get us both hospitalised with your driving,' Richard amended,

200

'in which case I'll sue your ass from here back to Chicago.'

***

The bar had the usual Saturday evening buzz going on. Tom waited for the landlord to finish with his order, one ear on the man's amiable chatter, the other trained behind him on the corner booth, where the regular group from the primary school had been joined a short while ago by Dean Mayer. Tom wondered if he would ever grow out of the feeling he was still ten years old when confronted with his old headmistress, and decided probably not: barely more than half Tom's size, where years ago she had towered over him, it still felt as if her eyes were boring into his back demanding to know where he'd hidden her board rubber.

Mrs Edwards and her husband met these other teachers in the pub most weekends, and seeing them engage Dean's attention the moment he'd come in, Tom couldn't help but wonder what they could possibly have in common. He'd soon found out when he heard his sister's name floating across the usual bar noise.

'It's only a matter of time of course, she's a bright young thing. Needs to spread her wings though,' Mr Edwards was saying now. Tom heard the others murmur their agreement and felt his defences prickling. Was he saying this place wasn't enough for Laura?

'I can remember yonks back, when she told me she was going to look for jobs in Plymouth,' Mrs Edwards put in, 'Her and young Michael were full of the idea. I reckon she would've done it too, if it hadn't been for –' Her voice was cut off short; Tom could almost see the urgent thumbs being jerked in his direction.

He picked up two of the drinks he'd ordered and,

turning to hand them to his pool partner hovering at his elbow, he affected to notice the embarrassed group in the corner.

'Andrew, Claire, Mrs Edwards, Mr Edwards, Dean.' They nodded and smiled back, and Dean raised a hand in greeting.

'Where *is* Laura tonight?' Mrs Edwards asked. Evidently she realised there was no point pretending they'd not been discussing her.

'Out for the day,' Tom said, trying to disguise his sourness.

'She's taken Richard to Land's End,' Dean added, 'they're making a day of it.'

'Mr Lucas? Now there's a lovely man,' Mrs Edwards said warmly. 'Are they courting already?'

'Good for them,' her husband declared. 'Never met the bloke, but she deserves a little bit of 'appiness, that one. When I think all the years she's just been wasted here, never really seen her 'appy though, not since –'

This time Tom saw the nudge, and shook his head in disbelief. As he carried the remaining two drinks away from the bar he heard Dean explaining how Laura and Richard were just friends. He didn't believe it for a minute.

The pool table was ready for a game of doubles, and Tom's annoyance, and the resultant large gulps of his beer carried him for the first few shots, but his mind drifted as play passed to the other team and he started to wonder: did the whole village think Laura was just wasting away here?

He leaned on his cue, and tried to remember back to when Michael had left. How had Laura been? A bit miserable, which was only to be expected, and of course, later that same day there had been the shock that had wiped out everything else.

But then what? Had Laura really planned on leaving until then? Why hadn't she gone with Mike on his travels if she wanted to get out so badly? But it was different and Tom knew it; he thought about conversations they'd had, and with a lurch of dismay he acknowledged that yes, Laura probably would have left long ago if their father had lived. A flash memory took him back further, to the day the vicar's dog had died. Hadn't she said then she would never stay here in Lynher Mill? As if the very idea was preposterous and it was a given she'd move to the city someday –

'Riley!'

'Sorry.' He moved in to take his shot, but skimmed his cue off the side of the ball and gave the winning two shots to the other team.

'Fuck's sake, mate,' complained his partner, 'what planet are you on?'

'Away with the fairies!' his opponent laughed, as he lined up on the black. 'Top right.' The ball rattled into the pocket. 'Geddon! Nice one. Cheers, Tom.'

'I'll see you later,' Tom said, and downed the last of his pint. Shoving the door open he took a deep breath of chilly evening air, letting the breeze carry away the Saturday night noises from the pub as the door shut behind him.

He crossed the car park and sat on the wall, and this time he didn't have to concentrate to remember. He saw clearly how Laura had been during the afternoon immediately before their father's stroke: chirpier, brighter, more animated than she had in ages. She had come to a crossroads, reached her decision, then left himself and his father arguing, over what he still couldn't remember, and later she had come home to the bewildering, heartbreaking news of Martin's heart attack.

Another crossroads. Again she'd chosen her path, but this one had led to a long narrow road that was taking her further and further away from where she wanted to be. And he'd simply accepted her being there all this time. When nightmares brought him to shuddering wakefulness, and a hand reaching for the phone could have her at his side in ten minutes, it didn't seem to matter so much that he himself couldn't leave the moor.

But she'd changed: her fire had fizzled and gone out, she'd let go of so many chances and with them her newly rediscovered exuberance. Until now. The whole village must have been talking about it for years. And now the realisation sent fingers of guilt snaking through him, replaced quickly by defensiveness. He'd never asked her to stay!

Right then, it was time to make it clear, to her and to everyone else in this nosy sodding place, that he'd never asked her to give up anything for him. He didn't need her to play the martyr, to make all these oh-so-noble sacrifices: if she wanted to leave she should bloody well leave, and let him get on with things – he didn't need her anymore.

He raised his head from his moody contemplation of the ground as a car approached. Laura's. She drew to a stop outside the shop on the other side of the square and Tom frowned as he saw the figure of Richard Lucas emerge from the passenger seat. At first he thought they were arguing: Laura's voice was raised and he heard the words 'Bog off!' quite clearly, but as she slammed her own door, her laughter rose and was joined by his, a low, pleasant sound that nevertheless grated at Tom's nerves.

They went into the shop and Tom waited, unsure how he was feeling, not wanting to blow into their path and cause an upset before he really knew what it was that was annoying him. Was it Lucas himself? If so, why? He didn't seem to be causing Laura any upset – quite the reverse in fact. Maybe it was this further proof she had a life beyond caring for him.

But he wanted her to have that! She was his sister, and he wanted her to be happy while she could, after all Lucas would leave eventually, after his little pet project at the school was done, and what then? God, what if she went back with him to America? Tom felt his heart tighten to the point of pain for a split second: feeling trapped could be the one thing that pushed her into leaving altogether, leaving her home, the country, leaving him. And no doubt Lucas would be quick enough to put the boot in, citing the tyrannical brother best left to his own devices.

He thought hard and fast, there was only one thing that might keep her close by; she must be persuaded back into her plans of living and working in Plymouth. Further away than he liked, but better than America – still within reach.

The shop door tinkled open and Lucas came out carrying a bottle of wine. He transferred this to his left hand to drape his right over Laura's shoulder, and Tom felt himself go taut again as Laura put her own arm around him, then relaxed as he saw her reach past and grab the wine instead. Lucas growled and made a half-hearted lunge for it as she danced out of reach and dodged around the car, putting the wine in through the open window, then stood in front of the door so he couldn't get it back.

Tom knew he shouldn't watch with such fascination, but he couldn't help comparing his own shy and ultimately passionless encounters with the scene before him. Lucas moved towards Laura as she stood, hands behind her and protecting the door handle and her prize, and she stared at him with a defiant tilt to her head. The laughter died, and he touched her cheek with a tenderness Tom could see even from this distance.

He took one more step closer and his body blocked Tom's view, but the long black coat flapped out sharply in the evening breeze, showing Laura's hands surrender their position on the door handle to rest lightly at his waist. The coat dropped again and Lucas dipped his head to Laura's. Tom got quietly to his feet and went back into the Miller's Arms, knowing he hadn't been seen and nor would he be, not by these two who had eyes and hearts only for each other

She had to stay, and so he must make sure she left.

Chapter Nineteen

S unday morning. Laura knocked at Tom's front door and, at his gruff response, pushed it open and dumped two carrier bags of clean clothes just inside. Tom was in the kitchen nursing an enormous cup of coffee. He tried on a smile but Laura could see it took an effort.

'Late night?'

Tom flinched. 'D'you have to shout?'

Laura opened her mouth as if she were going to yell properly, and Tom put down his coffee and covered his ears. Instead she mouthed, 'Your washing's in the hall.'

Tom dropped his hands away. 'Cheers.' He lifted his cup, then grimaced and lowered it again. 'Want one?'

'Not if it makes you pull a face like that,' Laura said, 'I'll make it myself thanks.'

She put the kettle under the running tap and looked for a clean cup, then, switching the kettle on she nodded at yesterday's dishes still stacked on the side. 'Want me to do those while I'm here?'

'Yeah, if you don't ... um, actually no. I'll do them in a bit.'

'I don't mind,' Laura was already rolling up her sleeves.

'I know you don't. That's the problem.'

'Not making sense again, Tom,' Laura said, and smiled, but he didn't return it. He waited until she'd poured her drink, then cleared his throat.

'Need to ask you something.'

'Okay.' Laura sat down and studied her brother. Now he was older she could see Martin in him more clearly, and as the usual ache rose in her at the thought of that gentle man, she forced herself to concentrate on Tom.

'Do you still want to move away?' he asked bluntly

She didn't give herself time to think about what he wanted her to say, his question surprised the truth out of her. 'Yes.'

'Then why don't you?'

Laura stared into own cup as Tom had done, and wondered what he'd seen in his dark, steaming drink: all she could see was a tiny dot of undissolved instant coffee getting caught in the spoon-swirls. Perhaps that was her, getting carried along wherever life took her.

'And do what?' she said at last.

'Anything you want. While you're still young enough to do it.'

'But what about you?'

'I never asked you to stay!' The words were blurted out as if they'd been building behind his lips, just looking for an opening in the conversation, however small. This had clearly been brewing for some time.

She chose her words carefully. 'I know you didn't. I've never made you feel guilty have I?'

'No.'

'And we've had this conversation before. I'm here because you needed me. You wouldn't, or couldn't, see someone else about your problem and so I stayed. What was I supposed to do, just bugger off and let you suffer those nightmares and all that goes with them?' She waved her hand at the mess on the sideboard, the over-full rubbish bin and the dirty laundry stacked ready for her to take back to her cottage.

Then she softened her tone and leaned across to touch his arm. 'Are you saying you don't want me around?'

'No! God, Laura no. I just feel bad about *you*. I heard that when Mike left you were thinking of moving out of the village, then Dad died and you felt like you had to stay.'

'I did have to stay, you know I did.'

'Yeah, I suppose. At first. But nothing's happened with me for a while now, and I just want you to know I realise what you gave up for me, and if you wanted to maybe move to Plymouth or something, that'd be alright. *I'd* be alright, I mean.'

'I know you would. And recently, I must admit, I've been starting to, well, to wake up again.'

'I knew it!' Tom said, smiling, and Laura felt relief peeling away the tension she hadn't even realised had been weighing her down.

She sat forward, eager to explain. 'The other night, when I took Captain out, I just had this kind of sense there was more out there I wanted to see. Not the far off places, not that anymore. Just life.'

'Then do it!' Tom urged. 'Get the paper, check out jobs in Plymouth. And flats; you could make a mint renting out your cottage. And when you visit you can stay in your old room here.'

'You've given this some thought, haven't you?' Laura observed. She sat up straight then, assuming a wide-eyed, excited look. 'Can you work your washing machine now, is that it? You had a revelation from Zanussi: a shiny alien came and showed you which cycle to put your non-fast coloureds on?'

Tom grinned. 'Never mind the washing machine, I'm only just learning how to work my sister.'

'And the shiny alien?'

'Mr Edwards,' he admitted.

'Mr *Edwards?*'

'Don't ask. Anyway, will you get the paper tomorrow? I'll come with you to look at flats if you like.'

'Will you be able to?' Laura sobered, remembering the

last time Tom had tried to leave the moor, just for the day: half an hour out of Lynher Mill he'd been sweating and grey-green with nausea, begging her to turn back.

'I can if it means me helping you for once. It's the least I can do, and it won't take long to look at a flat will it?' But he was looking uncertain now.

'I'll probably be looking at more than one at a time if I'm making the trek. You won't be happy and I'll be trying to rush it. Maybe Richard will be able to come with me if I need someone.'

She realised her mistake immediately; Tom's face closed off again and he drank his coffee in a few swallows. Her hand tightened on her own cup. 'What's your problem with him?'

'Nothing.'

'Come on! Ever since you first saw him you've looked at him like some kind of plague carrier.'

'He's a Yank, isn't he? Everyone knows they're all mouth and trousers.'

'And that's it, is it? Your considered opinion on the man who's actually made me happy for the first time since Michael left: "all mouth and trousers"? Well thank you for your vote of confidence, Tom. I'll get the paper tomorrow, I'll look for jobs in Plymouth and Liskeard, and *you*,' she deliberately left her coffee cup on the table as she left, 'can do your own sodding dishes.'

Laura had reached the end of the hall before her anger drained away. Sighing, she turned back and poked her head around the kitchen door. Tom was staring in surprise at where she'd been sitting and he opened his mouth, presumably to apologise, but Laura spoke first. 'It's cycle D.'

'Huh? What is?'

'Non-fast coloureds.'

Tom woke, freezing, assaulted by terror as he felt his breath coming damply back off the wall against which his face was pressed. Stone, running with moisture, a vast emptiness he felt as a solid thing at his back. Before he even had time to look around, to find out where he was, he knew: the cavern under the moor. Somehow he'd come here in the dead of night, driven by God only knew what, and now he was curled around his knees with his face pushed tight to the granite wall, as if he had tried to climb inside it.

He straightened slowly, listening for sounds in the huge cavern, hearing none except his own harsh breathing. He felt tears stinging the back of his eyes and nose, but he couldn't let them fall or he'd never stop. He strained for some source of light but there was nothing, and he stood up on shaking legs and groped around the walls until he found the opening to the tunnel.

By the time he emerged into the early morning light he had regained some kind of control. He'd dreamed of crossing the heath with easy familiarity, then the dream had faded into something altogether less pleasant: a foul, dusty taste in his mouth, and worse – a sense of his own mind shrinking under the onslaught of something much, much bigger. And older. Ancient even.

He'd fought against the invasion and felt the presence retreat, and in his dream he had wrapped himself in a thick cloak and curled up to sleep. He wished for such a cloak in reality now, hugging himself against the early morning cold, dressed only in the T shirt and boxer shorts he'd worn to bed.

He headed for the village, stumbling over the moors

and cursing under his breath as he slipped time and time again on the dew-damp grass. Where was the uncanny ease that had brought him here in the middle of the night? But this was better: at least each fall, uncomfortable as it was, was proof he was fully himself again.

His front door stood wide open and Captain, who'd been locked in the kitchen, nuzzled against him, hindering him while he tried to take off his wet clothes. But for once Tom didn't gently cuff him to one side, instead he abandoned the struggle with his clothing and pulled the dog close, pressing his face into the warm black coat and letting out a great gulping sob. Once opened, the flood gates would not be easily closed again and Tom held Captain close and wept while the dog sat, patient and unmoving.

The sun was rising by the time Tom wiped his eyes and removed his sodden boxers, replacing them with a clean dry pair from one of the bags Laura had brought back yesterday. He went to the sink and splashed cold water on his face, raising his eyes to look out of the window over the moors. A moment later he tasted bile in his throat and the first spasm hit, and he bent over the sink, heaving until he had nothing left. Gasping at the strength of the convulsions he remained where he was, his head resting on his arm and his body shaking so hard it ached.

*****

'How could it have happened?'

'Mother, I – '

'Hush, Maer, I need to think.' Deera turned away and Maer waited in silence. Tom Riley's appearance in the cavern last night had startled them all, and it had been hard to maintain silence but eventually he had left, never knowing he'd been watched by a hundred pairs of curious eyes.

Now Deera had called her family to her in a rare display of uncertainty. Maer saw Gilan was watching her closely, and he seemed even more tense than she was. Odd: it should be a time of preparation and decisive action, not this strange hesitation, bordering on panic.

'Should we ready ourselves for the change?' he ventured. Deera did not answer. Casta laid his hand on Maer's shoulder and silenced him with a look.

'Why were you not watching over him, Maer?' Deera said at last.

Maer scowled at Gilan. 'It was my uncle's duty. I am to take care of Richard, remember?'

'Oh. Yes, of course.' Deera faltered and Maer saw her frown briefly as she shifted her attention to Gilan.

'Ask him why he was *not* taking care of him then!' Gilan said, side-stepping the issue neatly. Deera would never allow that, Maer thought, but the queen's brow furrowed again as she turned back to him.

'Yes. Why were you here and not with Lucas?'

'Richard is not part of this problem! And he was safe with Laura last night.'

'Hah! What is "safe"?' Gilan snapped. 'The man could be run over in the street and you'd never know!'

'Or struck by a bullet in a shop doorway?' Maer flung back, furious at having his loyalty to Richard questioned by this vile creature. 'And what of Tom? He came here last night when he was supposed to be under your guard! What if he had fused with one of us? Taken my father? What could you have done to prevent it?'

'Then your father would have made a glorious sacrifice,' Gilan replied, his eyes shifting to Casta. 'He is a worthy creature for Loen to take, if take someone he must.'

'And if it had been *you* whose path he crossed, Gilan? Would you have been happy to make such a sacrifice?'

'What if, and what if, and what if! It was not and there is no point discussing it further! You are a tiresome child, Prince Maer!'

Their voices were rising, bouncing off the walls in the queen's chamber, soon the row would be heard outside in the cavern and Maer was aware Casta was looking to Deera to put a stop to it. Eventually Casta thundered out his own command for silence, and Gilan and Maer glared at each other, breathing hard, hatred crackling in the air between them.

'Gilan is right in this instance, Maer,' Casta said, rubbing his eyes wearily. 'We all came close to something terrible last night, but Loen was not able to effect the change, which is all that matters now.'

'Do you believe he is strong enough to do it?' Maer asked. 'And you, Mother? Because if he is, he is no longer safe to be near, and we must bring him to us with great care.'

Again Deera had retreated into silence, and Maer was about to ask again but Casta spoke up, his worried eyes upon his wife.

'No. Not yet, but it will not be long. His desires may have brought him out here, but Riley fought back. The battle exhausted them both and if Loen were ready he would not have been defeated. Riley is safe a while longer, but he must be watched closely now. Do you understand?'

'Tell Gilan this, Father; Tom Riley is his charge. Richard is mine.'

'Not any longer. Gilan will watch Lucas from now on.'

Maer's head snapped up, his heart hammering. Trust Richard's safety to this evil-spirited killer of mortals?

'Father, no! You cannot do this, he –'

'Enough, Maer.'

'But he doesn't care for Richard's safety at all!'

'You mean he doesn't care for the man himself, and that is good. He will bring him, without the sorrow or grief that might otherwise alert Lucas to possible danger.'

'You think Richard will trust him enough to follow?'

'He will be persuaded one way or another, I have no doubts. Now go, I must talk with your queen.'

Maer clutched at his father's sleeve, desperate to make him understand. 'Gilan killed Richard's friend, and his wife, and spares no concern for his wellbeing! It's his fault that Richard was –'

'He saved the man's life, thus proved his loyalty. I will come to you later and talk if that is what you wish, but for now, please ...'

Maer could see the distraction of deep concern on his father's face as he looked at Deera, and he withdrew, miserable and afraid. Outside in the main cavern he saw Gilan striding ahead of him, and called out to him.

'What is it, meddler?' Gilan said, not breaking his stride. 'I have duties to fulfil.'

'Oh, so now you care enough to do your job?' Maer caught up with him. 'I know what you did, to Amy and to Cait. I don't know how you did it, but I know you caused their deaths.'

'What precisely do you know?' Gilan taunted softly, turning back so quickly their noses almost touched. Maer only just stopped himself from shrinking away. 'Do you know Amy died thinking she had descended into madness? Do you know Cait died with her man's name on her lips and his face in her heart? Do you know that, when Lucas lay in the doorway, he wanted to die too?'

'You are an evil shadow on this land,' Maer whispered,

rigid with fury and his eyes fixed hard on Gilan's. 'If any harm comes to Richard you will pay with your life.'

'Any harm other than that which *you* have brought him to?' Gilan gave him a tight smile. 'Never forget, Prince Maer, you have brought this man here to be a sacrifice, you are the duplicitous one. I, on the other hand, have never pretended to care for him, to be his friend.' Before Maer could reply he spun away and vanished into the tunnel.

Maer took a long, shaky breath and turned back to talk to his father. As he drew close to his parents' chamber he heard them talking louder than usual. He hesitated, then started towards his own rooms – his father would be out soon enough and would be sure to keep his word and seek him out.

A couple of steps was all he took before his mother's words brought him to a halt, and he felt the icy cold he had always envied the mortals seeping through his veins.

'Lying to the boy as you did was foolish, Casta, and very, very wrong.'

'I believed we could do it, I knew nothing of the second curse! You should have shared Borsa's knowledge with me long ago, as you did with your son and your brother. It might have saved me a great deal of pain, knowing I have lied to my son.'

'I know, and I am sorry.' Deera said, 'I only told him when I felt I had no choice. He cares for the girl too, he will keep her safe until it is time for Loen to finish the task he has set himself.'

'Maer would have found a way to send Lucas away if I had not made that promise.'

'He would have been brought back, one way or another. Maer should have realised. I cannot believe ... unless ... Casta, do you suppose he means for the plan to fail? After all I have done to save his life?'

'No,' Casta said in weary tones, 'he would never go against your wishes – neither as a son nor a subject.'

'Then why has he not questioned this? He knows Riley's body cannot be allowed to live, no matter whose spirit is within it. Loen has sworn so!'

Maer's breath halted and he his head grew light. *Why* had he not realised? Richard's spirit would be in Tom's body, and safe yes, but for how long? Seconds, before Loen destroyed it. And he would have to help, as would his parents, or see the end of his own race. He leaned one hand on the wall for support. How could he have been so stupid? Instead of saving Richard he had almost sentenced him to death twice over.

He tried to think, but the voices from inside the chamber were rising further, and the swirling thoughts would not distinguish themselves beyond fury and helplessness.

'Look at the way you conducted yourself earlier, when Gilan and Maer were looking to you for guidance,' Casta was saying, 'you had nothing of your wits about you! It was left to me to answer their questions, to halt their ridiculous bickering, to dismiss them to their duties.'

'I cannot think, Casta.' Maer heard despair now, his mother sounded weak and uncertain.

'You cannot *think*?' Casta echoed, 'You are the ruler here, you must put these feelings aside and lead your people forward the only way you can; by giving them back their king.'

'I had thought to prepare, but everything is happening so quickly now. And Maer is almost unknown to me. He has changed so much –'

'Gather yourself,' Casta said, quietly now, but with an edge to his voice. 'You must understand you have wrought his situation, and accept what you have done to our son.'

'What I have done?'

'Deera, he has no-one. You sent him away when he would have been building strong, lasting friendships among his own kind, creating a life for himself. He had to befriend Lucas or go mad with loneliness. Now, at *your* bidding also, he must deliver this man, whom he loves, and watch him die. You have made our son into a killer of mortals, no better than your brother.'

'No – '

'You need to regain your position with our people now, not wallow in confusion and misery,' Casta said. 'What's done is done. Maer will never forgive either of us, we must just hope he does not realise you have played him for a fool.'

'Oh, you are too late, Father,' Maer whispered, heat replacing the ice that had crept through him. 'Such a fool I am, a fool you have both made me. But Richard will not pay for it.'

Chapter Twenty

'How about this one: two bed, DG, GCH – whatever that means –'

'Double glazing, gas central heating.'

'Okay, all the stuff you said, plus it says; overlooking the harbour –'

'Whoa, forget it, it'll be on the Barbican and cost an arm and a leg.' Laura shook out her own paper and sighed. 'Besides, before I look at places, I have to find a job. I can always commute for a week or so if I have to.'

Richard watched her scanning her situations vacant column. The change in her was really something miraculous. 'You really want to do this, don't you?'

Laura nodded. 'Since Tom brought it up I've thought of nothing else. I've really been ready for a while now, I think.'

'Right, then let's do it. What've you found so far?'

Laura pushed her paper over; she'd ringed three job adverts and put a question mark next to a fourth. 'Any of those would be great. I'll call and get application details in a minute.'

'What about renting out this place?'

Laura frowned and he understood why: her home had been bought with the money left by her father, helped by Tom buying her share of their family home, and she had put so much of herself into it she would find it hard to think of stranger living there. He thought back to his first impressions of this room and smiled. Who could blame her?

'If I want to rent somewhere in town I suppose I could do with the extra income,' Laura said. 'It'll be easy enough at peak season, but this is an odd time of year for holiday lets. I could ask Tom to take care of it for me until spring.'

'I was thinking,' Richard hesitated, unsure: it had made perfect sense in his head but now he realised it presumed a lot. Laura's eyebrows were raised, and she seemed impatient to get on with her job search, so he plunged on. 'I need someplace better to stay, until after Christmas anyway. Dean could share, chip in with the rent. Would that be okay?'

'You?'

'Well yeah, I mean I'd look after the place, pay you whatever you asked –'

'Oh god, how can I ask *you* for rent money?'

'By opening your mouth and telling me how much you'd charge Mr and Mrs John Q Public per month,' he said firmly. 'Look, I need to stay in Lynher Mill until the project is done, but the B&B is crazy money; too expensive for us to take two rooms. Between us we could pay you a better than decent rent for half what it's costing there. It makes sense, doesn't it? Unless you don't trust me, of course.'

'Oh, please! Of course I trust you. As long as you promise not to have wild parties that is.'

'Sorry, can't promise that, not with all the crazy people around here just dying to let their hair down.'

'In that case you'd better make sure you invite me,' Laura said. 'Okay. You and Dean stay here, but the first time I see dirty magazines in the bathroom the deal's off.'

'Sounds fair enough,' Richard said, 'I'll make sure they're kept under the bed.' He picked up his newspaper again. 'What about this; two bedroomed house for rent on outskirts of city, no pets.'

'Then *you* couldn't visit, my sexy rhino.' She ducked just in time to avoid the cushion, then picked it up and lobbed it back at him, grinning as it bounced off the side of his head. 'Right, now are you going to do something useful, or just keep distracting me?'

'Keep distracting you, of course.'

'Make yourself useful then, and put the kettle on, you might as well start learning where everything goes.'

The evening was mild enough, but later, as Richard walked back towards the bed and breakfast, he became aware of a creeping chill that started somewhere at the back of his neck. Only vaguely aware he was doing it, he removed his hands from his coat pockets and straightened his shoulders, trying to shake the feeling he was being followed. But the sickeningly familiar sensation remained and he shook his head, partly in negation and partly to clear the thoughts that had begun to whisper there. He turned his face a little to lessen the sound of the wind, and listened without slowing his pace, but there was no footfall in the road behind him. Still he had to fight the urge to scan the open moorland to his left, knowing if he saw what he half-expected to see he'd go mad, because now he remembered the last time he had felt like this.

The fear that had taken root back then, now had a hard, bright core of anger. Richard let it swell, drawing strength from it, but that strength wavered as Richard realised, with a shock of disbelief, that this was more than memory; Sharpe was here. Nearby. Right at this moment.

'Laura,' Richard breathed, and the fear returned like a solid blow, so hard the word was choked off in his throat and he stopped in the road. He stared across the darkening moor, but there was nothing to see except rising hills and the oddly shaped granite formations in the distance.

Behind him the road remained empty, and a scan of the gardens on the other side revealed nothing more sinister than shrubs and flower borders. Yet that feeling remained.

'Sharpe!' Richard shouted, not knowing he was going to do it, but his voice rang out, commanding and clear. 'Hear this, you evil son of a bitch; I will find you, whoever you are, and when I do you'll wish you'd been drowned at birth.'

Where the words came from he had no idea, but an authority he had not known he possessed turned the speech from bravado to pledge, and he felt the weight behind the words settle in his bones. But the deep current of fear for Laura remained.

When Dean arrived he looked tired and unsettled himself, and even more so when he saw Richard. 'You're white as a sheet. What's happened?'

Richard sat on his bed, rubbing his face hard as if by doing so he could erase himself from this situation and wake up somewhere else. 'It's going to take some explaining.'

'Try me.'

'Okay.' He let out a huge breath blowing his hair away from his eyes, and considered how to begin. Eventually he just came out with it. 'Gary Sharpe is here.'

Dean sat on his own bed and frowned but thankfully didn't scoff. 'Sharpe. Here. Right.'

'You believe me?'

Dean hesitated. 'I believe you believe it,' he said, carefully, 'and you're scared for Laura, right?'

'Damn right I am. With good reason.'

'You've seen him?'

Richard didn't answer. How to explain the feeling he'd had in such a way that Dean didn't dismiss it? Old friends they might be, and the best, but something like this might make Dean think he'd lost it for good this time.

'Richard? Have you seen him?' Richard shook his head. 'Then why are you so sure he's here?'

'Because I've felt him.' He told Dean all he'd experienced outside, and the way the words had sprung, unbidden, from his lips, 'I don't know where it came from, but I got the feeling I actually have what it takes to back it up. Does that make sense?'

'None of it makes sense,' Dean said, and his voice held a strange note that wasn't quite disbelief, more fearful. That hit harder.

'I'm not crazy,' Richard said quietly.

'No. Maybe just tired. A good rest will see you right.'

'People are always telling me I'm fucking tired! I'm not tired, I know what I felt out there!'

Dean went into the bathroom to splash water on his face, and Richard lay back on his bed and closed his eyes, trying to recreate the certainty he'd had in the lane, *knowing* Sharpe was there, knowing it without needing to see. But he couldn't do it. He could remember having felt it, but in this lighted room he could no longer imagine a fear intense enough to make his gut ache the way it had, his muscles so taut he'd barely had the control to walk. The longer he thought about it the harder it was to convince himself he'd been right.

Dean came back, electric razor in his hand. He crossed to the wall mirror and plugged it in. 'Your mind has been working overtime lately,' he said. 'Your song writing, your job and now this stuff with Laura. You're probably so scared of losing her, you pick the one thing that's stolen that kind of happiness from you in the past.'

'You should write a book,' Richard said. Then he sighed. 'You're probably right.'

'You don't sound convinced.'

'I am, I guess. But it makes me wonder how I can get

223

so spooked, because out there, Dean … out there it was *real*.'

Dean's eyes were on him in the mirror, looking thoughtful. 'There's something you should know about Lynher Mill,' he said at last. Richard waited; Dean was obviously unsure whether or not to say what was on his mind, but, as Richard had earlier, just spoke the simplest words. 'It's haunted.'

'Ah, come on. This is serious.'

'I'm not joking, Rich. There have been a lot of mining disasters in Cornwall, and one of them happened just over the heath a little way. Where the biggest derelict engine house stands now.'

'And so this means the village is haunted?' Richard tried not to let disbelief colour his words, but he knew he sounded, at best, sceptical. Dean went on, not emphasising the sinister aspect of the tale, just the terrible sadness.

'The engine collapsed into the shaft, it's why the mine was shut down. Fourteen miners were never found, lost in the network of caves and tunnels under the moor. It's said their souls are still trying to find their way back to their families.'

For some reason the thought of a lost soul looking for its home struck a deeper chill in Richard than the thought of some malevolent spirit haunting the moor. 'You're not yanking my chain, are you? You really believe this.'

Dean shook his head. 'Look it up, it's one of the most famous haunting stories in the South West, and the elem … god knows we've got plenty of those.' He shrugged. 'Anyway, the point is I've felt something out there myself, and I know at least two others who've experienced it first hand over the years. Just a chill in the air, a sort of, unsettling sensation.'

'Did you, or they, have a focus for it? Identify it?'

'For about half an hour I was convinced it was a vampire, but that was because I was reading Bram Stoker at the time.' Dean pulled on a clean shirt. 'You'd been thinking about Sharpe again, had you?'

'Not at the time, no. But as soon as I felt … what I felt out there, it came to me it was him. No doubts, I just knew it.'

'He's been on your mind though. Well then, maybe you've just experienced the same as me. "There are more things in Heaven and Earth, Horatio," and all that.' He smiled and put on a sinister voice. 'Cornwall's a spooky place.'

Despite the unsettling idea Dean had put forward, some of the suffocating fear for Laura eased and Richard was grateful for that at least. He checked his watch. 'There's something else I need to discuss with you, but if we don't shake our asses we're gonna miss dinner and if I eat in the bar every night I'll turn into a blimp. I'll see you downstairs.'

***

As the door closed behind Richard, Maer sank back onto his bed and his smile vanished. What was Gilan playing at? He was supposed to be remaining hidden, not purposely freaking Richard out. Although it was just like him to enjoy the fear on the face of the man he'd hated for so long. That was if he'd seen any at all; it sounded as if Richard had instead turned it right around. Gilan would not have liked that one bit.

Maer quashed a warm surge of pride: what right did he have to take pride in the strength of the man he was sworn to destroy? Richard's strength was his alone, whether he knew where it came from or not. But it would not be enough to save his life.

Maer had stopped at Tom's workshop after leaving the mine. Tom was tired and pale after his night-time visit to the mine, but Loen also needed time to recover from his premature attempt at total possession, and would doubtless lie low for a while now. Which might give Maer enough time to work out how Richard could be saved.

He remained there, watching Laura come and go with her brother's laundry: she'd clearly had a change of heart after their row. Today she seemed happy, luminously so, and knowing it was Richard who had put that light back in her soul was a source of both envy and that same misplaced pride.

But now this. Gilan seemed incapable of masking his malevolence as he masked his physical self; for Richard to have felt it spoke of its power and intensity, and the danger he and Laura were in. Maer thumped the wall in frustration and anger. No matter what the consequences, those two people must be kept safe, and as he thought about those consequences he felt the beginnings of a notion that terrified him, yet whispered coldly of being the only answer: he must revert to the correct order of things and present himself in Richard's place.

Despite Loen's natural desire for the body with which he was already connected, when it came down to the final choice, survival dictated he would take whoever came close enough. Maer knew his own spirit would struggle for life whether he wanted to or not, but he also knew Loen would win out in the end. He only hoped his own knowledge of Laura's history would be passed along with his body, just as Tom's abilities and knowledge were being absorbed now; the thought of his own hands harming her made him shudder in horror.

He felt sick with fear, and with regret at what this meant for himself, but this way his family and people would be safe, the curse of perpetual darkness and destruction would be broken with Tom's death, and Loen would have the all-but immortal body in which to take back the staff of absolute authority over his people. It was just as it should have been before Deera had determined otherwise; his destiny was simply reasserting itself.

There is something about a brightly lit room, and the smell of good food, that directs worried or frightened thoughts towards the positive. From the very first, men had dined well on the eve of battle, and raised their voices in song, and their strength had been increased by these simple acts of allowing the soul to breathe. It seemed little had changed in the fundamental make up of all species.

On the stairs, having made his decision, Maer had felt a quivering deep in his stomach, a basic fear for his own life, for what would be denied him, all he would never achieve. Yet the simple act of opening the door to dining room somehow put those terrifying thoughts to one side and gave him fresh appreciation of the time he had remaining to him. Leaving his fear behind in the dim stairwell, stepping into this large, light room filled with savoury smells, he straightened his shoulders and instead focused on what needed to be done to protect those he loved.

Richard was at a corner table, studying the menu, and the only other guests – a couple with a dog and a single, elderly man – were already eating.

The trembling in Maer's belly was replaced by a pleasant growling sensation and he slid into the seat opposite Richard. 'So what is it you wanted to talk about?'

'Okay, I don't know if you knew, but Laura has been looking for jobs in the city. In Plymouth, that is, and she – '

'Seriously? She's moving? When?' Maer felt his heart lighten further. If Laura was going to move off the moor, Richard would surely go with her.

'Take it easy!' Richard said, 'you trying to get rid of her?'

'Not at all,' Maer said, 'but I know it'd be good for her. What about Tom though?'

'You ready for this?'

'Go on.'

'It was his idea.'

'You're kidding!'

'Nope. Anyway, thing is, I suggested we rent the cottage off her for a few months so she's not hung up here trying to organise it. It's got two bedrooms, we could split the cost, and it'll give her time to ... what?'

'Nothing.' Maer studied the slip of paper that passed for a menu. He tried to sound calm but it was difficult. 'Aren't you going with her?'

'Now it's me you're trying to shake off?' Richard smiled. 'Look, Dean, she's starting a new life. I have stuff to finish here, she knows that. I thought a lot about what you said, and you're right, I'm probably jumping at shadows. But on the off chance I'm not, she'll be away from here, from me. And from Sharpe.'

'Forget Sharpe, thinking about him will drive you nuts,' Maer said. 'You do realise every bloke in a twenty mile radius is going to ask her out if you're not around?'

'Let them,' Richard said, 'doesn't mean she's gotta say yes.'

'Good point,' Maer conceded. There was a pause while they gave their order, and he took a sip of water to lubricate his throat, dry with worry again. 'Will you go and stay with her?'

'Maybe, but she'll be coming back most weekends. And I can make sure ...' he caught Maer's look, and stopped before Sharpe's name came out. 'Anyway, you want to split the rent on her place?'

'For how long?'

'Soon as you've figured out what you're doing you can either stay or leave.'

'And you?'

'When the project's over I'll have to make some decisions. Until then it's perfect.'

'I can't believe she's buggering off the minute she's met you,' Maer said. 'She'll be missed round here.'

'Yeah, I'm going to miss her too.' Richard looked momentarily morose. 'Even more than the kids will. But this is long overdue, and she's not leaving the country after all.'

'True again. Talking of leaving the country though, why don't the two of you do that, just for a holiday? She wants to flex her wings, take her back to Chicago, Canada even.'

Richard seemed to seriously consider the possibility, but shook his head. 'Too much to do here right now, Maybe after Christmas that'd be something we could do, while we figure out what we want long term.'

Maer wanted to yell, *after Christmas it'll be too late!* But instead he raised his glass to new beginnings.

Later he waited for Richard to go and call Laura, before slipping out to check on Tom once more. The few houses dotted along the lane had lights glowing in the windows, but there were no streetlights. It didn't matter: Maer had never needed light here, and he didn't need it now to know he was being watched from the garden wall.

As he drew alongside Gilan, he stopped walking but didn't look at him. 'He knows you're here. Are you trying to drive him away?'

'Me? Now why would I want to do that? Am I not loyal to my sister, as you are to your mother?'

'We should both be loyal to our queen,' Maer said, not wanting to dwell upon their familial connection; it was bad enough being of the same Moorlander race, but to admit such a close tie was poison in Maer's blood.

'And so we are. It is surely beyond such power as I possess to have any effect upon Lucas. Now, *nephew*, go about your own duties, let me be about mine.'

'You're not needed tonight, Richard is not leaving the hotel.'

'All the same, I think I shall remain –'

'He can feel you!' Maer hissed, anger dragging the words out into the night air. He shook his head: there was no sense in fighting. He had even considered allowing Gilan to drive Richard back to America, at least his friend would be safe there. But if he left, Laura's new found appetite for life would have nothing to sustain it and she would return, devastated, to Lynher Mill and the death that awaited her here.

'He thinks he has a power over me,' Gilan said, 'but he has not. You should pray to the elements he never has to find out what an adversary he might have in me, should he fall away from the queen's protection.'

'Very well, be the cause of his leaving, if you must,' Maer snapped back. 'But be aware that all our people will know whose hand has destroyed them.'

Despite his outward showing of righteous anger, Maer felt the full helplessness of the situation weighing on him. If only he could trust his parents he might tell them Laura was no true descendant of Ulfed, and beg them to allow her to remain under their protection, safe from Gilan. Just a short while ago he would have gone to them, and believed anything they told him that meant Laura might be safe – how fortunate then, that he had not, he would have delivered the girl directly into the hands of this creature who delighted in destruction, particularly of those Richard loved.

Maer felt Gilan's eyes on him as he walked away, but did not turn to look behind, he did not need to: whether he admitted it or not, Gilan had been shaken by Richard's fierce reaction, and Maer had the feeling his friend would not be subjected to any more "paranormal" experiences. Laura too, would soon be away from the moor – they would both be safe.

But the fact of Maer's own death loomed dark in his heart, and it hurt.

Chapter Twenty-One

November 2010.

The Tamar Bridge crawled with rush hour traffic. Headlights became blurred red and white smudges shimmering through the rain, and the wipers beat double-time to keep the windscreen clear. Laura turned the radio up to compensate for their regular thump-thump and for the roar of the heater, and tapped her fingers on the steering wheel as she thought ahead to an infinitely more comfortable evening.

Cornwall would always be home, despite the speed and ease with which she had settled into her new home and job, and this Friday night journey was as much part of her life as travelling to work each morning. She enjoyed knowing that at the end of this snarled up mess lay the familiar long, but soothingly empty road to Lynher Mill – and the worse the weather, the more she looked forward to the bliss of a roaring log fire, and curling into Richard's embrace on her old sofa.

The only grit in her now smooth-as-cream life was Tom. She'd barely seen him on recent visits home, he often cried off meeting arrangements with a brief text message, and when they did catch each other there was always some silly reason he had to rush off at the first opportunity: 'Got loads of orders for Christmas, sis,' or: 'Up late with the lads last night.'

'Yeah, right,' Laura muttered now, as she negotiated the roundabout at the top of the hill and took the Callington exit. Tom was in trouble and he wasn't letting her in, which could only mean one thing: he was dreaming again.

Laura had been relieved to note that, as her brother had grown, the dreams had faded and there had been no more instances of burning circles on his hands. Research had yielded the word 'psychosomatic' and that had suited them both, given them the peace they'd desperately needed. The last time he'd been so unsettled as a child had been around the time of their mother's death and that was only to be expected.

Laura's head was suddenly shot through with a dark, swelling thought: had Tom's hands been burned the day their mother had died? No, surely not, she'd have seen …but would she? He'd reacted predictably to the news his mother was pregnant, the thirteen year old boy with no interest in babies save for the fact that this one would usurp his position as favoured youngest child – there had been sulking. But after Vivien's death he'd spent months crying himself to sleep, there was no way he'd had anything to do with the accident. Laura cursed the twist in her own mind that had given rise to the notion; it said more about her than about Tom.

She flinched as a set of headlights swept around a corner on full beam, and thankfully her thoughts scattered. 'Concentrate, woman,' she said out loud, shaking her head. But with the newly awoken memories in danger of coming together in a picture she couldn't bear to contemplate, she knew she finally needed to unburden herself. With nothing more on her mind than seeing Richard and telling him everything, her foot pressed the accelerator and she turned the radio up again, wishing the miles away as they sped beneath her wheels.

The living room lights in the cottage were on. Dean often stayed out late on Friday evenings, sometimes all night, to allow her and Richard time alone. Hopefully he'd already gone out, she didn't feel ready for politeness and small talk. It was strange coming to her own home as a visitor; she never knew whether or not to knock, and settled for rapping on the front room window as she passed it and opening the door herself.

Richard was in the kitchen at the back of the house, rock music playing on the small stereo there, and clearly hadn't heard her knocking on the window. She stood in the doorway, resisting the urge to go straight in, and watched instead, feeling her tension falling away.

He was at the sink preparing vegetables, his movements timed to the music and exaggerated for his own amusement. He adopted an operatic pose, singing pompously to match as the sound swelled, and Laura couldn't stop the laughter from bubbling up. Richard swung round, his smile banishing the last of her shadowed thoughts and she dropped her bag and crossed the kitchen, meeting him halfway.

'You're early,' he said, his arms around her so tight she could hardly breathe, but she was holding him just as tightly and he didn't seem to mind either.

'Drove like a lunatic,' she said into his shoulder, and he snorted.

'Somehow I can believe that.'

She pulled back 'What's for tea?' she asked, knowing what his response would be. She wasn't disappointed.

'It's dinner, dammit! Tea is a drink.'

'When in Rome, or the West Country.' She followed him back to the sink where he continued his preparations, and saw the size of the broccoli head he was rinsing. 'Holy cow, that looks like something out of Little Shop of Horrors.'

'You could be right,' Richard held up a finger with a plaster on it. 'Damn sharp knives you have here. Maybe

234

I'll see if the broccoli wants some blood.'

'Good idea.' Laura rested her cheek against his back, her fingers playing blindly with the buttons on his shirt.

Richard laughed. 'Patience, babe.'

'For what, tea or you?' She worked at a button and opened it with a little exclamation of triumph, then groaned. 'T-shirt? Come on, that's not fair!'

'Hey, you're the landlady, you fix the heating.' Richard turned and draped his wet hands over her shoulders. He smelled of shampoo and toothpaste, and she smiled as she thought of him getting all cleaned up in her honour. His mouth lifted in an answering smile, and his hands went to the small of her back to pull her close. As he bent his head to hers she closed her eyes, released the last of the worries in her over-wrought mind, and let her body take over.

Stretched out next to her on their blissfully familiar bed, Richard's fingers brushed her skin, barely skimming the fine hairs as if he thought she might bruise with a firmer touch. His body was warm next to her, the smoothly rounded satin of his shoulders invited her teeth and lips, and she breathed him in as if he were life itself. Her hands knew the curve of every muscle, every hard ridge of bone, every sensitive inch of him, and while he gently coaxed her to tingling readiness with his fingers, she gripped and teased him with firm strokes until they were breathing hard in complete unison, heat between them, around them, through them.

Before he could roll on top of her she sat up and straddled him, sliding onto him with slippery ease, their fit perfect. She leaned down to nip at his lower lip, light-headed with anticipation and willing to draw it out while he kissed her deeply. Then she sat back, feeling his hands firm on her thighs, and began to move, the urgency increasing until, with a cry and a feeling that the sweetest release was just a breath away, she stopped, too deliciously weak to continue. His hands went to her hips and pulled her down harder as he rocked her, and the feeling changed, deepened, sweetened further. There was a flash of sensation in her lower belly and her hips began moving again, faster and faster, her breathless cries urging them both on.

When she slid off him, they were both shaking with the intensity of what had passed between them, and neither could speak for a long time as they lay tangled in the clean sheets and in each other's limbs, hands linked and breath mingling. Laura placed her free hand on Richard's racing heart and felt the wildness of her own in its echo. His skin was damp with cooling sweat, and she ran her hand down his chest to his stomach, feeling the strong pulse throbbing against her fingers as he fought to control his own breathing.

She turned her head so that her lips lay against his neck, and kissed him. 'Um. Wow,' she said, her voice cracked and weak.

'Sorry, who are you again?'

She growled, and he laughed. She enjoyed the feeling of his muscles flexing and relaxing under her hand almost as much as she loved the sound of his amusement, and the brush of his fingers on her temple as he pushed her heavy hair back from her brow. He turned into her and kissed her, and she closed her eyes, breathing slowly in the relief and miracle of him. They lay in silence for a while, then, each drifting in their own secret thoughts, and Laura was just on the verge of slipping into a blissful sleep when a shrill beeping made her jerk upright, eyes wide. Then she relaxed. Kitchen timer.

'Dammit,' Richard said with sleepy irritation. 'You don't really want to eat, do you?'

'Feed me, Lucas,' Laura sang, and prodded him in the ribs. 'Feed me now.'

Later, as they finished preparing the meal together, Laura found her mind reluctantly returning to her earlier worries. 'Have you seen Tom lately?'

'Only from a distance, in the bar. Weird, he never offered to buy me a drink.'

'Ha ha, funny.' Laura sighed and threw the broccoli into a pan of water. 'I know it's a lot to ask but I really wish you two got on.'

'Hey, not my fault,' Richard reminded her, 'I've tried. He's hated me from the minute I came into your life. Guess I can't really blame him though.'

'But he's got no reason to, it's not like you've come between us.'

'Can we talk about something else?' Richard said. He looked at her squarely, his eyes meeting hers with their usual directness. 'I miss you, Laura. Being here in your place, surrounded by your history is a pretty good substitute, but it can't compare to the real thing.'

Time was already slipping by too quickly. Soon it would be Saturday, and the day after that she'd have to leave him again. She shook the thought away. 'Have you thought any more about after the project is finished?'

'Hardly think about anything else,' he said. 'If you can stand having a lodger I'll be raiding your refrigerator and eating all your chocolate by Christmas.'

Laura glared. 'Touch the chocolate and you die.' She dried her hands and checked the oven. 'About ten minutes. Fancy a glass of wine?'

They took their drinks into the front room and Laura leaned against him on the sofa. Remembering the sight of him here on their first night together, rising over her, naked and glorious, she felt warmth stealing over her again and nestled closer.

'So, okay. What's troubling you?' His quiet tone surprised her as much as did the question.

'Troubling me?'

'You're obviously distracted. Is it Tom?'

'You said you didn't want to talk about it.'

'I can think of a hundred things I'd rather talk about than your brother, but they all come down to what you're thinking. Are you worried about him?'

Laura hesitated, but with the semi-darkness of the room to hide in, she knew if she didn't tell him now she'd never speak of it to anyone. And she had to, she must. Now.

She took a deep breath, sat forward and tried to find the words to begin. 'It's hard to explain, but there's some stuff in his past, *our* past, he has a hard time dealing with. It happened when I was thirteen and he was ten ...'

And then she couldn't have stopped talking if she wanted to, the words tumbled out, somehow arranged in the right order when in her head they'd just been a jumble of memories and images. The story didn't take long but when she'd finished she felt as if she'd been talking for hours. She stopped short of voicing the thought that had occurred to her in the car, somehow she couldn't bring herself to let that terrible notion out into the open, to have someone else even consider it as a possibility.

The kitchen timer beeped again, bringing her back to reality and the realisation of how insane it all sounded. Richard was sitting very still, she couldn't read his expression.

'I thought he was over it,' she said, 'but I'm not so sure now. Of course I know it was just some crazy old bloke living rough, but we were just kids then.' Her mind tried to show her the picture in the blue folder, but she shoved it away, uncomfortably aware of the irony of her next words. 'Tom's never been able to accept that because of what's happened to him. It'd mean he was losing it. Better for him to believe we saw something a bit, well, supernatural.'

She looked at him, and felt coldness in the pit of her stomach; in the shadows his face looked as if it were carved from the granite that littered the moor, and the light spilling in from the kitchen reflected in his eyes, making them appear lit from inside. She strained to see past the strange, shadowed stillness, concentrating on each small line at the corners of his eyes and the way his thick lashes dipped, so slowly, as he blinked.

And then he moved, and the illusion of otherworldliness vanished. She breathed easily again as he shook his head, frowning. 'Something you were saying kind of rang a bell somewhere in my head,' he said. 'I was trying to grab it before it disappeared, but it's gone.'

'You've heard of this happening before?'

'Not the psychosomatic stuff, the blister ring on Tom's hand, no. Not outside of TV shows anyway. But when you started talking about what it was like under the mine, it was like I really see it.'

'I tell a good story,'

'You must do. Also, there's that possibility of racial memories again. Let's eat, and you can tell me the rest.'

Over the meal Laura described how it had been in the years since the incident, the youth club burning down, and Michael's house too. 'Then it all just seemed to settle down,' she said. 'Fizzle out, really. I suppose looking back it was a bit strange that we just got on with life, but we do, don't we?'

'Yeah God knows how; it feels like you'll be freaked out forever, nothing will ever be normal again, but suddenly you look back and realise it hasn't crossed your mind for weeks, months even. So what makes you think he's not okay now?'

Laura looked at him for a long moment, her curiosity pricked by his words, then shrugged. 'He doesn't want to see me,' she said, 'and when we do meet up he's tired and irritable, like he's not getting enough sleep. He used to sleepwalk when the nightmares got to him, as if he was trying to escape something.'

'Must be tough. I know he's not my biggest fan, but I'd still like to help if I can.'

'There's nothing you can do, not for him anyway.'

'And for you?'

She smiled gratefully. 'Just be my dumping ground I suppose.'

Richard put down his knife and reached across the table. For a moment Laura thought he was going to take her hand, but at the last moment he swerved away and stole a roast potato from her plate.

'Hey!' Surprised into laughter she made a grab for it, too late. He dropped it onto his own plate. 'If I can make you laugh like that I'll count it as a good start,' he said, and although humour lingered around his eyes he looked at her seriously. 'I mean it, I'll do whatever I can to make you happy.'

'Then give me back my spud.'

'No way.'

'This is my house.'

'I pay the rent.'

'I'll put it up.'

'I'll still pay it.'

'Okay, the rent has now increased by one roast potato,

payable with immediate effect.'

'Damn, you're hard.'

'I have to be.' Laura leaned over and plunged her fork into the potato, and was about to retreat again when Richard caught her around the back of the head and pulled her lips to his. Feeling his laughter through the kiss, Laura felt a fleeting resentment towards Tom for threatening to spoil this precious and too-short time with Richard, then firmly pushed thoughts of her brother away: tonight was hers.

She sat back down and made a great show of enjoying the potato, and gradually the burden she had been carrying for so long lightened under Richard's gentle questioning and her own relieved responses. She made a decision, and blurted it out before she could change her mind.

'I have another picture, one you haven't seen.'

'Oh?' Then he caught her expression and his eyebrows went up. 'Something to do with that day and what you saw?'

'Yes. The little man in green.'

'Well if it's anything like the ones of your mom you showed me –'

'To be honest I can't remember exactly what it's like. I've never looked at it again.' She remembered she'd shoved the drawing of Richard into the same folder, and she'd not looked at that one either. 'I'll get it,' she said now, and went to the box, still tucked behind the sofa. Her heart was beating uncomfortably fast, and her hands felt clammy. Listening to Richard moving about the kitchen, clearing the table, she wished she hadn't said anything, that she was still in there helping him, feeling his hand brush hers as she passed him a plate, his breath on her neck as he leaned past her to gather up cutlery.

Instead she knelt on the hard floor, the plastic box in front of her, and a memory just within reach that might send her spinning into the same darkness as her brother. She took a deep breath and, with trembling hands she eased aside the stack of pictures of Vivien until her fingers hovered over the blue folder.

Richard had been gratifyingly effusive in his appreciation of the drawings he'd seen. She could tell he'd been prepared to be polite despite his genuine interest in seeing them and when he saw the first one his mouth had actually dropped open. She remembered his expression growing more and more awed with each shuffle of the papers, and wondered why she hadn't shown him the one she'd drawn of him. But looking now, at the folder in which it lay, she knew very well why she hadn't: the thought of accidentally glimpsing the picture of the little man had been too terrible to contemplate, and it still was.

Abruptly she shoved the box back behind the sofa, and stood up on shaking legs.

'I couldn't find it,' she said when she went back into the kitchen.

Richard looked at her steadily for a moment, then nodded. 'Okay.'

The understanding on his face brought a thick feeling to her throat, and she turned away to look for a distraction. 'It's stopped raining. Want to go for a walk?'

'Sure, that's probably a really good idea.' She turned back, and he met her questioning stare with deadpan innocence. 'You need to work off that extra potato after all.'

***

Gilan turned as Jacky Greencoat appeared around Lynher Mill Barrow. The creature's head was, as usual, hunched into his shoulders as if he expected a blow to fall at any moment. Gilan's irritation prickled and he had to curl his fingers into his palms to prevent himself from fulfilling the spriggan's expectations with a healthy slap. Where was the man's dignity? He'd lived on the moor for hundreds of years and, despite his lowly position and rank here, he was one of the oldest and strongest beings Gilan had ever met, far stronger than Gilan himself. Better he never realise that, of course.

'Oh, stop mumbling!' Gilan snapped, as Greencoat murmured apologies for his tardiness 'You're here now, stand still and pay attention.' Greencoat stood upright at once, raising his head, ready to do his superior's bidding. 'Better,' Gilan conceded. 'Now, have you given thought to the way in which you will despatch Lucas?'

'But sir, methought he would soon leave, followin' his lady, sir. To the new city.'

'I see. And *you thought* that would be enough, did you?'

'He will be out of His Majesty's reach, sir, and Prince Maer will be the only choice.'

Gilan's irritation flared into something much harder to suppress. 'And when exactly were you thinking of informing me of your carefully considered opinion in this matter?' Greencoat's head began pulling into his shoulders again, and Gilan reached out, grabbing his ear. Greencoat shrieked and stood upright, his face twisted in pain.

'Listen, worm,' Gilan said, keeping his words clipped and clear. 'I have given you a task. You will fulfil it.'

'But you said, you said that – '

'What? What did I say?' Gilan shook him and he yelped again.

'Sir, you said ...' Greencoat's voice abruptly changed,

becoming sharper, higher, eerily like Gilan's as he quoted; 'Get rid of Lucas, somehow. He must either leave the moor forever, or die ... either way, spriggan, see to it.'

Gilan let go of Greencoat, wiping his hand on his own jacket, his heart pounding uncomfortably. 'How did you do that?' he whispered.

Greencoat stared at him fearfully. 'Sir?'

Gilan peered at him carefully, then shook his head: mimicry, it was something and nothing. Not important. Although it had given him a nasty jolt to hear his own voice coming out of the huge mouth that slashed that ugly face from one side to the other.

'I have changed my mind, ' he said, 'there is no sense in leaving it to chance. Even if he does leave the moor he might return at any time. You will ensure this does not happen. Kill him, Greencoat. Do you understand?'

'But how, sir?'

Gilan sighed. 'Must I tell you how to wipe your filthy nose when it runs? How to eat the slops you concoct in your little hovel?'

'Can you not give me *some* help, sir?' Greencoat pleaded.

Gilan frowned, but the deed would not be done otherwise, that much was clear. 'Very well. I have studied his habits: it is his pleasure to walk the moors in the early morning. The poor weather does not deter him, indeed he seems to prefer to walk in the cold. On days when he does not teach, he is often out until the sun is mid-sky. His path often takes him out onto the tor beyond the farthest stack. Above the marsh.' He added this last part pointedly and, surprisingly quick to determine his meaning, Greencoat nodded.

'He will not return from the next walk he takes,' he vowed, and turned away.

Gilan kept his eyes on him until he'd disappeared into the distance. He had better be right, time was growing short.

Chapter Twenty-Two

Tom stared moodily at the half-empty grate in his front room. Roaring log fires were all well and good, but the bloody mess that needed sorting out afterwards was a nightmare. Still, it wouldn't help his cause to be seen knee deep in clinker and ash when Laura came around tomorrow, and there was no way he was getting up early to do it.

He felt a cool wetness on his fingers as Captain nudged at his hand, and ruffled the fur on the puppy's head 'She'll see, mate. We're alright, you and me aren't we? A few decent nights' sleep, and no wandering about in the early hours. Works wonders, eh?'

Captain huffed in agreement, his large brown eyes fixed on Tom, who sighed and unfolded a newspaper from the stack beside the log basket. He spread it on the carpet in front of the grate and knelt to begin brushing the ash out from the back of the fireplace.

Before long the dustpan was full, and Tom sat back on his heels, grinning at the sight of Captain sniffing suspiciously at the dust floating in the air around them. The dog sneezed once, twice, and scuttled backwards, knocking the brush out of Tom's hand into the dustpan.

A cloud of ash flew up into Tom's open mouth. Immediately the laughter stopped and he spat – the ash was dry and unpleasant of course, but there was something else about it: his head was full of noise and shadows, and the taste in his mouth grew even more sour.

Gagging, he lurched to his feet and stumbled to the tap in the kitchen, but his vision darkened until all he could see was a pinpoint of light sweeping erratically, jerking and trembling light that did not illuminate anything except grey stone.

He fumbled at where the taps should be and at last twisted the cold on full, cupped his hands and brought them to his mouth, swirling the water around and spitting it out; he didn't dare swallow any in case the ash went down with it.

He splashed more water over his face and head, and the darkness receded along with the madly jerking light his brain belatedly identified as torchlight: the torch wielded by a terrified girl. And oh, God! The dust in the cavern … He'd forgotten until now, how it had coated his tongue and lain so heavy in his mouth, but he'd had nothing to wash it out with then - he must have swallowed so much of it. Tom spat again but the dry, burnt taste was gone, and all that was left was the newly uncovered memory.

He moved away from the sink and allowed his trembling legs to take him back to the small front room, where he stared at the fireplace in mistrust and fear. The dustpan and brush lay together amidst the spilled ash, and Captain sat beside the mess, looking at Tom expectantly.

Tom shook his head. Cleaning up would have to wait, he had to get out. He gave a short whistle and grabbed his coat off the hook, took a deep breath, and he and Captain went out into the darkness together.

With the wind blowing drizzle in his face, the uneasiness faded, leaving his head clearer and able to think it all through. What had he remembered, and how much was accurate?

There was the little man in the green jacket, the jar of course – the dreams in the months following had ensured he would never forget the burning ring on his hand – and now that charred-tasting dust that he remembered clogging up his throat until he'd felt he was choking to death. So why were the memories resurfacing now?

'Maybe it's good,' he said to the dog. 'Maybe my head is letting go of all the old crap it's been hanging on to. Whatever's been sending me wandering in the night. What do you think, mate?' Captain sniffed at the stone wall and cocked his leg, looking around at Tom with his mouth hanging open happily as he relieved himself.

Tom grinned. 'Yeah, you could be right; I could be pissing in the wind, but I haven't walked in my sleep for weeks. I definitely feel better.'

His walk had taken him up the lane towards Laura's cottage. Of course it wasn't hers now, not really, the American had managed to persuade her to let him stay there. Tom felt his insides tighten; he'd never worked out what it was about Lucas that made him twitchy, but often when he passed the cottage knowing he was in there, he grew so tense he felt nauseous.

But he couldn't be forever worrying about his sister, she was a big girl and more than capable of taking care of herself. The American was in her life, and at the moment in her house, and since it was Friday night Laura would no doubt be with him. Yeah, there was her car parked alongside that crappy, rust-riddled Vauxhall Lucas had got himself. Cosy. A minute later he realised they hadn't been in the house at all, but were only now returning from a walk; Captain saw them first, and rushed to meet Laura. While she fussed over him, accepting his happy nuzzling and tugging at his ears, Tom and Richard exchanged polite nods and then Laura stood up and gave him a quick hug, promising to come down and see him first thing.

They parted amicably enough, and Richard was clearly taking care not to appear overly-affectionate towards Laura, but the closing of the door behind them couldn't have come a moment too soon for Tom. He tried not to think about what they might soon be doing, and kept walking, whistling to Captain to keep up. The last of the light from the village faded behind him, but there was thin moonlight now, enough to pick out silhouettes and shapes as he stepped off the road and onto an old beaten path, a part of the moor he rarely visited.

The hills were steeper at this end of the village and Tom enjoyed the feeling of pushing himself physically, it would make for another peaceful night's sleep. Captain bounded ahead now, happy to be off the road, cutting off the narrow path through a straggling barrier of granite lumps, and Tom was happy to let him go: the marshlands, where Kelpie had come so frighteningly close to drowning, were far out beyond the mines at the lower end of Lynher Mill. He ambled comfortably after the dog, taking deep breaths, becoming surer with each step that he was finally rid of the dreams that had sent him searching for god only knew what, night after night.

Of the mill that had given the village its name, little remained but a few broken walls and a rudimentary path, and most of the lower part of the stone tower which now rose to no more than ten feet. Tom sat by one of the piles of stone that had served as a wall during the civil war, and tried to remember what he'd learned of it.

Not much detail was known; the mill owner and his workers had put up a valiant but ultimately hopeless fight against the sudden attack by parliamentarians on their way down into Cornwall and some battle near Bude.

The grinding stone had then been used to prepare the attackers' weapons and, during the very battle for which these preparations had been made, a single lightning strike had all but destroyed the place: the upper, timber built tower and the sails burnt to nothing as the fire raged unchecked, and the mill had collapsed in on itself, burying the men who had died there.

'Got to be something weird about that,' he muttered aloud. Captain came back and licked his hand. Tom looked around, in this pale light it was hard to see such details as were left, but he'd been here often as a child, and remembered it quite well. 'Shame really,' he went on. 'I bet this could be a great place if it was done out, what do you think?'

The idea took hold as he sat there. Buying the land would be no problem: he could get a mortgage easily enough seeing as he now owned his cottage outright. A tingle started at the base of his skull, and he began to understand some of Laura's sense of liberation; a new life to banish the old one forever.

Re-creating the mill building would be no problem for skilled builders, there were plenty he could hire to help, and he'd make back any expenses in short order: Cornish properties, old and new were going for stupid money, encouraging the trade in this part of the country. A new project could be just what he needed – and when it was finished he'd have the choice of whether to move here himself, or rent it out and remain in the family home. Who owned this part of the moor anyway? Probably the Duchy. Prince Charles. Well, there were ways to find out.

'Bloody hell, Cap'n, this couldn't come at a better time. You and me are going to contact the Land Registry about this place first thing Monday. Hah! Welcome to our future, lad.'

***

On Saturday morning Laura found herself at Tom's front door, for the first time wondering if she should just turn and leave without seeing him again. Last night he'd seemed fine, but he was a proper Jekyll and Hyde character, lately. Eventually she raised her hand and knocked, then took a deep breath and pushed open the door.

'Hello, the house!' she called. It sounded falsely jovial and she wished she hadn't said anything.

'Enter and declare yourself!' came the cheerful reply from the kitchen, and Laura's heart gave a little flip of relief.

'Family, bearing sustenance,' she said, going into the kitchen and dumping a Tesco's carrier bag on the table.

'Thanks, sis.' Tom looked up from where he was washing his hands at the sink. 'Just been cleaning out the grate,' he explained. 'Coffee? Is Richard with you?'

'Um, no,' Laura said, surprised to hear him acknowledge Richard's existence without even a hint of rancour. 'Coffee would be great, thanks.'

'So, how goes it in the great metropolis?' he asked as he busied himself.

For a while Laura talked about her job and her new friends, then he put the coffee down in front of her and, knowing it was time to really test the water, she cupped her hands around it and braced herself. 'How about you, Tom?'

'How about me?'

'You seem better than you have lately. More rested.'

'Ah, and there's the thing. I've been sleeping like a baby.'

'Must be tiring,' Laura said.

'What?'

'Waking every four hours, demanding to be fed.'

He rolled his eyes and shook his head pityingly. 'Actually,' he said, sitting forward, 'I've got sort of a new

251

project in the pipeline.'

'Oh?'

'Yeah. I was thinking of buying the old mill and doing it up.'

Laura was jolted although she couldn't have said why, but Tom's enthusiasm put different words on her lips. 'Wow, that's a project and a half! Fantastic idea.'

'Yeah, Cap'n thinks so too,' Tom said. 'I'm itching to get started on it now.'

It was good to see excitement in his eyes again but also worrying to a degree; he seemed to have already pinned all his hopes on the place but there was the lurking possibility he wouldn't get funding, or lose it in some other way. What would he be left with then?

She pushed the thought to the back of her mind in case he read it and slumped back into misery again, at least he was happy for now.

'Will you do it out as a sort of heritage centre?'

'That's an idea,' he said. 'Hadn't thought beyond restoring it at the moment, but yeah, running it as a business would be good. Might make it easier to get the funding. Got a story behind it, so why not?'

Laura knew the story and it still made her shiver to think of real, living people, men with families and loves, clashing steel on these very moors – so much blood spilled on the ground where she had played so carelessly as a child. She wasn't sure she liked the idea of builders ripping the ancient heart out of the ruin, putting down plastic and metal in its place.

Perhaps it was visiting the Bude museum; seeing the armour recovered from bogs on the moor, and Richard's absorption with those artefacts, had made her look at it all differently. But that feeling of discovering a whole new life was such a wonderful, liberating one, she couldn't put the brakes on for Tom. 'If there's any way I can help, let me know, okay?' she said.

Tom nodded. 'Come with me and look at it, if you've got an hour. Tell me what you think?'

She hesitated, not really sure why, then nodded, forcing a smile and together they went up the hill, Captain enjoying his second long walk in two days. They poked around the ruin, discussing the gradually emerging possibilities. The local children never came up here anymore, it was considered too dangerous. Laura thought of the way she and her friends had behaved not so long ago; running around out here until it got dark, no way of keeping in contact with their parents … nowadays they weren't allowed on the school play equipment at lunchtime without written permission. Ridiculous.

Tom's thoughts clearly echoed her own. 'Have to fence it off from the surrounding moorland,' he observed wryly, 'everyone will be throwing themselves down mineshafts otherwise. Look,' he stepped over a crumbling wall. 'This was most likely where it happened.' After a moment Laura followed him, and, thinking about what had happened in here over three hundred and fifty years ago she shivered and involuntarily lifted her foot, half expecting to see blood staining the grass.

'Hard to imagine,' Tom said quietly. But for Laura it wasn't hard at all. She closed her eyes and could almost see it: the mill owner brutally cut down, his stone used instead to grind, to killing keenness, the edges of the Parliamentarians' blades. She saw hard working men reduced to blood-soaked sacks of flesh cooling on the ground; the mill would have been all eerie silence one moment, and swamped by the roar of the leaping flames the next as lightning ignited the roof beams, sending them crashing onto the bodies of the men who had raised them.

Tom was speaking but his voice seemed to come from a very long way away. Gradually she became aware of him looking at her, his expression concerned.

She shook her head, managing a smile. 'Just a bit lost in the past,' she said, and climbed back over the wall, feeling easier as she stood on the grass outside where the house had been.

The wind gusted, strong and sudden, making her take a step forward to keep her balance, and her foot struck something. A key ring lay in the grass, the fob a heavy silver oval with an ornate design of unusual shapes carved deeply into it, each with a heart of deep blue stone. And on the ring just one, fairly new-looking key. She turned the fob over in her hand for a while, enjoying the heavy smoothness, and the way the weak sunlight caught the blue-centred stones – she'd never seen anything quite like it before, someone would definitely be missing this. She slipped the key ring into her jeans pocket and then checked her watch, relieved to have a genuine reason to leave.

Tom came back over the wall to join her. 'You want to go back?' he said, clearly trying to hide his disappointment.

'It's not so much that I want to. I'd love to look around a bit more, get a feel for what you can do here.' How easily the lie came to her lips; she had never wanted to get away from anywhere as much since her thirteenth summer. 'I'm supposed to be meeting Richard for lunch,' she explained, and was once again surprised by Tom's calm acceptance of Richard's name cropping up.

'Okay, well by the time we walk back down it'll be getting on for half twelve,' he admitted, and with a last look of mingled wistfulness and excitement he led the way back to the road.

'You haven't lost a key ring, have you?' she asked as she followed him, feeling the bump of it against her leg.

Tom checked his pocket. 'Nope, got mine right here,' he confirmed. 'Find one, did you?'

'Yeah. I'll just hand it in at the shop.'

'Where'd you find it? Not up there?' He stopped suddenly and she realised he was already thinking of the ruined mill as his own, to tell him someone else had recently been there would deflate him like a balloon.

'No, just by the side of the road, only remembered it now, that's all.'

'Oh, right.'

The way he visibly relaxed told her she'd made the right decision, but she didn't like it.

As they rounded the corner at the foot of the hill Laura saw Richard crossing the small green towards the shop. His walk was unmistakeable: long strides that carried him quickly across the ground without any semblance of hurrying, and the easy grace of a man completely unaware of his own powerful attraction.

'Hey!' she called out. Richard turned and, as always, Laura felt her breath shorten at the smile that was for her alone. She said a hurried goodbye to her brother and caught up with Richard.

'Hey yourself,' he said. 'Ready to eat? I'm starved.'

'Actually I was going to pop in there first, too,' she said, gesturing at the shop.

'Pop? You're not *that* fat.'

'Oh, get knotted, you know exactly what I mean!'

He grinned. 'You're such a lady.'

Inside, she went straight to the counter while Richard fetched milk from the chiller at the back, and by the time he joined her she had laid the key ring on the counter and was writing on a card to put in the window.

'Where'd you get that?'

'Found it while I was out,' she said. 'You go walking a lot, not yours, is it?'

'Nope, it's Dean's. Only seen it from a distance before, but hard to mistake.'

'Ah. Okay.' Laura screwed up the card. 'Sorry,' she said to the shop's owner, 'no need for this after all.'

Richard was turning the key ring over in his hand as she had done, his expression rapt. He seemed absorbed in the design, peering closely, frowning as though he were trying to place a recognition just beyond his grasp.

'So that's the key to my place, is it?' Laura said. 'They all look the same to me. Doesn't he have any others?'

'No, no need for any. When we moved into your place, he had a spare one cut, and found this key chain in some little place near his parents' store in Liskeard.'

'Oh yeah, forgot he was working there now. I might ask him to get me one next time he goes, it's a bit gorgeous isn't it?'

'This design is supposed to mean something I think,' Richard mused.

'I don't know about that, but it's lovely. Can you pass it on to him?'

'Sure. He's home right now. I'll drop this milk back and meet you in the bar, okay?'

As Laura walked into the pub she reflected how unlikely it'd be that she'd ever be able to do this comfortably in Plymouth. This place was small, familiar and friendly and since that first night of grasping the nettle she'd never had the slightest qualm about arriving alone. The city though, that was something else again. No way.

She took her drink and a menu to a back table, and a few minutes later a shadow fell across the table. Laura looked up.

'Dean, hi,' she said. 'Richard at the bar?'

'Where else? Thanks for finding the key ring.'

'Welcome. Glad it found its way back home so quickly. Are you joining us for lunch?'

'Would you mind?'

' 'Course not. Sit down.'

Dean slid into the seat opposite, and picked up the menu. 'How's things in the big city?' he asked.

'Big. Citified. Work's going okay though, thanks. How about you, enjoying working with your parents? Sports shop, isn't it?'

Dean hesitated and started to answer but broke off, looking relieved as Richard joined them and took his seat. He seized the menu from Dean, ignoring his friend's protest.

'So, how'd it go with Tom this morning?' he asked Laura.

She told them about her brother's new found peace of mind, helped in no small part by the project he had planned. 'It's the old mill,' she said. 'You know the one, Dean.'

'Yeah, I know the place.'

'It was destroyed during the civil war,' she explained to Richard. 'One of the sails was hit by lightning and the place burned to the ground. I'll tell you the story sometime.'

'Maybe you can show me?' Richard said.

'Yeah. Tomorrow? And if we don't get around to it this weekend Dean can always show you.'

'Sounds like a cool place.'

'It is, isn't it, Dean?'

'Never been there.'

'But –'

'What?' Dean fixed his pale blue eyes on hers and she felt her skin shrink under the intensity of that look. Why was he lying?

'Nothing,' she said, keeping her tone light. 'I just assumed you'd been there, you know, as a kid.'

Dean blinked, and she saw the realisation in his face as he touched his pocket and, presumably, the key ring. 'Oh, yeah! Sorry, brain fart.' He rolled his eyes. 'I went up there just yesterday actually, just for a change of scenery. My stomping ground was always the other end of the village,' he added, 'beyond the mines, out that way.'

'Anyway, I want you to show me,' Richard said to Laura, tearing his eyes away from the menu and apparently not noticing the exchange. 'You'll be able to explain what Tom wants to do. If he's getting to be okay with me being in your life, maybe he'll let me help him.'

'Maybe,' Laura said, 'but right now this is his baby. You understand.'

'Yeah, sure, of course. So, what're we eating?'

'I wouldn't know, you stole the menu,' Dean said, and snatched it back, rapping Richard smartly on the head with it.

As talk turned to food, Laura watched him carefully. What could he possibly have to lie about? All the old questions were finding their way back into her head: how they could have spent their childhood in such a small place and never met; his mysterious appearance and equally strange disappearance; how he just happened to be hanging around outside the family home when Martin had had his stroke

If Richard Lucas was mysterious in a troubled, honest way, then Dean Mayer had a darker shadow trailing him. All at once, despite the dangers to be found in the city, Plymouth looked like the safer place to be.

Chapter Twenty-Three

Sunday afternoon. Richard walked up the road with Laura at his side, and although the wind whipped at their clothing and the drizzle plastered their hair to their heads he felt content, peaceful. Laura had been quiet yesterday afternoon, and a little distant through the evening, but after a drive out to St Austell Market earlier today she had reverted back to her usual sunny mood.

Even after leaving the road it was a fairly long walk along a rough lane, but eventually they stepped off, onto a rock-strewn path. Now they were close enough to see the remains of the mill house, she began to tell him more of the story behind it.

Richard wiped his wet hair away from his eyes and looked around him as she talked. The mist shrouding the top of the hill added to the impression of stepping back in time: nothing could be seen of the village below, or of the distant main road that ran towards Bodmin.

As with everywhere on the moor, Richard felt at ease here, but hearing the story of the slain millers brought a chill to his bones the wind and rain could not account for.

'One of the sails was hit by a freak lightning bolt, apparently,' Laura said. 'With no-one left alive to fight the fire, it burned to the ground. Of course no-one knows if anyone could have done anything about it anyway. That poor miller.'

'And his brothers.'

'Well, friends or brothers, or just workers.'

'No, they were his brothers.' As the words left his lips, Richard wondered where they came from, but only distantly; on a much more immediate level he was hearing

259

other sounds: the clash of combat, of someone crying out a name, 'Stephen!'

'How do you know that?' Laura's voice brought him back and he blinked slowly. She was looking at him the same way she had in the museum in Bude when he'd been similarly distracted. 'That they were brothers?' she urged. 'How could you know that when you didn't know anything about this place?' Now she was looking unnerved too, and he reached a hand out and took her hand in reassurance.

'You know what? I think we were right,' he said. 'I'm sure I have some kind of historical link with this place. You talking about the miller, I heard that, but I also heard something ... Jesus, the dream!' Richard took a step to the low, broken wall, on legs that felt as if they'd had the bones stripped out, and sat down.

'What dream?' Laura sat beside him, and now she didn't look worried but excited, fascinated. On an impulse he leaned in and kissed her, She tasted cold and fresh, and he felt her smile against his lips, so he kissed her again.

'I dreamed about this place,' he said, when they broke apart. 'Not specifically here, but there was a battle, one of my ancestors was in it, I'd swear to it. I've got to read about this racial memory stuff, Laura, I don't know a damn thing about it. But it's so *strong!*'

'I know it's a recognised thing, I've checked it out a bit,' Laura offered, her lips still so tantalising close he wanted to kiss her again. Instead, he put his arm around her and pulled her in so she could rest her head in the hollow of his shoulder. She didn't seem to mind the heavy wetness of his coat, and he felt her arms go round him.

'I can remember most of the dream. I guess it couldn't have happened exactly that way, but I put details in it I could never have known about: the armour, stuff like that.

And I always thought armies just used swords until I saw those pikes in the museum, but I, *he*, was carrying one. Sawn off to about fourteen feet.'

'What side was he on?'

'He was a Royalist. Named Stephen something. No question. There was such an anger in that dream, I can remember it like it was last night. Someone told him about the mill, his friend it was: John - John Bartholomew.'

'Oh my god! You even have names in your head?' Laura sat up, away from him, and he laughed, feeling feather light with relief.

'This John told the guy in the dream that the miller and his brothers were dead. There was lightning, way over the hill.'

Laura shook her head. 'This is incredible! Do you think, maybe, that business out on the moors, when you scared us both stupid, that was a kind of historical flashback?'

'I guess. That part's pretty blurred, but this, it's as if someone's playing a movie in my head. Right now.'

'So what happened in the battle?' Laura wanted to know.

Richard thought for a moment, but shook his head. The dream was clear right up until he that name called out. 'I don't remember that part, I think the guy's friend was hurt.'

'Bartholomew?'

'Yeah. We may be able to check that out. God, I can't tell you what a relief this is. I remember waking from that dream, it was just after Cait ...' his throat tightened and he couldn't speak for a moment. Laura squeezed his arm and they sat quietly, looking around the ruined mill.

'So, Tom's going to get this place working again?' Richard said at last.

'That's the plan.'

'Let's take a look around.'

There wasn't much to see, but Laura painted the word pictures Tom had given her, and it was easy to envisage: the full story of the tragic miller and his brothers would be preserved forever. But Laura suddenly seemed anxious to leave, telling him about Tom's plans seemed to have taken the shine from her eyes. They started towards the path and she stopped and frowned, looking at the grass.

'What is it?' Richard asked.

She didn't reply for a moment and he wasn't sure she'd heard, then she shrugged. 'This is where I found Dean's key ring.'

'Yeah? He said he was walking up here.'

'But first he said he'd never been here. Why would he say that?'

Richard frowned. 'Are you sure he knew you were talking about this place?'

'There was only ever one mill here. He knew. Richard, do you think he could be doing something illegal here?'

'Like what?' Richard's first instinct was to laugh but he could see Laura was serious. Of course she didn't know Dean like he did.

'Drugs maybe? This is a really out of the way place,' she pointed out, 'it'd be perfect. And Cornwall does have a fairly notorious coastline.'

'Dean doesn't do drugs, babe.'

'Not himself, no. Or if not drugs, then maybe guns, alcohol, cigarettes? Where does he go every day?'

'To work at his parents' place while they're away. You know that.'

'Have you ever been there?'

'Laura, please, think about this. He walks in a lot of places, he was probably distracted at first when you mentioned it. He was pissed at me for stealing the menu, remember?'

He could see the thought made her pause and he was glad: she was making him uncomfortable because no, he'd never been to Dean's place of work, he didn't know for sure that was where he went, and Dean had seemed pretty anxious for her to leave the village. Shit, *he* was even questioning his best friend now.

He shook his head. 'I've known him since I was fifteen,' he said. 'Whatever the reason, if he is lying about being here it won't be because of drugs, or weapons or any of that stuff.'

'Okay. But please, Richard – if he's involved in anything he shouldn't be, don't get pulled in.'

'I won't.' He felt her let out a heavy sigh and relax against him. 'Is this why you were weird at lunch yesterday?' he asked.

'I just couldn't understand why he'd be lying,' she said. 'He's always seemed a bit mysterious, but it didn't occur to me that this would be a perfect place for hiding stuff until just now.'

'So you seriously think he may be stashing stuff here?'

'It's possible.'

'Want to take a look around?'

She shook her head. 'No time, I have to get back. Besides, it'll be really well-hidden.'

'*If* it was here.'

'Yes. Will you keep an eye out?'

'Okay. It's all I can do.'

'Thanks. Because if Tom takes this place on and finds something –'

'Yeah, I understand. Don't worry.'

As they left the mill behind he tried to recapture his relief at finding an explanation for his strange feelings, but his thoughts kept straying to Dean, and where he spent his days.

Mingled with the niggling and disturbing new doubt was the ache that always set in when it was time for Laura to leave, and less than twenty minutes later, after Tom had called in to say his goodbyes, Richard was lifting her bag into the trunk of her car. He held her close one last time before releasing her to slip behind the wheel. 'Call or text when you get home, okay?'

'Nope.' But she would, she always did, no matter what time it was.

'Stay safe,' he said, the last part of their ritual, and she blew him a kiss and, for the first time ever, responded:

'You too.'

Richard waited until her car was out of sight, then turned to go back inside. As he did so he saw a figure in the lane, unmistakeably agile, and moving with considerable speed. And heading towards the mill. His heart sank, and he debated whether or not to follow, but accepted he had no choice when he realised his feet had already started in that direction.

Dean was gone from sight by the time Richard came to the hill and he started up quickly, hoping to see him walk past the turning, or stride away over the moor, anything rather than confirm Laura's suspicions.

When he himself arrived at the rock path, it was almost dark. He was walking with a light step, but found himself holding his breath in any case, listening out for evidence he'd been noticed. He peered at the crumbling walls of the cottage and the dark shadow of the tower base.

There was no sign of Dean. For a second he thought he saw him, standing beside the back wall, but when he peered harder there was nothing but shadow.

Richard sat down on the wall, wondering if he'd

imagined the whole thing. The conversation with Laura must have been weighing more heavily on his mind than he'd realised, but could he really have projected a picture like that onto the evening canvas? There had been no doubt at the time, no doubt at all, but the guy couldn't have just disappeared. He must be losing it.

Then the voice spoke behind him, and it wasn't Dean.

***

Maer heard Richard's approach, saw him peer directly at him and, heart hammering, twisted the shadows further to make doubly sure he was no more noticeable than an individual blade of grass. He watched, eyesight easily piercing the gloom as Richard sat down, bewildered.

Tom had headed here the moment he'd said goodbye to Laura, and Maer had followed of course, never realising until now that Richard had, in turn, seen and followed him. It was obvious why: Laura's suspicions were not something she could have kept to herself. There was nothing he could do now but stay out of sight and pray that Loen was sleeping tonight, gathering his strength.

And now Tom appeared from behind the tower. The shadow loomed tall above the seated figure, who had not heard his approach.

'Piss off, Lucas. This place is mine.'

Richard was on his feet before the first word was complete. There was anger on Tom's face and Maer tensed, but even he was not prepared for the speed of Tom's attack.

Richard opened his mouth, probably to explain he'd been following Dean, but was sent stumbling as Tom's fist smashed into his jaw, snapping his head back. Richard fell, hit the ground and immediately rolled away, and

265

Tom's boot, aiming for his ribs, struck the wall instead.

Maer's own hands were clenched in an agony of fear: there was no telling what might happen here. Thankfully Richard had regained his wits and come to his feet quickly, alert and ready to protect himself. Blood was seeping slowly from a graze along his jaw.

'What the hell was that for?' he demanded, his voice rough and furious.

Tom's eyebrows drew together. 'I said piss off. Leave me alone.'

'I'm not looking for you.'

'Well you've found me.' Tom lunged again and Richard took a step back, hands held out in front of him. He clearly did not want to strike back, but Maer saw one hand close naturally into a fist as his back came up against the tower – he was ready.

The wind started to pick up. It tugged at Richard's coat, and blew the hair back from his face but it worked against Tom, whose own fringe flapped into his eyes. He wiped a hand across his forehead, but the wind blew stronger still, and then a wall of heavy, thundery rain swept down across the moor. Maer stared at Richard, who did not seem surprised by the worsening weather and had his entire attention fixed on Tom.

The wind changed abruptly, blasting into Tom's face and temporarily blinding him. He shook his hair from his eyes and grabbed at Richard, and then the two of them were locked together, Tom howling in fury, Richard silent and tight-lipped as he struggled against his taller, heavier assailant.

Maer wanted desperately to come forward but Tom had hold of Richard's coat and was shaking him from side to side, and all Richard's strength was going into trying to loosen that hold before he was flung headfirst into the stone wall; to distract him now might be fatal.

The wind raged around the two men, and just as Maer was about to intervene he saw lightning step down nearby, followed by a crack of thunder so sharp and sudden the two men jerked apart in shock. Richard fell to his knees and Tom was clutching at his chest, breathing hard, eyes wide with fear and confusion.

He backed away from Richard, and Maer saw him look to the sky as the rain stopped as suddenly as it had begun, and the wind fell to no more than the chilly breeze it had been before. He turned and, with one last look at Richard, broke away and ran.

Maer passed by close behind his bewildered friend in order to follow, and as he did so a thought struck him: Richard had seen and identified Maer's presence earlier without realising conventional sight had nothing to do with it – an acute sense of the spirits around him that mortals rarely achieve.

Maer let out a shaky breath. Gilan had not deliberately allowed himself to be seen after all, Richard was becoming something different here on the moors, his elemental self was coming to the fore – a development that would make him even more easily accessible to Loen. Maer waited at the top of the path until he saw Richard stand, and, reassured his friend wasn't hurt, he took off swiftly into the night.

***

Richard clambered to his feet, pressing his fingers to his jaw, and winced as the ache told him he'd be bruised pretty damn good by morning. Tom was gone, Laura had been right about his claim to this place but obviously his feelings ran even deeper than she'd realised. Unless ... he stopped for a moment, frowning. What if it were Tom doing something illegal? No, he'd never have brought Laura here if so. He hadn't attacked because he'd been caught doing something he shouldn't, he'd attacked because he had a hatred that just wouldn't let up.

Richard started the walk back, his muscles still tense with fury. For Laura's sake he'd promised to make things right with the guy, but it was kind of hard if he was going to get his jaw busted just for being in the wrong place. 'Asshole son of a bitch,' he said aloud, enjoying the freedom of saying it without hurting her.

Her reproachful face floated in the front of his mind and he sighed. Okay, fine, he'd give it one more shot. Call in on Tom, explain he'd been looking for Dean but he'd been mistaken, tell him he'd never set foot on the damn mill land again and couldn't they just get along for the sake of the one woman they both loved?

It sounded good, rattling around in his head, and although the friendly light of home called to him on the way, he walked past Laura's house and carried on into the village.

As he drew alongside Tom's cottage he paused, unsure. Maybe it was too soon? The first knock brought no reply, just yelping from Tom's dog, and after knocking a second time, louder, Richard bent to look through the letter box. The front room beyond was well lit but there was no sign of Tom, so he moved to the window where the curtains stood parted a few inches.

He stepped carefully over the narrow flower bed beneath the window and framed his eyes with his hands to help him focus. A second later he stumbled back, not caring what he crushed, and shoved the front door open.

Tom was lying on the floor, his hands by his sides. Captain sat at his head, licking his face and whining, then looked round at Richard with a helpless, pleading tilt to his head. There was no sign of any alcohol – maybe Tom was epileptic? Heart attack was also a grim possibility: he was a big guy, and didn't eat too wisely most of the time. He didn't look as if he'd been convulsing, more as if he'd just passed out cold and fallen backwards where he stood.

Richard dropped to a crouch beside him. 'Tom! Can you hear me?'

Tom turned his head a little and mumbled something, and Richard sighed in relief and tried again, reaching out to shake Tom's shoulder.

'Hey, it's Richard. I – ' A light sparked behind his eyes as a large hand swung up, hit the side of his head and knocked him off balance.

Even as he felt a wave of anger at having been struck twice by this oaf, his own hands flashed out with gratifying speed to steady himself, but before he could retreat he felt the painful grip of fingers fastened tight to his shoulders, and he gasped.

Something was pulsing into him. Sudden, agonising pressure, rooted deep in his guts and spreading right up into his head, as if he had too much … *self* for his body. Through the confused roar in his ears he thought he heard a whisper, soaked in desperation;

'Mine!'

He was overflowing, his blood vessels expanding and filling with something he couldn't accommodate. In sudden, possessive outrage he lashed out, striking Tom under the chin. It was a lucky blow, the man fell and Richard scrambled backwards out of his way as Tom landed heavily on his side, unconscious once more.

Captain's furious, protective yelping sounded as if it were coming from a long way away, but the nip on his fingers was close enough. Richard jerked his hand away from the angry puppy and stared in disbelief – had Tom even woken? He didn't think so. God, the man was lethal, even in his sleep.

He looked down at himself, expecting to see his chest and stomach as tight and bloated as they felt, but his rain-drenched shirt remained buttoned, unripped. The trembling disorientation began to fade and Richard stood, feeling the blood pounding in his throat and head, every pulse point still seemed to be bursting from his body, as if there was still too much life to fit inside his skin. His nerve endings tingled as he ran a shaking hand through his hair, he could feel every root tugging at his scalp.

Abruptly the swollen sensation vanished, leaving him light-headed and nauseous,

'Holy shit,' he breathed, and as he took another step back the floor seemed to tilt under his feet and a rush of motion sickness hit. He braced his hands on his knees and let his head hang for a moment until the urge to vomit had passed. He took a deep breath and leaned over Tom to make sure he too was breathing, then backed out of the house, loathe even then to take his eyes off the man.

As he walked back towards the cottage, Richard felt a prickling all over as he recalled exactly how it had felt. But beyond the pain and the sickening, crawling sensation of something trying to force him out, to make way for the vastness of whatever was trying to claim him, beyond even the horrified realisation that it had conquered his body, and was trying for his mind … beyond all that had been absolute, white-blazing fury and he felt it again now, burning in his chest, his head tight with it. What right did *anything* have to make him feel like he didn't belong in his own body?

Abruptly he stopped, the anger displaced by a freezing memory: the voice hissing, 'Mine!'

'No,' he whispered back to the night, turning around slowly in the deserted road, only vaguely aware he was saying it out loud, and not understanding why he was saying it at all, but feeling it deep in his bones nevertheless. His own voice hardened. 'Never. *Mine,* dammit ...'

Chapter Twenty-Four

Maer waited, television on but unheeded, and finally he heard the front door open. Richard came into the front room, his eyes worryingly distant. The graze on his jaw was matched now by a red mark on the same cheekbone, and Maer frowned. He'd seen Tom to his home and then reported straight to Deera but maybe he should have stuck around instead.

'Are you okay? What happened?'

'I'm fine. I'm gonna go take a shower.'

He turned without another word and went upstairs. A moment later, Maer heard the water running and he sagged, covering his face with his hands; it was all happening too fast now. But he held onto his despair, knowing that if he let go the intensity of it would take voice, and the cry would carry to the farthest reaches of the moor.

As time passed Maer's apprehension only increased: Richard never took this long in the shower, he'd been in there at least twenty minutes now. At last the water clicked off and a minute later there were footsteps on the stairs, and he composed himself as Richard appeared. He wore only a large towel around his waist and had rubbed his hair so hard it stood in semi-dry spikes all over his head.

Maer seized upon the chance to make a joke, to ease the ache in his heart, and was about to comment when he realised that wasn't the only thing that had been scrubbed with more than the usual vigour. 'Christ, Rich!' he breathed in horror.

'Guess I was going for the Silkwood scrub down,' Richard said, a hint of humour briefly touching his eyes. Maer didn't smile, he felt ill: Richard's body no longer showed an all-over, healthy, light tan, instead it was hot and pink, rubbed raw, spotting blood in places.

He shook his head, precluding questions, at least for now. 'It's okay, I'm clean.'

'You're *peeled* is what you are!' Maer retorted, fear sharpening his voice into anger. He stared at his friend, noting the obsessive attention to hygiene seemed confined to Richard's face and torso, his arms and legs retained their natural colour. 'You're going to need some kind of cream on that,' he pointed out, and Richard nodded.

'Yeah, I got some of Laura's aqueous stuff right here.' He screwed the lid off and applied the water-based cream to the worst of the raw patches. Then, body daubed with thick white blobs, he faced the large mirror over the mantelpiece and Maer saw the look of fear flash across his face, quickly replaced by a cheerful, patently false grin. 'Good thing Laura's away for a few days,' he observed, squeezing more cream onto his fingers and smearing it across his forehead.

'Why'd you do it, Rich?' Maer asked quietly.

Richard grew still and met his eyes in the mirror. 'I don't know,' he said, troubled now. 'I got in the shower, and I felt this weird urge to scrub. As if the dirt was inside.' He pressed a hand to his body, then let it fall away – Dean saw blood mixed with the white cream and felt sick. 'I had kind of a fight with Tom, up by the mill,' Richard went on, 'he just attacked me out of nowhere. So I went to his place to try and, you know, patch things up for Laura's sake.'

'And?' Maer knew he should've sounded more surprised about the attack by the mill, but he was too desperate to hear what had happened since. Gilan had been shirking his duties again.

273

'He was lying on the floor, I thought he was sick or something so I went in.'

'And then what?'

Richard shook his head, and had to try twice before he could speak. His words told a vague story, a sense of crushing tightness, intense pain, but little more: his memory of the event was clearly fading fast, yet as he listened Maer's desperation to get Richard at a safe distance from Lynher Mill threatened to stop him breathing.

'Maybe you'd better get away for a few days,' he said. 'Go and stay with Laura, or take some days out by yourself. Just get away from here for a little while.'

'I can't let that guy run me out of the village. I'll just stay away from him 'til he's over whatever it is that makes him want to kill me.'

'What about the other stuff, the weird stuff?'

Richard looked blank for a moment, almost as if Loen's possession attempt had been swept from his memory already. Then he frowned. 'I don't know. I can't explain it, I'm probably making it sound a way bigger deal than it is.'

He sighed and dabbed more cream on a raw spot on his collar-bone. 'This looks crazy but to be honest I can't even really remember what it felt like. All I know is I feel as if I belong here just as much as Tom does, whether that makes any kind of sense or not I have no idea. But I'm not letting him win.'

He left the room and Maer's heart trembled: he knew his own part in this was coming, and he had to be the catalyst, give himself to Loen now instead of waiting for the appointed moment. Courage, that was what he needed, and the right opportunity ... and that opportunity must present itself before Laura's return on Friday.

Jacky Greencoat waited, twisting the dart with trembling fingers. This would put an end to the plan – to his queen's plan … his breath hitched in panic at the thought, but the image of a furious Gilan in his mind's eye made him shake even harder. Gilan would be the restored king's advisor when Deera was disgraced. He was the dangerous one.

The dart lay still now in Jacky's grimy hand: once the curare-based poison was in the half-mortal's blood it would be a matter of moments until he was paralysed, unable to breathe, and Jacky would be able to drag the body while it still lived, the better to hide it more quickly. It would take little time to get it to the marshy ground and watch it disappear beneath the moor forever, and he would likely never know if death came in the form of drowning or of suffocation, but it would come, nevertheless.

He lifted the hollowed stick and examined it once again for obstructions, peering through it at the brilliant blue sky. He had only seen Lucas from a distance, a few days ago, walking with familiar assurance over the pathless hillocks and tufts on this otherwise deserted part of the heath. At first he'd thought it must be Tom Riley, but as he'd drawn closer he'd seen the difference in more than stature: Riley moved with ease through this difficult terrain, but this man almost seemed to drift. Jacky's heart had thumped hard and he'd turned away, back to his own granite covered cavern hidden in the hill.

But today he would remain out here in the open. He would carry out Gilan's orders and destroy this man whose body would, ultimately, have failed the king. That could not happen: Loen must have Prince Maer's fine, strong form or risk another terrible death. This act of apparent treason today would save Loen's life.

Having satisfied himself that he was, after all, doing the right thing, Jacky waited, his bones growing numb from sitting on the rock. He was on the verge of accepting Gilan was wrong about Lucas's habits when he heard it; a man's voice, raised absently in song, coming closer over the moor. The raw beauty of the sound made Jacky shiver in reluctant delight and his hand clenched on the dart. Oh, that he must destroy such a song!

But he fitted the dart into the stick and lifted it to his lips. Lucas appeared over the hill and stopped to gaze over the glory of the vista spread out before him; Jacky understood the reaction well.

A smile touched Lucas's lips as he looked about him and Jacky closed his eyes, unable to look on this display of simple pleasure lest it sway him from his duty. He knew he could not be seen, but still he shrunk down until he judged that clear green gaze had passed him by, then he raised the stick again.

His choices were limited: today the long, black coat was open, tugged away by the brisk, snapping wind, and although the shirt beneath it was thin the dart could not pass through cloth. It must be bare skin. As if lending his assistance, Lucas raised his face to the sky, offering his throat to the barb that would kill him. Jacky was close enough to see the pulse that beat steadily there – the pulse that must soon be stopped. He drew a deep breath and closed his lips on the stick, preparing to send the dart spinning through the air.

And then Lucas looked right at him.

Jacky gasped and dropped the stick - Of course Lucas had not seen him, but that gaze had seemed to burn a hole right through his face! He felt at his feet with shaking fingers and found the stick, the barb still lodged in the tip, and lifted it to his lips again. Raising his gaze to take aim once more he paused, then lowered the stick to his side, letting the dart fall into his hand. He did not raise it again.

He stared instead, at Lucas. He saw thick black hair, breeze-lifted away from a fine, clear brow, saw a smile curve the lips and lighten the eyes, saw the graceful body braced against the wind ... but he saw something else also, something that encompassed that fragile mortal beauty and gave it meaning. At last Jacky understood.

Chapter Twenty-Five

Tom jerked awake to the sound of crashing on his front door. He leaned out of his bedroom window, surprised and annoyed to see Dean Mayer out there, and flung the window open.

'What the bloody hell are you playing at?' he yelled.

Mayer glanced worriedly behind him, as if he was expecting someone to come and drag him away at any moment. 'It's important, it's about Laura. Can I come in?'

Once Mayer was inside he didn't seem to know what to say, and Tom grew more and more worried. 'For God's sake, what are you here for? What about Laura?'

Mayer found his voice at last. 'All you need to know is that she mustn't come back here. That's all,'

'Why? Is it that bastard Lucas? What's he —'

'No! Richard would never harm her, you know that.' He seemed to come to a decision, and sighed, and as he stepped forward as if to tell a confidence, Tom felt light-headed, and a fluttering in his chest made him take a deep breath. Mayer's expression also paled and he moved back a little, a hand rising to his head, resting at his temple. 'Fact is he's the one who's in danger; someone's followed him here from Chicago. An old enemy — he's tried to kill Richard before and he'll do the same thing to anyone who gets in his way, like he did Richard's wife —'

'His wife?'

'She was killed eleven years ago, and he was badly wounded. Look, Laura's the first one he's let through to his heart since, that's why I know he would never do anything to put her at risk.'

Tom was surprised to feel a stab of sympathy for Lucas, but it was quickly overshadowed by worry for

Laura, and fury at the danger the American had brought into her life. He turned away and pulled open the front door, one hand raised ready to push his visitor out.

Mayer grew desperate in his pleading. 'Please! You have to stop her from coming back here, but –' his voice dropped and he glanced over his shoulder – 'You can't tell her why.'

'Why not?'

'Because she loves him, you idiot! Do you think for one minute she'd stay in Plymouth if she knew someone was planning to kill him?'

'Yeah? What about the police?'

'We've told them, they're looking into it, but they've told us to keep Laura away.' Mayer's eyes flickered but when he fixed them on Tom again they held only honest fear. 'Call her, Tom. E-mail her, something. Anything. Just, please, keep her away from here for the next few days until we can get this sorted, okay?'

'I'll call her tonight, she'll be going to work in a minute.'

'E-mail her then, at home and at work. But don't tell her too much. If Richard gets in touch with her first he may say the wrong thing and get her back here without meaning to.'

Tom scowled. 'Just let me tell you one thing though, Mayer –' At the sound of his name Mayer's eyes widened, then he shook his head and motioned for Tom to continue.

Tom took a deep breath and controlled himself with an effort. 'If your friend does, or causes, anything to hurt my sister, *I* will rip him limb from limb. Do you understand?'

Mayer's eyes narrowed and fixed him with a look that brought the power squarely back into his own quarter. 'Just make sure she doesn't come back.'

And then he was gone. Tom stared at the closed door for a moment, momentarily unsure whether the exchange had taken place at all, it had such an air of unreality about it. Dean was a weird one and no mistake. He checked his watch: he really needed to be at his doctor's appointment today of all days; a prescription for sleeping pills was starting to look good. He went back upstairs, trying not to dwell on what kind of trouble Lucas might have brought with him from America.

Once dressed he opened his e-mail client and started a new message.

Laura,

Just want to tell you I'm going to spend a couple of days in Bude from tomorrow, but in the meantime your boyfriend is acting a bit high and mighty and frankly it's pissing me off. It's no big deal but I'd rather not think of the two of you discussing me when I'm not here to put my side forward, so promise me you'll stay put and let him and me work this through? We'll do it better on our own, and don't worry, we'll be civilised about it - Dean is determined we'll be shaking hands instead of throats by the time you come back!

We'll sort it, ok?

Love as always, Tom.

Tom read it through to satisfy himself he had told Laura enough without worrying her. As his eyes moved over the text he felt his vision blurring slightly, the words mingling into a lump of black and white misshapes. God, he was so tired, maybe he didn't need sleeping pills after all. But then there was the terror of waking in the mine – at least pills would knock him out properly. Something about the place seemed attractive to him now though; it would be cool, dark and quiet down there, he would be able to sleep for as long as he wanted …

He woke twenty minutes later, his head lolling back on the leather chair, a thin line of spit cold on his chin. Jerking upright with a look at the clock, he reached out and switched off the monitor, grabbed his keys and left, picking up his crash helmet on the way. Halfway down the path he couldn't remember if he'd sent the e-mail, and hesitated. Then he shook his head; he'd miss his appointment if he went back now, and a couple of hours wouldn't make any difference, Laura wasn't due home for days.

The duty GP peered into Tom's eyes, asking him various questions about his sleepwalking activities … none of which Tom could answer truthfully; he couldn't bring himself to tell the doctor about waking in the mine, and simply said he had woken outside the house.

'You stressed about something?' the doctor asked 'Work going okay?'.

'Work's fine.'

'Well look, I'm sure you've got nothing to worry about. Take a few days off if you can, and you could try some herbal sleeping tablets, or some St Johns Wort. If they don't work, come back to me and I'll make out a prescription for something stronger. That do you?'

'Yeah, thanks. Frankly I'm so knackered right now I'll probably manage without anything at all.'

'Keep some handy – sometimes tiredness can work against itself.'

It was a little after ten when Tom left the surgery in St Tourney, and headed back towards home. As he rode he thought about the mill, and his plans for it. He needed to get hold of the land registry plans, and contact the Duchy of Cornwall, and someone who knew about restoring windmills, and ...

A sudden and frightening realisation brought him to a skidding stop in the middle of the quiet country lane and the bike stalled, ticking hotly. He could hardly account for any of the time he'd spent up there yesterday evening. He had heard people say they didn't know where the time had gone during their holidays, or that they had simply idled it away and relaxed, but this was different. He strained to remember what he had been doing there to begin with, and encountered only blankness after saying goodbye to Laura.

His hands began to weaken on the grips of his motorbike, and he ripped his glove off with his teeth to see his fingers shaking uncontrollably, and the knuckles of his right hand grazed. His heart was thudding fast and light, and he leaned the bike over onto its stand and braced his hands on his thighs. He bent over, waiting for the tremors to subside and his pulse to return to normal.

A sweat broke out on his forehead, and when he tried to reach up to release his chin strap his fingers fumbled ineffectually and the road seemed to tilt towards him. A hard smacking sound told him he'd fallen from the bike and smashed his crash helmet into the tarmac, but he didn't feel it. Blackness closed in.

***

Loen felt the strength flowing into himself again as Tom lost consciousness. He was becoming a little easier to control when he was awake, but Loen was not yet strong enough to take over completely. He had pushed and pushed at Tom's mind this time, until the conflicting commands had overloaded, and Loen was able to use the confusion to bring himself forward.

This boy could have no idea of the way fate had played him: when he had breathed the remains of the most ancient of kings into himself he had accepted the shape of his own destiny, and it was a cruel and ugly shape indeed – as befitted the last in the line of that accursed chief. Once the sister was gone Loen could dispose of this frail human form, and take possession of a true faery body in which to reign as was his right.

He had felt the nearness of such a body just a short while ago and surged towards, it but checked himself at the last moment: desirable as that body was, it was wrong. There was another – the one whose pain had shocked him into a new understanding a few short cycles ago, the same one he had almost claimed so recently. That spirit had fought back hard, and its strength made Loen all the more determined to take it. The temptation of the first healthy form to come within reach must be subdued, but before he could claim the body of his descendant, the last threads of this glorious weaving must be brought together and the ends tied: Laura Riley must come home.

***

Tom woke on the floor of his living room, aching and exhausted. For a moment he lay still, re-orientating himself, then abruptly he sat up, a whimper caught in his throat: there was nothing in his memory between stopping in the road with the feeling he was either going to pass out or be sick, and waking here, now.

Climbing to his feet he blinked at the computer, the screensaver informing him of the time: 11.52 am, over two hours lost. He checked again, his spine crawling. He knew he'd switched off the monitor this morning, it was habit.

Feeling nauseous all over again he hit the space bar on his keyboard and the screen saver vanished, replaced by his e-mail client. He checked his sent items folder, breathing a sigh of relief as he saw he had sent the message to Laura after all, and opened the mail to reassure himself he'd said nothing to worry her.

Shock brought a bitter taste to the back of his mouth. He rose and backed away from the computer, re-reading the short, unfamiliar message with grainy eyes.

'Somethings happening im scared please come home.'

He moaned aloud and, with frantically trembling fingers, seized the phone and stabbed the speed-dial for Laura. No reply. He tried her mobile with the same result – she was probably driving out here by now. He left a message on her voicemail, then he threw the phone down and sank onto the sofa.

A moment later he was up and hunting for his keys. Not there. He must have walked home, leaving his bike a good three miles away near St Tourney, and by the time he walked back out to it Laura might be here, and there would be no-one to warn her of the danger she was in.

The low rumble of thunder outside sounded far too sinister; something about it made him stare in superstitious fear at the prematurely darkening day. A moment later, a flash brilliant enough to make him turn away left squares of vivid blue behind his eyelids, and he blinked rapidly to clear his vision.

All he could do was wait, and hope she came to him first.

***

Maer headed out towards the mine. It would have to be tonight: his watch duty would take him to Tom's house, and there he would force Loen to take him – it had almost happened earlier, when he'd stepped too close, he'd felt a pressure building in his body that gave him some inkling of the assault Richard had experienced.

He knew now that, whether he wanted to or not, Loen would take him if he was close enough: the basic instinct for survival would be paramount, at least for long enough for Maer to tempt him. But first he had to see the queen, try one last time to reach her, as a son to his mother. Perhaps then she would be able to forgive him later when she discovered what he'd done.

As he started towards the mine he heard a shout, and turned to see Richard on his way back from his walk.

'Hey. What are you doing here?'

'Looking for you,' Maer only acknowledged the idea as the words left his mouth.

Richard blinked. 'Huh? Why, what's the problem?' Then he tensed. 'It's not Laura is it?'

'She's okay,' Maer said quickly and, as he'd hoped, his reply had the opposite of a soothing effect.

'What do you mean "okay"? What's happened?'

Maer put a hand on his arm, realising with a painful catch of breath that it was the last contact he could make with this man. 'She wanted me to tell you, she had a small accident. A small one,' he repeated as he saw Richard's face drain of the healthy colour walking had given him. He wondered if it had even occurred to Richard to question how quickly his skin had healed after his assault with the scrubbing brush yesterday.

He went on, 'She's fine, but she's hanging around waiting for an X-ray on her wrist, and she's a bit miserable. She tried to call you but your mobile's out of signal so she called the house. Why don't you take the afternoon off and go to her? I'll call in at the school for you.'

'I'm going.' Richard started to walk away, then turned, walking backwards, and raised his hand. 'Thanks, Dean. I'll call you later.'

Maer watched him taking long, urgent strides back towards the village, and his heart hurt. Really hurt. It was a confusing mixture of relief and crushing terror, and his breathing turned short and shallow with it. He watched Richard out of sight, and prayed to all the spirits of the moor and beyond to keep him and Laura safe.

He put one hand on the wall of the engine house and tried to draw strength from its solidity, from the knowledge that some things prevailed in this world … a tiny piece of dry moss flaked away and crumbled under his fingers, and his heart twisted further; yes, some things prevailed but others, no matter how long they had stood against all weathers, were reduced to nothing by a single, careless act.

'Your Highness! Sir! Prince Maer!'

Maer recognised the green jacket, pulled close around the misshapen figure hurrying across the heath. 'What is it, Greencoat? I have no time for – '

' 'tis about Mr Lucas, sir.'

Maer listened, and his anger grew and burned, eclipsing his grief. He slid to the ground at the foot of the chimney as Greencoat talked, and as the pictures unravelled in his head he knew he could not give himself to Loen until he had made his uncle pay the price for this treachery.

When Greencoat had finished, Maer took a deep breath. 'Listen to me,' he said, fixing the little man's eyes with his own and reading in them that same mad mixture of relief and fear. 'No harm will come to you as a result of disobeying Gilan's orders. You have done well, but you and I must work together, do you understand? Here is what you must do now.'

***

Gilan waited for Greencoat to arrive at the agreed meeting place. He didn't trust the little earthworm to do this job properly any more than he trusted himself not to blink in the light of the sun, any more than he could trust a child not to cry in the wake of a nightmare, any more than ... ah, but here he was, scurrying as usual, more like an insect than a worm.

'Well?' he demanded.

Greencoat stood, his face lowered, twisting the bottom of his jacket in his fingers until it lost its shape altogether. 'Done, sir.'

'Look at me when you address me, spriggan!' Was it his imagination or was Greencoat particularly slow to raise his face today? And it was less reluctance than defiance, it seemed. His confidence was clearly renewed, it must have gone well. 'Now. Tell me everything.

'Sir, I waited, with my barb. Tipped with the herb the humans call curare.'

'And Lucas was alone?'

'Yes, sir. Singing, he was. A wonderful sound, if I may say so, sir.'

'That does not interest me!'

'But you said tell you everyth ...' Greencoat trailed away at Gilan's look, then finished limply; 'The barb struck him true.' He raised a hand to his own scrawny neck.

'And then?'

'He, he fell, sir – he lies silent and cold beneath the

287

moor, sucked down by the marsh.'

'Good. Glad I am to hear it Greencoat, your name will be honoured when Loen is king once again.'

'Thank you, sir.'

Gilan waited, but Greencoat did not leave. 'Well? Why do you still stand there?'

'I was wonderin', sir, do you wish me to carry out any further duties, for the good of the king?'

'Such as?'

'Such as bringin' the news to the queen?'

Gilan kept his tone even, with an effort. 'I suggest you do not seek to advance yourself in her eyes. She will be told, and you will receive all praise and gratitude due to you, but for now it's best not to speak of this to anyone. I am sure you would rather not spark jealousy that *you* have been chosen to be the instrument of Loen's restoration.'

Gilan watched Greencoat leave, but now he wasn't scurrying, he was walking with his wizened little head held just a little higher than usual. Gilan let him go, he would do well to resume his old subservient ways soon lest he draw attention to himself, but for now let him revel in this feeling of success. In years to come Gilan would have need of someone who could grow to enjoy killing.

Chapter Twenty-Six

ichard drove fast, grateful for the lack of traffic: remembering to drive on the left was a problem at the best of times and there was no way he could concentrate on that now. He'd been worried enough to begin with, but the longer the journey went on the more time he had to think, and the more frantic he became.

He approached the Tamar toll bridge in record time, steering with one hand while the other fumbled tickets out of the glove box, tearing them in his haste. Not for the first time he wished fervently that he'd gotten around to getting a toll tag for the car, and swore he would do it first chance he got.

Negotiating the tight turns on the country roads he'd told himself to calm down, she'd had a minor accident and hurt her wrist, but something in Dean's face had bothered him, it felt like maybe there was more he wasn't telling him. Flashes of Amy's accident and Cait's murder were going off in the darkness of his mind, and the more he thought about having sensed Gary Sharpe, the more he was convinced he'd not been imagining it after all.

Had Dean been deliberately playing it down so he wouldn't risk life and limb getting to Plymouth? What if Sharpe had somehow gotten to Laura too? Whatever had been going on for all these years was coming to a head, Richard felt it. He didn't know how, or what it meant, but something about this place had the feel of endings, conclusions, the final coming together of all the confusing threads in his life that had been unravelling since the day Caitlin had died, and Gary Sharpe had everything to do with it.

Derriford Hospital proved a parking nightmare, but Richard finally found a space, illegal though it was, and each passing second felt like another wire snapping inside him. Dean wouldn't lie – he'd looked a little weird, but not guilty, more sad. Oh, Jesus – what if it had been too late all along? He ran the length of the parking lot, following the signs, past people in dressing gowns clutching at portable drips while they used their cell phones, and at last found the A&E department at the foot of a short hill.

The duty nurse told him he had no record of a Laura Riley being admitted.

'I was told she was here, and waiting for an X-ray,' Richard insisted.

The nurse shook his head. 'She'd have been admitted after triage and sent to the radiology department, but we'd still have a record of it,' he said. 'Look, maybe they dropped her off, she took one look at the queue and decided they'd over-reacted. People do.'

'So why would she have said she was waiting for treatment?' Richard asked.

'I'm sorry, I can't help you,' the nurse said, already looking past him to the next person in the queue and beckoning her forward. 'As you can see we're really busy, maybe the main reception desk could help?'

'Yeah, sorry. Thanks.' Richard walked out slowly, and once outside he called Laura's cell. He let it ring all the way back to the car, then snapped it off. Okay, so she'd be at the flat, feeling sorry for herself and probably having a bath. He somehow found a smile as he imagined her big grey eyes looking up at him from a mess of steam and bubbles, her face tilted in the familiar, bewitching mixture of flirtatious innocence.

But that simple pleasure faded as Sharpe once more pushed his way to the front of his mind. Richard gave his thoughts free rein as he drove, looking for answers he felt certain now would never come. Dean's explanation of the paranormal aura surrounding the village had fit so neatly at the time but Richard knew he'd been too keen to accept it: paranormal he had no problem with, but why should his mind turn it into a certainty it was Sharpe? Why would that freak have needled his way into his head again just when everything had been going so well?

He frowned; was it *because* everything was going well? Each time Richard had encountered that man his life had been on an even keel, he'd been happy, loving and loved in return. Then Sharpe had cast his blacker than black shadow – had he been there when Richard's parents had died? No-one but Sharpe would ever know.

By the time Richard turned onto Laura's street his head was bursting with vivid pictures of Amy's smiling face as he'd waved her off to her beach party, and of Cait in her coffin, her hands folded around their wedding picture. He felt sick.

It was easy to find a parking space opposite the flat on a Monday lunchtime, and within moments he was letting himself in, calling out as he took the stairs three at a time.

'Laura! Hey, you okay?' Even as he opened the inner door to the first floor flat he was thinking back to the space outside and a fact that had only just clicked into place: Laura's car had not been there. He looked around the front room, saw the computer switched on, a slideshow of pictures taken on various days out playing across the screen.

His own smiling face appeared on the monitor and scrolled across it, and Richard was about to tap a key when his phone buzzed in his pocket. His heart leapt with relief, but it wasn't her.

'Don't let her come back here, Rich,' Dean said before Richard had time to speak. 'Both of you, please, stay where –'

'You lied, you son of a bitch,' Richard bit back. 'She never went to the ER. I'm at her flat, so where the hell is she?'

'She's not there?'

Dean sounded scared and Richard felt sweat prickling along his brow. 'What's going on?' But before Dean could answer he spoke again, his voice hard and flat. 'Forget it. It's Sharpe, right? I got a lot of questions about you and him, and how come he never showed up back home when you were there. You've been lying to me for the longest time, my friend – I'm going to find Laura, and then you'd better have some answers.' Unconsciously echoing Tom's actions he reached out and hit the space bar, and the screensaver vanished. Laura's e-mail window was still open beneath it.

From: Riley, Tom
(lynhermill-frames@btopenworld.co.uk)
To: Laura (ladylaura77@hotmail.co.uk)
CC: Riley, Laura
(riley.l@manadon-hill .plymouth.gov.uk)
Subject:

Somethings happening im scared please come home.

Richard's eyes froze on the screen. Dean's voice was becoming more and more urgent as it buzzed in his ear, pleading with him to keep Laura away from the moor, and here was the proof she was on her way back there right now. He was having trouble breathing.

'She's headed back to Lynher Mill,' he managed. 'Got some crazy e-mail from Tom saying he wanted her there.' His forehead tightened. 'Anything happens to her, Dean, I swear to God –'

'You're in more danger than she is! Look, don't worry, I'll take care of her.'

'I'm on my way.'

'Stay where you are!'

Richard snapped his phone shut and powered it off so Dean couldn't call back. Then he immediately turned it back on and called Laura again. With a sense of bleak inevitability his eyes went to the jacket hanging on the back of the door, and the faint sound of one of his own songs coming from the pocket.

***

Maer threw the phone across the room in frustration. He checked his watch. It would take Richard over half an hour to get here, but how long before Laura arrived? He had to get to Tom's place fast – try and divert her from there and away to somewhere safe.

He grabbed a piece of paper and, writing in block capitals to disguise the handwriting, he printed:

LAURA. I CALLED YOUR PLACE BUT YOU MUST HAVE ALREADY LEFT. SORRY FOR THE CRAZY-SOUNDING E-MAIL, I OVER-REACTED. BUT I DO NEED TO TALK TO YOU, WILL WAIT FOR YOU BY THE MILL.

TRY NOT TO WORRY!

LOVE, TOM.

He picked up the roll of sellotape from kitchen drawer and took it with him to Tom's house. As he approached he felt a tingling in his scalp that told him all was not well within. He stopped by the gate, his heart racing with fear, for himself and for his friends. Someone was inside this place but it wasn't really Tom. Not anymore.

Working quickly, Maer stuck the note to the door and risked a glance through the window. He noted the crushed plants by his feet, and remembered Richard's story of peering through this same window to find Tom lying unconscious on the floor. This time there was no prone figure; Tom was curled in the corner, his hands over his head, and his back was hitching: he was weeping. Captain was, as ever, sitting protectively at his side.

Maer felt tears start to his own eyes and cursed his weak, humanised nature: that he should care so deeply for these beings was almost more than he could bear. But Tom was lost now, Loen had come forward and was crushing the very last of the man he had been. The human mind was not equipped to fight such an onslaught and if Loen hadn't taken so long to come to full strength himself, Tom would never have been able to fight it for this long.

Maer backed away and checked his watch again. Around twenty minutes before Richard came within the circle of danger this place held for him. He took the quickest route back out onto the moor, and found Jacky.

'Go to the Mill, Greencoat,' he ordered, fully prepared, for the first time, to use the full force of royalty at his command. But Greencoat nodded immediately.

'The girl will come to you, looking for her brother,' Maer continued, 'You *must* protect her. With your life if necessary, do you understand?'

'I do, sir. I will.'

'Go then. And be aware Gilan will be searching for her.'

'And what of the ... what of Mr Lucas, Your

Highness?'

'I will do everything in my power to see Richard is safe. I don't know how much time we have. Go!'

Maer watched Greencoat head across to approach the Mill from the back, with the ease of a long time inhabitant of the heath. When the spriggan had dropped out of sight behind the hill Maer turned and ran back to Tom's cottage, unseen by the few villagers out and about on this drizzly Monday afternoon.

He had been at the cottage for only a minute when he heard the car. Laura parked outside the gate and Maer watched her go to the door and read the note. His heart thudding, he prayed she wouldn't ignore it, or worse, that she would go to the window, but luck was on the side of good at this moment and she visibly relaxed, though still looked irritated as she tore the note off the door and got back into the car.

Maer had been hoping she might have chosen to walk, but there was no time for empty wishes now. She would be safe, at least. Praying he could do the same for Richard, Maer began to run again, this time along the road that led towards Plymouth.

***

Laura's car wound up the hill, and her mind was crowded with questions. The e-mail from Tom had come as a bolt from the blue after their successful weekend, and he'd over-reacted to what, a dream? Another sleepwalking episode? A bit of bad news from the Land Registry? What?

And that stupid note on the door 'try not to worry' indeed! He dragged her all the way back here on a workday, and she'd had to call in sick for the afternoon which hadn't gone down too brilliantly for starters. Of course she'd only remembered her computer was still on when she was already halfway across the Tamar Bridge. Electric bill through the roof again then.

She parked at the side of the road and got out, thinking of the positive aspect: at least she'd be able to spend a bit of time with Richard once she'd sorted her brother out, a bonus for a Monday. The thought lifted her step, and she found herself smiling as she took the rocky path to the mill. It was chilly and she'd left her jacket at home, but her thick grey jumper cut out the worst of the cold ... maybe this would turn out to be an okay kind of day after all.

As old as the churches around which so many villages were built, the mill had the feel of so much history, all piled in with these broken stones and the moss covered remains of the tower, it was impossible not to be moved by it. Tom shouldn't change it, let bunches of tourists with flashy cameras swarm all over it. It had seemed a good solution, both for Tom's well-being and to keep the memory of the millers' tragic sacrifice alive, but now it felt more as if that memory would be sullied rather than preserved. She wondered what he would say if she tried to explain, she wasn't even sure she understood it herself.

Tom hadn't arrived yet. He may have been still in the house when she'd arrived, she realised, and swallowed another sigh of irritation. She patted her front jeans pocket and groaned; her mobile was in her jacket pocket so she couldn't even call him. Well he'd be here soon enough, in the meantime it was peaceful here, and it was nice to be out, even up here. She sat on the damp wall, closed her eyes and turned her thoughts away from the millers, instead she let her mind drift, and other, real memories came easily, rich and full of colour. Herself, Tom, Jane and Michael – until that school Christmas disco when those two had taken her heart and stamped all over it – others that came and went. They'd played all kinds of games up here; treasure hunts; hiding games with forfeits; character games from TV … this old place had been such a huge part of her childhood and yet she'd barely given it a thought in years. It was out of sight, out of mind and not somewhere you'd happen to stumble across, you had to come here deliberately.

The realisation gave way to another memory, more recent and far more sour. Why *had* Dean lied about being here? He had to be up to something. Maybe Tom had found something to implicate him, and been initially convinced Richard was part of whatever was going on too – she had to admit her own cold thoughts had strayed that way for a second, but his incredulousness at her theory had been genuine, she was sure of that if nothing else: if Dean was into something illegal he was in it on his own. Hopefully the note on the door was an indication that Tom had discovered that too.

A footstep crunching on the flint-strewn path brought Laura to her feet again and she looked expectantly towards the track, ready for Tom's explanation. But he wasn't there. When she heard the sound again she realised it was coming from behind the mill tower, and as a figure stepped into view the words of greeting froze on her lips; her picture had come to life. Small, he was. Dressed in green. An ugly face, with a mouth stretching the width of a huge head that balanced on a thin neck and narrow shoulders … every detail had been right.

Laura choked on the breath that would not loosen. Her vision spun and darkened, and she saw another figure appear behind the first, his arm raised to strike: a tall, thin man in outlandish dress and, as Cait had done eleven years before, she instinctively knew he was death.

Chapter Twenty-Seven

There was little traffic that afternoon but each time Maer saw a car in the distance he felt his heart speed up, only for his worry to increase when none of them proved to be Richard's. At last he recognised the white Vauxhall Richard had bought just a few weeks ago. He stepped out into the road and waved his arms, seeing Richard's mouth fall open in shock when he didn't move aside. The car screeched to a halt, and in seconds Richard was out and coming towards him, his face darkly furious.

The temptation to back away was strong, but Maer remained where he was, his hands out in front of him. 'Richard, listen! At least let me explain, and then you can yell all you want. But first, please?'

'Is Laura safe?' Richard said, his voice tight with the effort of restraint.

'Yes. Now she is. Someone's looking after her.' Richard's eyes closed briefly and he let out a shaky breath, and Maer took advantage of his moment of relief. 'Look, I need to explain, and you're not going to find it easy to hear, but if you want to help Laura you have to trust me, okay?'

'Get in the car, we'll talk on the way.'

'No. Park up, we're going onto the moor.'

'What the hell? Are you *ordering* me?'

'Yes.' Maer stared at Richard, focusing all his persuasive power on him – this close to home it was considerable. 'I'm the only one who can take you to her, Rich, and I won't until you've heard me out.'

Richard clearly realised he'd get nowhere until he'd done so, but at the same time there was a hardness and an unnerving, laser-fierce light in his own eyes. 'The second I decide you're bullshitting me I'm out of here.'

'Understood. Move the car out of the road, I'll be waiting.'

Maer watched as Richard got back behind the wheel, wondering if he could trust him not to drive off and look for Laura himself. It seemed to cross his mind but, after another searching look at Maer, he manoeuvred the Astra onto the verge and switched off the engine.

They walked a short way onto the grass and Maer was acutely aware of Richard's tightly controlled anger; a glance at his profile revealed a muscle jumping in his jaw and although his face was now turned away Maer easily recalled the furious intensity in his eyes. How could he have once believed there may be someone more suitable to rule? But since Loen would not rest until he himself was king once more, his descendant would never fulfil the role that was rightfully his.

And neither would Maer. Greencoat had his orders for when Loen had taken Maer's body, but Maer still wondered if the terrified spriggan would be able to do it. He felt his own fear like a fist in his gut, clenching and unclenching, one minute loose and fluttering, the next crushing him so he could barely breathe. Would it hurt badly? Would he feel only relief, after the pain of Loen's assault, when Greencoat stepped in? He knew had to try and put that aside, for now at least, but oh it was hard, and so utterly terrifying.

After they had walked in difficult silence for a couple of minutes, Maer gestured to a collection of granite lumps. They were not comfortable to sit on, but he sat anyway, if only to hide the trembling in his legs. Richard did not. He stood in the same way he had walked, tense and alert, his shoulders square, his fists tight.

'Talk to me,' he said, 'and start with Sharpe.'

'His name isn't Gary Sharpe,' Maer admitted. 'He has one name only: Gilan. He is my mother's brother, and sent, as I was, to protect you and bring you home when the time was right. Neither is my name Dean, it is Maer.'

He told it all. The time was creeping on towards late afternoon, and after a bright morning, rain was now falling again in a fast, steady drizzle. The two of them faced each other as the story unfolded and, angered beyond reason, Richard twice went to walk away. Each time Maer stopped him with a word, the first was Amy, the second was Laura.

Richard sank down onto a boulder opposite Maer, his head in his hands. When Maer reached the point where Tom had attacked Richard at the mill, Richard looked up, his eyes filled with disbelief.

'First of all you expect me to swallow this crap about being a goddam *fairy*? And then you tell me you were there when Riley tried to beat my brains out against a wall, and you didn't raise a hand to help?'

'It was too dangerous. Besides he wouldn't have killed you, he needed you, he still does: you're healthy and strong and you're his own descendant! He was simply trying to subdue you so he could effect the change. I know you barely remember it, but he tried it again in the cottage. And you fought him off, Rich, you didn't need me.'

'The hell I didn't!' He took several deep breaths, then he quietened but sounded no less angry. 'Know what? I don't know what you've been taking but Laura was right, it's got to be something pretty heavy.' He was on his feet again now, pacing. 'I came up here, agreed to listen because, stupidly, I was worried about you, about what was going through your mind. I believed you when you said Laura was safe, but now I don't know what to believe. Damn, why'd you get into it, Dean?'

'I'm not on drugs! Look, I can prove the truth to you, of who I am at least.' Maer closed his eyes and concentrated, working the grey afternoon light and folding it around his form so he became as one with the background. He opened his eyes again, expecting horrified realisation, and ready with his explanation.

Richard merely stared at him. 'Forget it, I'm going to find Laura.'

'Can you see me?' Maer stood directly in front of him, his heart hammering – Richard's lineage was reasserting itself more by the minute, exposure to the land was strengthening history into now.

'Get out of the way.' Richard tried to push past him, but Maer stood his ground.

'Are you saying you can see me right now?'

'I said move!'

'Look at this,' Maer pulled his key ring from his pocket and pushed it into Richard's hand. 'Look at the runes, tell me they mean nothing to you!'

Richard automatically gave the intricately designed key ring a glance, and Maer's heart flickered with hope as his friend's eyes widened slightly. But Richard shook his head, as he dropped the key ring into his own coat pocket.

'If you think I'm letting you back into that house you're even crazier than I thought.'

He started to walk away and Maer sighed in desperation. 'Look, okay, deny that if you want, but how do you explain Sharpe?' he said.

Richard whipped his head around, fixing Maer with a look that pinned him in place.

'I'm telling you right now, he lays a hand on Laura and I don't know which one of you I'm going to kill first.' His fury rendered him barely recognisable; all white-knuckled

301

fists and flashing emerald eyes, and Maer had never seen him look so terrifying. It gave him further hope.

'I'll sort it,' he said. It was pointless trying to convince Richard he was descended from a Cornish moorland elemental, this born and bred Chicago boy, with a reputation he'd earned since he was old enough to fight. This was outside his realm of understanding, and yet there was something so fundamentally right about his being here he'd felt it himself although he hadn't understood it.

The sky had clouded over and the rain now fell harder. There was a low rumble in the distance and Maer had one last try. He grabbed at Richard's arm as he turned to leave once more.

'Hear that?' he said, '*You're* doing it. You have that power, it's in all of us.'

Richard leaned in close, until their faces were almost touching, and Maer could feel heat burning across the minute distance between them. 'Bullshit,' he whispered. He shoved hard and Maer stumbled against a boulder, losing his balance.

Richard began to walk away, and was clearly caught off guard at the speed with which Maer had caught up with him, but shook his arm out of his former friend's grasp.

'Look, if you don't believe me about the other stuff, fine,' Maer said, 'I just thought you had a right to know. But at least believe me when I say I'll sort it. I'll make sure Laura is safe and brought back to you –'

His words were cut off as Richard swung a blow into his face, smashing him back so he fell flat, stunned.

'Believe you?' Richard yelled, rain running down his face, distorting his features as he stood there, soaked to the skin and more furious than ever. 'How can I believe you? You've lied to me this whole time, brought this evil bastard into my life. You weren't there when Amy died!

You weren't there when he killed my wife, Dean, my *wife!* And now ...'

His words were choked off and he could not continue, but wiped his hand across his face, pushing his dripping hair away from his over-bright eyes. His confusion and sorrow were worse to witness than the anger, and Maer felt his heart shrink.

'Richard, let me help. You're in serious danger if you go to Lynher Mill.'

'*I'm* in danger? And what about Laura, she the bait? Well it worked: whoever it is, and whatever they want me for, they finally got me. I'm hooked and reeled in. Fuck you, Dean.'

This time Richard's own departure was too swift even for Maer, who, still shaky and disorientated by the force of the blow, could not bring himself to rise and follow. Instead he watched Richard cross the moorland, without the supernatural speed he did not yet know he possessed, but with a taut urgency and fluidity that spoke clearly of what he was.

***

Laura swayed but kept her feet. She stared, dry-mouthed at the man, who cocked his head at the sound of distant thunder and frowned.

He stepped forward and grabbed her arm. 'We're going for a walk, you and I.'

'We're not!' Laura jerked free, and the man grinned but did not seize her again. Still, she knew it was pointless trying to get away; as dizzy and terrified as she was he only had to reach out those narrow fingers and she'd be caught instantly. 'Who are you?'

'You may call me anything you like,' he offered. 'My

real name is Gilan, but you may have heard of Gary Sharpe.'

'No.'

'He didn't tell you about me?'

'Who, Tom?'

'I was referring to your lover.'

'Richard knows you?'

'Oh, I gave him terrible troubles in his younger years, poor boy.' He sounded anything but contrite. 'He might have learned a valuable lesson from your brother, who has at last learned not to touch things that don't belong to him.'

Laura's head jerked around. 'What's happened to Tom?'

'As I've said, we will talk as we walk, no time for dallying up here.'

'No, please, tell me here.' She looked around at the mill, little more than a heap of stones, yet it gave her a kind of strange, indefinable strength.

'Why do you harbour such an affection for this place?' Gilan said irritably. 'Your family are not from here, you shouldn't feel the connection like this.'

'You know my family?'

'Naturally. You and your brother are descended from Chief Ulfed, who tried to murder the king's son. Why do you think Loen has decreed you both must die?'

In the confusion of otherwise meaningless words, the last stuck like a poisoned thorn in Laura's heart. 'Oh, God ...'

Gilan leaned in and grabbed her arm again. She cried out as his fingers sank into the flesh just above her elbow. 'I'll tell you as we go,' he repeated, and jerked her forward, pushing her ahead of him towards the slope that would take them higher up over the moor. 'I think it's best we stay away from the road, don't you? Come on, we don't want to miss out on all the fun.'

Laura stumbled in the long, rain-soaked grass, Gilan always beside or behind her to hurry her when she slowed. As they went, he told his story, and it all slipped into place horribly easily. She must have realised some of the truth all her life, because she did not fight the knowledge now; out here, with nothing of her modern life beyond her own clothes to tell her who she was, anything and everything was possible.

The news that Richard was descended from some other being just like this vile creature jolted her, but when she thought of the frighteningly intense way he had reacted to his surroundings, that too made sense: he was linked to the moor more closely than either of them had suspected. Knowing he had been brought back here deliberately by his best friend, only to be betrayed by him, made Laura feel sick, and helplessly furious.

'But in my defence,' Gilan was saying, 'I saved his life once. He wasn't supposed to die, not back then.'

'And now?' Laura managed at last, and the words were not even a whisper, they were a breath leaving her body, they were her hope, her life. Gilan did not hear.

'The queen has made herself believe Lucas to be the one, and if it is revealed I have disobeyed the reigning queen I will never have the power and respect I deserve when the king is restored.'

Laura's anger returned, edged with incredulousness. 'So all this is because of your ambition?'

No! *All this* is something that has been pre-ordained for longer than you could possibly comprehend. Your foolish brother set it in motion, luckily he made a convenient host. But he is not enough and never could be.'

Oh, God – poor, lost Tom …

'So Loen wanted Richard instead.'

'Wrong again. That was the queen's notion; if it were not for the spriggan's knowledge of the child Lucas, her own son Maer would be the one. She sought to save his life using that knowledge, and I am merely putting things back in order. Lucas will not be there when the time comes, Maer will. Him who you call Dean. And he will give himself willingly in order to make amends for what he has done.'

'Good!' Laura hissed, 'Richard doesn't deserve to die for your stupid people.'

She was disturbed even further to see the nasty smile lurking at the corners of Gilan's mouth. Her breath faltered, but she shook away the thought that probed at her mind, looking for a way in. She wouldn't let it.

'I have very loyal servants,' Gilan was saying.

'The green man?'

'He wears green, but The Green Man is, as you should know, a far greater being. A God. This servant is loyal, but a deity he most certainly is not.'

'He *was* here, wasn't he? And he was there, in the cavern, when I was a child.'

'Oh, congratulations, common sense finally wins the day. Your family has certainly not made this easy: Loen swore to end your line, and of course, when he discovered there was to be another child he had to put an end to it.'

Laura stopped, shock worming through her as it had when she had first considered the possibility. But this time the truth was there, stark and impersonal, spoken by one who had nothing to gain by either confirming or denying it.

Gilan's hand sent her stumbling, and she fell, hitting her shoulder on a rock hidden in the long grass. Pain flowered from neck to fingertips and she bit back a cry; her captor would no doubt use any weakness he sensed in her. He reached down and yanked her hair until she stood, tears flooding her eyes so she could barely see to walk, but she still refused to cry out.

She kept her voice steady, but it took every ounce of self-control she possessed. 'Where's Tom?'

'Loen is ready to leave him,' Gilan said. 'Humans are never strong enough to fight when a spirit invades, unlike the one who will, ironically, give himself freely. Yet that one too will be defeated in the end: he is weakened by the knowledge he is unworthy to live after what he has done.'

Laura wondered how it would feel seeing Dean's familiar form taken over by his ancient ancestor, and shivered. He was trying to make it right, giving himself up to save Richard's life, did he deserve to be destroyed as senselessly as Tom had been?

Fresh grief … it was crippling. Tom's life had been blighted from the moment he had broken the jar. Even the knowledge of his part in Vivien's and Ben's deaths did not ease the sorrow, or the bright anger that burned inside her as she looked at the narrow, horribly handsome face of the man who led her now, to her own fate. He had killed those Richard had loved, would have no compunction in doing the same thing to her, but he had at least fulfilled his original task: Richard was safe from Loen.

Chapter Twenty-Eight

Richard drew up opposite Tom's cottage. The day had darkened and he experienced a moment of disorientation: what time was it, how long had he been out here with Dean? A glance at his watch told him it was still only mid-afternoon, the premature dusk was a result of the storm that had been curling towards them across the moor.

The storm. Dean had seemed convinced he and Richard both had the power to change the weather ... the story had washed over Richard in a flood that stank of someone high enough to believe his own delusions and his heart clenched at the tragedy of that, but there were more urgent matters at hand now.

He crossed the road, checking the garden, half expecting to see Gary Sharpe standing in the shadows and pushed away the insistent question of what that would mean, but it was a question he didn't have to answer: there were only the shrubs, buffeted out of shape by the force of the storm, and the rain-slick path leading to the front door.

There was a torn scrap of paper flapping in the wind, all that was left of the note headed by a capital L, the remnant held in place by a single strip of sticky tape. All thoughts of caution disappeared at the sight of that tiny white triangle: Laura's fear for her brother, used against her. So much deception, so many lies.

He hammered on the door, then lifted the latch, not surprised to find it unlocked: he was getting used to the way people in Lynher Mill trusted each other, rightly or wrongly.

'Laura!' he shouted, ducking through the door into a

long, narrow passageway. On his right was another door, lying ajar: the living room. Last night's bizarre and frightening encounter came crashing back in vivid detail, and Richard was suddenly, coldly, aware he had no protection should Tom Riley or Gary Sharpe turn out to be armed and waiting.

He checked his pocket, felt only Dean's key and dropped it back as if it had burned him, his anger rising further: *runes, for Chrissake?* He glanced down the passageway and toyed with the idea of finding a blade of some kind, but a sound from the living room stopped him. He reached out and pushed the door wide with his fingertips.

No-one sprang out from behind the door, and he let himself relax a little, until he saw the figure in the far corner. His breath caught in shock and he took a step closer. The man rocked and moaned, unaware of Richard's presence.

'Tom?'

The hands that had been covering Tom's head dropped away. He raised his face, and his eyes, fixed on Richard, seemed dead. Even Captain had slunk away, to lie trembling in his basket.

'I'm going to try and help you, but I need to know where Laura is,' Richard said as gently as he could despite the urgency.

He crossed the room and as he put out his hand to help he noticed a deep red circle blazing on the palm of Tom's right hand. He winced at the sight of the weeping, blistered skin and opened his mouth to express concern, but once again Tom caught him off-guard.

His own swift reaction came as almost as much of a surprise: he stepped lightly back as Tom rose with his hands outstretched, and watched him stumble as his arms closed on nothing. Compassion turned to anger at the speed of light.

'Where the hell is she!' he yelled. Tom lunged again, but this time Richard's back was against the wall and he had nowhere to go. Tom seized his shoulders. Richard's breath was choked off and as he saw the light of determination illuminate Tom's features, he suddenly knew Dean had been telling the truth. Everything he had forgotten, or tried to forget, came crashing back into his mind, everything he had desperately tried to explain away, everything Laura had told him about what had happened when they were children.

This creature, whatever had taken hold of Tom Riley, wanted his body – no, *needed* it. It was as if desperation and urgency was giving it the strength to fight off its physical weakness, and along with the pressure in his body came the creature's deadly intention, in a series of images of such clarity Richard could almost believe they had already happened. Himself, walking towards Laura, smiling; one of his hands reaching for her and then her sweet, trusting face going blank in shock as the other hand plunged a blade through her heart. This creature, insane as it was, would use *his* body to carry out its filthy work, and Laura would die believing the man she loved had killed her.

'Mine,' Tom said, in a strange, calm tone, fingers sinking into flesh.

'No!' That bizarre feeling of expanding inside himself was now heavily laced with pain, and he grew dizzy with it. He didn't know how much longer he could stand against the attack: he was exhausted, his shoulders burned, and it felt as if his ribcage might burst apart at any minute.

Desperation leapt anew at the realisation of what this thing intended to do with the body it won, and the second

Richard realised physical strength was useless, he understood there was another way to fight. All his effort went from keeping Tom at arm's length, to concentrating his will against the invader. He pushed with his mind. Hard and sudden.

Tom faltered. Hope lifted Richard's heart briefly and he did it once more, letting anger and fear harden into mental strength and pure force of will. But even as he pushed, Tom seemed to collect himself and drove him back. No, not Tom, something else. Dean's words thundered through his mind, this being was an ancient king, and he himself was descended from it. But there was something else, something even more important – Richard struggled with the memory, knowing it was vital, and then it came to him: *he needed you, he still does: you're healthy and strong ...*

He let himself go completely limp, and as Tom's grip slackened he was able to get a hand to his coat pocket. The key seemed to deliberately elude his fingers as Tom shifted his fingers and bore down again but at last Richard seized the oval fob and dragged it out, holding the key so the serrated edge protruded from his knuckles.

Tom spared no more than a glance at the puny weapon, but Richard had no intention of using it against him. Instead, his eyes fixed on Tom's, he lifted the key and pushed it against his own throat just below the angle of his jaw, hard enough to make his resolve clear. A trickle of blood ran down his neck.

Tom's grip tightened. 'You do not dare!'

Richard closed his eyes and took a deep breath. He did dare, and the king knew it.

***

Laura saw the engine house in the distance. She tried to pull away, but Gilan's fingers dug into her arm, sending pain spiking into her bones.

'No you don't, dearie ' he panted, 'there is someone down here who would like to see you.'

All her hard-won self-control fled. The thought of death was horrific and yet somehow numbing, but to know these were the last moments of daylight she would ever see filled her with a terror so complete she could barely stand. 'No, please it's so dark –'

'Rubbish! It's only dark when we want it to be. When there are meddlesome children around, for instance.'

Once again she was thirteen years old, but this time there was no friendly dare bringing her here, this time there was only death in the shape of this oddly dressed man.

'Don't worry,' he said, as if reading her mind, 'it won't be me does the honours, much as I'd like to. The destruction of Ulfed's last living issue is for Loen to carry out. Imagine his gratitude when I deliver you to him.'

Ulfed's last living issue … Laura felt her fear retreat a little: as long as they kept believing that's what she was, she was safe here. Until she was brought before Loen anyway, and then nothing she said to the contrary would make any difference; who would believe her?

The passageway she and Tom had crawled down so long ago now seemed like a spacious pedestrian subway, and Gilan had been right, it was as bright as daylight. Once inside the huge cavern that had caused the mine to close down, Gilan led her to a crack in the wall that opened into a further group of chambers beyond.

He brought her to the covered opening of one of them, and called out, 'Deera! Look what I've brought.' He pushed Laura through, and she caught her breath as she saw a woman standing by a curtained bed chamber. Tall and extravagantly beautiful, she was so clearly related to Dean that any doubts Laura may have had about Dean being a prince were instantly swept away; this woman exuded royalty from every line of her elegant form.

'You are Ulfed's last child?' the woman said.

'No, Majesty,' Gilan corrected, 'she is the elder of the two. The male is the last child, but soon he will be no more, of course.'

'He is already no more,' Deera snapped. 'His body remains but that is all.' Laura felt the pain of loss tearing at her heart once again and she slumped, but Gilan pulled her upright.

'Stand straight before royalty, stupid girl,' he hissed, and in doing so he did her the favour of re-kindling her anger. She jerked her arm away and gave him a look of hatred that clearly surprised him. He frowned and was about to speak again but Deera spoke first.

'Before your brother's body is reclaimed by the ground it will perform one last task,' she said, 'this has been explained to you?'

'You mean he's going to kill me. We like to use plain English where I come from,' Laura said, as coldly as she could manage.

The queen smiled, but it was tight and humourless. 'Very well, in plain *English*, yes. Loen intends to kill you. He is not a cruel king, you understand, but it was his dying declaration in revenge for his son. We will endeavour to make it possible for him to fulfil it. We will tend to you here until the time comes to take you to him.'

'Dusk, I suppose.'

'I beg your pardon?'

'Oh come on, it's all a bit obvious isn't it?' Laura said, trying to inject boredom into her words. Gilan shook her and she was unable to keep a tiny cry from breaking loose, but she stood straight again and stared at the queen, who frowned.

'Explain yourself, child.'

'One, I'm not a child, and two, it's always dusk! It's so bloody …' Laura waved her free hand, unable to find the word. 'Why couldn't it be lunchtime, or five-thirty, or twenty past eight?'

'Dusk is when the sacrifice took place, and when Loen swore his oath,' the queen said. 'It is the death of the day, the fitting time for sacrifice –' She broke off as the curtain was swept aside to admit a tall, striking-looking man with dark hair.

'Oh, hello. You're the *current* king then, are you?' Laura said before he could speak. His eyes held none of Gilan's or the queen's distaste. They were the same glorious light blue as Dean's, and the way his fine brows drew down gave him an air of compassion that took Laura by surprise and made her regret her outburst, though she refused to show it.

'No, I am not king,' he said. His voice was rich and deep, and Laura tried not to be lulled by its softness.

'So what are you? Apart from Dean's Daddy Dearest?'

To her further surprise, a smile flickered in his eyes, but he bit his lip to prevent it touching his mouth. 'My name is Casta. I am, as you say, the father of Prince Maer but I am not king here, I am proud to be consort to Queen Deera.' He lifted a hand towards the woman, whose own expression softened slightly as she watched him.

There was something about these two; different yet the same, and they clearly loved each other. So why was she so bitter? To have the love of such a man … Laura's thoughts flickered again to Richard, and sharp agony pierced her to the bone. Let it be enough that he, at least, was safe, that the strange, skinny man, as wicked as he was, had decided for his own reasons to thwart Deera's plan.

'We will take care of you until the time comes, and we will try, as best we can, to ease your fears,' Casta was saying, and now there was sympathy in his eyes and Laura felt tears pricking again. Easier when she could be angry, rude even, but this compassion held such a note of finality that the truth was set now, as solid as the stone surrounding them – she would die today.

***

Maer stumbled into Tom's front room and stopped in blood-chilled shock: the key might be small, but with enough pressure it would sever the artery and Richard would be dead in moments. Richard's eyes were closed, as yet unaware of Maer's presence, but the determination and regret that creased his brow told Maer he was serious in his intent. His head was forced back by the pressure of Tom's large hands at the base of his throat, the skin was pulled tight – it would be all too easy, providing he was strong enough to drive the key deep enough with one push. And he would be.

Maer took a deep breath and reached over. He lay his hands flat on Tom Riley's broad back, and opened his mind as wide as he could. He reached out and sought the king's spirit, finding it almost immediately as it flowed between the two men, a mess of pain and confusion.

He pulled, drawing the spirit towards himself, but Loen did not want him, he was already connected deeply to his own flesh and blood, and although Richard was fighting hard he was comparatively young, inexperienced in using the hidden power of his mind, and his fury was all that was keeping Loen at bay. Maer saw his trembling fingers shift on the key, getting a better grip for the final plunge, and he cast around and saw the poker lying by the fire.

Remembering the curse, he checked the force of the blow as he swung it at Tom's shoulder, hoping simply to break his hold. But Tom collapsed, unconscious, and the key dropped from Richard's fingers as he sank to a sitting position against the wall. He focused on Maer through half-closed eyes and tried to speak, but only a small, exhausted sigh breathed past his lips.

Maer squatted in front of him and reached out, gently wiping away a rich, dark bead of blood with this thumb. Then he looked over at the still form of Tom Riley – the battle was not over yet.

***

As Richard slipped under the thick blanket of darkness he felt the floor under him change, carpet becoming hard wood, stability becoming a rocking motion, and the sensation of the ground flying beneath him was making him nauseous. He dragged for a cleansing breath and felt dust settling in the back of his throat. He coughed …

***

August 1849, California.

The dust of the road was choking, but the tiredness was at last dropping away. Will glanced at his wife sitting beside him, her hold on the wagon seat as precarious as ever, but her eyes shining with renewed excitement as they grew closer to their destination.

'We're really doing this, Will!' she said again, and he smiled like it was the first time. He turned his face back to the road but out of the corner of his eye he saw her take out the land title document.

He winced. 'Sweetheart, would you put that away? You're gonna lose it.'

'But it's just so magical, I have to keep looking at it in case it turns into a grocery list!' She laughed, and despite his worry he couldn't help laughing with her.

'I know. But please, for me? I didn't slog all this way out here just to lose everything for want of a piece of paper.'

'Maybe you should've left it with Gabriel back at the claim.'

'I had to bring it to show you, didn't I? Besides, it's got the place marked right there on the plan. By the time we get back there'll be God only knows how many more people working the place, and everything will have changed.'

Lucy sighed, although the smile never left her face, and tucked the document back inside her bodice. Will let his eyes linger on her, appreciating the swell of her breasts, and the thought of the precious paper nestled against the warmth of her gave him a warm glow he couldn't ignore.

'You wait 'til I get you off this thing and onto the bedroll,' he promised, and she faced him with an expression of innocence, belied by the heat in her skin.

'Will Deacon, are you planning something?'

'Yes, ma'am I think I am,' he grinned, and pretended to doff his felt hat in her direction. She turned away again, her smile not quite hidden by the brim of her bonnet, and he let out a long, slow whistle, flicking the reins to urge the pair of horses on to greater speed.

When it happened it was too fast to make sense of.

One minute they were flying along paths beaten easy by thousands of pioneers before them, the next moment the horses had reared, screaming, and the wagon was skidding and sliding into the rough scrub.

The wheels caught in the clumps of grass, and before Will could do more than shout a warning to Lucy the wagon flipped, sending them both spinning from the seat. Will landed hard on his side and lost his breath, along with sight of everything except the blur of sharp, dry grasses flicking into his eyes as he slid along the ground.

He stopped and lay still for a moment, trying to orientate himself, and then lurched to his feet and cast around desperately for his wife. The wagon lay on its side, one wheel shattered, the other still spinning, and through the gathering shadows of the evening he saw the small figure sprawled a short distance away.

'Lucy!' he croaked, dust flying into his eyes and making them water. He lowered his face to pull his bandana over his mouth and nose and started towards her. The next second a heavy impact across the back of his neck knocked him to the ground. Realising what was happening, and angered beyond reason he tried to rise immediately, and made it to his knees before a boot hooked up under his ribs into his diaphragm.

As he fought for breath yet again he heard feet shuffle beside his head, and steeled himself for another kick but it didn't come. Instead he felt someone grab at the shoulder of his waistcoat and jerk him over onto his back, pulling the bandana away from his face.

Blinking against the light of the sky, Will saw two men standing over him. Dressed much as he was, though with their travelling coats still on, they were clearly men of as little wealth as himself and intent on acquiring more.

'We'll just pick up what you've got and be on our way,'

one of them said politely.

'We, we don't have anything,' Will gasped, dragging air into lungs that felt like rocks.

'Oh, I don't know so much,' the man replied, and his glance over towards Lucy gave Will the strength to drive out with his boot, catching the man in the lower leg hard enough to send him stumbling.

He was on his feet in a heartbeat and his voice was back, edged with steel. 'Touch her and I'll kill you.'

'She's very pretty. You married?'

'Don't do it,' Will warned.

'We'll just take a look in there, sir.' The man nodded to his companion, who stepped away and around to the back of the broken wagon. Will felt heartsick at the loss of their life's belongings but they were just things after all and, for the most part, replaceable.

'Got some nice silverware here,' the second man called back, 'and some fancy silks. Fetch a good price I'd say.'

'Take it!' Will snapped.

There was a pause. Will kept his eyes on his attacker and the huge Arkansas Toothpick he wore sheathed into his belt, then the second man spoke again and this time he sounded almost awestruck.

'My oh my. Look what I found!'

Will looked, and to his horror he saw the man had moved over to where Lucy lay. No doubt wanting to get his filthy hands on her, the man had bent over and sliced at the strings of her bodice with his own blade, a smaller, spear-pointed boot knife.

But he'd found something even more pleasing to him than unfettered breasts, and withdrew the piece of paper that held Will and Lucy's entire future: their land claim to work the California gold.

He flicked it, grinning at his companion. 'This will be

easier to carry than all that other stuff I reckon,' he said. 'Thank you, darlin', I believe I owe you a little something for this.' Turning, he planted a foot either side of the unconscious woman and knelt, putting his hands on her breasts and rising over her in a crude parody of the act of love.

Will shoved furiously at the man in front of him, and lunged across the space between himself and Lucy. He grabbed the thief's shoulder to drag him back, and the man turned and his own fist flew out, punching Will hard in the chest.

Rocked by the impact, Will tried again to pull him away but the strength seemed to run out of his fingers and they lost their grip. His arms went limp and his legs could no longer hold him up.

He dropped to his knees, dizzy and weak, and saw the man who'd been pawing at Lucy stand suddenly and move away. Will could not raise his head as far as the man's face, but his eyes fixed on the knife that hung at his side; it was glistening dark red.

With realisation came pain, like a doubled fist behind his ribs. Will's hand went to the wound and felt the sticky warmth of his blood there. He tried to speak but couldn't hear himself through the shrieking noises in his head, and the shocked, accusatory shouting of the two men who'd attacked them.

Then they were gone. Will's own horses stamped and snorted, and Will turned back to his wife, breathing hard but getting little air, forcing the words out past rapidly numbing lips. 'Lucy, I'm sorry.'

He put his free hand over her heart, reassured to feel the strong, steady beat beneath his fingers, and after a moment he saw her eyes flicker open. She looked confused for a second, then rose to her elbows, wincing as she touched her head.

'Will! Thank the Lord you're all right. The wagon ...' Then she looked at him properly and her face went white with shock. He swayed and, sitting up quickly, she leaned forward and caught him, then struggled to a kneeling position to ease him to the ground.

'They took it, I couldn't stop them,' he whispered.

'Hush. Lie still.' Her fingers were shaking and she couldn't work the buttons well, but finally she was able to loosen his waistcoat, and carefully open the thong securing his shirt. Finding it wouldn't open far enough to be able to see the wound, she gave a frustrated cry and ripped at the linen, and Will groaned as the impact jarred his body.

As darkness crept in he tried to tell her again: 'They took our future.' But all he could hear coming from his own throat was a wordless, hopeless mumble. Her voice though, reassuring and determined, followed him down into the blackness; 'You're going to be all right, Will, I won't let you die.'

Light filtered through his eyelids. Flickering shadows as someone moved above him, sometimes blocking it out, sometimes allowing it through. His skin was both hot and chilled, but his chest was pure fire. He managed to open his eyes and saw Lucy bending over him, her hands holding a blood-soaked, wadded cloth over the wound, high on his left side. He wanted to tell her it wouldn't help, she had to let go, to let *him* go, but again he couldn't speak. He swallowed, and by that he let her know he was awake, and she lifted her face to his.

The tears had cut clean trails in the dust on her cheeks, and her eyes were red with crying.

'I know it's gone, but it doesn't matter,' she told him. 'Gabriel will be okay, he's got men. And someone will pass by, there will be help for us too.'

He managed to shake his head, and found the strength to speak. 'Don't go to Gabe, they'll be there. Go home, Luce.'

He closed his eyes and felt her kiss on his forehead, her tears falling warm on his skin. Her face rested against his, her slender body shaking, denying the truth as her hands moved over him, sobbing his name over and over again. He felt her wildly beating heart pressed against his, felt her arms finding the strength, from somewhere, to lift him so that she held him in her lap rather than let the unfeeling ground steal his last moments.

She rocked him, her despairing little moans hurting his heart, and her hands gripped him as if they'd never let him go, but of course, they must. He wanted so much to ease her pain even as his own receded, but he felt the tears shuddering through her as she bowed her head to bury her face in his neck, as if she could breathe her own life through his skin into his weak, fluttering pulse.

And then he was pulling away. Upwards ... and when he saw her there, bending over him, it all seemed terrifyingly familiar.

White. Vast emptiness, and unfamiliar sounds, shapes shimmering, serene in the distance while others flew past at horrific pace. Such a sense of urgency, but no pain, not even residing in that broken body, but gone forever, no home for it here.

And it seemed to him that the body down there was not Will Deacon, but a young man named Jack. And the figure bending over him no longer Lucy, but Jack's dearest friend Roland, rifle hanging limp by his side, shoulders shaking with grief and horror. Will recognised the young

Jack Trevithick, knew all the hopes and dreams that had come with him from Cornwall to America to work the copper mines, and he knew Jack's friend Roland, who had shared them.

On the long awaited day off they had managed to get invited on a hunting trip. Roland had bagged himself something, he was waving his gun in triumph as Jack rode towards him. Roland's excitement transmitted itself to his horse, which began skittering around under the scant control of its rider. There was a flat-sounding explosion, Jack's body rocked under sudden, shrieking pain, and then nothing.

Another dizzy turnabout and the vision of Roland weeping over Jack's body was gone, replaced by that of a man killed in battle, his chest wound mirroring the wound that had killed the young miner. Mirroring his own. This man too, he knew: Stephen Penhaligon – fighting for his king in the English Civil War.

Back, and back; names, faces; scenes of death replayed over and over, and each time the man had been struck down by a blow to the chest, from bullet, blade or some other weapon. This man: an arrow finding its mark as he defended his home against raiders. He stumbled to his knees, his hands going to the shaft to tear it loose but unable to find the strength. He fell on his side, blood bubbling from the wound to soak his jerkin and mix with the dust of the yard.

That man, handsome enough to drive another to murderous jealousy, impaled upon one of the tines of a two-pronged pitchfork, his body pinned to the ground while his rival stood over him, and his lover wept in terror in the corner of the barn.

As the faces raced past, every one stared up at him with the same shocked green eyes, eyes just like his own

323

and each one seemed to see him, to acknowledge him, to plead with him.

Back, back through time. Every hundred years or so; the clothing changed, the scenes changed, but so often there was someone bending over the prostrate body; sometimes it was the one who had taken the life, sometimes it was some loved one who sobbed and tried to bring it back ... sometimes that was one and the same person.

Will watched the faces spin and fade, cry out and die, and the screams mingled and wound together until they became a terrible, discordant song. And in that song Will heard the plea that this must never happen again. This cycle had to end.

Chapter Twenty-Nine

Maer watched Richard's ragged breathing slow again as the dream faded, and when his eyes opened they held a story so ancient, twisting back into their shared past and beyond, that Maer felt the weight of it pressing in on him without understanding what that story was.

Richard struggled to sit upright. 'Laura,' he managed, and Maer stilled him with a touch on the shoulder.

'She's safe.' Jacky would have found her by now. 'What were you dreaming about?'

'I remember them,' Richard said, sounding unbearably tired. 'All of them. It's like I knew them myself, how they lived and died. Everything.'

'Ancestors?'

Richard nodded. 'They all died the same way. The way I should have died back in that gas station.'

Maer helped Richard to his feet. 'Maybe, or perhaps that part was the dream. Your subconscious would probably project something familiar on them, since you have no way of knowing how they really died.'

Richard considered, then nodded. 'I guess. It would explain that part at least.' For a moment he braced his hands on his thighs, regaining his equilibrium, then he straightened and gestured at Tom's still figure. 'What are we going to do about him?'

'Nothing for now. It has to run its course.' Maer held up his hand to forestall Richard's denial. 'We just have to keep you out of his way for a while longer, until all this is over. We'll go back to Laura's place for a while.'

Captain crept towards Tom's still form, growling softly, his tail thrust between his legs, and Richard and Maer went out into the front garden. Richard took an audible breath and Maer saw him staring at the road, at his car, and back at the house. Then he shook his head and rubbed his hands through his wet hair and down across his face. The action seemed to focus him, and he shoved his hands into the pockets of his coat, before sinking onto the wall.

Maer looked at the key he had picked up from the floor, at the design carved into the fob. He saw Richard's eyes on it too, and knew without asking that he understood the meaning of every line etched into it. Faery Runes, blue for wisdom, and neither of them had ever needed it more.

The charm was intended to ensure the safety of loved ones; for Maer it had been his way of helping him protect Richard, and for Richard it had almost turned out to be the surest way of protecting Laura that there could be. Maer dropped the key ring onto the ground and stamped it into the mud. Richard's eyes followed the action but he did not question it.

Maer watched the evening race towards them across the moor. 'So you get it now, you understand?'

Richard looked at him levelly for a moment. When he spoke he sounded calm, controlled. 'When that stuff was going on in there I felt more than some entity, trying to claim me,' he said, 'I felt my own life starting to make sense.' Maer nodded. 'I guess I just passed out afterwards,' Richard went on, 'but it didn't feel like that, it felt like I was taken somewhere, so I could see the ones who've gone before.'

Maer sat down on the wall next to him. 'Do you think they were there to convince you of what I told you?'

'No, it wasn't that.' Richard cast about, if searching for the right words. He seemed, if anything, embarrassed. 'I think they all wanted me to help them, it's as if they could see across time when they died, and knew that someday I could do something. But what? They're long gone. It's over for them.'

'Maybe it's revenge they want?' Maer suggested.

Richard turned troubled eyes on him. 'I always thought my life had started coming undone the day Cait died,' he said, 'but another way to look at it, is it started unravelling the day I should've died myself. All those people I saw ... it wasn't like a dream, it was like they were calling to me, like they can't rest. Why should I have lived when they didn't? So maybe it is revenge, yeah. On the guy who saved a life that shouldn't have been saved.'

'Gilan?'

'Sharpe, Gilan, whatever he calls himself. But what am I supposed to do? I don't know if I can just kill someone no matter what he's done.'

'All I know is every moment you're here you're in danger, you have to get out.'

'And leave you to fight this?' Richard shook his head. 'Can't do it.'

'It has to be done. Loen has cursed our race through his own pride. If he is not restored our kind will be destroyed – if he cannot be king, no-one will be. I must allow him to take me before Tom's body dies.'

Richard's brows drew in as he looked back at house where the fallen body of Laura's brother still lay. 'His body? Is there nothing left of him at all?'

'Nothing we can save. As of right now everyone believes Laura to be Tom's sister, so she's safe as long as she does not come near Loen. He has sworn that he will destroy the line himself, by his own hand. That hand might have once been yours, but if not it would have been Tom's. Either way she'd have trusted her killer. But when he takes my body, he'll take my knowledge, and he'll know the truth. Tom's physical form will die, the last of the line. Loen will be in his rightful place and my people, *our* people, will be safe.'

'And you?'

'I may have a chance – I have the strength of will to resist to a certain degree.'

Richard's glare was direct, penetrating. 'Yeah? And then what? You know as well as I do you can't hold him off forever, I've felt that strength, remember? You might be fully of their race, but you don't have the power either.' Maer dropped his gaze first, but he'd underestimated his friend's capacity for understanding. 'You're going to kill yourself aren't you? Or have someone else do it?' Richard spoke in wondering tones at first, then his voice rose. 'As soon as Loen has restored his rule and your race is saved, you're going to destroy yourself and him!'

'It's what you were going to do with that key!'

Richard shook his head. 'It's not the same thing; I had no choice, but it wouldn't have mattered anyway. Your people need you.'

'Wouldn't have mattered? What about Laura? How would she have felt, losing her brother and you in the same day?'

Richard gripped his arm. 'You swear she's safe?'

'I swear,' Maer said. 'More than likely she's at the cottage. You must get her away from this place, Rich. She'll know all about who you really are by now, she'll listen to you.'

'We're really going to leave Tom here?'

'We have to. Everything will happen as it will.'

For a second Richard's expression held a trace of his old humour. 'You've been watching too many old movies, buddy.' Maer found a small, tired smile, and stood up, and together they left the garden and started up the hill.

When they got to the cottage it was immediately obvious Laura wasn't there. Maer frowned, but pushed away the feeling of disquiet; Greencoat might have considered it too dangerous to bring her here, and that was probably wise, in fact.

'Where is she?' Richard demanded.

Maer laid a hand on his arm to soothe him and felt the tension in the muscles there, even beneath the thick coat. 'She's safe,' he repeated. 'Sit down, you need to regain your strength.'

Richard headed for the sofa, but he didn't follow Maer's advice. Instead he went around to the back, knelt, and pulled out a semi-transparent plastic box. Maer moved closer, curious, and saw Richard pushing aside a pile of stunningly life-like pictures of a pensive-looking woman with short hair and large eyes. Vivien Riley. His attention was snagged by the only framed picture in the box, clearly a child's drawing but one that drew his eye back every time it tried to slide away; a woman with only the suggestion of features, but an enquiring and alert tilt to her head and dressed, not in the pretty dress he might have expected from a little girl's imagination, but in the clothes of a traveller. For a moment he stared at it, wondering at the little tingle it gave him, and then Richard drew out a blue folder.

'It has to be this one.'

'What does?'

Without explaining, Richard opened the folder and Maer caught his breath. There were two pictures inside, and the top one was a likeness of Richard that was unnervingly accurate. Although … he squinted at it, trying to understand what made it less vital than the pictures of Laura's mother, but he couldn't quite get it. Richard picked it up and gave a soft laugh, but Maer thought he sounded more sad than amused, and then his gaze fell on the picture that had been revealed beneath it. His mouth went dry.

Richard lifted the drawing out and together they stared. The little man looked back at them, his tears bright and terrified, his leathery old face. 'Who is this?' he said in a broken whisper. 'She told me they saw him, down that mine.' He turned to Maer. 'Who is it?'

'His name is Jacky Greencoat,' Maer managed at last. 'A spriggan.'

Richard turned back to the picture, and Maer saw an odd expression on his face; a kind of puzzled affection. But it quickly faded, and Richard shoved the picture back in the folder and dropped it back into the box. He stood up, kicked the box back under the sofa with sudden savagery and fixed Maer with an ice-cold gaze. 'Where's Laura?'

***

Left alone in the chamber, Laura tried to sort everything into some kind of order but it was dizzyingly unreal; how had she ended up here, below the ground, guarded by creatures that should never exist outside children's tales? Such a short time ago she'd been settled, in love, excited by her new life – now she was terrified for that life, and for the man who'd helped her find it.

She searched for anything that might make this more immediate, but it only pushed her deeper into the realm of disbelief: exquisite goods made by the most careful of hands for beings who claimed the highest esteem. Heavy velvet curtains, tables carved from beautiful dark wood and covered in ornately designed lace cloths, even the bed upon which she sat was built for royalty, it showed in every notched join and in every hand-stitched seam.

Then she caught sight of a decorated jar, and the past crashed in again, bringing a feeling of such tight, icy terror she didn't even know how she could breathe. That jar – its twin had been the cause of all this. Tom's excitement at finding it; the shock of the green-jacketed little man; the raised, blistered circle on Tom's hand. And the dust. Remains of the ancient king, now at work destroying what was left of her brother.

Laura felt the scream building in her chest and she knew that once she let it out she wouldn't stop until the last breath left her body. Her mind was crowded, seething with images and memories; reasons; explanations; realisations ... and now she was ready to die, because this pressure inside her head, this pain and terror twisting her gut until she moaned aloud, wouldn't end until she did. Madness was swirling just beyond her thin armour of reason, ready to descend and steal her away.

Richard. His smile, his strength, the sound of his voice ... the thought of him held that madness at bay, but not the knowledge of what must inevitably be. She kept him at the front of her mind and drew her courage from him; if she must die she would do so knowing herself as she was, not as some screaming, insane stranger.

Barely aware of what she was doing, Laura rose from the bed and swept aside the curtain that covered the doorway. Beyond it lay the cavern, now pitch dark once again – to her eyes at least. She stepped forward into the blackness and felt a hand close on the back of her head.

There was light now. Gilan was holding her, and his vision was hers. The cavern was full of creatures: small and large, tiny and human-sized, and the grip of the fingers on her scalp nearly rent from her the scream she had been biting back. But she did not cry out.

'Kill me then,' she whispered instead.

But as the words left her lips she knew that wasn't what she wanted after all. Back there it had seemed the only way to escape the pressure, and the horror that crawled, squealing inside her skull. But out here seeing life – of whatever kind – going on around her, she knew she would fight for what was hers until she was utterly spent. Which was not yet, not by a Cornish mile.

'No, you don't want that, missy,' Gilan whispered back, and she could feel his smile curving against her ear.

'Does the queen know you're planning on destroying her?' Laura said in a normal tone, and Gilan's hand clamped shut on her head. She winced and sucked in a breath: his fingers were like sharp little pieces of stone against her flesh.

'You'd better be keeping little snippets like that to yourself, or I might grant your little request after all.'

'It's not for you to do, remember?' Laura said with a tight smile of her own.

'Terrible dangerous place, the moors,' Gilan said. 'Everyone would understand if I wasn't able to protect you.'

'You would still be punished.'

'Yes. And you would be dead. Let's keep some perspective, shall we? Anyway, I was just coming to find you, it's time.'

His words, although expected, sent a small current of shock through her. But she had no time to think as Gilan pulled her through the cavern towards the tunnel. All around her the dwellers of the heath stopped and stared, nudging one another, clearly familiar with who she was, and with the fate that awaited her.

Out, they went, and up. Onto the moor, where the late

afternoon was creeping across towards them, the sky dark in places, patchy-light in others. She had thought she'd never see natural light again, and although the relief was fleeting, she accepted the strength it granted her. As she peered through the descending gloom she saw a tall figure making his stumbling way over the grass towards the stones: Tom. Laura finally started to cry, but they were not tears of terror, they were deeper than that; they were born of a sorrow that began at her centre and pulled at every part of her until she could do nothing except give in to it.

***

The rain fell steadily on the broken down walls of the old mill, and swept across the moss-encrusted tower stump. Richard's stomach twisted with a hollow fear that was echoed in Maer's voice as he called out for Laura.

Then he called another name, 'Greencoat! Show yourself, I command you!'

Richard started. 'What –'

'He's the one protecting her, he was to meet her here.'

'Wait. You didn't see her safe yourself?'

'I had to find you,' Maer said, 'to explain. You would never have been able to fight for so long if you hadn't known what you were fighting.'

'And that little goblin guy is the one you put in charge of keeping her safe?' He was shouting now. 'What the hell were you thinking?'

'He was the only one I could trust. I'll explain how I know that, but now isn't the time.'

Both of them were pacing the area as they argued, looking for some kind of sign Laura had ever been there. Richard bent and plucked something from the gorse bush beside him.

'Now *is* the time,' he said bleakly. 'How do you know you can trust him?' He held up the scrap of rain-soaked cloth, it was dark green. Maer took it from him and held it draped across his fingers, while he struggled with his reply.

'Because he was supposed to kill *you*, this morning. He had orders from Gilan.'

'Guy's showing his true colours at last.'

'He had the poisoned dart all ready, but he couldn't do it. I saw him just after I sent you to Plymouth, you had just escaped with your life, had you but known it.'

'So how come he couldn't do it?' Richard had thought nothing more could shock him, but he felt light headed with the knowledge of how close he had come to instant, invisible death.

'Greencoat says he saw you for what you are.'

'And what is that?'

Maer shrugged, still staring at the cloth. 'Rightful heir to Loen's rule, the king of the Moor. He must have sensed you were born to rule in your own right, not just to give your body to Loen.'

Richard was startled but saw no guile, no clear attempt at persuasion, only sorrow as Maer looked at the cloth in his hand. 'What about Laura, how come you trusted him with her, or doesn't she matter?' he said, more brutally than he had intended. Maer's eyes showed him how wrong he was, the pain there was unmistakeable.

'His loyalty would be to you, and I believe he gave his life for her because of who she is to you.'

'You're not making sense!' Richard's heartbeat was once again rapid and fierce, and as he looked at the piece cloth Maer's words began to sink in. 'Sharpe,' he said dully. 'He has her doesn't he?'

He didn't need an answer, nor did he wait for one. Instead he bean to run. Instinct told him the quickest way and he took it, flying over the heath with only one thought pounding through his consciousness, pulsing in his veins and propelling him onwards: Laura.

***

Maer was momentarily staggered by the swiftness of Richard's departure, then he took off after him. Once over the rise it took longer than he'd have guessed to catch up; Richard's earthbound flight was as graceful and silent as the shadow of a hawk. Maer dug deep, put on a burst of speed he himself had not even realised he possessed, and drew close enough to catch at Richard's coat as it flew out behind him.

Richard tried to shake him off, but Maer hung on, and Richard shot a furious glare over his shoulder as he tried to wriggle out of his coat. 'You won't stop me.'

Maer shook his head, transferring his grip to Richard's arm. 'I'm not trying to. But listen to me! Richard finally slowed and Maer went on, 'Let me take care of Tom. You concentrate on Laura.'

Richard stopped, and turned to him. The truth lay between them, as readable as the runes on the key ring that had failed them both. 'You're going to give yourself to Loen again aren't you?' he said, 'or die trying.' He shook his head. 'But it won't achieve anything since your little sidekick won't be around to put an end to your body after Loen gets a hold of it.'

'That's why I want you to do it,' Maer said, sounding far more resolute than he felt.

Richard flinched. 'I can't believe you'd even suggest that.'

Maer dropped his gaze, worried the fear was showing in his eyes. He tried to inject his words with a persuasive, confident note.

'But it won't be me, not really. It's as you said: neither of us is strong enough to fight off Loen's spirit for long – I'd be absorbed into him, there'd be nothing of me left.'

'That's not what you said before, but putting that hypocritical bullshit aside for a moment, how exactly do you expect me to do it?'

'Gilan will have a knife. Not about his person, but hidden somewhere in the stones. He has them all over the moor. Find it, use it. You have to, Richard. Please.'

Richard's shoulders sagged, his eyes finding Maer's and filled with bewildered grief. 'God, how can you ask me –'

'Because it's going to save Laura's life! If Loen doesn't believe she's not Ulfed's line, or even if he does, and he *doesn't care*, he's going to use my hands to kill her. Can you stand by and watch that?'

'Are you trying to make me hate you enough to do this?' Richard backed away, his face pale. 'What if there's no knife?'

'There will be. What were you going to kill Gilan with?'

'I told you, I'm no killer. I'm just going to get Laura away from him.'

'Or die trying?' mimicked Maer gently.

Richard held his gaze a moment longer, and Maer saw the last of his fear melt away, his expression now cold and still. 'You said it.'

He took off again and Maer heard his own words: *can you stand by and watch that?* and he groaned. Had he really just made this man, whom he cherished above all, choose between his friend and the woman he loved? No wonder Richard was still utterly furious; he'd been lied to all his life by the person who'd professed to be his friend, and now that friend was trying turn him into a murderer.

He caught up as Richard crested the hill, and searched for a way to explain, to express his regret, but Richard had stopped dead and was staring down at the stones with clenched fists. Maer followed his line of sight, and all the words he had wanted to say dried in his throat. Without speaking, he took the track that led to the stones, and saw Richard move too, directly into the path of the cold-hearted killer of mortals and his prize.

**

Laura felt the stones before they reached them – all the years she'd lived and played here and she'd never felt the power of these lumps of granite the way she did now, it was as if history itself were leaking out of them and wrapping her in its cool embrace. Each tiny glistening piece of quartz and mica within the rock shone more than it should on this early November evening, even magnified as they were by the steady rain.

But the wonder that stole over her was involuntary, and quickly obliterated by Gilan's fingers tightening on her arm.

'Young Maer will be here soon, to make his oh, so noble sacrifice,' he said as he nodded towards Tom. Laura looked again and her heart contracted as she saw Tom stare straight through her, no recognition in his eyes.

'It's not him, not Tom, not anymore,' she chanted softly. The ache inside was terrible.

'Your majesty,' Gilan said. 'I have the girl: the last in the line of the chief who tried to kill your son.'

'Tried? What are you saying?' Tom's mouth moved as the king spoke, but his body was slumped against the central stone, his eyes fixed ahead. Laura couldn't have gone to him even if she'd felt safe to do so, Gilan's grip was tight and painful.

'Ulfed struck awry. The child did not die.'

'Then there is no crime to answer. The girl may live.'

Laura's heart leapt, and she gave a tiny gasp of pure relief. Dear god, thank you …

But Gilan shook his head. 'It is true he did not kill your son, My Lord, but he grievously wounded him. His evil intent remains unchanged. Your words, passed down through Borsa's line, declared your intention to end Ulfed's line if he *harmed* your son.'

There was a long silence, and Laura started to shake in renewed fear. When Loen did not answer, Gilan spoke again, his voice hard. 'My Lord and King, your words have sustained your people ever since you uttered them, you cannot deny your own curse. This girl is Ulfed's get. I offer her to you as a gift to show my loyalty, and express my regret that you must take an inferior being to that which you chose. Be assured the culprit has been dealt with.'

'Inferior being? Why? And what culprit?'

Gilan smiled. He leaned in close to Laura, although his words were addressed to Loen. 'The spriggan who killed Lucas.'

Laura's heart tightened so fast and hard she thought it would burst. Everything went dark, and her knees lost the strength to hold her up but Gilan's grip stopped her from falling.

'You are a fool, Gilan. Lucas lives.' Tom's hand rose jerkily and pointed, and Laura found her breath again as she saw two figures covering the ground with startling speed.

One of them, his black coat flying behind him like

huge, dark wings, was heading straight for her and Gilan. His hair blew back from a face set as hard as the stones at her side, and she felt everything coming together in that one instant: the equation of her feelings for him with those of the wildness of the moor, the tight, controlled energy she had sensed the first time they had met – all this flashed through her mind in a split second, before it was replaced by horror at the realisation that his destiny, as hard as Maer had tried to fight it, was being played out right now.

She opened her mouth to scream a warning, but Gilan's hand was suddenly filling her face, his fingers clamped on her jaw, sending jagged shards of pain through her head. She could taste sweat and dirt on his palm, and gagged, but Gilan gripped harder.

'Let him come, lovely, let him come,' he said in her ear, and as his breath brushed over her skin she felt her self-control struggling with mounting hysteria. 'You can't take her,' Gilan called as Richard drew close. 'You're no match, and besides, I have a little something you don't.'

He bent quickly, dragging Laura with him, and reached down. There was the scraping sound of metal on stone, and when Gilan straightened again he was holding an ancient looking blade with a broken handle. Another second and it was pressed against her throat.

Richard's expression had not changed, he looked like the carved statue of some beautiful, deadly creature, something not of her world. She would have been terrified of him if she had never seen that face softened by love, animated by laughter. Now she was terrified for him. He glanced over at Maer who, she saw, had stopped on his way to Tom and was watching with a horror equal to her own.

Richard turned back to Gilan. 'I can go to him now,'

he said calmly, inclining his head towards Tom. 'I can give myself to him if that's what he wants. Or I can give myself to you, in return for Laura.'

'She's a gift for the king,' Gilan said, but Laura could already feel the hand that held her face slackening off, although the blade still pricked the skin at the side of her neck.

'She's no good to the king,' Richard said, 'she's not the right blood.'

'Then she's expendable,' Gilan said, clearly surprised but covering it well. 'You shouldn't have told me.'

'Loen would have killed her anyway, and he would have used someone she loved to do it. So, do I go over there now and let Loen take me over?'

'No!' Maer cried.

'He'll kill her, Maer,' Richard said evenly, not taking his eyes off Gilan – splashes of Arctic seawater in an icy-still face. 'He always meant to, we both know that.'

'Well I do have something of a history, after all,' Gilan said softly, taunting. 'Third time's the charm, don't you know?'

Laura saw pain flash across Richard's face, followed by the same dead, expressionless stare as before. He took a step forwards, and now he was close enough to touch. More than anything Laura longed to reach out to him, but the press of the blade point against her neck paralysed her.

'Let her go, Gilan,' Richard said. The other two might as well not have existed, there were only the three of them now and Laura stood between Richard and Gilan, feeling the hatred charging the air around them. She felt the blade twitch, drawing a drop of blood that was immediately washed away by the rain. Richard's gaze fixed on the diluted blood as it trickled away down her neck. When he spoke his voice was low, but tight, and she recognised fury and anguish in equal measure.

'Hurt her again and your king will destroy you using these hands.' He raised them, then reached out and caught hold of Laura's arm. Gilan allowed him to pull her away and guide her to stand behind him. At his touch, Laura began breathing again, only now realising she'd stopped as the blade had drawn blood. Her hands went around his waist from behind, and she rested her bowed head against his back, feeling the tension in him that pulled every muscle tight.

'Go stand by Maer,' he said, too quietly for the words to carry to where Maer stood. 'He loves you, he won't trust himself to go through with it if you're close.'

Gilan heard, however, and his face twisted in anger. 'You dare to interfere with fate?'

'Why not? You did. Maer was never meant to be the one.'

'Wrong, Lucas, he was *always* meant to be.'

Laura saw the blade come to rest over Richard's heart, and felt his breathing becoming shallower as he readied himself. He had no intention of giving himself to anyone. She stepped away from him, then turned to go towards Maer and Tom, but stopped with a hollow cry of despair: Maer and her brother were locked together, Maer's face was a mask of pain but he was holding on to Tom's shoulders, forcing her brother's body back against the rock. Too late …

***

The head hurt. The shoulders hurt. And the hand throbbed and burned. Everything hurt; this body was dying and the spirit that had inhabited it was no more than an echo in the back of his mind. Loen had come

341

forward too quickly, taking advantage of Riley's grief at failing his sister, and this terrified heart had faltered, quickened, faltered, quickened, and now it beat with a fluttering irregularity that told Loen it would soon cease altogether. He must leave before that happened, let this child of Ulfed die, and then put an end to the girl.

The half-mortal body he had almost seized earlier was coming too, he could sense it, and once he was in that glorious form he would have the girl's trust and then her life: no matter what her brain told her, her eyes would see only the man she loved, and her heart would take over.

Burning with hunger, Loen had watched the speed with which his black-clad saviour covered the ground between himself and his quarry. He felt his spirit yearn towards this, his descendant, and the link established so long ago made the pull hard to resist but he sank back down beside the large central stone, and folded Tom's arms across his chest. He waited.

After a moment he felt sticky warmth on the chin he wore, and realised he was chewing on the lower lip; the flesh was torn, it caused him more pain and he moaned softly and made himself stop. As he did so he became aware of a lifting sensation, although he knew he remained firmly on the wet ground. He felt as if he were elongating, then rising, lifting through the top of this head. He raised the eyes with difficulty: Maer stood beside him and the pain in the shoulders was from Maer's hands, gripping tight while he worked his demon's magic.

'No,' Loen whispered. He closed the eyes, tried to remain anchored in this body he detested, but his survival instinct was winning out: this barely animated corpse was only too happy to reject him, and without it he was just a wisp, helpless and formless, unable to be heard, unable to seize hold of the body he needed and force himself into it.

Without that contact he would find refuge in the first body that came close, *but this wasn't the right one.*

Maer gripped tighter. Loen tried to shrink into the ground itself, pulling down hard, finding the nerve endings in Riley's body, picturing fingers, toes, forcing himself to reach into those extremities and hang on.

But as he felt himself pulled inexorably towards the healthy form that offered itself to him, he suddenly wondered why he was fighting: wasn't he strong enough to subdue this youngster? Couldn't he merely use the fresh form as a way of getting closer to Lucas?

Could he risk it?

Chapter Thirty

Richard felt Laura step away, and although relief swept over him, Gilan had the knife against his heart and he was seventeen again and pinned against a tree; he was standing by the shores of Lake Michigan, terrified by a shade that appeared from nowhere; he was back by his car in the parking lot at O'Hare.

But that Richard Lucas had been little more than a child.

Even as he felt the press of the blade that had so recently let Laura's blood, he felt no fear, only familiar, bitter fury. He heard Laura's despairing cry and could not spare a glance so could only guess at what was happening. His anger grew, but he let his expression go blank and met Gilan's mocking stare with empty eyes.

'You've waited long enough, right? This time you're going to do it. So do it.'

'I'll do it when I'm ready.'

'Waiting to make sure the other part of your plan goes through first?' Richard indicated behind him.

'Shut up, whelp, I'll do it when I'm ready,' Gilan repeated. Richard leaned closer, deliberately letting the blade pierce his shirt. The skin tore and blood flowered there, tiny but bright, and Gilan pulled back the knife slightly. As he did so Richard brought his hand up hard, striking Gilan's wrist and sending the weapon spinning away into the long grass.

Gilan let out a roar of anger and lunged after it, but Richard seized him and dragged him back, smashing a blow into the man's jaw that spun him around and back. But Gilan was faery too, and faster than Richard realised, and as Richard closed in again he threw his arm out and blocked the punch that would have sent him into oblivion. His own foot came up in a vicious, high kick that drove his booted heel into Richard's stomach.

Richard slammed back over the central stone, striking his head, and from where he lay momentarily stunned he saw Gilan dive for the knife once more. Gritting his teeth against a groan, he rolled, coming to his feet as Gilan found what he was looking for, and the two of them circled each other and the stone. Richard's breath began to come smoothly again, and the crippling pain in his gut was receding, reduced to a dull ache that pulsed with each beat of his heart.

His vision sharpened again as the dizziness from the blow to his head faded, but as he moved around the far side of the stone his attention was stolen for a crucial second by an horrific sight: Tom's body slumped, eyes wide open to the sky, and Maer, kneeling still and watchful beside it. Maer had done it, taken that final, terrible step, and was now as lost to him as Tom was to Laura. Grief struck Richard harder than any physical blow, and he knew the pain of it would not fade as quickly, if ever. He heard Laura's soft weeping but could do nothing.

His shock had already cost him dearly.

Gilan had seen his momentary distraction and leapt onto the central stone. Now he stood above Richard, the knife in his hand, triumph all over his narrow face as he saw what Richard had seen. Slowly he flipped the knife over so he was holding it by the blade, balanced on his fingertips ready to throw. And Richard knew he wouldn't stand a chance.

He also knew exactly where the blade would pierce him, already he felt the scar burning beneath his shirt. In quick succession the images flashed behind his eyes: the soldier dying in the mud, the excited Englishman out hunting, the young prospector and his wife... would it end here after all then, in failure?

Then his heart jolted: coming through the stones, echoing through the circle and filling the air all around them, Tom's voice, yet older, deeper. The voice of Loen.

'Gilan, born of Borsa's line, hear me! Your wickedness will not go unpunished, but lay down your weapon and you will be allowed to live.'

Gilan dropped the knife in an instant, it clanged onto the stone at his feet and spun in a circle, the wet blade reflecting what little light filtered through the grey drizzle. He stared around in evident terror but Tom was still slumped, and Maer seemed in a state of near catatonia, only the way his eyes were squeezed shut betrayed any sign of life.

Gilan turned back and, still confused, stooped to seize the slowly spinning knife. Richard realised he had a split second in which to act, and vaulted onto the stone, kicking the blade away. This time his blow struck hard and true, and Gilan was unconscious before he hit the grass.

The voice had fallen silent. Where had it come from? Richard looked out over the moor through the rain, towards the source of the sound, and saw three figures approaching, two full-sized: one male, one female carrying a large stick, and one much smaller. He could not see features clearly, but something about the little creature spoke of maleness, and also struck a chord of familiarity that went beyond his recognition of the picture he had seen. A feeling of disconnected affection washed over him and he jumped down from the stone. That feeling faded as he hit the ground, but his gratitude was undeniable: Maer was gone, Tom was gone, but both he and Laura were safe and that was entirely thanks to this ... what had

Maer called him? A spriggan.

The little man did not walk stooped, as would have been natural judging by the roundness of his shoulders, instead his head was held high, as if he walked at the side of equals. But when his gaze met Richard's he stopped short, bowing his head. He called out, this time in his own voice.

'My king! Jacky has deceived you, plotted your death, failed your lady, deserves to die himself for –'

'Stop it!' Richard yelled, and the little man did, but remained where he was. His companions stood silent at his side. Richard walked towards them, and as he stopped before Greencoat he saw blood encrusted on the side of the spriggan's head, and frowned. He adopted a gentler tone. 'Look, I'm not your king, Loen never got to me.'

'But that is –'

'And you saved my life back there, so I don't want to hear any more whining, okay?' Greencoat looked bemused, making slow sense of the unfamiliar speech, then relief crossed his face. Richard gestured to the wound on his head. 'Did Gilan do this to you when you were protecting Laura?'

Another nod. 'My lord, Jacky is grievously sorry for failing Your Majesty, for allowing Prince Gilan to take your lady.'

'Doesn't look like you had much of a choice,' Richard said, and touched the little man's shoulder. 'You did your best, thank you.'

Greencoat looked as though he'd been presented with a sack of gold, and couldn't speak. The taller man stepped forward, and Richard realised who it must be, he saw Maer looking back at him through those bright blue eyes and felt a stab of pain.

'You must nevertheless understand what we must do,'

the man said, and his face held an expression of honest regret. Richard inclined his head, acknowledging the other's royal prerogative, but letting him see he was anything but ready to acquiesce. A hint of respect touched the older man's face, while the woman stood cold and rigid.

Greencoat was staring at Maer's father, aghast. 'Sir, you cannot! I explained –'

'You explained nothing,' broke in the woman. 'You brought us here to witness the rebirth of Loen.' She looked around, suddenly worried. 'Where is Maer? Where is my son? Casta, what has he done to –'

'Peace, my love. Lucas, where is the prince?'

'Maer's done an incredible thing,' Richard said, his voice shaking as he took in the enormity of the sacrifice. Maer's eyes were open now, but stared ahead, no more animation in his face than in the bleak, darkening horizon. Deera gave a cry and started towards him, but Casta stopped her.

'He has given himself? And you let him?' he said to Richard. Words of apology hovered on Richard's lips but he would not utter them – he had nothing to apologise for.

'There was nothing I could do,' he said instead. 'It happened too fast. No matter how mad I was at him I would never have wanted this to happen.'

Casta nodded, though grief for his son carved deep lines in his face. 'You had to save the one you love,' he said softly, 'Maer knew this better than you realise.'

'But I loved *him* too!' Richard cried, undone by Casta's compassion. No, he had nothing to apologise for, but sorrow and guilt twisted his guts into agonising knots … he could only imagine the pain Maer's parents were in.

Laura came to stand at his side, and glared at Deera.

'Your precious brother is to blame for Dean's ... for *Maer's* death,' she said, and despite the tears in her eyes her voice was steady and cold. 'He's planned this for a long, long time. He even arranged for him,' she gestured savagely at Greencoat, 'to murder Richard so that Maer was the only one who could replace him. So much for family loyalty.'

'Then why did you *not* kill him?' Deera demanded, turning on Greencoat who did not shrink beneath her fury.

'I saw.'

'Saw what?'

'Who he is. What must be.'

'Stop talking in riddles!' Deera snapped. 'Tell us what you saw that meant your prince must die in the place of this stranger.'

***

Greencoat looked at each one of them in turn: Gilan was awake, and Casta was preventing him from rising by placing a foot on his scrawny chest; Maer's eyes were also open, although blank; Deera's eyes were locked onto him, her hands wrapped across her middle; Laura had moved to Richard's side and they held one another, giving and receiving strength equally. It was well. And it was time.

Greencoat made his way to the central stone, climbed upon it and closed his eyes. In a voice that began as little more than a whisper but grew stronger with each word, he re-told the story of Loen and Magara, of the terrible decision Ulfed had made to save his people, and of the storm that had struck Loen down in the midst of his horror and fury. 'Borsa gathered up Loen's dust and swore to uphold the king's promise of vengeance.'

'What became of the woman?' Laura asked. 'Was she punished as well?'

'Punishment enough to lose her child,' Deera said, and she sounded bleak as she gazed on her son's empty face.

'She took the babe and ran,' Jacky said, and as he looked at Richard he faltered again, but the clear, ageless green eyes both steadied and commanded him, and he drew a long breath, squaring his stooped shoulders, and began the rest of the tale, the part that had waited too long to be told.

The distraught woman fell upon the spriggans out of the storm, her murdered baby son wrapped in her cloak, and the fear among them had been echoed by her own horrified realisation: these were creatures to be despised, unlike the one she had lain with. But her grief was fresh and she had begged them to shelter her, and to allow her to bury her child with honour and decency.

But as the elder spriggan had gently lifted the limp, blood-drenched infant from his mother in order to prepare it for burial, she had felt a fluttering below her fingers and declared the child alive. Using every piece of medical lore passed down through her line she had nursed the child, and cared for him, and the babe had healed. This alone told the spriggan he was not fully human.

She had questioned the woman, who had remained close-lipped, clearly terrified, until the baby cried aloud for the first time since the storm, a sudden, lusty cry, indignant at his discomfort. Magara had broken down in gratitude and relief, and told the gathered clan everything.

The child was not merely half faery then, but from Magara's description, and the appearance of the child himself, the spriggans recognised King Loen as his father.

Kin of both a chieftain and the king of the Moor; this child was born of such nobility he could be nothing less than king himself one day.

When the boy had lived eighteen cycles his mother made the decision: she would take him back to the village and show her people the child they had wanted to kill. She would dare them to deny the wickedness of their act when they saw what he had become, for the child had grown into a good-hearted, pleasant-natured young man of startling beauty, with the ethereal grace of his father, the human strength of his mother, and the calm, natural authority of both. The spriggans had watched him grow into this singular creature with all the pride of true parents.

So Magara and her son made their way back across the moor to the settlement where the boy had been born. Neither realised they were being watched, but the creature who would carry this tale back to his people would remember every word, every gesture and every expression, and tell it faithfully through his tears of grief.

The journey had been short, less than a day – Magara's flight from the scene of the sacrifice had ended abruptly on stumbling on the spriggan clan, and she and the boy had remained welcome there ever since. But now she came upon her old village and her determination wavered, and her trepidation was clear to the eyes that watched among the tufts of gorse.

They passed through the stone circle, and, as they drew close to the centre stone Magara turned to the young man at her side. 'Tir, there is much I must tell you, and I would do it now.'

Tir frowned. 'But surely we are almost at the village, can we rest there and talk?'

'No, you need to be prepared in case they do not

welcome us as we hoped.'

'Very well. Shall we sit here?' He made for the centre stone but Magara caught his arm.

'No, but look on it a while. Then I will tell you what you have to know.' She waited for a moment while her son did as he was told. 'Does that stone bring any feelings to life inside you?'

Tir stared at it, frowning and clearly impatient to know what his Mother was being mysterious about, shook his head. 'No, nothing at all.'

'Come and sit with me, I will try to explain everything to you.'

They moved away from the stones and Magara sat down on the grass, her hands clasped between her knees, her head bowed. Tir sat beside her, his arms resting on his raised knees as he waited for her to begin.

'You know we are different from those with whom we have lived?'

'Yes, of course.'

'I am far, *far* different. You, my beloved, are not.'

'Of course I am, I don't look like them any more than you do.'

'Differences are not only made in the eyes, Tir.'

'Mother, please, we are both tired and hungry, can we not – '

'Hush!' Magara's tone tightened, and when Tir smiled his beauty was almost heart-breaking to behold.

'That's better,' he said. 'I thought my stern, chieftain mother had gone forever.'

Magara looked at him, and she found a smile so like his they almost appeared twins for a moment. Then she turned away again, her hand brushing his, and began to tell him everything: the king coming to her in the night, the certainty he was something otherworldly, the ease of the birth and the terror of the decision brought upon them by her kinsman. Her smile had long since fallen away by now.

'Ulfed had to do it,' she whispered, and her grief was shaking her body anew but this time it was grief for her lost family, and for what they had wrought in the name of their deity and protector. 'You were not permitted to have a name but in my heart I called you Tir. For the land, from where your father came that night. And when you lay upon that stone and I heard you crying, oh, my sweet boy, you were so angry!' She smiled through her tears and her son moved to put his arm around her; he was taller than she, and she seemed the child in his protection.

After a moment she was able to continue. She told of the storm, of the blade flashing down and of Ulfed, standing there stunned and disorientated, staring at the apparently lifeless infant on the slab and the rain water running, blood-reddened, off the stone.

'But you had moved in your anger, and Ulfed struck with his blade but it did not pierce you through the heart as everyone thought.'

Tir's hand went to the his chest where the scar lay beneath his tunic. It had been a long, twisting scar when fresh, but remained the same size as he had grown, and now formed a short mark midway up his ribcage. He had never considered it was something he hadn't been born with.

Magara laid her own hand over his and told him how she had seized him and run blindly across the moor, only caring about getting her child's body away from the terrible scene.

'I believed you to be dead, and you might still have bled to death, but the reason you healed so well was because you are more like those creatures who took us in, than the one who tried to kill you,' she said. Tir was silent for a long time, clearly struggling with everything he was learning.

'But if I am also of their race, why do I not look like them?' he said at last.

'There are many spirits on the moor,' his mother said. 'I learned much during our life with the spriggans: your father and his people are the most powerful of all the elementals, and the spriggans and their like serve them. That is in part why you were so cherished among them – they can see royalty in you, as I can, and are bound to serve.'

'But you are all wrong!' Tir's cry was rich with misery. 'If you speak the truth now, then I am human, yet I am elemental spirit, and I have no place with anyone because I am both and I am neither. I am nothing.'

He stood and walked a short distance away, staring out over the hills as though they held the secret of where he belonged. Magara rose too, and went to him, touched his shoulder. He did not look at her, but his stiff posture relaxed a little, and he let his clenched fists open at his sides.

'How can you say you are nothing when you have the love of so many?' Magara asked softly.

Tir turned, and for the first time since childhood there were tears in his brilliant green eyes. 'And what have I done to earn it? An enchanted birth, a lucky escape, and since then I have done nothing but be waited upon by a race so kind, so wise and so generous, acting out of a duty I did nothing to deserve.'

'You have worked hard,' Magara protested. 'You have done your share of wood cutting and hunting, you have learned at their feet as their own children have, and you have brought joy to them. The royalty for which they love you is not simply your birth right, it is the way you are.'

Tir stared at her as if he wanted to believe her, wanted it with all his heart, but then he shook his head. There was a silence between them, it drew out for many minutes before Tir spoke. 'Do you really want to return to your village?'

Magara looked over her shoulder towards the place she had fled eighteen cycles ago. 'It is over and done. They must take me back, and yes, more than anything I want to be among my own people now,' she said. 'I know you have lain with mortal girls of other villages,' she added with a little smile as he flushed. 'You should be looking among your own people for a mate. Even the highest born among them would be blessed to claim you.'

Through the tightness of his expression, the ghost of Tir's own smile reappeared. 'Then we must be sure to arrive before dark, in case I make any promises I should not like to keep once the sun comes up.' He held out his arm and Magara took it, and together they walked into the village.

Evening was painting its shadows over the ground and the people as Magara and her son walked side by side, towards the hut of the chief. The skin hanging over the doorway was askew, letting the evening cool waft inside, and through the gap Magara could see the man within was not her brother.

'Your pardon, but where is Ulfed?' she asked a passer-by. The woman turned and Magara flinched, recognising the old face and thankful she herself stood in shadow.

'Who are you to seek out the disgraced one?' the woman said.

Magara glanced at Tir. 'What happened that he should be disgraced?'

'Cast out. Many cycles past. But since you are clearly a

traveller, perhaps word did not reach your settlement.'

'No, we have heard nothing,' Magara said truthfully. 'Please, tell me so I do not appear foolish in the chief's eyes.'

'You heard about the babe? The evil child?'

'The one who was killed, yes.'

'Killed? The fool could not even manage that!' The woman was warming to her tale now. 'Ulfed's hesitation brought the wrath of The Goddess upon us and it was because of him our village was plagued for so long – the storms were terrible, we lost our crops.'

'So the baby lived? How can you know?'

'I see much that is hidden.' Magara fought a wave of sick remembrance at the familiar words. 'The babe lived, I saw this. But my sight is not what it once was and I could not be sure when it died, but it will have been soon after, for Ulfed at least managed to wound it. The mother ran away with ...' The woman tailed off and stared hard at Magara who tried, too late, to turn away. Then her eyes lit on Tir and they flew wide open. 'You!'

'My name is Fema,' Magara said quickly. 'This is my –'

'He walks among us,' the woman breathed, stepping back, and Magara shook her head.

'Please, hush! You are wrong –'

'Demon!' the old woman suddenly screamed, louder than seemed possible from such an old throat. The beaten earth path was suddenly full of people, and Magara's arms were seized. She twisted around to see Tir caught in the same way, and struggled to reach him, but she was held firm.

The skin covering the doorway of the chief's hut was jerked aside and a large man erupted, fury all over his face. 'What disturbs me this night?'

'She has returned,' the old woman said, pointing at

Magara. 'The one who lies with evil. She brings death to our home once more.'

Panic was spreading through the gathering crowd, and the chief held out his hands for quiet. 'You are Magara, sister of the disgraced Ulfed?'

'No, my name is – '

'Do not think to lie.' He peered closely at her. 'Yes, I recognise you now. And the woman there knows of the death you bring with you.'

Magara sagged. 'Very well, yes, I am she. But this not that baby; the child died on the same night. Tir is born of another –'

'Tir? You have named him for the land? Why is that, I wonder?'

Without waiting for an answer, the chief turned and ordered Magara and Tir taken away and closely guarded while he took counsel.

As the woman and her son were led away another shout went up, and they were abruptly released. Ulfed stood on the grassy mound beside the rough track, his face set and determined.

'Magara!' he bellowed. He started towards the woman, and every line on his face spoke of hate and betrayal. 'You cost me my life!' No-one moved as he came closer, and Magara did not shrink back, but squared her shoulders and stood as tall as she could, almost matching her brother's height.

'I did no wrong,' she declared. 'Tir is a good man, honest and hardworking – he would benefit the village greatly. Why not let us stay?'

'The village has suffered great ill, and I am merely tolerated now, burden instead of leader.' The words were forced out from between lips that were tight with fury.

He stopped a short distance away from his sister and

his gaze swept over the young man. For a moment hesitation took the place of his anger and he looked at the newer chief, who had been so stunned by Ulfed's arrival he remained speechless, uncertain how to deal with this unexpected upheaval.

Now he too looked at Tir, and nodded his answer to Ulfed's unspoken question. 'It is not the child's fault,' he said. 'Cast him out, but let him live.'

Ulfed addressed the crowd again, 'Your chief has spoken wisely, but *she* has brought ruin upon us!' He gestured at his sister, then grabbed at the front fold of his cloak and when he withdrew his hand he held a filthy blade, ornately carved at the handle but covered in mud, as if it had been recently dug from the ground. He turned and lunged at the stunned Magara.

There was a grunt and a scuffle behind her, Magara was pushed roughly aside and in her place stood the young man she had named Tir. Ulfed could not stay his hand as it drove forward, and the mud-encrusted ceremonial knife cut through the scar it had once marked on Tir's chest. But this time it was no glancing slice.

Tir gasped but his expression did not change beyond the closing of his eyes and his brows drawing together. He remained on his feet, held there by Ulfed's hand on the knife, and as Ulfed tore the blade free and stepped away, horrified, Tir opened his eyes again. Blood began to spill, soaking his tunic, and he took a faltering step forward and caught hold of Ulfed's arm. He snatched a sudden sharp breath and groaned, and Ulfed caught him as he stumbled to his knees.

Tir looked into his killer's face and his breathing was short and ragged, but he held on to Ulfed until the old chief knelt in front of him. Their eyes were locked on each other, and Magara's weeping could be heard, a soft, helpless sound, without hope: her son had defied death once and now he had given the life he had won, for hers. She could not demean the sacrifice he had made by dishonouring him with a display of grief, no matter how deeply she felt it.

'It may be I have not earned my place in this world,' Tir managed, and now his face told of his agony and the struggle for breath, and his body was bent against it. 'But I will see the end of your line, Ulfed.'

Despite Tir's bitter words, Ulfed still held him, bearing him up while he spoke. Then he nodded, his face dark with sorrow. 'You have done a noble thing, Son of The Land,' he said. 'You will go to your rest a man of honour.'

But Tir shook his head. 'No,' he whispered, and cried out, doubling over the wound. Magara lurched forward instinctively but was dragged back. Tir straightened again, one hand on his chest, the other clutching at Ulfed's cloak. 'I have nowhere to go.'

'Tir, you –'

'Nowhere,' Tir sighed, and fell. Ulfed held him, his forehead laid against that of his young kinsman until he was forced to let go, and was led away, leaving Tir's body lying in the dust of the road.

'The spriggan watching from the shadows, remembered every detail, and through all these years not a word has been lost.' Greencoat looked up, found Richard's eyes still on him, and knew there was no need for further explanation.

Chapter Thirty-One

The silence drew out, and the group remained as motionless as the stones around them.

Then Richard sank back onto the central slab. 'Not ancestors,' he said, and the words seemed to rip their way out of him.

'And not racial memories,' Laura added softly. He knew she was looking at him, he could feel her gaze but he couldn't take his eyes off the little man in the now sodden green jacket.

Greencoat looked terrified to speak beyond the necessity of imparting his story, but he did so. 'Little wonder the storm that killed Loen could not be quelled by him alone; Tir's infant anger fuelled it also, father and son together.'

Richard turned to Maer, and addressed his new-found father through his best friend; it made him feel like crying. 'Loen, you must spare Laura, she's not Ulfed's line and you know you have no right to take her life. But what of Maer? You were a worthy king once, will you let him live?'

'He is safe in there?' Deera said, hope propelling her forward to seize Richard's arm. He looked down at her hand where it lay, white and elegant against the black wool of his sleeve. She seemed to realise the incongruity of her actions, given that she had been planning for the last twenty years to bring him here to his death. But she met his eyes and did not let go until he nodded.

'I think he's hanging on in there, despite what he wanted.'

He walked over to where Maer now stood, hoping his apparently catatonic state was an indication that he was, indeed, struggling to hold on in there somewhere. Nature and the desire to live often take over, how well he knew that; he'd wanted so badly to die when Cait had, yet he'd fought for his life with every last piece of strength he'd had left.

But Loen was in the forefront now. 'My own born son,' he said, and the words coming from Maer's lips, in his familiar voice, were both bizarre and touching. 'Tir, I recognise and greet you.'

A silence fell over the group, and Richard felt hope lift his heart as he saw Maer's body begin to slump: Loen was leaving him. But was he going out into the air to drift forever?

'You are of royal spirit indeed, Loen,' Casta said quietly.

Gilan had taken advantage of the shock that had fallen over them, to push Casta's foot aside. Now and was on his feet. 'Royal?' The word was filled with disgust. 'To give up that which we have slaved for so many cycles to prepare for you? That is not an act of royalty, it is an insult! This man is our gift to you, your chance to rule in your own right, with your own blood!'

'Which you did your best to spill,' Laura said furiously. 'Why should you care now?'

Gilan ignored her. 'Loen, this fool of a so-called son has fought you at every turn, mocking your strength and your wisdom, and your very right to rule! Why do you believe what a stupid spriggan tells you?'

'Silence!' Casta snapped.

'What of the curse? You must rule, you said so, and you must do it before ...' he stopped, staring at the body of Tom Riley, then turned to Deera. 'Curse?' he said, softly mocking.

Deera did not flinch away from his gaze, though she

flushed. 'There had to be *something* else, something to make Maer see sense. He kept finding reasons why Loen would not need Lucas, and I knew it would be the death of him if he believed that. So I told all of you the same story. I had to! But … no.' She sagged. 'There was no foretelling of darkness, only Loen's desire to end Ulfed's line.'

Richard held her in the cold prison of his gaze as he realised how hard Maer had tried to avoid bringing him here, and how much deceit there had been. But it wasn't all lies. He stepped away from Laura and crossed the circle to where Tom lay.

'Loen and me, we both swore to be there at the end of Ulfed's line,' he said, his heart hurting a little bit more with each beat. 'Him to end it, me to witness it.' Laura had followed him, and now crouched beside her brother once more. His hands lay open, and Richard saw no sign of that fiery, blistered ring. 'I'm so sorry, for all of it,' he said. She shook her head, but kept her face down, and Richard saw her tears falling freely onto Tom's slack face.

He heard Gilan taunting Loen again but it was coming from somewhere distant. Even the cries of warning were just a far off buzzing in his ears and he was completely unprepared for the shock of Maer's hands falling onto his shoulders, forcing him easily to his knees.

This time the assault was explosive and swift, and even as Richard fought back against the all too familiar crushing pain, he sensed things he should never have been able to feel, as if the moorland winds were inside him, the rain falling on his soul instead of his skin, and he realised with a horrified jolt that he was almost beaten, his body was almost taken from him.

He drew on all the energy he could find flowing in and around him. The fight was on once more, and this time

362

Richard understood what he was fighting for – his place. The end of the horrific cycle that had brought him back time and time again to the same point: death with no promise of rest.

***

Laura had heard him speak, heard the regret in his voice, but could not look at him again, not yet: he was partly responsible for this loss, she couldn't forget he had sworn to see this death. It was on his hands as much as his father's.

Then she heard him cry out, and jerked around to see him on his knees in the churned mud, his hands tearing at Maer's as they gripped his shoulders. All thoughts of blame fell away, history vanished and there was only a man struggling for his life. Maer's strength was terrifying to behold, and as those hands slipped up and closed about Richard's throat, Laura screamed out in rage and flew at the battling pair.

She vaguely registered Casta moving towards them too, a blur in the corner of her eye, and then she felt a violent tug on her hair and was jerked back off her feet, landing hard, the wind knocked out of her. Gilan still had hold of her hair and began to drag her backwards. Laura screamed again, in pain this time, and reached up to her scalp as some of her hair ripped away.

Gilan stopped, but relief turned to terror once more as he bent to retrieve something from the grass. The old ceremonial knife, the one that had killed Tir and had drawn her own blood. Gilan rose with it in his hand and, yanking her head back by her hair, he brought the blade down. She closed her eyes.

In the split second left to her, Laura had only one

363

thought: like Vivien and little Ben, and like Richard's parents, she and Richard were going to die together. It was just as he'd said it must be.

But the knife never completed its deadly arc. Laura heard a dull thump on the grass beside her head, and opened her eyes to see Gilan, a bemused look on his face, the hand that had dropped the knife now going to his neck. Then he fell, half landing on Laura, winding her again as his head crashed onto her chest.

Shocked and revolted, she shoved at him and wriggled away. Jacky Greencoat was standing nearby, a thin tube at his lips, a look of absolute terror on his face as he turned to his queen; he had killed her brother. Deera, visibly shaken, was staring back at him, but a tiny twist of her head said she bore him no ill will.

'Richard,' Laura whispered, still trying to get some air back into her lungs. She climbed to her feet, searching anxiously for her bearings through the dizziness. And there he was, lying on the wet ground next to Maer, his face to the sky and his coat flung open around him like some hideous black shroud waiting to be sewn shut.

Maer was gazing at him in horror and misery but he raised his face to Laura as she stepped closer, as close as she dared. Half fearful, half longing, she searched his eyes but saw no sign of the ancient Loen. It could only mean one thing. Despair drove her to her knees but there were no tears; her eyes were hot and dry as she knelt and rested her hand at Richard's shoulder, gently brushing her thumb over a fresh, ragged cut on the side of his neck. He stirred beneath her touch and tried to speak but Maer spoke first, his voice thin and drained after his long battle.

'Move away, quickly.' He stumbled to his feet caught at her arm. 'Please, Loen is ...' he broke off and shook his head, tears spilling over as he stared at his friend. 'He's insane, Laura.'

She shook her head. 'He's not. He knows who Richard is now. He was prepared to let himself go into nothing –'

'And Gilan has once again twisted him! He's been so long caught between worlds he has no understanding of either any longer. Please, just move away.'

But she couldn't. She was tied to Richard's side as if ropes bound them, and the feel of warm skin under her fingers, the life that still flowed through him, gave her hope that he'd been strong enough after all.

'Tir is gone.' Deera's words were, for the first time, spoken gently. 'He gave my son his life back, and he has saved his race. He will be honoured.'

'Screw your race,' Laura flung at her, low and savage over her shoulder. 'He's not *your race*.' She looked up at Maer in desperation. 'He may still be in there, you have to get Loen out while there's still a chance!'

'Laura?' The voice, husky and faint as it was, slammed into her heart like the bolt from a crossbow and she looked down: Richard's eyes were open and fixed on her, and the calm intelligence looking back at her told her there was no-one in there except him.

'Y'okay?' he managed, but before she could answer his eyes slipped shut again. As he struggled against whatever it was that kept trying to pull him back down into darkness, Laura looked around fearfully at the gathering dark.

'Stay with me, please,' she urged. 'I don't know if it's over yet, Loen might be –'

'It's alright,' Maer said suddenly, in an odd voice, 'Richard's safe.' He was staring at his father who leaned on a nearby stone, wheezing slightly and bending over, his hands braced on the wet granite. As Laura watched Casta stood straighter, steadied himself for a moment and then stepped over to where Richard lay.

He dropped to one knee beside him. 'I am sorry for striking you, My Lord.'

Taken aback at both the title and the admission, Laura saw Richard's hand rise to the back of his head. He eyed Deera's staff, lying on the ground nearby.

'That's where the headache came from, huh?' he said, his voice gaining strength. 'Well I guess I can hardly complain.'

'He almost had you,' Casta said grimly. 'It momentarily confused him when you lost consciousness; he believed, for a vital moment, that you were dead. It gave me the tiniest chance but it was enough.'

'Casta?' Deera stepped towards her husband, her expression a mixture of concern and not a little fear. 'You are ...' she shook her head in wonderment. 'And you are whole?'

He smiled up at her, and spoke softly. 'I am whole, my love. My age has served me well for once.' He rose with fluid grace, belying his rueful comment, and his smile broadened, the resemblance to Maer stronger than ever. 'It's quite extraordinary, I believe Loen has taken nothing from me, but instead given something that was uniquely his to give. I feel more than I was, not less.'

Laura felt Richard's hand on her arm, and she and Maer helped him to stand. She caught a movement from the corner of her eye, and turned. Deera had taken up the staff and now knelt before Richard with the ornately carved wood laid across her palms.

'Tir, son of Loen, we honour and recognise you, and we offer the Lightning –'

'The what?' Richard looked drawn and terribly tired. 'Look, it doesn't matter. I never wanted to rule,' he said, 'just to belong. You are still queen, and Maer will be king after you.'

But Deera shook her head. 'I am not fit to hold the staff,' she said, and rose to her feet. 'I have done dreadful things to my people, and to strangers who have done nothing to deserve it.' She looked at Tom as she said it, and Laura closed her eyes against a fresh wave of grief.

'You did what you had to do,' Maer said. 'You are my mother first and foremost, and as my mother you had to try and save me. As for Tom, his death is a tragedy and no-one is more sorry for it than I. But it was no more your fault than was the accident which brought him here today.'

'All the same, I have behaved foolishly, thoughtlessly,' Deera said, 'and I became a lesser queen because of it.' She crossed to her husband, bent at the knee once more and held the staff balanced across her raised hands. 'Take it up, Casta, if Tir will not. Use your wisdom and Loen's to guide our people, teach your son to rule after you. We honour and recognise you.'

Casta reached down and took the staff, drawing Deera to her feet with his free hand. There was a visible strength and sureness in his touch, and Laura began to understand how he had been able to subdue the insanity of the once great king Loen. The real miracle was that what had made Loen great was still there, absorbed into Casta to form a being at once ancient and new.

Casta seemed to sense her thoughts and looked directly at her, his expression gentle and filled with silent understanding, and she nodded, accepting it. What was done could not be undone, but Richard was safe, and order had been restored to the world of these strange, complicated people; her brother had given them his future, wrapped in their past. Wordlessly she moved to Tom's side and knelt beside him. She closed his eyes and kissed his brow, and folded his blameless hands across his chest. There was a look of peace about him now that he hadn't had since he'd been ten years old, and, knowing the reality of her loss had yet to hit her properly, she numbly accepted that that would have to be enough.

**

Richard stood in the light rain, looking down at the fallen body of Gilan, and tried to find forgiveness in his heart but it would not come. The part of Loen that had risen to destroy Laura's family was no longer, but at least the wisdom and honour remained; in Gilan there had been no such honour with which to balance the cruelty. Loen's fate had been shaped by circumstance and his own terrible love for his child; Gilan had been driven by greed, jealousy, and black hatred. No, there could be no forgiveness, no understanding for him. As Richard watched, Gilan's body seemed to become … *less*, somehow. The texture of his skin altered, turned dusty in appearance, and then it began to sink into the bones, outlining the shape of the man beneath the bright clothes. It was both horrifying and fascinating, and hard to look away from.

A touch on his arm brought his attention back, and he turned to see Maer at his elbow. 'No loss,' Maer said, also looking down at what remained of his uncle, and his eyes were so hard that Richard wondered if any part of Loen remained in him at all. Perhaps that wasn't such a terrible thing, not if it made him as strong as he looked now.

A thought occurred to him and, amazingly, he felt a smile touch the corners of his mouth.

Maer saw it and raised an eyebrow. 'What?'

Richard gestured at Casta, who had taken Deera's hand and was leading her back towards the mine. He felt an odd sense of pride in the man, and he welcomed the feeling. 'I guess now he's my father too.'

Maer started, and his eyes lost that hard look, and widened. 'Which makes us –'

'Brothers.' They said the word together, quietly, both staring after Casta's tall form as he moved easily over the rough terrain of the heath.

Richard sneaked a glance at Maer, and his smile broadened. 'I'm the eldest, so I'm in charge.'

'Hardly, I'm nearly two hundred in mortal years, don't forget.'

'And I'm getting on for three thousand.'

'Yeah, good point. You might want to take it easy, wrinkly.' Maer sobered then, as he looked over at Laura. 'Do you think she'll be okay?'

Richard's own grin faded, and he turned back to see her rising from her brother's side. She started towards him, an expression of wary relief on her face, and he felt the breath catch in his throat and wondered if his father had ever seen in Magara what he could see around Laura now; the beginnings of his child in a glistening aura that fell about her like a cloak, formed of some exquisite fabric only he could see.

With Thanks:

To everyone who's had to listen to me banging on about this, the first book in the Lynher Mill Chronicles, since I started writing it in 2006. Most especially to my Mum and Dad, Anne and Eddie Deegan. Anne is the talent behind the lightning and blade and Lynher Mill logos on the back cover.

Particular gratitude goes to *Ian Brown*, for his wonderful illustration of little Jacky Greencoat (p.6) and his constant enthusiasm for my project; to my friends and family (see first line of these acknowledgements!) and to *Jeanine Henning* for her stunning cover design. I'm also grateful to *Richard Clark*, who gave his permission to use the gorgeous black and white photo that graces the back cover.

Special thanks also go out to *Sean Ryan*, whose brilliant manipulation of what started out as a rather ordinary photograph has turned it into the cover-photo dreams are made of (or should that be: "of which dreams are made"? Who cares, I've finished the book now!)

Finally, to those who've read part, or all of this book and said they've enjoyed it, thank you too; you've given me the push and the confidence to finish it. Thank you, *Shelley Clarke*, for telling anyone who'll listen that it's better than Harry Potter! And *Tonya Rittenhouse* who's been there from day one, my long-distance cheer-leader and "sister."

The Lynher Mill Chronicles continues in:

Book II: The Lightning and the Blade

A royal marriage promises to unite the Moorlanders and their old enemies on the coast, but bad blood runs deeper than the underground caverns in which the couple choose to make their home. As ugly truths come to light, and old hatreds rise again, the two races embark on a collision course that threatens to destroy them both, and the land that protects them. With elementals playing their wicked weather-games, and a mortal woman rapidly sliding into self-destruction, the two worlds become more closely entwined than ever, leading to heartbreaking tests of loyalty and strength.

Scheduled for release June 2014.

Book III: The Western War

They face each other across the expanse of moorland that covers the West of Cornwall, a reluctant king on one side, a misled lord on the other. And while the elementals clash swords in the name of vengeance, the mortals fight to put right the twist in destiny that has brought them all to the edge of annihilation. As the battle builds and the stakes are raised, one woman races to protect her child, and to uncover a truth that will either save them all, or plunge the land into perpetual darkness.

Scheduled for release June 2015

Visit the author's website at www.terri-nixon.co.uk

Follow on Twitter: @TerriNixon

Printed in Great Britain
by Amazon.co.uk, Ltd.,
Marston Gate.